OLD DOGS, OLDER TRICKS

JAMIE MCFARLANE

PREFACE

FREE DOWNLOAD

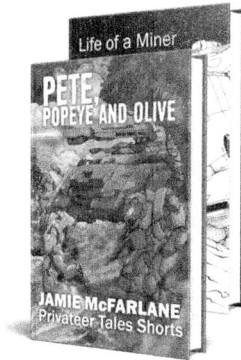

Sign up for my newsletter and receive a free Jamie McFarlane starter library.

To get started, please visit:

http://www.fickledragon.com

1

GILDED CAGE

"What a pile of crap," Albert Jenkins said. "Beverly is royalty. You'd think she'd have access to a nicer place than this damn windowless hut."

"Any word from her yet?" Darnell asked. The two men were stretched out on opposite ends of a thickly padded couch. Their friendship had been forged decades ago while serving together in Vietnam.

"Not a freaking peep," AJ grumbled, waving at a wall panel to switch from an old Diamondbacks baseball game to an even older Arizona State football game. Greybeard snuffled at the edge of the couch and scratched softly at his leg. AJ lifted the heavily muscled dog next to him and smoothed his gray fur back. "Seriously, would one window kill them? We've been trapped in here for days. I'm about to go insane."

"I got a glimpse outside when we transferred from the shuttle," Jayne piped up from an overstuffed chair. "There wasn't much to see. It was all red dirt and mountains. Hard to imagine how any species evolved in such a place." Doctor Amanda Jayne had been a late addition to the close-knit team, although, she too had earned her stripes in Vietnam as a surgeon.

As if summoned by AJ's grousing, the image of a ten-inch-high woman wearing a formal black robe appeared on the edge of the table between AJ and Darnell. "I apologize for my extended absence," Beverly announced. "There were many questions regarding my team's survey mission to Earth. It is not too strongly said that Mother was quite angry I undertook such a dangerous mission."

"What's the plan, BB? Is the Galactic Congress going to send a ship back to Earth and run those damn Korgul off planet?" AJ asked. BB was the nickname he'd assigned to her ... Beverly from Beltigersk.

"The Galactic Congress Subcommittee on Sentient Rights has formed a panel to review the data gathered from the survey. After initial review, the panel's recommendation is that the Sentient Rights subcommittee formally review this data for future presentation to the congressional subcommittee on interstellar trade practices," Beverly said, uncomfortable in her delivery. "I requested that the Sentient Rights panel send a delegation to Earth to gather additional data in order to expedite the elevation of Beltigersk's complaint against Korgul. That request is under consideration."

"Holy crap, BB," AJ said. "I feel like you just used a hundred words to tell me the Galactic Congress doesn't give a shit."

"That's a wildly inaccurate oversimplification," she said, her tiny cheeks growing red. "Beltigersk representatives filed a request to censure the Korgul for illegal mining on planet Earth. This action could be completed within eighteen to twenty-four months. If enough representatives vote positively for censure, Korgul could face significant trade sanctions and even tariffs on all goods suspected to have originated on Earth."

"Hogwash," AJ spluttered. "We need action. Those damn Korgul are stripping Earth. According to that survey, more than two-thirds of the Fantastium and Blastorium have already been removed. We don't need a bunch of politicians running around, rubbing their hands together."

Greybeard, AJ's English Bulldog, barked loudly, seemingly in agreement with AJ's outburst.

"Hold on, AJ," Jayne said, interrupting the anger she knew was about to boil over. "What would you have the people of Beltigersk do? They're a tiny, nano-meter-sized civilization. Negotiating *is* their strongest action."

"I wish we could do more," Beverly said, staring at the table her virtual projection stood on. "Is there anything I can do to make your stay more comfortable?"

"We could do with some windows," AJ grumbled. "When can we get out of here? If you won't do anything for us, I'd like to go home and join up with that resistance group. We need to take more direct action – *politics* through other means, if you know what I mean."

Beverly shook her head. "I don't think you understand. I'm home. Beltigersk won't let me leave. I have responsibilities."

"What? Ever?" AJ asked. "What about Jayne? Darnell?"

"Beltigersk is not a common destination for trade. We have few material needs and we produce nothing. Finding a way back to Earth is quite difficult. This is now your home."

The words were too much for Jayne. "*This*, as in *Beltigersk*? Or *this* as in this small residence?"

"The residence is configurable. You should find it quite comfortable. For example, the windows you asked about are simple." Beverly waved her hand. A three-foot-tall transparent strip appeared at roughly waist height and encircled the rectangular room.

For the first time since they'd arrived, the group was able to see outside. The bright red landscape of Beltigersk Five closely resembled photographs AJ had seen of Mars. Now visible at the bottom of a valley were roughly fifty white rectangular structures resembling the size and shape of their own habitat.

"Are those living spaces for hosts?" Jayne asked.

"That is correct," Beverly replied.

"And those are ships?" Darnell asked. "It looks like most of 'em haven't been used in years. Why, some of them are almost buried."

AJ huffed in frustration. "Nothing more than a prison planet. You Beltigersk are no different than Korgul. To you, we're just a bunch of dumb raccoons and this is our cage."

"That's a bit harsh, don't you think, AJ?" Jayne said. "Beverly and her crew put their lives on the line for humanity. I can't believe they intend to keep us in a cage."

"It's not like that," Beverly said.

"Oh?" AJ said. "Then what's it like?"

"The residents of those homes are here voluntarily," she said. "For most species, it's a great honor to join with a Beltigersk. The rooms are locations for their corporeal bodies to rest while the hosts virtually intermingle with Beltigersk society."

"You want us to intermingle? What about Jayne? She doesn't have a rider anymore," AJ said.

Beverly dropped her head. "No. Humans are considered limited sentients and are therefore precluded from this possibility."

"And you're okay with this?" AJ swallowed hard. "I thought you didn't buy that whole raccoon thing."

"If you could be part of Beltigersk society, would you?" Beverly asked, her eyebrows lifting. "I would negotiate on your behalf. I must go, but will return in a few hours. Please, if there is anything that would make your stay more comfortable, do not hesitate to ask."

With her point made, Beverly disappeared, causing Greybeard to bark.

"I know, boy," AJ said, moving the dog's legs from his lap to the couch. "Pisses me off, too. Did all our Beltigersk buddies take off or are you still in there, Seamus?"

Greybeard barked and held AJ's gaze. The Beltigersk rider, Seamus, had made a tremendous sacrifice by bonding with Greybeard. It was an odd pairing, but Seamus had been unwilling to separate from the dog, knowing Greybeard wouldn't survive the separation.

"2-F is still here." Darnell referred to his own rider, who Beverly had explained was immature and therefore either unable or unwilling to project himself visually. Instead, 2-F's interaction with Darnell was primarily through a virtual HUD only Darnell could see. "BB is the only one wrangling with the political types."

"Good," AJ said.

"What's on your mind?" Jayne asked. "I see those gears churning. You're not thinking what I think you're thinking, are you?"

"Big D, ask your buddy, 2-F, what the Beltigersk atmosphere is like," AJ said.

"Not directly breathable, but not toxic. Atmospheric pressure isn't bad either. 2-F has a filtration mask that just needs a small support tank," Darnell said, walking over to the manufactory. The machine had, to date, only produced replacement clothing and unexpectedly good replications of Earth food dishes.

"AJ?" Jayne pushed, but he didn't seem to hear her. "You're not thinking ..."

"Right now, that's all I'm doing," AJ said. "For some reason, every alien out there believes they can push us around, including Beverly."

Greybeard barked. It wasn't immediately clear whether Seamus was irritated or supported AJ's statements.

"But we're trapped on an alien planet," Jayne said.

"See, there you go," AJ said. "Hitting the nail right on the head. Way I see it, as long as we're trapped, we're not much good to anyone, so we work the problem."

"Well, hell. That wasn't too hard," Darnell called, lifting a thin mask from the outfeed tray of the residence's manufactory. "Think you can get what you want with thirty minutes runtime, big man?"

"What are you going to tell Beverly?" Jayne asked.

AJ shrugged. "Darlin', me and Big D are just going out for a walk, that's all." He caught the mask Darnell tossed at him. Greybeard barked again and stood on his hind legs next to the manufactory. A moment later, a more conical mask plopped onto the outfeed. "And it looks like Greybeard is coming."

"Count me in," Jayne said. "I don't know if you noticed, the door we came in isn't there anymore."

AJ raised his eyebrows when he glanced at the blank patch of wall that had once been an entryway. "That does present a problem. See if you can find a seam or a latch or something." He joined her near where the entry had once been.

After several fruitless minutes of searching, Jayne stood and placed her hands on her hips. "I swear it was right here."

"It was," Darnell said. "2-F says it's a reconfigurable Vred bulkhead. Since we're not expected to go outside, they probably didn't think we'd need the hatch."

"Well, ain't that a pickle," AJ said, slamming his fist into the wall partly for emphasis and partly to get a feel for the structure. "It's plenty solid."

"There's got to be a way out," Darnell said. "Maybe Greybeard can break into the software and do some of that voodoo cypher crap he does."

Greybeard growled and shook his head.

"Maybe we eat dinner and think about it," Jayne said. "I, for one, am getting hungry."

"Yeah, my blood sugar's getting low and I'm feeling grumpy," AJ said.

"Couldn't tell," Jayne deadpanned while raising an eyebrow in exasperation.

AJ chuckled and turned away from the wall. "Big D, you suppose 2-F could program that wall thingy to make something resembling steak? And maybe a bottle of Scotch?"

"Not like you to give up so easily," Jayne said.

"Who said anything about giving up?" AJ asked. "Or have you forgotten that I'm an engineer by trade."

"What's that mean?"

"We tried to find an existing exit. No luck. Therefore, our next option is to make one. Sure, it'd be easier if Beverly were here to help, but that kind of takes the fun out of it," he said. "I was thinking. If those masks Darnell made are a mix of oxygen and nitrogen, how hard would it be to load one with pure oxygen and another with acetylene? All we'd need is a rig to control their mix. Add a spark and voila, Bob's your uncle, we've got a cutting torch."

"Let's say that works and you make a hole in the side of this building. What if we can't get it closed back up?" Jayne asked. "Your masks are only good for thirty minutes."

"Glad you asked. Probably something we should think about. But Big D already said we don't have pressure problems. We'll make duct-tape. It'll make me feel good to have some on hand, anyway," he said, shrugging. "Good questions, Doc. We make a good team."

She shook her head. "This is insane. So many things could go wrong."

"That's why we're having Scotch and steak first."

"WE'VE ONLY an hour of daylight left," Darnell said, crouching behind AJ.

AJ had just eased a stream of the mixed gasses from his newly manufactured torch. He adjusted his dark glasses and grinned as the acetylene caught fire with an audible pop, then plunged the white-hot tip into where the door had once appeared. Black smoke billowed back at him from the burning material, forcing him to retreat.

"Get those masks on," he called over the torch noise, following his own instructions. Air from the mask smelled funny, but it was more breathable than the rapidly darkening air within the habitat.

"You should stop," Jayne called. "That smoke looks toxic."

"I slagged off a chunk of the lining inside the structure. We'll be through in a jiffy." He plunged the flame back into the wall. This time, the flame met a heavier material that absorbed the torch's heat.

"Seriously, AJ. Maybe this isn't a good idea," she pushed again.

"Doc, I got this." AJ held the flame in place. Finally, light appeared through a widening hole and the flame flickered as Beltigersk Five's atmosphere rushed through the new opening. With a practiced hand, he drew the flame up the wall, allowing the material's melting point to set his pace. He'd just turned the corner at the top of his makeshift door when the flame popped out, the torch dousing itself as the gas was exhausted.

"Want me to cool that wall?" Darnell asked.

When AJ turned, he saw the entire room was filled with the

pungent black smoke. "You better make a few more cartridges for these masks. Where'd Jayne go?"

"I'm not sure," Darnell said. "There's a replacement oxygen canister by your foot. I think you still have acetylene."

AJ switched out the oxygen canisters. "We'll quench the wall once I've finished the cut. I don't want things cooling down too much."

"Copy that."

AJ gritted his teeth and fired up the torch. As he cut, black smoke continued to fill the room and he started to question the sanity of his approach. Ten minutes later, he shut off the flow of gas to the torch and kicked at the now loose panel. A plume of red dust billowed up as it fell into the dry Beltigersk Five landscape.

"Give way," Darnell said, dumping a pan full of water over the wall, allowing it to run down onto the heated material. Wind whipped past the three-foot-tall, two-foot-wide opening, pulling a small trail of the black smoke behind it, although not substantially clearing the room.

"Did you make those additional canisters?" AJ asked.

Darnell gave him a sharp nod. "Copy. On the counter."

A sudden strong breeze pulled through the opening, venting the sooty interior atmosphere through the ceiling. "We should have found that switch before we started," Jayne said plainly, standing next to a control panel near the manufactory.

"I had it handled," AJ said defensively.

"What, were we going to sleep with these silly little half-hour masks all night?" she asked.

He knew better than to argue with an irritated Amanda Jayne. Instead, he stepped through the hole. "Well, that's not something you see every day." Some twenty miles from their position, fiery slag was thrown into the air by an active volcano.

"Does anyone else think that's closer than it should be?" Darnell asked, sliding the still hot panel away from the opening.

"I wonder if that volcano is a new feature or if it's been erupting for a while," Jayne mused. "Maybe getting off this planet isn't such a bad idea."

AJ chuckled. "Pick your poison, Doc."

"Pardon?"

AJ pointed up the valley. "Best I can count, there are at least a dozen abandoned spaceships. We need to find something compatible."

"Then we survey the lot of them," she said. "Or maybe, 2-F or Seamus have ideas on what might be suitable for human habitation."

"2-F says, other than Korgul, Vred are the most physically compatible. The only problem is, Vred companies supply hulls for a lot of different species, especially smaller ones. It'll be hard to tell which ships are Vred without opening them up."

Greybeard barked excitedly and spun in place.

"Seamus, if you have an idea, we're all ears," AJ said. "Lead on."

They trudged through the loose Beltigerskian soil with Darnell muttering complaints the entire time. "Geez, this stuff is impossible. It's like walking over fresh snow. It's going to take most of our oxygen to just get to that first ship."

"Don't give up, Big D," AJ encouraged. "We're learning a lot. If we only look at one ship, that's a good first trip."

He inspected the closest ship which sat next to an entirely opaque habitat. The ship was thirty feet long and tapered from a point at the bow to wide-swept wings at the aft. It was clearly designed for atmospheric flight and a small payload.

"What do you make of it?" Darnell asked, panting as he pushed to keep up.

"Isn't good," AJ said. "This one's not much bigger than a fighter jet, but it's still worth checking out. Who knows what we might find?"

Darnell sighed as he continued forward, inspecting the sleek ship that looked like it hadn't been on Beltigersk Five longer than a year.

"We'll have to make this quick. I've only got five minutes left in my first canister," AJ said. "Next time we bring extra."

"We need a rebreather," Jayne said. "We're exhaling oxygen for no good reason. Carbon dioxide scrubbing isn't that complex and it would give us a longer range."

"Could you explain enough to 2-F or Seamus to make one?" AJ asked.

"I think so," she answered.

Darnell said, ducking beneath the belly of the ship, only three feet off the ground. "This looks like the hatch." Looping two fingers into a small d-ring handle, he gave it a twist. "Doesn't even feel locked."

The d-ring handle slowly extended, stopping when it reached ten inches. The circular hatch, which was a foot in diameter, disappeared upward, into the ship. Darnell stepped back as a tiny ladder articulated downward, embedding itself into the soil.

"Those steps are only five inches apart," Jayne observed. "The only one getting through that hatch is Greybeard."

Greybeard, hearing his name, ran over and placed his paws on the ladder, looking up into the hatch. He growled, shook his head once and barked for good measure as he pushed away from the rungs.

"How's your O2, Seamus?" AJ asked. The dog padded over and pushed the side of his face against AJ's leg. AJ bent, swapped out Greybeard's canister and then swapped out his own.

"Those are some tiny aliens," Darnell said, pushing his head into the open hatch. "Everything is shut down. Nice looking ship, though."

Jayne's intellectual curiosity got the better of her. "I want to see," she said, her voice bright with excitement. Darnell ducked out so she could look in. "Remind me to make a flashlight. You're right, these guys can't be more than eighteen inches tall."

"I guess that scratches one ship off the list," AJ said, ducking and sticking his head into the open hatch as Jayne made way for him. "Too bad, too. Been nice to find one close."

"2-F scanned the interior so we can review it," Darnell said. "Let's head back. We're already pushing our oxygen supplies and I'd hate to get caught out here."

The small crew made better time as they followed their footprints back to their own habitat. Once inside, AJ set about repairing the hole he'd cut in the wall. He looped duct tape around the top and then left the tape much looser on the last two passes, creating a sort of handle to grab so he and Darnell could pull the panel back into place. He held the piece upright while Darnell and Jayne applied more tape to the seams.

"Smells like an electrical fire in here," Jayne observed as she removed her depleted mask.

"Do you think Beverly will notice?" Darnell asked. "What will you say to her?"

AJ shrugged. "I'll tell her the truth. We got bored and went for a walkabout."

2

GET 'EM, RAY

The eighteen-hour Beltigersk Five day was evenly split between day and night, which had thrown off AJ's already unpredictable sleep schedule. Having been his constant companion since bonding, he found Beverly's absence disturbing.

"Are you awake?" Jayne asked, her voice quieter than Darnell's rhythmic snoring.

"Just thinking," AJ said. "I feel like I should apologize. Cutting that hole in the habitat was reckless. I'm just not very good with cages."

"Darnell said you were captured by Viet Cong."

"I got off easy. They only had me for a couple of days. It's not really something I talk about."

"Sorry," she said after a pause.

"The soldiers that got us were spread thin. Ten of 'em to hold twenty of us. We were all kids back then, full of piss and vinegar. VC stuck us in a hole for a couple days, but one of our patrols stumbled across our position. When the shooting started, we fought. I don't remember much other than being stuck in that hole, but I tell you what I'll never forget; the faces of the boys who rescued us."

"Have you kept in touch with any of them?"

"I used to. Haven't recently," he said. "Last I heard, only Lefty Johnson was still alive. As Rangers, life expectancy wasn't all that high. Three of them made it out, but Maury Thompson got exposed to something over there and brought it back with him. Never made it to fifty."

"Sorry to hear that."

"Any luck on that rebreather you were talking about?" AJ asked.

"Not really. 2-F says it's beyond our manufactory's capabilities. Darnell recycled our canisters and requested two dozen more," Jayne said. "Kind of hard to believe your duct-tape patch would work so well. I thought you were crazy."

"One of the six wonders of the world. You know, next to the Grand Canyon."

"It's seven wonders," she said with a chuckle. Then she grew serious. "What do you think humanity will do once they learn about all this?"

"You mean, aliens?"

"Yeah."

"They're gonna be pissed that those snot-balled bastards have been stealing our stuff. Other than that, it's not really that much of a stretch. Have you ever wondered if all those books and movies were government sponsored?"

"Not sure I'm following."

"All those space movies with aliens and spaceships. What if it's just a propaganda tour to get the public ready?"

"Is that what you think?"

"I guess I'm saying that when word does get out, most folks won't be real surprised," he said. "Sure, there'll be an adjustment period. Remember how we showed Darnell what was what? You made a movie. I'm just saying, what if the government already makes those types of movies?"

"I hope not. Some of them are pretty dark. Can you imagine if Godzilla was a real thing?"

"I was thinking more like *Star Wars*."

"I only caught the first one of those," she said. "Not really my thing."

"Are you guys going to talk all night?" Darnell asked. "Or should we get up and do something?"

AJ sent Jayne a chagrined look. "Sorry. It's still dark."

"You're right. Advanced alien species probably can't manage to make flashlights," Darnell growled, sitting up. "Any word from Beverly? I was kind of expecting her to show up and ask about our new hole."

"Not so far," AJ said. "Probably best if we didn't get her royal highness involved any sooner than necessary."

"She's four-hundred nanometers," Darnell said. "What's she gonna do?"

"They control your visual cortex," Jayne said. "Trust me, it can be quite disturbing."

Darnell grunted. "Seamus used scans of the valley to identify a couple of ships that might be worth checking out. They're quite a ways out, but I got to thinking about how Jayne suggested the dirt is powdery like snow."

"I was the one who said that," AJ argued.

"Point is," Darnell said. "I made snowshoes. We should give 'em a try."

"I'd vote for a trip," Jayne said. "This time we take water and something to eat. I bet the sunrise here is spectacular."

"VOLCANO SEEMS TO HAVE SETTLED DOWN," Darnell observed as a large, glowing hunk of slag slowly arced across their view.

"I feel like I'm a duck." AJ struggled against his new shoes.

"Try a slow jog," Jayne said. "That worked for me on snow."

"Oh, here we go," AJ said. "Ms. Lifestyles of the Rich."

"Snowshoeing is an affordable activity for all kinds," she said defensively and picked up her pace. "Personally, I prefer cross country skiing."

"Don't let him get to you, Doc," Darnell said. "He's looking for soft spots to pick. Makes him feel better."

"Shut up, you big dummy," AJ said.

Darnell increased his speed and caught up with Jayne.

"We're just going to burn more oxygen by going faster," AJ argued. When neither of his companions answered, he picked up his own pace and discovered that indeed, the faster movement kept the shoes from sinking in, making them easier to maneuver.

After twenty minutes, the group stopped so Darnell could hand out fresh canisters from his backpack.

"It's beautiful," Jayne remarked, pointing behind them to the lightening sky. A small brilliant dot had formed behind a mountain ridge allowing the morning sun's first rays to enter the valley.

"Do you suppose downhill will be easier or harder?" AJ asked, looking down the steep slope they'd just come up. "I can't believe we climbed all that so easily."

"Nice to have a young body again. I'd bet we'll find the experience a lot like hiking. The descent will be harder on our knees and quads," Darnell said, "but we won't breathe so hard. We'll definitely feel it tomorrow."

"It's so barren here," Jayne said, distracted by the alien sunrise. "I'd love to know how the Beltigersk people evolved. No opposable thumbs. No primordial soup. It's such a mystery. It just shows how little we really know as a species."

AJ offered his hand to her, who had plopped down onto the soft dirt. "Break's over. We have a ship to steal."

She accepted his hand and then brushed self-consciously at the dust sticking to her suit. He was distracted by the attention the old surgeon brought to the new curves of her body.

"What?" she asked, defensively. "The dirt sticks to everything."

"Seriously, it's like we're at summer camp with you two," Darnell said, resuming his jog toward their destination.

"What's that mean?" Jayne asked, trailing behind him. "How is this like camping?"

Darnell ignored the question, focusing instead on the effort of the climb. Twenty minutes later, they pulled to a stop beneath a much larger, rectangular ship.

"I see a hatch." AJ walked beneath the ship. "I can't reach it, though. Might need a boost."

"2-F says this ship is made for a much larger species, but the atmosphere should work for humans. He doesn't want to invent an English species name until Beverly gets a shot at it," Darnell said.

"See if you can get me up there," AJ replied.

"We'd have better luck getting Jayne up."

"Fine. Doc, let's try this," AJ said. "We need to add a ladder to our gear."

After struggling with balance, the trio finally lifted Dr. Jayne high enough that she was able to touch the bottom of the ship. Unlike the previous ship, she was unable to find a manual release, which prompted Greybeard to bark.

"2-F says you'll have to put your hand into that slot on the end. Curl your two smaller fingers over, like you're pointing a gun with your index and middle fingers," Darnell instructed. "Once you get your fingers in, you have to push up, hard."

She yelped and pulled her hand back. "It cut me."

"Doc, we can't hold you forever," AJ complained as he and Darnell wobbled under her weight.

"It doesn't look too bad," Jayne said and stuck her hand back into the slot. "The stupid thing bit me!" This time when she withdrew her hand, she did so with enough force that it knocked their impromptu human pyramid to the ground, landing her directly atop AJ.

Greybeard barked excitedly, catching Darnell's attention. "Move!" he exclaimed.

AJ cuffed Jayne on her side and rolled the two of them away, just in time to make way for the base of a wide, telescoping ramp. By the end of the rolling, he was on top of her.

"What was that about?" she asked, initially angry, until her eyes fell on the ramp that hadn't existed moments before. She channeled her irritation by pushing him. "Get off."

"Don't need to get all handsy, Doc," he said, swinging his leg off and pushing to his feet.

"Uh, yeah, I don't think this is going to be our first choice," Darnell called from the end of the ramp.

AJ offered his hand to the still flustered Jayne. This time she swatted it away and stood on her own. "I'm not an invalid."

"Never said you were." He made his way to where Darnell looked up into the ship. "Ugh."

The room in front of the hatch was only four feet tall, surprising, given the volume of the ship. He pulled back as soon as he saw the long, gooey, wet streamers of green gunk hanging from the ceiling.

"That's more reasonable," Jayne said. "I'd guess we're looking at something akin to Lumbricus. Worms."

"2-F just showed me a picture," Darnell said. "You're right."

"What's with all the material hanging from the ceiling?" AJ asked.

"Dermal transfer," Jayne answered. "They probably absorb nutrition and even information through those streamers."

"Smart worms, but I'm with Darnell on this one. Not my first choice." A familiar body brushed past his leg as Greybeard barreled up the ramp and disappeared behind the curtain of oozing material. "What's up with him?"

"Seamus is checking Fantastium reserves and looking to see if he can interface with the controls," Darnell said. "Looks like no good on fuel. The Fantastium is completely depleted."

"This sounded easier when we started." AJ sat on the edge of the ramp as Greybeard searched the ship. "Who knew there would be so many different aliens?"

"Every xenobiologist ever," Jayne said. "Do you think it's a coincidence that life on Earth is so varied? Did you really believe it'd be any less on other worlds?"

"Just hopeful, I guess," AJ said.

Jayne's face softened. "I'm sorry. I don't mean to be such a grump," she said. "I'm hungry and that thing bit my hand, and then you hit me."

"You hit her?" Darnell asked.

"Only to save my life," Jayne said, quickly coming to AJ's defense.

"Well, at least we can fix one thing." AJ pulled granola bars and water from the pack he'd been carrying.

"I swear I told that manufactory to add berry flavoring," Jayne said, grimacing as she chewed on a bar. "These all taste the same."

"I'm tasting peanut butter," Darnell said.

"Vanilla?" AJ asked.

Greybeard barked as he appeared at the top of the ramp and ran down to join AJ. After removing the dog's mask, AJ fed him one of the bars.

"We could survive in this ship," Darnell said. "We'd have to get fuel and clear some of that worm moss. Seamus thinks he could interface the flight controls. It wouldn't be pretty, but the ship is in working order."

"We have nine more ships," Jayne said. "I'd like to investigate at least one more before we go back."

AJ pushed a water bottle into his backpack and stood. "Sounds like a plan. At least they're all downhill from here."

"I CAN BARELY MOVE," Jayne said, plopping onto the couch next to AJ after grabbing a hot cup of what the Beltigersk manufactory considered coffee.

Over the last three days, the team had set out on seven sorties and visited all the abandoned alien craft in the valley. Their visits had considerably broadened each team member's view of the diversity of sentient species, but there had been no silver bullet, no ideal ship fully loaded with fuel and set up for human habitation.

"If we gather all the Fantastium we found and load it onto that worm ship, are we even close?" she continued, tucking her feet beneath her for warmth.

AJ shook his head. "Not even if we took the smallest ship on the mountain. Darnell was saying 2-F thinks they salvaged the Fantastium instead of leaving it aboard the ships."

"It's worth too much, I guess," she said.

"How's that hand doing?" AJ asked. Jayne pulled the bandage back to expose the wound that was slowly knitting back together. "Doesn't look like infection or anything bad. Do you miss having a rider to fix you up?

"Not even a little," Jayne said. "You have no idea how painful it was when Jack separated himself from me. It felt like every nerve in my body was on fire."

"I listened to you scream. It was hard to hear."

"Anyone want eggs?" Darnell called as he entered the room.

"I hope we didn't wake you," Jayne answered.

"Nope. I was just thinking about going out for a run this morning."

"No eggs for me," AJ said.

"Me, either. And before you ask, I don't care that the Beltigersk riders can so easily repair our bodies. I'd rather be sore. Nothing is worth the physical pain and mental anguish that asshat put me though." Greybeard whined and crawled over AJ to rest his head on Jayne's lap. In response, she patted his head. "Not your fault, Seamus," she said, using her doggie voice.

On the end table next to where Jayne and AJ sat, Beverly appeared, wearing her formal long black gown. "I see you've had time to visit your neighbors." She did her best to look disapprovingly at AJ. "If you'd asked, I would have presented an opening in your habitat."

"Like we had any idea if her royal princess was coming back," he sneered.

She ignored the jab. "Did you find anything interesting?"

"How long are the Lumbricus?" Jayne asked.

Beverly's smile was genuine as she turned to Jayne. "I'm not sure they would appreciate the comparison to the worms of your planet," she said. "But between us, I'll admit their resemblance is uncanny. A mature Lumbricus can reach four hundred pounds and nine feet in length. Although that would be an unusual traveler. Ambassador Wormy is one hundred eight pounds and four feet in length."

AJ chuckled. "Wormy? I thought you were being careful.

Beverly shrugged. "The names I create are simply for the purpose of communication. Like Fantastium, I believe it is easiest if nouns, especially, resemble what they describe. You didn't answer my question."

"We're short on Fantastium," AJ said. "How irritated would Ambassador Wormy be if we swiped his ship?"

Beverly smiled. "I wondered if you would see past the minor incompatibilities, especially in light of your current living arrangements."

"Ah, there it is," Darnell said, triumphantly.

"What?" AJ asked.

"Is it not clear? Beverly has already thought this through," Jayne said, nodding at Darnell.

"Thought what through?" AJ asked. "What are you guys talking about?"

"Are you being intentionally dense?" Jayne asked. "She knows what we're looking for. I might even think that she purposefully stayed away so she wouldn't have to report our activities. She's as trapped here as we are."

"But it's her home," AJ argued.

Beverly's formal black robe transformed into a World War II flight suit complete with a leather bomber jacket and sheepskin collar. "I believe you said it yourself. I'm only four hundred nanometers long. How am I going to stop you from stealing a ship if you're of such a mind? And even as small as I am, where the body goes, so goes the mind."

"You're down for all this?" AJ asked.

"You're asking what my choice would be if you were to put yourself to the task of stealing a ship?"

"I suppose."

"Well, it might not be up to me," she said. "Certainly, you understand that I'd be in mortal danger if harm were to befall my host?" She switched her bomber jacket for a yellow southern belle style gown and a paper fan which she flipped back and forth. "Why I'd be forced to help you, if only for my own survival."

He grinned. "I've been a bad influence on you."

"Two peas in a pod, if you ask me," Jayne said, shaking her head. "Even if we squeeze into the Lumbricus ship, we still have a fuel problem."

"We'll need travel supplies," Darnell said. "How long is the trip back to Earth?"

"That depends on the ship we take. I'd count on at least forty-five days," Beverly answered.

"But we got here in less than three," Jayne said.

"We were on a Tok freighter," Beverly said. "The Tok have by far the most advanced propulsion. There are no abandoned Tok ships on Beltigersk Five as they are too valuable."

"We need to think this through," AJ said. "Let's say we make it home. What's to say the Korgul won't just shoot us down. Or let's say we make it to the surface. Won't they just hunt us down? We need more of a plan than to hijack a worm ship and race back to Earth."

"Daunting problems to be sure," Beverly said. In front of her, a drafting table popped into existence and a sheaf of rolled papers appeared in her hand. "I took the liberty of speaking with an old family friend. We spoke hypothetically about the Korgul problem on Earth and the issues presented to the human resistance we encountered."

"An old family friend?" AJ asked. "You've been plotting this for a while."

"Of course, mon ami," Beverly tutted, this time changing her outfit so she wore a red beret and a red scarf around her neck. "The largest problem is, of course, the ease with which Korgul gather intelligence. All they need is to take over a human host who has information they require. It is impressive that the human resistance has remained isolated from the general population."

"What happens when your friend rats us out to your mother?" AJ asked Beverly. "Seems like she might have something to say about you returning to Earth. I bet she could lock this place down if she was of such a mind."

"Your assumption about how Beltigersk see humanity is wrong," Beverly said. "There are many who are sympathetic to humanity's plight and want to help. DLG2209TVX has already done considerable research on the Korgul data we brought back and he's offered his help. He just has one requirement."

Jayne held up her hands defensively and walked backwards. "Oh, no."

"What?" AJ asked.

"He's nothing like Jack," Beverly said. "He's adopted the name Thomas and I assure you, he's a perfect gentleman – more than a perfect gentleman."

"He wants to hitch a ride with Jayne?"

"I'm not doing that again," Jayne said. "The last time nearly killed me."

"Hear me out, please, Dr. Jayne," Beverly said.

Jayne gritted her teeth. "There's nothing to hear."

"What if, with your help, the two of you were able to manufacture a compound capable of rendering humans incompatible with Korgul?" Beverly asked.

"You can't ask me to do that," Jayne said quietly, shaking her head.

"We're getting ahead of ourselves," Darnell said. "Without Fantastium, we're not going anywhere. And, without a plan to get past the Korgul patrols around Earth, we're just as lost. I'm all for hitching a ride in the worm-mobile, but we need a better plan than *Get 'em, Ray*."

"Really? Now we're quoting *Ghostbusters?*" AJ asked.

"What's a ghost buster?" Jayne asked.

"Never mind," AJ said. "Darnell's right. We were nearly worm food when we tried to escape Earth last time. I'm not showing up in the worm-mobile just so Korgul can finish the job, although you gotta admit there's a certain poetic balance to it."

"You're an idiot," Darnell said.

"Mother calls." Beverly switched back into her formal black gown and her face grew serious. "Perhaps you should have 2-F or Seamus consult the galactic atlas. Maybe you have just enough Fantastium."

"Wait, before you go," AJ said. "Any chance you recorded any old movies? Jayne needs an education."

Beverly took on the visage of a green ball of slime with a goofy smile. Turning toward the wall, she raced forward. A wet slap sounded as she seemed to pass right through, leaving a trail of translucent goo dripping down the wall.

3
___

A PLAGUE UPON

"What do you suppose she meant by *just enough* Fantastium?" Jayne asked. "Is there a refueling station nearby?"

"2-F is looking," Darnell said. "How would we pay?"

"Do they use money?" AJ asked.

"I've seen references to Galactic notes," Darnell said. "That's basically what dollar bills are. Doesn't matter, though. We don't have any."

"Do you think they're just going to let us leave?" Jayne asked. "Beverly acts like she's afraid of her mother. You have to believe that if Beverly knows what we're up to, it's likely others do, too."

"No gas stations. At least not in range of the worm-mobile," Darnell said.

"What if we scraped residual Fantastium from all the ships?" AJ asked. "It wasn't like we didn't find any at all."

"No good," Darnell said. "The worm-mobile is heavy. Best bet is three jumps. It'd get us about a tenth of the way home."

"Get a piece of paper," AJ said, suddenly missing Beverly's presence. "We need to list every system within three jumps."

"There are forty-two," Darnell said.

"Seriously? In three jumps?" AJ growled. "Why in the hell was she so vague? Like it would have killed her to just tell us."

"Maybe she was being monitored," Jayne offered, taking a spiral notebook and pen from the manufactory. "Darnell, what's the first system?"

"Do you want their number or name? Because the names don't make a lot of sense," Darnell said.

"Numbers are too easy to confuse," she said.

"Names won't be any better."

"Just have 2-F assign names from the chart of periodic elements." She held her pen ready. "List habitable planets, moons, cities and space stations."

"That's a big list." Darnell blinked as three-inch-thick booklets plopped onto the counter from the manufactory.

Jayne retrieved them and handed one to AJ. "I assume you don't need a booklet, Darnell?"

He gave her a look. She shrugged.

For several minutes, the trio scanned the information, trying to make sense of it. "How about the city, Argon-3? Population isn't real big. Maybe we could bring something with us and trade for Fantastium," AJ said. "It's inhabited by Rosengul."

"2-F says Hafnium-8 is similar and has a rural Vred population," Darnell said.

"What's wrong with Rosengul?" AJ had barely gotten the question out before a projection popped up on the wall. A saggy, yellow-skinned alien with an egg-shaped torso, spindly arms and thick, stubby legs appeared on the wall. Next to the alien a projection of Darnell appeared, towering over the tiny alien who only came up to Darnell's knees. "Ugly little suckers, aren't they?"

Jayne blew out a breath. "We just need something to trade, right?"

"There are a dozen ships out there we can salvage," AJ said. "Come on, it's what I do."

"Vred have tons of technology. Why would they need to trade with us?" Jayne asked.

"That's like saying humans invented cars, so nobody wants a new car," AJ said. "No, it's all about finding a motivated buyer. Trust me, you wouldn't believe the junk people buy. Aliens ain't gonna be any different."

"2-F agrees," Darnell said. "Given the inventory of the ships we searched, he's come up with a list of items most likely of interest to Vred."

"Do we have another choice?" AJ asked.

"Not an easy one."

"Let's get some rest and hit the ground running in the morning."

"THIS REALLY ISN'T THAT BAD," Darnell said, resting his forehead on a cushioned bar AJ had fabricated to make the Lumbricus ship easier to pilot.

Instead of a ship where blocky rooms were connected by rectangular corridors, the Lumbricus designed their ships with a series of rounded, interconnected tunnels that periodically opened into wider spaces, usually at the ends of the largest, most sweeping curves. According to the images they'd seen, Lumbricus had eyes located forward and centered on plump, tuberous bodies. The only way for humans to access the low controls and data displays was to lie on their stomachs, push up on their elbows and crane their necks back. It was an impossible angle for anyone to maintain for more than a few minutes.

To solve this problem, AJ cut away a section of the bulkhead beneath the cockpit to accommodate human legs and positioned a narrow platform to take the weight of the pilot's chest allowing them to stretch out and lean forward. A soft pad held the pilot's forehead at a comfortable angle allowing visibility through the hole in the platform to the displays.

"I got the idea from a massage table," AJ said.

"When did you ever get on a massage table?" Darnell asked.

"Don't answer that," Jayne quickly interjected, causing both men to laugh.

"Do you think you can fly her?" AJ looked worriedly at the rows of thick, pencil-like controls that stuck up from what Darnell had informed him was the flight control surface.

"Lumbricus proboscis aren't nearly as dexterous as human fingers and they don't have ten of them," Darnell said. "Although, I imagine if you got frenched by one, you might think differently."

"Ah, geez, Big D. You really had to put that in my head?"

"I did," Darnell said. "The fact is, this ship is easier to sail than that Korgul ship we bought on Earth. Overall, the ship isn't particularly maneuverable, but she should get us from point A to point B. My guess is, Lumbricus combat pilots aren't in high demand."

"My fingers may never unprune after this," AJ said, flicking his hand to remove the ever-present layer of what they'd come to call *juice*. Short for AJ's originally coined name of Lumbricus juice, the simple mixture of protein, sugars and water exuded from nearly every surface of the ship.

"The Lumbricus are an amazing species," Jayne said. "All these juicy surfaces allow intra-ship communication while providing nutrients to the inhabitants. If human skin was like theirs, we'd never have to eat or drink anything while aboard."

"Thanks for the biology lesson, Doc," AJ said, "but like everything else on this ship, that's disgusting."

"Have you warned Beverly that we're leaving?" she asked.

"I didn't want to burden her," he answered.

"How will that work? Will she lose contact with whoever she's talking to when we get too far away? Is her consciousness split? What if it hurts?" She peppered him with questions.

He put his hand up. "Slow down, Doc. I didn't say I wasn't going to talk to her, just that I haven't. She shows up every couple days, which makes her due tonight. We should have the ship loaded and ready, so we can spring our departure on her just before we roll. I'm pretty sure she's expecting it."

Jayne nodded. "I have a batch of supplies waiting on the habitat manufactory. I'll fetch them now since you tell me she could show up at any time. Darnell, do you need anything while I'm out?"

"No, I'm good," he said. "I was just going to work on the head a little more. I feel like we aren't going to love the way it works."

"I don't plan on using it much," she said.

AJ laughed. "Like that's an option."

"I'll conserve on liquid and solid intake. We're ten days from Hafnium-8. I should be able to last."

"Didn't pick you for being shy about that sort of thing."

Jayne placed an atmospheric mask over her face and slithered her way back to the exterior hatch.

"Smooth," Darnell said, once she was gone.

"What?" AJ asked. "She's a doctor, for crying out loud. It's no mystery how that end of things works."

"There's no privacy, AJ. We're crouching over a hole. Not exactly dignified."

"No different for us."

Darnell shook his head in mild disgust.

"I could make an opaque sheet and hang it. Would that be better?" AJ asked.

"She tried that. Couldn't get it to stick, what with all the slime."

"Oh, I can get it to stick."

Darnell nodded. "Then what are you waiting for? Go."

AJ gave his friend a perplexed look and slithered down the narrow passageway on his stomach, flipping his legs under him as he dropped through the hatch. "Doc, wait up," he called, jogging over the loose dirt after strapping on the makeshift snowshoes. As he ran, AJ marveled at his body's renewed strength and agility. They had all adapted quickly to the snowshoes and AJ knew his legs, at least, were stronger for their efforts on Beltigersk Five.

"Did you forget something?" Jayne asked as he caught her.

"Darnell said you tried to put up a sheet around the head, something about you couldn't get it to stick," he said.

Jayne shrugged as they ran. "There's nothing to attach to."

"I could make a spring pole," he said.

"I'm not following."

"Not worth explaining. I can get your sheet in place."

"Really?" She flashed him a broad smile. AJ's breath caught in his chest. Her straight black hair was shiny with Lumbricus juice. Matted like it was to her head, the sleek locks made her look like she'd just emerged from the ocean. Her grin widened as she recognized his interest. "Keep looking at me like that and we're going to end up making Darnell very uncomfortable."

"You've always been a real looker, Doc," AJ said. "You couldn't hide it behind fatigues in 'Nam. You can't hide it here on Beltigersk Five."

"You're not really one to mince words, are you? The older I get, the more I appreciate that."

"You don't look a day over twenty-five."

"You clean up pretty good, yourself." She suddenly increased their pace. "But this is hardly the time or place for this conversation."

"What do you think Hafnium-8 will be like?"

"2-F says it is wetter than Beltigersk. Kind of fits with the whole alligator-man, Vred thing, don't you think?"

"This whole evolution thing is weirdly consistent," AJ said. "Don't *you* think? I mean, if you ignore Korgul and Beltigersk, there are more humanoids than not, even though there's variance in size. Nothing really new in the skin department either: reptilian, wormy, furry. Eyes – plural – but, so far, not more than two."

"I don't find that weird at all," Jayne said as they arrived at the habitat and ducked through the opening.

"You describe the same type of variance we see on Earth, just not necessarily sentient. In wet climes, reptilian skin has an advantage. Colder climes, fur would be more valuable. Two eyes, or really duplicate of anything, just makes sense. A species with two of anything critical would survive longer because of the backup."

AJ thought about her comments as he programmed in his idea for holding a curtain in place. "Sounds like confirmation bias to me," he said, knowing that he was goading her into a longer conversation.

"Hardly. My observations are just that," she said. "We've seen species outside of our experience. Korgul are a good example, as are Beltigersk. The idea of parasitic evolution will cause quite a stir in the scientific community."

A trio of poles extruded from the manufactory and AJ set them to the side as he watched Jayne stuff her remaining supplies into a large backpack. "Do you think I'm making a mistake?"

"To leave here? That's the second time you've asked," she said. "Do *you* think we're making a mistake?"

"Seems like our odds of survival drop quickly once we're in space."

"And if we stay here, we're little better than domesticated dogs trading comfort for safety. I was never more alive than when I put you boys back together in 'Nam. I hated every moment of it, but all the same, I knew there was no place else I should be. I made a difference, AJ. Those boys got a second chance at life."

"Preaching to the choir," AJ said, tapping the old scar on his chest where Jayne had operated on him so many years ago.

"This is my second chance, AJ," she said. "I don't care if I have to lie, cheat or steal if it pushes those Korgul puss-balls another inch off our planet. If I die in the process, so be it. That's the same contract you had when you fought in 'Nam. Why should I expect anything different?"

"Feel like I touched a nerve there, Doc," AJ said. "But I was asking about this potty screen. Do you think I'm making a mistake in the design? Will you be okay with a curtain?"

Jayne's face contorted in surprise. After thinking a moment, her eyes narrowed and her lips pressed together. "You're an asshole, Albert Jenkins."

He grinned. "Yup."

"There have been reports of copious utilization of manufactory supplies." Beverly appeared on the counter where the final pieces of AJ's spring pole screen had finally slid out. "Further, there have been reports from our visitors that property has gone missing."

"Odd," AJ said, wrapping his spring poles in a tarp. "Doc, you good to go?"

"You need to tell her, AJ," Jayne said, shrugging on her backpack and working her way to the exit.

"Hypothetically speaking, of course," AJ said, "what would happen if you were off visiting your family when my body moved a considerable distance?"

Beverly slowly tipped her head to the side and smiled. "It would cause no harm. Just as hypothetically, if an investigation were already well underway, whoever was involved might only have a few hours before steps were taken."

AJ nodded in understanding.

"Mother, no," Beverly suddenly said. "It is not done!"

"What's going on, BB?"

"Run, AJ!"

Jayne pushed open the flap that had served as a door to the surface of Beltigersk Five and slipped through. AJ raced after her. Just as he thought he would clear the opening, his head slammed into something hard. Stunned, he fell back into the habitat.

"AJ?" Jayne called back. "What are you doing?"

"I hit my head," AJ answered, trying to get up. Suddenly, a high-pitched sound filled his ears. The noise was so loud to be almost incapacitating. He dropped his poles and pressed his hands tightly to his ears, trying to stop the pain. Somehow, he could still hear Jayne talking from the other side of the flap, but just barely. "AHHH!" he screamed.

"What is it, AJ?" Jayne asked, looking in to find him lying next to the opening. When he didn't respond other than to groan in agony, she pulled on his arm. "Come with me."

AJ felt her hand on his arm, but the pain was so overpowering he was unable to do anything more than crawl toward the opening. "The noise! We've got to shut it off!"

Jayne shook her head, hearing nothing. "It's Beverly. She's overloading your auditory," Jayne yelled back.

Suddenly the world went quiet. "Oh, shit, that's better." AJ looked around, grateful for the change. "I think that was Beverly's mother," he shouted. "She's overloading my senses."

"Can you hear me?" Jayne shouted back.

"I can't hear you, Doc."

"Let's go," she said, motioning to AJ so he'd understand. "I'll help you."

"I've stopped her for the moment," Beverly said, hovering in front of AJ's face. "You need to move quickly!"

AJ had no trouble hearing Beverly and though his hands trembled, he pulled his snowshoes on and set off after Jayne. The trek back to the Lumbricus ship would take twenty minutes and he had no idea if Beverly could buy them that much time.

"We need to protect Darnell," AJ said. "Without 2-F, there's no way he can sail that ship."

"I understand, AJ," Beverly answered, appearing next to him wearing a flight suit and rocket pack. "There are those who will help us, but it will come at a great price. Mother will stop at nothing to bring me back."

"Including sending Tok ships for us?" he asked, panting as he and Jayne pushed their pace. "No way is that Lumbricus ship outrunning a Tok."

"I don't think immediately," Beverly said. "She will want to keep my defection quiet. It is one thing to have your daughter embark on a mission to provide aid to an impoverished species and quite another to help free a small group of..."

"Say it," he growled.

"Raccoons," Beverly said. "Pets. Limited sentients. You were right all along, AJ. The bigotry against humanity is widespread. I've been arguing for why Beltigersk should engage more directly with Korgul because there are things we could do. We are not without resources. But Mother would hear nothing of it. She said it was the responsibility of the Galactic Congress and that we'd done everything possible. It's not right, AJ. How can we stand by and let this happen?"

"You're not exactly standing on the sidelines, darlin'," AJ said.

"It's not just me," she said. "There are hundreds of Beltigersk who will join us. I just need to get the word out."

"As long as you can do that and keep your mom out of my head, I'm all for it," he said.

"Albert Jenkins!" The voice came from nowhere and everywhere all at once. It was as if the entire valley was filled with the sound.

"Mom?" AJ asked, perhaps a more sarcastically than necessary.

"I am your master, Albert Jenkins," the voice said. "You will cease your actions or I will bring your life to an end."

"What, so I can live in a forty-by-forty cell in a dead valley while Korgul enslave my people and strip my planet? What gives you the right?" he shouted back.

"My daughter has attached herself to you," the voice answered. "Her life is more important than you could possibly understand. There are others who have taken up the mantle of protecting humanity. Would you have me withdraw our support? Without my ambassador to the Galactic Congress, there will be none who would speak for you humans. You are surprisingly noble for such a lowly creature. Prove this again and give yourself to my daughter so she might take up her rightful position at my side. What stronger advocate could you ask for?"

AJ shook his head angrily, not sure what to say, but it was Jayne who answered. "What kind of sentient would bargain the life of her daughter for an entire species? There are nine billion lives in the balance. Do you consider her life worth more than all of these? Are we so low in your estimation?"

"Humanity is a violent species of limited intelligence. You would become a plague on the peoples of the galaxy," the voice replied. "Korgul have done all of us a great favor by limiting your capacity for intergalactic travel."

"Mother!" Beverly gasped. "Stop. You can't possibly mean that."

"Why is that, daughter? What do you see in humanity that is so worth saving?"

"It is not our question to ask," Beverly answered. "Humanity has much more to offer than Korgul, yet we allow them to operate freely."

"If it were up to me, Korgul would be cut off just as humanity has been," the voice responded. "Why can you not understand this? The greed and violence of humanity, as well as theirs, cannot be allowed to propagate. It would be the undoing of us all. It was a fortunate day indeed when Korgul discovered Earth."

AJ reached the bottom of the ramp leading into the Lumbricus ship and flung his payload upward. "Beverly, are you still with us?"

"I am," she answered. "But my strength will not last long."

"Big D, we need to get this tub out of here. Doc and I are loaded," AJ said, retracting the loading ramp.

"It is already too late. I am in charge now." Darnell's voice was pinched as he delivered his final message before a scream burst from his lungs like steam from a pierced boiler.

4

THE WHOLE IS GREATER

The howl of pain that echoed through the Lumbricus ship was worse than anything Jayne had heard in her many years as a doctor. At the same moment Darnell's anguished screams reached her ears, AJ grabbed his head and toppled over, wailing in agony. There was no question that Beverly's mother was now in charge.

Glassy-eyed, AJ looked up as Jayne bent to help him. "AJ, can you hear me?"

"You were wise to refuse a bonding, Doctor Amanda Jayne." Tears streamed down his face as he writhed on the floor. "I like to think we treat pets with dignity on Beltigersk Five. You have been very naughty, though. It is an extreme act of disloyalty to kidnap one of the royal family for personal gain. What if we were to visit Earth and inhabit your elected officials? Would you not defend yourself from this?"

"Surely, you see the parallel between your words and what the Korgul are doing on Earth?" Jayne shot back. "We are not pets. We are an intelligent, self-aware species. You have no right to play god with our future. Your daughter understands this and I believe your people do as well."

"You know nothing of my people." The queen's words were spat from AJ's mouth.

"You would find good company with the petty tyrants of Earth," Jayne said, forcing herself to crawl away from AJ. "You have shown yourself today."

"Where are you going?"

Jayne continued backing into the ship until she reached Darnell. His screams had diminished but had been replaced with a wild look in his eyes. "No!" he said, flailing his arms as if to block her from getting closer to the ship's controls. "Don't!" Before she realized what was happening, his fist struck her in the face, dropping her to the deck.

Fighting against the pain and the desire to fade into oblivion, Jayne grabbed at Darnell's leg and scooted back. Her goal was to trip him and get him down, but like a wild man, Darnell kicked at her, easily fending her off.

"There is nothing you can do, Doctor," the queen said through Darnell's mouth.

Greybeard barked angrily as he lunged through the passageway. Jayne was suddenly afraid. While she could fend off Darnell's aimless kicking, her skin was no match for the powerful bulldog's jaws and sharp canines. Bullishly, Greybeard dug his claws into the slippery passageway and churned with his chubby legs. Instead of latching onto Jayne, the dog sunk his teeth into Darnell, growling and shaking his head as if trying to snap the neck of much smaller prey. Jayne absently wondered at the damage being done to the man's leg. Greybeard mulishly pulled Darnell toward the back of the ship.

"What, can't you even control a dog?" Jayne taunted.

"I... there is no rational thought," the queen sputtered.

Jayne seized her advantage and crawled across Darnell's body. Bracing her hands against the forward bulkhead, she pulled her legs to her chest and placed her feet unkindly onto whatever surface she could find on Darnell, which happened to include his head. She uncoiled her body and pushed against him, helping slide him down the passageway.

"I can't believe this is what we're down to," Jayne said, positioning herself on the makeshift pilot's bench fashioned for Darnell. "Eight levers to fly a spaceship," she muttered, grasping at the thick paddle-shaped handles.

"You'll not succeed!" the queen howled from Darnell. "I've disabled your pet. I'll soon master your friend. Give up now and I'll allow you all to live out your lives in this valley. You will want for nothing. I'll even require our ambassadors to make their pleas for humanity. If you resist, you will lose everything!"

Jayne reached for one of the middle handles and nudged it forward. In response, the ship lurched forward, sailing across a shallow swale only to embed itself into the rise on the other side. The dirt barely slowed the ship's forward movement, even as Jayne released the paddle and attempted to pull it back into its original position. As she fumbled in the bumping ship, Jayne managed to make things worse. She found out the hard way that the paddle didn't just move back and forth, but also twisted. Not too surprisingly, the ship responded in kind and turned on its side.

"Keep it up, Doctor Amanda Jayne," the queen taunted over the screeching of earth against the hull. "You'll destroy yourselves and we'll have no trouble recovering our people."

While she had no experience sailing spaceships, Jayne was quite familiar with the critical, terrifying moments when the unexpected occurred. Dealing with catastrophe was a lesson every surgeon learned, and she drew on past experiences to push aside her panic.

"Observe, react," she chanted to herself, even as the ship skidded into the hillside. As she focused on the eight sticks, she recognized that two were out of alignment with the well-defined centerline on the console. When she nudged one control forward, the next in line moved on its own the same distance in the opposite direction. In a flash of inspiration, Jayne recalled the description of the Lumbricus. They were beings that manipulated the world with a protruding tongue, which meant the Lumbricus could push against the paddles much easier than they could pull.

"There you are," she said smoothly as she pushed the lowered paddle, causing the adjacent one to retract. With her actions, the ship stopped moving, jostling its inhabitants as it belly-flopped back onto the loose Beltigersk soil. Noticing that the first paddle she'd touched was still out of alignment, she realigned it with its neighbors.

"I've got you now!" the queen growled triumphantly as Darnell's heavy hand landed on Jayne's back.

"Think like a worm," Jayne said to herself and reached for a third paddle, nudging it forward.

Darnell's fingers closed and his strong arms wrenched her from the bench. More importantly, however, the Lumbricus ship leapt from the small valley. "No!" Jayne said as she swung her leg, reaching for the controls. Her toe hit the lever she knew would make them go up, but this time, with less control, she pushed it forward several inches. The response was instantaneous. The ship's occupants were smashed against the floor and the ship rocketed skyward.

"You fool! You'll kill them all," Darnell gurgled, releasing her.

Alarms sounded within the ship as statuses displayed on the forward panel. While she couldn't understand the shapes and symbols, the danger to the ship and its inhabitants was obvious. They were rocketing out of control, well beyond the ship's limits.

Jayne blinked back the tunnel vision of excessive g-forces and painfully reached for the ship's controls only inches from her fingertips. What should have taken seconds seemed to take forever as she willed her body to stay awake. Blackness took her.

"COME ON, DOC," AJ said, cradling her head in his lap. "I know you're in there."

"Her cardiac rhythm is restored but there is significant pooling of blood in her vessels," Beverly announced as she appeared, wearing a white lab coat complete with a stethoscope around her neck. "The patient will recover over time, although there is increased danger of aneurism."

"Did we do it?" Jayne asked.

"You did it, Doc," AJ said. "That angry lima bean had Big D and me on the ropes."

"Lima bean?" Jayne asked groggily.

"Just the mental picture I got of Beverly's mother," AJ snorted at his own joke. "How'd you figure out how to fly this thing, anyway?"

"At first, I didn't," she said, struggling to open her eyes. "What about Beverly, 2-F and Seamus? Are they okay?"

"I guess you can't hear them anymore, can you?" AJ asked. "BB's standing on your belt after giving you a full exam. She says you check out okay but might have issues later with aneurisms."

"I heard her. She must be using the ship to project. Her mother is terrifying," Jayne said. "How could the leader of such an advanced species be so narrow-minded?"

"I'm sorry," Beverly said, looking forlorn as she stared at the deck. "Mother does not want to believe that humanity is fully sentient. It is a common sentiment within the territory governed by the Galactic Congress. It will take time to change this perception. It is also not an excuse."

"What happened to your buddy?" AJ asked. "You know, the one who had an invention that'll let us gas people so Korgul can't infect them?"

"Thomas has no invention yet. He simply has an idea he would like to explore with someone who has a scientific mind. I hope you are not offended, but Thomas has taken up residence in your dermis, along with several others," Beverly said. "There was no time to ask for permission."

"Mi casa and all that," he said wearily.

"After Mother's tirade, I find that I more clearly understand Dr. Jayne's reticence in hosting a Beltigersk. I knew Mother did not hold favorable views of humanity, but I did not understand her bigotry was so deeply embedded. My faith in my own people, my own family, has been shaken."

"Sounds familiar," Darnell said.

"Are we really going there?" AJ asked.

"Just saying," Darnell needled, but was cut off by Jayne.

"Beverly, do you trust this Thomas?" she asked.

"Yes. Thomas is highly respected within Beltigersk society," Beverly answered.

"That wasn't my question. As far as I know, Jack was respected too. If you recall, you said nice things about him."

"The fault was mine," Beverly said. "I allowed the immediacy of our peril to cloud my judgment. I was aware that Jack was not a perfect candidate for bonding with a human. While subtle, his views were often expressed as jokes where humans were the punchline. I should have seen the danger."

"Ma'am, you'll need to step to the back of the bus," Darnell added.

"Big D. We get it. Will you let us have this conversation already?" AJ asked.

"We're coming back to it," Darnell warned.

"I know."

"Thomas does not hold the view that humans are lesser sentients," Beverly continued. "He would also like me to communicate that he will be most respectful of your privacy. May I inquire as to why you've had a change of heart?"

"It's not that complex. My fear of joining with Thomas endangered our crew," Jayne said. "If I'd agreed earlier, I wouldn't have struggled to gain control of the ship. Thomas could have explained the extraordinarily simple Lumbricus controls."

"That is not an entirely true statement, Dr. Jayne," Beverly said. "Mother would have disabled your body, just as she did the others."

"I am ready, Thomas," Jayne said.

"You simply need place your hand on AJ's skin." Beverly's rocket packs lifted her from Jayne's belt. She puttered toward AJ's foot and with a laser pointer, illuminated AJ's right ankle.

"Just how many travelers do I have down there?" AJ asked, looking at his ankle as Jayne pulled at the cuff of his jeans.

"I've chosen eighteen volunteers," Beverly answered. "More were interested, but I was selective, choosing personalities that are likely to successfully bond with humans."

"What was your selection criteria?" Jayne said.

"My highest-weighted criteria was a strong belief that humanity deserves a full seat on the Galactic Congress. Almost as important was a flexible mind that did not require control of the host."

"Thomas fits both these categories?"

"Yes, although he is considerably older than the other candidates. As a scientist, his mind remains flexible and I am certain the two of you would be well matched. I could set up a link so the two of you could become acquainted," Beverly said.

"Are there others who could develop a mechanism for humans to resist a Korgul infestation?"

"In short, no. It is true that some who have come along are quite intelligent. It is also true that they lack the experience Thomas has in studying the Korgul and Beltigersk condition."

"Why do you do it?" Jayne asked.

"It?"

"Merge with lesser sentients. You could just as easily construct mechanical means to provide mobility or only communicate by electronic means. Surely your bodies derive no benefit from joining."

"Tell me, doctor, what is the physiological response to fear?"

"When a human experiences fear, chemicals known as adrenaline and cortisol are released, increasing the heartrate. There are a number of side effects that support what we call the fight or flight reflex."

"And when you experience joy?"

"Endorphins, oxytocin, serotonin and dopamine," Jayne answered. "Are you saying Beltigersk riders are addicted to human biological responses?"

Beverly laughed. "I've never heard it presented that way, but I suppose in some manner, you're not far off. Throughout Beltigersk history, we've discovered that if we join with other species, we're able to accomplish significantly more together than if we simply take an outside advisory role."

"Makes sense," AJ snorted. "Who's going to listen to a four hundred nanometer lima bean?"

"Be serious, Albert," Jayne chastised. "I think Beltigersk advisors would be highly sought after."

"Thank you, Dr. Jayne," Beverly said. "But AJ is not incorrect. Advisors are easily ignored, but trust is gained through shared experience. I believe humans have a saying – the whole is greater than the sum of its parts."

"So, experiencing physiological responses are just an added bonus?" Jayne asked.

"It is more than that," Beverly said. "Those responses provide much needed incentive to the host and rider alike. Beltigersk people live long lives but have little in the way of passion. Have you ever wondered why I so enjoy experimenting with fashion?"

"The question has crossed my mind."

"Because it's fun," she said. "It also helps me better communicate with AJ."

"Feels dirty when you say it like that," AJ grinned.

Beverly switched into a skin-tight purple leather bodysuit, complete with a hoodie, mask, stilettos and pointed ears. "Feels dirtier when I say it like this," she purred.

"Now you're just playing with me."

Beverly switched back to her flight suit and rocket pack. "Contrary to what he would lead you to believe, AJ's mind is not consumed by thoughts of wild women and drink."

He frowned. "Whoa, how'd this get so personal all of a sudden? I'd like to argue that point."

"AJ is significantly more inspired by problems. While the catsuit grabs his attention for a few moments, he derived significantly more satisfaction while engineering an escape from Beltigersk Five. Even the catsuit pales in comparison to his response to your approval, Dr. Jayne."

"Now, that's enough," he snarled. "That's not your information to share, BB. Go back in your hole."

Beverly looked both surprised and chagrined by AJ's outburst. Without further hesitation, she popped out of existence.

"That was kind of harsh, don't you think?" Jayne asked.

"There are lines, Doc. How I feel about someone is my business."

"You might want to rethink that banishment, buddy," Darnell called back from the makeshift cockpit. "2-F and I have been chatting up here. We think there's gonna be trouble on Hafnium-8."

"What kind of trouble?"

"The kind of trouble caused by a general alert for a stolen Lumbricus ship and a kidnapped princess. It appears that BB's mom put out the equivalent of an APB on us," Darnell said. "2-F thinks the authorities on Hafnium-8 will likely take us into custody and send us back to Beltigersk Five."

AJ closed his eyes. "How long before we reach the inter-system transit point?"

"You have time. Two days to reach this system's transition point and another eight to get us to Hafnium-8," Darnell said. "According to 2-F, there isn't much space travel through there, so we shouldn't see trouble until we're inside the planet's territorial boundary."

"What's the boundary?"

"The Galactic Congress defines planetary territorial distance as ninety-one thousand miles from the surface of any occupied plane-toid or moon."

Between Jayne and AJ, a green and blue planet appeared. Like earth, large oceans of water separated several continents. At first blush, the percentage of land looked to be larger than the one-quarter of Earth's surface. A translucent purple sphere encircled the planet at roughly half the distance to the planet's two orbiting moons, one of which had its own translucent orb.

"That's cheating, BB," AJ growled and the display blinked out.

"Nonsense," Jayne said. "Have her bring it back, AJ."

AJ sighed. "Fine, bring it back." For a moment, Jayne and AJ stared at the empty space between them.

"Maybe use the magic word?" Jayne suggested.

"Oh, hell," AJ growled. "BB, would you *please* bring the projection of the planet back?"

The planet and moons reappeared.

"Be nice to her," Jayne said. "She's still learning the nuances of human interaction and she doesn't need you yelling at her."

He rolled his eyes and muttered, "Shoot me now."

"Don't tempt me," Jayne said. " Beverly, I assume this is Hafnium-8 and its moons. It looks like one of the moons is occupied. Should we expect to be apprehended on both the planet and moon?"

When Beverly didn't answer, Jayne glared at AJ with a raised eyebrow. He considered digging in but decided to take his lumps. "Beverly, I apologize for yelling at you. Would you please return to our conversation?"

Beverly appeared, sitting atop the planet, her heels resting comfortably in the ocean. "I also apologize. My comments were intended to be witty, but I realize I shared information to which I alone am privy."

"How likely are we to be taken into custody on Hafnium-8?" He was in no mood to discuss his feelings in public or anywhere else for that matter.

"Ninety-five percent chance within the first two hours in any location with a population in excess of ten thousand," Beverly answered. "Less populated locales would reduce that percentage to seventy."

"What about the moon?" AJ asked, pointing at the moon which boasted several cities.

"The surface of the moon, Celestarn, is inhabited and would present a much poorer choice than the planet itself," Beverly said.

"Why would they go to space when they still have room on the planet?" AJ asked.

"Hafnium-8 was originally inhabited by a limited species. I'll call them indigenous Halfnies for the sake of translation," Beverly said. "When Vred settlers arrived, they set up a base of operations on the moon, Celestarn. Over a matter of centuries, the Vred settlers moved planet-side, pushing out the original inhabitants. The poorly organized indigenous, originally welcomed the Vred. However, as the Vred settled a majority of the planet and became known by others as true Halfnies, the indigenous became resentful and retreated to a few protected colonies on the planet."

"Don't tell me I'm the only one seeing this," Darnell said.

"Seeing what?" AJ asked.

"If you want to take something, you identify the species as *limited* and then take whatever you want," Darnell said. "Kind of like what Europeans did to the American Indians."

"Right," AJ said. "Good thing we have the PC police along. I'd hate to miss an opportunity to wring my hands in self-loathing."

"You're an asshole."

"Hard to argue with that," AJ said. "So, tell me what's on that other moon called Farst. Why isn't it claimed if there's such a shortage of space?"

"It's covered in debris," Beverly said.

"What kind of debris?"

"Everything. Due to a high-water table on the planet and a desire to clean the ecosystem, Vred offloaded centuries of waste onto Celestarn-2 or Farst. It was an expensive endeavor, but the ecology of Hafnium-8 is now pristine and protected by strict environmental law."

"Sounds like a fun bunch," AJ said, sarcastically.

"What's it gonna be, AJ?" Darnell asked. "Are we turning around? It's not like we can go anywhere civilized at this point."

"I assure you, you would all be treated well on Beltigersk Five if you were to return," Beverly said.

AJ chuckled. "You just told me about the biggest junkyard in history. Now, you want to know if I'll go back and turn myself in?"

5

MAELSTROM

"I didn't think the smell would be this bad," Jayne complained, shifting the plastic barrier to cover the entrance to the team's semi-private facility.

"Downwind of the latrine is always a bad spot," AJ said. "I'd like to say you get used to it. You don't. I'm surprised the ship doesn't have some capacity to dispose of waste."

Beverly appeared on the slick passageway wearing knee high rubber boots, long rubber gloves and her hair pinned back with a red scarf. In her right hand, she held a long plunger. "I've been communicating with the ship," she said. "It refuses to recognize the material as waste. In fact, the Lumbricus would consider the current conditions to be quite favorable, delightful even."

"I don't know if I can take another eight days of this," Darnell called from the makeshift cockpit.

"Have you been successful in communicating with Thomas yet?" Beverly asked. "His knowledge of chemistry might prove most useful."

"I am aware of his presence, but there has been no attempt at communication. That might be voluntary on his part," Jayne said. "I still have significant trepidation in sharing my body and consciousness with another being. I believe he is showing restraint to gain my trust."

"If he can fix this smell, you might consider giving him a nudge, Doc," AJ said. Jayne gave AJ a concerned look and nodded. "I'll be right here with you."

Next to Beverly, a wrinkly old man with bright white hair, colorful bowtie, and white lab coat appeared. "Thank you for the invitation to join you. My dear Dr. Jayne, I assure you, I'm as harmless as a fly and I will endeavor to regain what you once entrusted to your previous guest," he said, his voice carrying a hint of a German accent.

"Thomas, my analysis is that there is a significant rise in the levels of hydrogen sulfide and ammonia," Beverly said, pushing a gas mask over her nose.

Thomas smiled gently at the ten-inch-tall woman standing next to him. "Your bond with Albert Jenkins must be quite significant that you experience his physical discomfort to the olfactory. I assure you, the levels of the gasses you've mentioned, while an irritant, are quite harmless. I would, however, like to process a few samples of the interior walls. This moist environment and substrata allows for quick replication of bacteria."

"Not to mention pruning me up like an old man," Darnell added.

"You *are* an old man," AJ shot back.

"Don't look like one."

"AJ, perhaps while Thomas and I look for equipment to sample the ship, you and Beverly could do something about the constant feed of this mucus that coats everything," Jayne said.

"Did she say mucus?" Darnell groaned. "How am I gonna get that outta my head?"

"I'm not sure what we have in the way of tools," AJ said. "Exactly how would a worm work on a spaceship, anyway?"

"The Lumbricus, like many species, are not known for mechanical aptitude," Beverly said, walking into an adjoining passage previously used only for the storage of potentially tradable parts. Totally immersed in the experience, Beverly's boots made a wet slapping sound as they hit the floor. "It is unlikely they were prepared for in-transit repairs."

"Where are you going?" AJ asked.

"Vred engineers customized this ship for the Lumbricus ambassador. In searching all available information, I believe I've identified the hatch the Vred used for maintenance on the lowest level."

AJ half crawled, half slithered behind her, doing his best to push Jayne's mucus characterization from his mind. "Explain how Lumbricus are considered smarter than humans, given they can't maintain their own ships."

"Lumbricus do not procreate like species who require a male and a female to join in some manner," Beverly said. "Instead, a sufficiently large Lumbricus splits into between two and four segments, each retaining the knowledge and experience of the parent. The Lumbricus were not the dominant species of their home world and were hunted by numerous natural predators. The pressure to survive and their ability to retain generational knowledge facilitated their first spaceflights."

"So, they didn't give the Galactic Congress a choice," AJ summarized. "They just started firing off into space. Nothing anyone could do about it."

"That's the essence of it."

"Now I feel like we've been going in the wrong direction."

"One moment, AJ, there should be a spring-loaded panel on the wall which will give us access to the mechanical control section." Beverly watched patiently as AJ slid his fingers beneath the layer of slime and found the panel. "Now, please explain what you believe the metaphorical *right direction* is."

The panel popped out as AJ released it. In response, a two-foot square section of the wall receded into the ship. Cool, dry air flowed through the new opening. AJ slid his body through the hatch and onto a deck made of metal grating.

"That feels fantastic." He closed his eyes in pleasure as he stood to his full height. "What were we talking about?"

"Right direction?" Beverly prompted.

"It's an old Earth saying. *It's easier to ask for forgiveness than to get permission*," AJ said. "Lumbricus didn't ask for anyone's permission. They just did what they needed to do. That's what we should be doing."

"Like stealing a Lumbricus ship?"

He nodded. "Exactly. You know what a hungry raccoon does when it finds a garbage can with food in it?"

"I don't understand your obsession with raccoons."

With a patronizing smile, he said, "The raccoon knocks over that can and makes a buffet. I'm just saying, I'm getting hungry."

"There are those who will not treat unsanctioned species gently."

"You're missing the big idea. Your mother would have *gently* kept us as prisoners. Maybe look up what old Ben Franklin said about trading liberty for security and you'll know just how we feel. Now, how about we look at drying this ship out?"

"My analysis suggests that would be unwise," Beverly said. "The ship's systems are designed to operate with a constant coating. To change that mix would potentially cause failure in ship components."

AJ looked around the maintenance room. The ceilings were low, barely seven feet. Even so, standing here was a huge improvement over the short tunnels. The room was filled with machinery, but most equipment was separated on all sides by a four-foot-wide work zone.

"What's this?" AJ asked, discovering an alcove that held a heavy square metal table eight feet on each side and three feet off the ground.

"A simple workbench," Beverly said, using a jetpack to float over the table. "Vred engineers place equipment on the bench and use magnetic clamps to hold the piece in place. I'm surprised it is unfamiliar."

"What's the temp in here, seventy?" AJ asked.

"Seventy-three point four degrees Fahrenheit."

"How many ship's systems are controlled by equipment in this room?"

"I would need access to ship information," Beverly said. "I've attempted but a cipher is blocking me. It will take time to break the encryption."

"Big D, tell Greybeard to find me," AJ called, hoping Beverly would establish a communication channel.

"He must have heard you," Darnell answered. "He just ran off toward the back of the ship."

Excited barks drew AJ's attention. He walked back to the entry hatch and sank to his haunches. "I hear him. In here, boy!"

"What'd you find?" Darnell asked.

"Have 2-F show you on the HUD. I found a dry spot."

"Is there anything like lab equipment?" Jayne asked.

"Not sure. Could be. There's room for all of us if you want to come down." Greybeard popped his head through the hatch and looked happily up at AJ. "Hey, buddy, see if you can get Seamus to pop the cipher for BB, would you?"

Greybeard barked and jogged around the room, stopping to relieve himself on a particularly tall piece of equipment.

"AJ?" Jayne's voice carried through the opening. "Are you in here?" AJ crouched again and was met by the top of her head as she squirmed her way through the hatch. She stretched languorously as she stood. "Oh, that's nice."

His eyes grew wide as he took in the soaked, wet fabric of her suit clinging to the curves of her body. As she brought her arms back down, she raised an eyebrow, clearly aware of his stare.

"Sorry, Doc, it was just right there in front of me."

"Been a long time since I earned a look like that," she chuckled, flicking her hand to knock off the goop clinging to it.

"Always been a looker, Doc."

"Humidity is forty-two percent," Jayne said. "It's cozy, but we'll be much more comfortable."

Greybeard's barks drew their attention to a video console. "Seamus is very good at code breaking," Beverly said, putt-putting over to where the dog stood on its hind legs. "There's good news and bad. We have no way to reroute flight controls to one of these mechanical bays. However, I have discovered plumbing suited to humanoid needs, including wash stations."

"Showers?" Jayne asked, hopefully.

"No, but the pH of Vred skin is similar enough to that of humans, making the cleaning products left behind perfect to facilitate removal of the Lumbricus lubricant," Beverly answered. "There is a large basin and a spout similar to a kitchen sink. I'm afraid the water will be considered quite cool at sixty-five degrees."

"Perhaps our experimentation with bacteria could be postponed given this new development," Thomas said, appearing on the large metal worktable still in his white lab coat and bowtie.

AJ began systematically removing crates from where they'd been strapped onto wire metal shelving. "BB, can you inventory this as I go?"

"What are you looking for, AJ? The Vred have good records of the material left behind," she answered, puttering over next to him.

"Something soft. If I could make beds, we'd be more comfortable." AJ pulled a long piece of netting from a crate. "Or this would do it."

"Netting?" Beverly asked.

"By itself, not that interesting," AJ said, dumping the contents of the crate onto the table. "Add this cabling and now we've got something."

"I'll be in the restroom," Jayne said. "I'd appreciate it if you gave me some privacy."

"Not what you said earlier."

She rolled her eyes. "Don't get fresh, soldier."

AJ sighed as he watched the surgeon disappear down the narrow hallway. He found it odd just how much he'd come to care for the woman in such a short period of time. Turning his attention back to the pile of materials, he spread the wide netting out over the table and used the pocketknife he'd manufactured on Beltigersk Five to cut off a seven-foot length. Working steadily, he tied off two ends of the netting with the cabling and then attached the cable high on the walls. As was common, he lost track of time and was surprised to look up and see Jayne leaning against the wall.

"Is that a hammock?" she asked.

"Depends."

"On?"

"If I got that cable attached well enough. Want to give it a spin?"

She slowly shook her head. "Feel like that's the job of the inventor. I'm not sure I want to be your guinea pig."

"Where's your sense of adventure?"

"I'm standing in a spaceship stolen from a race of worms, on the run from a vindictive, four-hundred-nanometer queen, headed for a moon covered in junk and you think I need more adventure?"

"So dramatic." AJ put the material for a second hammock back onto the table. "Maybe you could help me get in, then."

"Feels like a trick."

AJ's head shake did little to relieve her of the notion, but she joined him anyway at the side of the untested hammock. "We used to make these things all the time back in 'Nam. Better than sleeping in the mud. Just give me your hands for leverage."

Jayne offered her hand and AJ sat back carefully into the netting. Unfortunately, the material was so stretchy that he sank much further than expected. Refusing to let go, he pulled Jayne in with him. Growing taut just before hitting the floor, the hammock held the two suspended before flipping over and depositing them on the hard floor. The entire turn of events took only a second or two, landing AJ atop Jayne on the deck.

"You planned this," she said. He grabbed her waist and rolled so their faces weren't quite so close together. She folded her arms up between them but didn't push him away.

"Not sure that could've worked out better," he said. "Always appreciate a soft landing."

"Soft, eh?" Jayne asked, pushing on his chest.

"Only in all the best places." AJ grinned and moved off to stand up.

Jayne swatted at his butt harder than she'd intended. The resounding slap echoed through the machine room. While she didn't say anything, a flush raised on her cheeks. AJ's wicked grin widened as he offered his hand to help her up. "Don't worry, Doc, there'll be plenty of time for all that."

"How far out do you suppose Halfnium-8 will start tracking us?" AJ asked. The trip through the solar system had been totally uneventful.

"They're already tracking us," Beverly said, sitting on the forward bulkhead. It was almost the end of AJ's last shift in the pilot's chair, the job amounting to nothing more than making minor adjustments every twenty minutes or so. With only an hour left of deceleration, they would reach Halfnium-8's moon, Farst, in roughly three hours with Darnell at the helm.

"And that's not a problem?" AJ asked.

"They already know this ship has limited engine capacity and nothing in the way of weaponry," Beverly said. "Safety protocols won't let us crash-land in a population center. I expect they'll just wait and see what we do. Space flight is extremely expensive and nobody's going to come too close until they have to."

"Is that why you have us lined up like we're headed to Celestarn instead of Farst?"

"That's right." She held a compass and ruler on top of a virtual map table and mimicked drawing a line between two points. "The alignment of the moons was particularly fortuitous. At the point they realize we're headed to Farst, we'll be well past. Even if they decide to chase, we'll have a significant head start. Tell me, what's your plan once we arrive on Farst?"

"I guess that depends on what the Halfnies end up doing," AJ said. "How much staff do you suppose they have on Farst? I know you said it isn't claimed by anyone, but surely there are caretakers."

"To our combined knowledge, there are no full-time residents on Farst," she said after a moment. "As you might expect, there is limited gravity, approximately fifteen percent that of Earth. With limited gravity, there is an extremely thin atmosphere, its pressure unsuitable for humans. The suits we've created with the ship's manufactory will be difficult to maneuver in. Our design focused on safety, after all. I'm still fuzzy on what you expect to accomplish."

"Well, that's just it. I don't know exactly," AJ said. "The fun thing about junkyards are the possibilities they open up. Going into this with a firm plan will lead to nothing but disappointment. It's just like when I burned a hole in the side of the habitat on Beltigersk Five. Did I already have a plan to swipe a worm ship and make a run for a junkyard in orbit over an alligator-infested planet? But look where we are now."

"Worm and alligator are not flattering comparisons for the Lumbricus and Vred," Beverly said. "Both are peaceful, highly intelligent species."

"Respectable galactic citizens. Folks who don't like getting too far out of their comfort zone, even when they see something bad happening. Trust me, I'm all sorts of impressed."

"I don't understand this side of you, AJ. I think you would find that Vred are similar to humans. They raise families, strive for personal independence and participate in bettering those around them."

"Exactly what would these family-Vred types do if they caught us?" he asked.

"We talked about this. They'd send you back to Beltigersk Five because of your status. Surely, you don't expect every sentient race you make contact with to immediately take up the plight of humanity. How would they even know what was happening on Earth?"

"One action I have a problem with is when they get in my way," AJ said. "Beyond that, they can sit in their mud springs and sip anchovy Mai Tais for all I care."

"I could go for a Mai Tai," Darnell said. "How we doing up here?"

"BB says Halfnies are already tracking us. They aren't sending a greeting party because they figure we'll come to them," AJ said.

"Makes sense. Not a lot of options. Say, 2-F and I have been working through some old scans of Farst. Looks like there's a buildup of older ships near the southern pole. Might be a good place to start looking."

"I believe the odds of finding residual Fantastium in the abandoned ships is unlikely," Beverly said. "I don't understand how you expect us to leave Farst once we land. We will have exhausted our own reserves."

AJ slid out of the horizontal bench that made up the helm and rolled his head, attempting to stretch neck muscles sore from poor positioning. "Have a little faith, BB."

"I thought you said we weren't expecting company," Darnell said.

"We're not," AJ said. "Where?"

"There's a ship coming up from Celestarn," Darnell said. "Looks like they're planning to intercept."

"This is not good," Beverly said. "The ship is requesting a communication link."

"Or what?" AJ asked.

"There was no threat levied."

She constructed a virtual display, showing the position of the two moons, their ship, and their pursuer. The unknown ship was accelerating in a wide arc away from the planet, lining up to travel in the same direction.

"How long before they get here? And more importantly, are they armed?" AJ asked.

"The ship is Galactic Police," she said.

"Police? That's gotta be your fault, Big D," AJ said.

"Very funny."

"Who are Galactic Police? I thought this was a Vred-settled system," AJ said.

"The Galactic Police are a branch of the Galactic Congress," Beverly said. "They provide enforcement of Galactic Law."

"That can't be good."

For several minutes, the three stared at Beverly's rendering of the moon and the converging ships. "The ship is within a mile and requesting we change our navigation so we fall into orbit around Celestarn."

"Are they going to shoot at us?" Darnell asked.

"I would not think so. Shooting a member of Beltigersk royalty would be counter to their objective."

"Kind of like diplomatic immunity," Darnell said. "Bet Mom didn't see that wrinkle."

"They're not breaking off," AJ said. "They're going to keep following us."

"Who?" Jayne asked, joining the group.

"We've got a tail," he said, calmly. "Cops. We're making a run for it."

"Why does this not surprise me? How soon 'till we get to Farst?"

"Not long now," Darnell said, adjusting the attitude of the ship.

AJ was disappointed to see that as Darnell bent their ship's path to match Farst's orbit, the Celestarn police continued to follow. "How much jurisdiction does that guy have on Farst?"

"Considerable. Farst isn't inhabited. They see this as a rescue mission," Beverly replied.

"Are you sure Farst isn't inhabited?" Darnell asked. "2-F is picking up radio traffic near the south pole."

"That is odd," Beverly said.

With little atmosphere, the ship experienced only minor turbulence as it sailed in toward the moon's surface.

"I'm not seeing that much trash," AJ said.

"It's an entire moon," Jayne said. "What were you expecting?"

"That," AJ said, pointing through the narrow window. The Halfnium system's star shined brightly on the moon's southern pole, illuminating miles upon miles of forgotten litter deposited long ago. From a distance, the trash resembled towering sand dunes that stretched as far as the eye could see.

"How does this help?" Beverly asked. "The outcome will be the same no matter what. Once you land, the Galactic Police will capture us. Your extra vehicular suits aren't nearly sufficient to allow us to make a run for it."

"How bad do you suppose they want us?" AJ asked.

"Better be darn bad." Darnell chuckled as he slowed even further and drove the nose of their ship into the side of a mountainous dune, throwing massive plumes of junk in every conceivable direction.

AJ watched with satisfaction as the virtual representation of the patrol ship veered off in its attempt to avoid the maelstrom of dislodged trash.

"You never cease to surprise me, Albert Jenkins," Beverly said.

6

PICKLE

"BB, Darnell, power down everything that won't kill us," AJ said.

"I don't understand how you can crash-land this ship without causing more damage," Jayne said. "We barely moved."

"According to 2-F, the Lumbricus aren't known for their landing skills," Darnell said. "This hull can take a lot more than landing in a sea of soft garbage."

"What do you think, BB? Is that patrol ship equipped to locate us after all that?" AJ asked.

Beverly now wore a flight suit, bomber jacket and aviator shades. The grin on her face gave away her answer before she could even speak. "Our engine heat signatures would be the easiest to locate. Darnell's approach vector suggests we have come to rest beneath roughly twenty yards of material. If that weren't enough, the ship's impact created a mushroom cloud of chaff that will cover a twenty-mile radius before it settles."

"How long will that take?"

"Given the moon's low gravity, some of the lighter material could take days. To answer your question, I don't believe a constable's patrol ship will be prepared to investigate such an event. That may work against us, though, as they could decide to send a larger team."

"So, we need to be gone before that happens," Jayne said.

"Seems right," Darnell agreed. "2-F was just showing me a line of old junked ships we caught sight of before we ditched. It's only a couple of miles from our position. I figure we give the dust an hour or so to settle and do a bit of exploration."

"I thought you said the suits weren't good for moving around," Jayne said. "How are we going to make it miles?"

"Low gravity should help," AJ said.

She grimaced and shook her head, unconvinced.

"Might be worth bringing the ship up to the surface while we've got cover," Darnell said. "Low gravity or not, I don't think we want to try to tunnel through twenty yards of junk."

"Just take it slow," AJ said. "With crap falling everywhere, I doubt you'll be too noticeable."

"Couldn't we just run the ship over closer to those junk ships?" Jayne asked. "Why's that different than surfacing?"

Darnell tipped his head to the side as he considered her idea. "Don't see why not, though it'd be helpful if I could get an idea of how deep we really are."

"Without the additional velocity of the crash landing, this ship will find it difficult to make significant progress through the trash without leaving behind an energy trail," Beverly analyzed. "Debris will also fall in behind where the ship vacates, creating a ridge that a Halfnie AI would likely identify. I suggest bringing the ship to an elevation where a majority is still submerged. The energy trail will be beneath us and leave no telltale trail on the surface."

"Any objections?" AJ asked.

"She's probably right," Darnell said. "I'll bring us up, nice and slow-like and stop once the forward viewport is clear. That work for you, BB?"

"It is brilliant, Darnell." She flashed him a big smile.

"We need someone to stay on the ship while the others are out,"

AJ said. "If those Halfnies return, I'd hate to get caught out in the open."

"We could suit up while Darnell is repositioning," Jayne said. "My last try at sailing this tub on Beltigersk Five didn't go all that well, so I'm not volunteering."

"Work for you, Big D?"

"Sounds like a plan."

"Our sensors are unable to locate the Galactic patrol ship," Beverly announced as Jayne and AJ worked their way down to the maintenance room where they'd left the suits. "Unfortunately, that doesn't mean they're not there, just that our sensors are currently overwhelmed."

"As long as it works both ways." AJ slid into the maintenance room, eliciting a happy bark from Greybeard who'd been curled up, sleeping in a pile of rags. AJ turned his attention to the bulldog and raised his voice. "You want to go with us? You'll have to wear that suit we talked about." Greybeard danced around, his response much like every dog *ever* throughout history.

"Are you sure it's wise to bring him?" Jayne asked. "I'd hate for him to fall in a hole."

"Bulldogs are natural rodent hunters. He'd love falling in a hole," AJ said. "Besides, if we run into any crazy electronics, we'll need Seamus's expertise."

Jayne shrugged. She'd adopted the role of devil's advocate. To her, AJ and Darnell were as brilliant as they were devious, but they tended toward leaping before looking. The approach stood in stark contrast to a surgeon's training, where every step was measured and each outcome predictable.

"How much time will we have outside?" she asked.

"Four hours max," AJ said. "We'll turn back when we've used a third of our O2. That should give us plenty of buffer."

Beverly appeared between the two as they struggled into the soft-sided suits. She wore a shiny silver spacesuit made popular in the 1960's TV show *Lost in Space*. "We may find oxygen reserves in the old ships," she offered. "While I'm certain the Vred will have salvaged as much Fantastium as they could, there would have been no reason to capture oxygen."

"I wish we'd brought a rocket pack or two along," AJ complained as he tapped what looked like a transparent fishbowl onto his over-sized suit. He waddled toward a hatch at the back of the mechanical bay and then turned back to make sure both Jayne and Greybeard followed. He couldn't help but laugh as he thought about how ridiculous they all looked. With pressure in their suits, it was as if they were living inside human and dog-shaped balloons gathered at their necks, waists, wrists and ankles.

"I hope movement gets better once we're outside," Jayne said, stacking up behind him, her arms held out at forty-five-degree angles due to suit inflation.

"Darnell, we good to go?" AJ called.

"Roger that, AJ. Your hatch exits at twenty feet below the surface. I slid the ship forward a bit, so you should have an open pocket where you can climb out."

"Good thinking." AJ twisted open the manual airlock, pausing to consider the volume of the tiny room. Even one at a time, using the airlock would be a tight squeeze. "Jayne, there's not much room in this airlock. You'll need to lower the pressure in your suit and run the cycle on your own. I'll walk you through it."

AJ released half the volume in his suit and lowered himself into the lock. Reaching up, he pulled the door closed and turned the wheeled handle to lock himself in. Only after accomplishing this did he see Beverly's projected indicator that said he could open the outside hatch.

"Can you see anything?" Jayne asked after he closed the exterior hatch behind him.

"Just be warned, it's a drop to the ground. And yeah, I can see daylight. Good job, Big D."

"Glad to be of assistance."

With oversized glove fingers, AJ tapped on the suit's controls on his forearm, instructing a return to full pressurization. A moment later, Greybeard and Jayne dropped next to him, their disturbance causing an avalanche of loose garbage to roll down the shaft opened by Darnell.

As if he'd been climbing his entire life, Greybeard dug into the side of the column of garbage and scaled it easily, disappearing over the lip. "Guess that answers that," Jayne said, also pressurizing her suit.

"Looks like he's hot on the trail of something." AJ pushed his comically large arms into the pile of garbage and worked his way up.

"Hey! You're covering me," she complained as garbage tumbled down and filled in around her feet.

"Just dig in. Use arms and legs. We don't weigh much here, so you don't need a lot of force," he said. "It's easy."

She followed suit, finding the climb to be significantly easier than she'd expected. Escaping her temporary prison, Jayne gasped in awe at the sight of the green and blue planet directly overhead. "I feel like I can almost touch the planet," she said, gawking unabashedly. "It's so beautiful."

"Astronauts say the same thing when they EVA," AJ said. "Something to do with the lack of atmosphere."

"I never thought I'd see anything so gorgeous."

"Um, you have something stuck to your suit," AJ said, brushing his bulbous fingers across her midsection. "Not coming off. Must have been heated up by the ship and it's not frozen again."

She looked down and discovered a sickly yellow patch of slime holding a narrow piece of tin or steel onto her suit. "Careful. I don't want a puncture. Best to leave it there."

"Looks like the lid to a can of soup." AJ detached the metal from her suit but was unable to remove the mustard yellow stain. "BB says this suit material is just about puncture proof."

Jayne shook her head. "I'd like not to find out. Now, where are we going?"

AJ pointed his puffy arm at a ridge across the shallow valley ahead. "That's our mountain."

"Lead the way."

Thup. A refrigerator-sized piece of debris fell onto the surface a few yards from their position and disappeared from view.

"Crap, that was a big one," AJ said. "BB, are we in trouble out here?"

"Statistically, the chance of either of you being struck by a large enough object to cause damage is low," she said. "It would be safer, however, if you delayed your trip for twenty hours or greater."

"How low is our chance? That shit storm is our cover."

"Point five percent," Beverly answered.

"One in two hundred aren't great odds," Jayne said.

"Doc, if you want to go back, I'll understand."

"No. I'm not sure our odds of survival improve if we're captured. Perhaps we should focus on learning how to navigate this field," she said, her leg sinking into a previously hidden hole. Surprisingly, however, when her over-inflated abdomen hit the hole, she merely bounced out. Kicking against the ground, she lifted above the surface and sailed several yards before bouncing unceremoniously, not once but twice, before coming to rest.

"Bravo, Doc. Might need to name that move after you."

Jayne laughed as she scrabbled back to her feet. "I feel like an oversized beach ball at graduation. I never imagined these oversized suits would actually work to our advantage."

AJ shook his head, trying to make sense of the analogy. Not coming up with anything, he tested a bouncing run and caught up with her, the only issue coming when he tried to stop. "When we get back, you're going to have to explain what beach balls have to do with graduation."

"Keep going," Jayne said, finding her feet and bounding toward him, not wanting to get too far behind. "It's not a hard reference. I've attended a number of graduations for colleagues. It is not uncommon to see beach balls loosed during these ceremonies."

"You're saying a bunch of stuffy doctors play with beach balls at graduation?"

"No, not them. Undergraduates."

"You really lived on the wild side, didn't you?"

The pair accelerated across the landscape, daring to take longer and longer strides. In minutes, they'd chewed up a distance they had thought would take hours.

"Sometimes it was balloons," she continued. "The deans and professors were always annoyed by the breach of protocol, but I always thought the activity was a good representation of the transition from adolescence into adulthood."

"You needed to get out more."

"I'm currently jumping across a garbage heap on an alien moon. Is that *out* enough?"

"Definitely a start," he said. "That's disappointing." The trio had arrived at the middle of a mile-long aisle of dilapidated ships. As far as the eye could see, the ships had been stripped to their frames and garbage had silted into the openings. "These ships have been picked clean."

"Don't give up," Jayne said. "We just got here. There are hundreds of aisles. This can't be all that's left."

"Where should we try, left or right?"

Jayne considered the question and shrugged. "Right."

"Right it is," AJ said and set off at a slower pace. "BB, Darnell said something about radio signals. Are you picking up anything?"

"2-F continues to monitor but has not detected anything more," she said.

"Let me know if you that changes."

"This is getting better," Jayne said as the quality of the wrecks improved, if only slightly, on either side of the aisle.

"There's a lot of organization here for a supposedly abandoned moon," AJ said. "Why line these up if you're just dumping them?"

"What are you saying?" Jayne asked.

"Junker's intuition," he said. "Doesn't matter if these vehicles are alien. They have value. Any intelligent species will have people who recognize that value and figure out how to do something with it."

"You're saying someone lives here?" Jayne asked. "Is that why you're interested in the radio transmission?"

"Lives here or regularly visits. Point is, there's a junker about. If you ask me, that's good news."

"How do you figure? You all live by a code? Have a secret handshake or something?" She chuckled. "You know surgeons have one."

"Really?"

"No. It's not a thing."

"Sassy. I like it," he said. "It's the same way I knew there'd be someone picking this stuff. A junker knows how to make a deal. That's all I'm saying."

Greybeard's barking interrupted their conversation. Even though the dog was half a mile ahead, he sounded like he was only a few feet in front of them due to the bridge created by the Beltigersk riders.

"Sounds like Greybeard found something."

They found the dog digging furiously around a delivery-truck-sized vessel stuck deep into the landscape.

"Look at that," Jayne said, doing her best to crouch in her oversized suit.

"What do you have?" At AJ's feet, the overlay of a large old-fashioned CRT-style console TV appeared. The image centered in the screen clearly showed that Jayne was looking at a boot print. The track outlined in the dust on top of a rusty steel panel was too long to be human by several inches. Plus, the wide toe split in two toward the end.

"Smurl grulp flargul zertargen!"

AJ spun toward the sound of a hissing voice. A seven-foot-tall alien appeared from nowhere and towered over Jayne, holding a long metal pole. AJ flung himself at the alien, doing his best to wrap his arms around the giant's waist.

"Gargun!" the alien yelled. AJ's momentum had propelled them about ten feet and he had the huge alien pinned to the side of a vessel.

"AJ, stop!" Beverly said. "You're attacking a Vred. They're peaceful!"

With Greybeard barking furiously at his back, AJ tried to land a punch, but his puffy fist only rebounded off the alien's suit.

"Gargun!"

"I don't know what Gargun is, but you need to drop the pole!" AJ growled.

Surprisingly, the alien complied, allowing the length of steel to fall to the ground.

"You needs be stopping!" A new voice demanded. "We gives you what you wants. Be no hurts."

Sensing no resistance from the alien beneath him, AJ stopped trying to figure out how to pummel the beast and turned to see who was speaking. Another alien, wearing a suit similar to the giant, stood next to Jayne. AJ pushed off, dove for the steel stick and brought it up in his hands as he rolled inelegantly to his feet.

"AJ, these Vred are no threat," Beverly said, appearing in front of him in a referee's uniform, holding her hands out.

"Oh, yeah? The big one was about to clobber Jayne," he said, quickly looking back and forth between the two aliens.

"Sharg not clobbers scary alien," Gargun said. "Angry alien takes what wants, leaves Sharg and Gargun safe."

"Is this really your best translation, BB?" AJ asked.

"Sorry, they're using a cheap common language unit," she answered. "Sharg, turn off translator. We speak Vred. We're peaceful." The last part sounded like AJ's voice instead of Beverly's.

"Why did you attack my mate, Sharg, if you are peaceful?" The baritone alien's voice had a slight hiss to it but otherwise sounded human. Unlike the seven-foot-tall alien who had threatened Jayne, the speaker was only five-and-a-half feet tall. Green reptilian skin shone through the transparent face shield.

"Because Sharg was threatening my ... well, Dr. Jayne," AJ sputtered, loosening his grip on the steel pole, but staying ready.

"What are you?" the large alien asked with a feminine contralto voice. "You are not Tok as we originally thought. You are much too tall."

"Human."

"Human? What is human?" Sharg asked.

"Yous are not," Gargun said, scoffing. "Humans do not sails the stars. They are barely more than conscols. I've seen information videos on humans. You are not them."

AJ chuckled. "Fine. You got us. We're just really pale Vred. We came up for a romantic afternoon. Wanted to get away from the little gators back in the nest and all."

"AJ!" Beverly said, aghast. "That's insulting."

"What is gator?" Gargun asked, irritated.

"Gargun, don't be so grumpy," Sharg said. "This is my mistake. I startled the male. What is your name, male?"

"Albert Jenkins. People call me AJ," he said, offering the large alien her steel pipe back.

"Two names? How unusual," she said, accepting the pipe. "Will you join us for a meal? We felt vibration from the small animal and came to investigate."

"Meal?" AJ asked, his mouth hanging open.

"We'd love to join you," Jayne said, stepping up next to him. "It is our custom to shake hands to signify peaceful intent. I am Amanda Jayne." She extended her puffy hand to Sharg. The large Vred's suited hand completely swallowed Jayne's but her grip was gentle.

"A lovely custom."

"Thieves not welcomes. If human, they're little better than ... than ...."

"Raccoons?" AJ offered. "Humans have been given a bum rap around here. And explain to me how we could be considered thieves by Vred who hang out in a dump? Are you saying you own this dump?"

"More than you do," Gargun answered, angrily.

"Gargun, you will be civil. The one named Amanda Jayne and I have shaken peaceful hands. You will not upset this important meeting. You will open our home to the humans and demonstrate our civility."

Gargun turned in a huff toward the large vessel Greybeard had been digging around. Surprisingly, he stepped through a sidewall and disappeared within.

ument42

68 JAMIE MCFARLANE

"That's kinda cool," AJ said. "Is that some sort of electrostatic pressure barrier?"

"Dielectric," Gargun grunted, sticking his hooded head back through the barrier. "I'm not sciences."

"What brings humans to the system of Halfnium?" Sharg asked, walking to where Gargun had disappeared. "And why would you visit Farst? It is a moon with few resources. Surely you would be better received on Halfnium-8 or Celestarn."

"Well, to be honest, we're in kind of a pickle," AJ said.

"Most unusual. You must be referencing a human idiom, otherwise, a preserved vegetable does not make much sense. Please, join us inside. The pressure is steady at point eight atmospheres. I am unsure what your species might consider poison for gas composition, but hopefully you do not find argon and nitrogen so, our planet has considerable volume of both."

"You'll be fine," Beverly's voice whispered in AJ's ear.

"*Pickle* means we've run into some trouble," Jayne said. "Our atmosphere has higher concentrations of nitrogen, but argon for a short period of time will not cause too much trouble. I assume you also expel carbon dioxide and consume oxygen given your warm body temperature."

"Is that a thing?" AJ asked. "You can tell by that?"

"It's an efficient mechanism," Jayne said. "You'd expect to see it in a majority of carbon-based evolutionary chains."

Passing through the wall felt like a whisper. AJ blinked several times as he took in the new surroundings. Everything was both alien and common in the same moment. There were tables, chairs and even video screens. The chairs had open backs, the tables were covered with a rich green carpet of moss and the video screens displayed an alien scene of reptilian humanoids interacting. Glass bowls containing clear water sat on the countertops and tiny schools of fish moved rapidly about within them.

"Are we the first Vred you've met?" Sharg asked, doffing her broad helmet and hanging it on a hook near the entry. AJ depressurized his own suit and removed his helmet, carefully testing the home's atmosphere. It had an unusual smell, but he didn't pass out, so he was probably okay.

"First Vred," AJ said, his eyes wide as he nodded in agreement.

"You're much smaller than your suits suggested. Now I understand *human*. I had forgotten what your species looked like and the bulbous creatures you appeared to be beneath those suits did little to prompt my memory."

"We needs be careful, Sharg," Gargun growled.

"Nonsense. I would ask you to make tea so that we might learn of Albert Jenkins and Amanda Jayne's pickle."

7

WELCOME TO THE TRIBE

"May I touch you?" Jayne asked, staring at Sharg intently.

"Doc, we don't have a lot of time," AJ protested.

Sharg gave an oddly human-like nod. "I would return the request."

"Of course," Jayne said, pulling off her deflated glove and extending her arm toward the much larger, reptilian-skinned woman. At the same time, Sharg reached for the exposed, milky-white skin of Jayne's upper arm. When Jayne's long, slender fingers touched the Vred's chest, she pulled her hand back with a surprised gasp.

"You're so warm," Jayne said.

"And your skin is so soft ... like dipping my fingers into the waters of a cool river."

Jayne smiled. "Such a poetic description."

"Poetry and politics. Bah! Why are they here?" Gargun interrupted. "They've led the Galactic Police to our very door. We must leave, Sharg."

"Calm, Gargun. The humans have shown no violence that cannot be explained by protectiveness. It is the way of the Staros to explore and communicate above all else," Sharg said, not taking her eyes off Jayne as she ran her fingers through Jayne's shoulder-length black hair. "The variation in our galaxy is remarkable. Tell me, Amanda Jayne, how is it that you understand my speaking? I do not believe humans partake in Galactic Trade and, therefore, I find it unlikely you have a translator." Sharg tapped a rounded ridge of skin on the side of her own head where an ear was likely located.

"Look, I'm gonna level with you," AJ said, stepping closer to Sharg. His movement caused Gargun to step quickly between them. "Calm down, big man."

"Gargun, will you make tea as your attended has requested?"

"Yes, Sharg." Gargun gave AJ a final suspicious look and trundled into the kitchen but not before brushing his shoulder against AJ's.

"You were about to bring us to level," Sharg prompted.

"Right," AJ said, inspecting the tall reptilian woman's features. "It's just ... you're so ...."

"Alien? Personally, I am more surprised by our similarities than our few differences. We should first level your pickle."

AJ chuckled at her attempt to combine the two idioms. "The bottom line is, we're trying to get home and we're out of gas," he said.

"Fantastium is available on Celestarn," Gargun growled from where he stood in front of a heating pan of water.

"Galactic Police do not follow those who are allowed legal trade," Sharg said, pulling a translucent robe from a nearby hook and wrapping it around herself.

"Are Vred sex organs ordinarily visible?" Jayne asked, unable to contain her curiosity. "The skin on your back is darker and appears thicker, but there are no obvious breaks in front or back, save possibly beneath your tail."

"Jayne, are you serious?" AJ asked.

"I apologize," Jayne said. "We just met a sentient species who are at roughly the same point in evolution as humanity and, well, I don't think the most important question is about running out of gas."

The smile on Sharg's face extended across her short, flat muzzle. Her pointed teeth became evident for the first time. "The warrior and the explorer. It is a time-honored bond amongst Vred as well. Albert Jenkins, AJ, I believe we can both satiate Amanda Jayne's curiosity and discuss your immediate needs to provide safety for your attended. No, Amanda Jayne, the female Vred's sexual organs are hidden from view by the same pouch of skin that provides our offspring's first comfort. We excrete waste from beneath a point where our tails join with our spines."

"Things shoulds not be said," Gargun growled.

"I'm with Grumpy," AJ added.

"We use clothing to cover ourselves," Jayne said. "If I understand correctly, these anatomical features are similarly located on our bodies."

"How does a human feed it's offspring?" Sharg asked. "Once a child is free from our pouch, we continue to feed from our chests."

Before AJ could object, Sharg reached for one of the two large bumps on her scaly chest. As she pulled back the skin, the end of a very human-looking breast was exposed.

"God save me if we have to go through this with every new alien we meet," AJ grumbled.

"AJ, these are fundamental questions. There is nothing to be embarrassed about," Jayne said.

"I agrees with the angry human," Gargun said. "No talk of breeding."

Jayne cupped her own breast but saved AJ further embarrassment by stopping there. "Human females are similarly equipped, except we utilize clothing to cover ourselves."

Sharg nodded, then asked, "AJ, what of this pickle you would level?"

"Back on Earth, I own a junkyard," he said. "I store lots of things humans think are past their expiration. Turns out, that stuff still has value if the right person shows up. You're correct, we can't just go to Celestarn to fill up on Fantastium. First problem is, we don't have any Galactic funds. Second, we're kind of being chased. Turns out we had to swipe a ship on Beltigersk Five to get this far and we're just about out of gas. We were hoping to scrape out enough leftover Fantastium from the junk ships to get us down the road a bit."

"There is no Fantastium on Farst," Gargun said, carrying a platter of steaming cups over and placing them on a table. "I made garb tea with tenchies."

"Delightful, Gargun," Sharg said. "Let us sit."

As AJ settled onto the small platform, he slowly sank until he was nearly to the deck. Without being prompted, Sharg came up behind him, clamping her long fingers around the metal support attached to the seat. With little exertion, she lifted the platform until he was at a more comfortable height. Heat radiated from her body as she brushed against AJ, causing him to blush as he caught Jayne's eye. She shook her head in amusement.

"What?" AJ asked.

"You're blushing."

Sharg turned back to look at AJ. "His skin color is darkening with a red hue. Is that blushing? What is the significance?" She reached for his neck, her eyes searching his for permission.

"Fine," he agreed. Her fingers were hot on his neck, which caused him to blush further. "I can't believe this is happening."

"What is the significance of the additional blood flow beneath his skin?" Sharg's fingers strayed upward, running along the line of AJ's chin and then to his lips. "So delicate but yet, I felt your strength. Such contradictions."

"Blushing shows embarrassment," Jayne said. "I'd say he's attracted to you."

"Jayne ..." AJ's voice held warning.

"Or perhaps he's just overly aware that your unclothed skin is only inches from him." Jayne smiled as she continued to needle him.

"Thank you, Albert Jenkins. You pay me a compliment this moment," Sharg said. "I assume that this is an involuntary response and you have no intention to verbalize your interest."

"The thing is, we need a ship," he said, closing his eyes. "The ship we stole is modified for Lumbricus. We can't possibly sail it back to Earth, even if we had the Fantastium. Are you sure there aren't any ships here?"

"Wees did not says there be no ships," Gargun said. "Wees says there be no Fantastium. But humans have no funds. Gargun not shows good ships to humans."

"Why are you on Farst, Gargun?" AJ needed to change the conversation so the Vred male was less hostile.

"Like you, we have come to Farst to mine its forgotten wealth," Sharg answered. "In turn, we have also found ourselves a pickle."

AJ raised his eyebrows at the small shapes darting beneath the surface of his darkly brewed tea. "What kind of pickle?"

"Our estimate of Fantastium was incorrect," she said. "We are stranded here much like you."

"Sounds like a pretty basic calculation," AJ said. "How'd you miss that?"

"Gargun not good at maths," Gargun said. "I do not needs shame. It is nots my place."

"It was Gargun's estimate?" Jayne asked.

"We operate as a team. There is no value in reviewing history," Sharg said. "We have survived many months in the delicate bliss of solitude, yet I will admit that I have found joy in our meeting. Perhaps when the Galactic Police arrive, they will offer us assistance in returning to Halfnium-8."

"Galactics no helps," Gargun said. "Galactics jails Vred for helping humans."

"That does sound possible," Sharg agreed. "I fear my curiosity may have brought trouble to our table. But all is not lost. Are we not stronger as four than as two?"

Greybeard barked and ran up next to Sharg, pushing off so his stubby front legs rested against her.

"About that," AJ said. "We're a lot more than two."

"Was I incorrect in my assessment?" Sharg asked, scooping Greybeard from the floor and holding him so she could stroke his fur. "I had believed this one was a non-sentient companion."

AJ and Jayne exchanged a look as Beverly appeared, sitting on the table between them. "I don't think you'll make it any worse at this point. They already know the Galactic Police are after us. And you were totally looking at Sharg's chest, AJ."

"She was behind me!" AJ exclaimed. Since Sharg couldn't hear Beverly's side of the conversation, a look of concern and confusion moved across her face.

"We haven't told you everything," Jayne said. "One more of our crew is back on the Lumbricus ship. He stayed in case the Galactic Police show up."

"What will he do if this occurs?"

"We have enough Fantastium to land on Celestarn or Halfnum-8, just not enough to get home," Jayne said. "We were thinking of making a run for a city on Halfnium-8. Try to blend in. Find some fuel."

"I sense this is not everything," Sharg said. "For purpose of clarity, I do not believe you would blend in on any of Halfnium-8's cities."

"Do you really want to know everything?" Jayne asked. "It could make future decisions sticky for you. Right now, you're just helping a couple of limited-intelligence sentients who crash-landed. What conscientious Vred wouldn't do the same? "

"You, my friend, defy the description you present. I find the intellect of both yourself and Albert Jenkins to be quite sharp. The description of limited is not correctly applied," she said.

"But it's handy for those who came to our planet to strip it of Fantastium and Blastorium," AJ said, angrily. "Even handier for those who want to look the other way while it happens."

Sharg sighed. "I wish this was an uncommon story. And yes, Amanda Jayne, I would understand as much of the truth as possible. I do not hide from unpleasant truth any more than I support taking advantage of a society's lack of technical advancement. Tell me this truth you fear to share."

"We have joined with Beltigersk riders," AJ said. "These riders, along with courageous Vred, took a mission to Earth forty years ago to collect evidence of Korgul crimes against humanity. The Korgul tried to stop this mission by killing the Vred hosts. A few months ago, I was approached by a Beltigersk princess who we call Beverly. She not only saved my life but helped me gather evidence and bring it back to Beltigersk Five where it was presented to the Galactic Congress."

"That is fantastic," Sharg said. "I am surprised that news of this has not spread. The Korgul are a vile species and action is clearly called for."

"Yeah, you'd think," he said. "Apparently, the evidence is now buried in subcommittee."

"That's not entirely fair," Beverly said. It was quickly evident that Sharg could now see Beverly, as her focus snapped onto the small woman's projection. Beverly wore a formal black robe and stood on the table between the soup bowls. "Humanity's case *is* being heard but these matters take time. It will take a great adjustment and decades to modify how the Galactic Congress recognizes humanity. Ours was but the first step of many."

"And meanwhile, BB's – or Beverly's– mother, queen of the fart-smelling volcano, wants to keep us as pets on Beltigersk Five because I'm joined with her daughter," AJ said, growing impatient.

"AJ, sarcasm doesn't translate well," Jayne said. "Suffice it to say that Beverly's mother is in a position to make trouble for our return to Earth."

"Ahh, that is quite a tale and I am familiar with the smell of sulfurous ejections," Sharg said, grinning. "You were wise to initially withhold this information. You are equally wise in sharing it with me as Gargun and I have little love for Galactic rule, a sentiment you will find amongst many of the Vred people. We have given up much freedom to gain peaceful existence. One might wonder if the conflicts of our history were exaggerated to gain control of the masses."

"Wees found ship for humans," Gargun said. "Wees takes Lumbricus Fantastium and goes home, we could."

"Wouldn't the Galactic Police just track us down to Halfnium-8?" Jayne asked.

"We have access to Fantastium once we get home," Sharg said. "The Galactic Police would not need to know of our involvement. There is no love for Galactics in my family. I do, however, believe that your spectacular landing has left your pursuers close to Farst, watching. If we attempt to leave this moon, they will no doubt give chase and all will be lost."

"What kind of ship?" AJ asked. "And what's in my tea? I've got swimmers."

"Those are tenchies," Sharg answered.

"Plankton," Beverly clarified. "High in protein. I think you'll find they taste a little swampy, but they won't hurt you."

"I don't suppose you have anything stronger?" AJ asked hopefully.

Gargun's eyes narrowed. "A bites, you ask?" Quick as lightning, a cylinder containing a clear liquid appeared in his hand. "Maybes human not so different."

Gargun took a quick short swig before AJ reached over. He was slightly surprised when Gargun grinned and handed him the cylinder. AJ sniffed the top. The unmistakable tang of alcohol filled his nose and he smiled.

"AJ, I don't think that's wise," Beverly said. "I don't know what's in there."

"I think me and Gargun are finally bonding. I'm only doing this to improve human-Vred relations. Consider it a sacrifice to diplomacy." AJ tipped back the vessel and grimaced as he swallowed. Involuntarily, he coughed and considered it a minor victory that he only coughed a single time. "Holy crap, Gar! That's liquid fire. Where'd you get that?"

Gargun's grin was predatory as he accepted the cylinder back from AJ and took a longer drink, managing not to cough. "Gargun has still. Gargun makes from trashes of Farst."

AJ held out his hand and beckoned. "Trash, huh?" He took a second swig and coughed again. "My friend, that's pure rocket fuel. You might have just invented Blastorium."

Gargun's grin widened. "Gargun likes Albert Jenkins. Is nots Blastorium. We would have many riches with so much Blastorium. Human is strong to drink twice from Gargun's still."

The alcohol burned as it raced down AJ's chest. His vision started to swim. "Damn son, that has quite the kick to it. Are you sure you're not from Kentucky? My wife's family brought something like that to Christmas one year."

"Are all men like this?" Jayne asked, looking at Sharg. "We're talking about saving the planet and they bond on hooch?"

"I don't suppose you have a bit more of that? My boy, Darnell, would probably like to take a run at it," AJ drank deeply from his teacup, hoping to put out the fire in his stomach. "Oh, hell, that tastes like mud puddle. Don't mind the crunch, though."

"How can you be so relaxed?" Jayne asked. "If the Galactics are waiting for the dust to settle, surely they won't have trouble finding us? Making a run for it isn't going to work."

"That, my dear, is why we drink," AJ said. "Gargar, buddy, set her up with a hit."

"No. This is no time to get drunk."

"BB, show me Halfnium-8 and the two moons in real time," AJ said. Hovering over the table, the planet and two moons appeared. "What would you say the distance between Celestarn and Farst is compared to the distance between Farst and Halfnium-8? Kind of looks like they're about the same right now."

"It is one hundred ninety-eight thousand miles to the surface of Halfnium-8 from our current location," Beverly said. "Only ninety-four thousand miles separate Farst and Celestarn."

"So it's not a perfect plan," AJ said. "Any idea how many Galactic ships capable of spaceflight are on Celestarn?"

"That is not public information," Beverly said. "I would estimate in the low hundreds. Perhaps fewer."

"More than a couple, though," AJ said. "Then why didn't they send more after us?"

"How many policemen do they send when a raccoon knocks over a trashcan?" Jayne asked.

He chuckled. "Touché, Doc."

"I don't see how we're going to get away from the cop who's already here," Jayne said.

"I hear you. Gargs, how about you show us this ship you were thinking about. I don't suppose it has any guns on it, does it?"

"Weapons are not allowed on non-military vessels in civilized space," Sharg said. "You will need to don your space suits if we are to visit the ship Gargun speaks of."

"Albert Jenkins is friend, but pays must be," Gargun said. "It is rights."

"I would not cheapen the first meeting between Vred and humanity by requiring payment," Sharg said. "We will work together and demonstrate the morality of all Vred."

AJ shook his head. "That's not right. You came to Farst to make money, I'd bet so you can have little Gargs and Shargs running around. Am I right?"

"I find your observation stunningly perceptive, Albert Jenkins," Sharg said. "Is there a reason you have changed my attendee's name?"

"We call 'em nicknames. Like AJ instead of Albert Jenkins. It's my way of saying welcome to the tribe," he said.

Sharg nodded her head. "Limited sentients, indeed."

"BB, show the kids the trade goods we brought along," AJ said.

"What is this?" Sharg asked as projections appeared of the parts they'd stripped from the derelict ships on Beltigersk Five.

"Think you could sell this stuff?" AJ asked. "I think most of them are Vred design."

"Where did they come from?"

AJ shrugged. "We didn't just take the Lumbricus ship from Beltigersk Five. I figured we also needed hard goods for raising a little capital when the time came. Far as I can tell, our time is now. Think you could sell those and make some cash?"

"It might take some effort," Sharg said. "But yes, I have family that could help in such an endeavor. Some of this equipment is quite valuable. What is your intended trade?"

"Well, I showed you mine, maybe you should show me yours now," AJ said, his head still swimming from the alcohol.

"AJ, must you be so crude?" Jayne chastised.

"Oh, honey, I'm holding back," AJ said, his words slurring. "Look, I'm on a ship in an alien junkyard with a hottie reptile woman who's half naked and my new buddy is loaded with grain alcohol. I just slugged down a half a million baby krill with my mud tea. Not to mention the cops on my tail. Trust me, this is the mild version of the laugh track playing in my head."

"Sounds like someone needs to sober up."

He stood and grabbed for the table as he almost blacked out. "Whoa! Are we moving?"

"I apologize, Albert Jenkins," Beverly said, flitting up in front of him wearing a white lab coat over conservative black slacks and gray turtleneck. "I believe Dr. Jayne is correct."

AJ hung his head, shaking it back and forth. "Aww, BB, don't do me like that."

A moment later, his head cleared and his bladder urgently demanded attention.

He sighed.

8

DUST OFF

"Now, this is a ship," AJ said, squeezing his bloated suit through a floor hatch.

From the outside, the ship was hard to pick out because of the debris covering it. About all AJ could see was the long sweep of wings attached to a squat body of undetermined size. The interior was clean, well-lit and had more than sufficient headroom to stretch out his six-foot tall frame. He leaned over and offered Jayne a hand as she worked her way up the metal ladder.

"Olds," Gargun said. "Leaky. Rigid necks who sits to makes monies no likes. Pollutes, they says."

"Were you trying to take it back to Halfnium-8?" Jayne asked.

"There are many parts that would fetch a good number at auction," Sharg said. "There are limitations on what can be brought back to Halfnium-8. This ship, or whatever remains after we salvage what can be sold, would have to be returned to Farst within thirty days or fines would be levied. We have already salvaged parts from two ships of similar composition. Gargun didn't want to start on this one until we figured out our return trip. It is in the best shape of all we've discovered."

"And you'd trade it to us?" AJ asked.

"No." Gargun said, simply. "Likes human Albert Jenkins. Not good trades."

"Are you trying to get home?" AJ asked.

"Needs Fantastium," Gargun said, pulling the hatch closed. Steadily, atmospheric pressure was restored to the ship.

"Where I'm from, shipping can be just as expensive as the item," AJ said. "What if I said we could get you and your parts home? We'd even throw in the parts we brought from Beltigersk. We just need a load of Fantastium once we get back to Halfnium-8."

"You seem to be implying that you have sufficient Fantastium to fuel the Lumbricus ship, our vessel and this atmospheric cruiser," Sharg said. "Even if that were true, the Galactic patrol ship would follow us home and bring with it trouble."

"BB, let's say we don't need the Lumbricus ship. Do we have enough Fantastium to get two ships planetside?" AJ asked.

"Yes – and you would have a small reserve," Beverly said, appearing in a bright red and pink stewardess uniform from the late sixties, complete with mid-thigh skirt, matching hat and knee-high boots. "This particular vessel is a passenger liner designed for comfortable mid-range trips for wealthier clientele."

"Can it go interstellar?" AJ asked.

Before Beverly could answer, Sharg stepped in. "Accessing a transition point is a simple matter of applied physics. Most Vred vessels capable of extra atmospheric travel are equipped with technology to access these points."

"Not exactly answering my question. I'll assume that was a *yes*," AJ said. "Here's my proposition. We load this ship and yours with go-go juice and make a run for it once the dust settles. Your payment is the Fantastium necessary to get you home. Once we're home, you hide us long enough to take possession of the parts we are trading and get us a load of Fantastium. If there are leftover funds, you guys keep them. Deal?"

"There appears to be a significant overlooked consideration in your plan, Albert Jenkins," Sharg said. "The Galactic patrol vessel will gain full maneuverability once the debris settles. We cannot afford to have it follow us to Halfnium-8. Even now, more vessels could be inbound from Celestarn."

"There are not," Beverly said. "It would appear the local Galactic Police are not overly concerned about the crashed Lumbricus ship."

"So, here's the deal. Right now, the Galactics don't have any idea we're in cahoots. They also believe we're a limited-intelligence species, which we reinforced by crash-landing into a pile of trash. We're going to use that bias against them. All I really need to know is if you're in."

"What would prevent us from simply departing once you've provided Fantastium for our ship?" Sharg asked.

"I've already considered that scenario," he replied. "If that occurred, the Galactic Police would chase you down and we'd use that distraction to improve our circumstances. You'll forgive me for not elaborating more."

Sharg's already narrow lips thinned even further as she grinned. "I have to wonder if it was humans who propagated the notion of your own limited intelligence."

"Now, that'd be a great long-con," AJ said. "I'm asking you to trust me when I say we'll depart from Farst without a tail. I don't want to get into the details."

"We will not participate in behavior that would endanger the Galactic Police members. They are likely citizens of Celestarn who were recruited and are executing their duties faithfully," Sharg said.

"I don't even own a weapon," AJ said, holding his hands up.

"I find your terms satisfactory," she said with a sharp nod. "We will trade this vessel, which Gargun has repaired, for sufficient Fantastium to return us to our home on Halfnium-8. Further, we will broker the trade of machinery brought from Beltigersk Five for the purpose of procuring sufficient Fantastium to transport this vessel to Earth."

"Sounds like we have a deal," AJ said, holding his hand out to shake. Sharg looked at him quizzically but mimicked his gesture. Gripping her large hand, AJ gave it a single pump.

"Does that signify your acceptance of terms?" Sharg asked.

"Indeed, it does. Nice doing business with you," AJ said.

"You've had some dumb ideas, but I feel like you've outdone yourself on this one," Darnell said. "You know this thing fails for a million reasons, right?"

"Just working with what I've got." AJ finished lugging the last of the machinery into the small, boxy vessel Gargun and Sharg had utilized to travel to the moon.

"What if the big girl decides to bail on us and the cops don't follow because she warns them? This ship has a radio." Darnell said.

AJ held up a small phial of Fantastium. "That, my friend, is an excellent point, but a moot one," AJ said. "We are working from a considerable disadvantage, but I would draw your attention to something you quite often draw mine to."

"And that is?"

"Cop behavior."

Darnell narrowed his eyes. "I don't follow."

"You think I'm doing the *black thing* again." AJ grinned.

"We'll see. Get on with it."

"If Sharg and Gargun take off, do you really think the cops would let them go, even with a phone call?"

"Not if they're anything like cops on Earth. Matter of fact, they'd probably stop everyone, empty both vehicles, and call a dog out to search the car," Darnell said, nodding. "I see where you're going. Still feels like you're messing with me."

AJ waggled his eyebrows. "Only fun if I can do both."

"Sharg says Galactic patrol approaches," Gargun said. "Needs Fantastium."

AJ held the phial out to the shorter Vred. "Here you go, my good man."

Their two Vred friends exited the ship and Darnell clasped his buddy's puffy shoulder. "This could get intense. You sure you're up for it?"

"What's the worst they could do?"

"I bet even enlightened cops carry guns."

AJ pursed his lips. "If you get a chance to get free and I'm not gonna make it, I need you to promise me you'll take the *out*. Lisa is still back on Earth and you need to get home to her. Jayne, well, she deserves better than all this."

"Sure, buddy. Will do."

"You're a horrible liar."

"You're a horrible friend."

AJ chuckled to himself as he bounded across piles of garbage with Greybeard barking at his heels. "Greybeard, go back," he said. "BB, tell Seamus to get Greybeard loaded in with Big D and Jayne."

Beverly blinked into view, wearing her silver *Lost in Space* suit and a rocket pack. "Seamus says that Greybeard is ignoring him."

"He can do that?"

"Greybeard's loyalty to the pack is instinctive. The portion of his brain that responds to rational commands is overridden by his expectation that you will be in danger. It also does not help that you are running and he enjoys the chase."

"Crap." AJ scanned the horizon. In the several hours since they'd landed, met with Sharg and Gargun, and then loaded their parts for trade, the sky had cleared significantly of debris. "Can you pick up the patrol vessel? I can't see it."

"It is twenty miles out," she said. "It also appears you have been spotted. They have adjusted their course," she said.

"How soon will they arrive?"

"You should increase your pace."

AJ's stomach soured as urgency drenched his system with adrenaline. Having made the trip back and forth a few times, his skill at navigating the piles of junk had steadily increased. Marveling at how his age-defying new body responded to strenuous tasks, AJ grinned broadly, pushing himself faster and faster.

"You're going too fast," Beverly finally warned as the Lumbricus ship quickly grew in front of them.

AJ angled his legs each time he landed, absorbing as much inertia as he could before he lost contact with the surface again. "Aw, crap, this is gonna hurt!" he exclaimed, just before slamming into the side of the ship. His vision flirted with the black edges of consciousness as he fell into the hole, which would give him access to the hatch.

"AJ, you are concussed. I'm going to help you through this," Beverly said. "The Galactic Police landed their vessel twenty yards away and are preparing to disembark. It is imperative that you find the strength to enter the ship. It is likely they will deploy non-lethal means of capture. You cannot afford to be caught out in the open."

AJ shook his head. For a moment, he was right back in Vietnam, hunkered behind sandbags, bullets whizzing overhead. Blinking quickly, his head pounding, he became aware of Greybeard's insistent barking. Beverly's words hadn't registered. It sounded like she was talking underwater.

Suddenly, a bright red arrow like one would see in a *Tom and Jerry* cartoon snaked between his feet and pulsated upward in front of his face. Struggling for consciousness, AJ's eyes followed the arrow's path. With his mission reduced to a single action, AJ knew what he had to do. He jumped. Unfortunately, on the first try, his helmet struck the underside of the ship and he fell back onto the piles of junk. On the positive, the impact didn't further damage him and he took a second try. This time, he landed inside the maintenance bay's airlock.

"Greybeard, get in here!" AJ shouted, struggling to grab the handle on the hatch he needed to close. A moment later, Greybeard leapt in, striking AJ squarely in the chest.

"You need to calm, AJ," Beverly said. "Your blood pressure is spiking."

AJ pulled the metal door closed as something blurry slid through. "Any idea what that was?" AJ asked, spinning the wheel closed. With Beverly's help, he found the interior hatch and waited as atmosphere transferred into the lock.

"I believe it was a restraint device," Beverly said. "Either quick-expanding foam or an electrical charge. The device was not in visual range for sufficient time to identify it."

"Man, those guys move fast," He spun open the inner hatch and pulled himself inside. "You coming, boy?"

Greybeard barked, catching up with AJ who was already inside the worm tracks that made up the main corridor of the ship.

"There are two individuals preparing to deploy some sort of countermeasures," Jayne said.

"What kind of countermeasures?"

"I would expect to disable electronics," she said. "I believe they are having difficulty due to the position of the ship within the garbage dune."

"Garbage dune. Nice visual." AJ wriggled into position at the helm, his slippery worm-ejection-covered suit sliding easily onto the pilot platform. "Show me that patrol vehicle in relation to my ship, BB."

"Aye, aye," Beverly answered smartly. Her image appeared in his peripheral vision, this time wearing the blue uniform of a Naval seaman.

The Galactic Police vessel was a quarter the size of the large Lumbricus ship and had been positioned aft and to the left of the central bridge. It was a strategic spot to park, AJ imagined, since most ships took off going forward, accelerating in a long arcing curve. The thing was, however, due to the limited dexterity of the Lumbricus pilots, their ships required three hundred sixty degrees of flexibility, happily sacrificing speed in the tradeoff.

"Where are those patrolmen?" AJ asked.

"Directly aft. It looks like they're considering entering the hole that gives access to the hatch," Beverly said. "They appear hesitant."

"Smart," AJ said. "Raccoons bite if they're cornered."

"I wish you would stop with those references," Beverly said. "I do not see you or any human as a raccoon."

"Know your enemy," AJ said, nudging the ship's controls.

The Lumbricus ship jumped straight up almost ten yards, showering garbage onto the ground below. Without hesitation, AJ jammed forward on the stick, causing lateral movement at the same time he lowered the ship.

"Crap, did I miss?" AJ asked as the ship plunged back down into the pile of garbage, the star's light disappearing as a mountain collapsed atop him.

"Were you aiming for the Galactic Police vessel?" Beverly asked.

"Yes."

"Then you did not miss," she said.

"Good."

Taking a page from Darnell's playbook, AJ scooched the ship up and forward. Slipping from the helm, he glided expertly on his stomach all the way to the maintenance bay, grateful for the inflation of his atmospheric suit.

"You know, if you're a worm, this ship is actually laid out pretty well," he said, grabbing the edge of the maintenance bay hatch and swinging his legs onto the slotted metal floor.

"I'll be sure to send a note to their ambassador," Beverly said. "I am sure he will appreciate your critique of his ship."

"If he didn't want it stolen, he would have put a lock on it," AJ reasoned.

"I do not believe it would have stopped Seamus."

"Good point. Now to make sure we keep that patrol ship where it belongs for a few days." AJ opened a small panel and extracted the remainder of the Fantastium. Tucking the vial into a pocket, he made his way to the airlock.

"I still question how this will suffice," Beverly said. "Galactic Police are still on the surface. They will simply capture you."

AJ worked the ring on the airlock and jumped down into the small space. With a little urging, Greybeard joined him.

"What are the odds those boys have seen combat?"

"I do not believe it is clear that they are male. Vred have not engaged in war for over a century, so it is unlikely they've experienced combat."

"Then they've probably never experienced what we call *a dust off*."

"Dust off?" she asked, as AJ pushed aside loose trash and scrabbled out the other side of the airlock.

"Check out your Vietnam archives. Big D didn't always fly

gunships. He started out flying slicks. If those Vred boys don't have something better than foam, they're in for a rude surprise."

AJ glanced up and realized he'd somewhat overdone the compression of the two ships into the garbage dune. He was at least forty feet from the surface. His head felt just like it would if someone was beating on it like a steel drum and every movement seemed to take way too much energy. He tried to climb, churning his arms and legs, but his efforts did little except dislodge the trash around him. He watched jealously as Greybeard scampered up the side of the pit. AJ took a breath and tried again, soon finding purchase to slowly follow.

"You will cease movement or be shot!"

AJ held up his arms as he turned toward the voice. Forty yards over, two figures wearing matching uniforms struggled to cross the uneven floor of garbage. Greybeard barked madly, spinning in a tight circle as he ran at the approaching police and then back to AJ.

"AJ, hit the deck!" Darnell's voice boomed in his ears. AJ didn't need to be told twice and he dove away from the approaching figures.

AJ's body didn't hit the ground so much as the ground rose up to meet him. Debris struck, not stopping him, but instead carrying him several yards away. Unable to mitigate the impact, AJ tumbled, struggling to regain his footing.

"Get in!" Jayne's voice was tight with excitement.

Small tornados of debris swirled all around as he searched for Jayne in the chaos. He caught the glint of steel and an overlay of the restored passenger liner popped up, thanks to BB. Their new ship rested on the garbage only yards from where he now lay. He experienced the same feeling of salvation he'd had so many years ago when he'd been racing over swampy ground to the welcome embrace of a Huey. With no urging required, he threw himself at the airlock where Jayne stood beckoning him.

"Greybeard, we gotta move!" he exclaimed.

"Now, AJ," Jayne pushed.

Seeing the small, bulbous bullet that was Greybeard rocketing toward safety, AJ leapt into the hatch and did everything he could to bring his legs up beneath him. A moment later, the small furball, still wrapped in what might as well have been an innertube, smashed into him.

"We're in, Darnell," Jayne called, slapping a panel on the sidewall that closed the exterior hatch.

"How are those GP boys doing?" AJ asked.

"Knocked 'em over," Darnell answered. "They're both moving, though."

"Damn good flying there, Skippy," AJ said, accepting Jayne's outstretched hand.

"This thing is a cream puff," Darnell said. "What kind of messed-up society mothballs a ship like this because they think it's too leaky?"

"We're holding atmo, right?" AJ asked, suddenly curious. "Seems like we'll care about that."

"Not that kind of leak," Darnell said.

Jayne pulled off her helmet and nodded at the airlock, which AJ was currently blocking.

"What kind of leak are we talking about?"

AJ pointed at a panel that looked like the one Jayne had used on the other end of the lock and got an affirmative nod from her. He pressed it and was rewarded with the airlock releasing them into the main section of the ship.

"Apparently, it has waste lines that leak small amounts of unrecyclable material," he said. "Overall, it's not good stuff, but its microscopic. According to 2-F, the ships are considered toxic to Vred."

"Are they?"

"It is still a matter of discussion," Beverly said, joining the conversation. "There are reports of Vred who have neurological disorders associated with the waste in question. There is broad speculation the reports were financed by a competitor, however."

"I'll risk it," AJ said, working his suit gloves off. "What are the odds those police will get a comm off to home base before we make it to Halfnium-8?"

"Not good," Darnell said. "This baby has some punch to her. We just caught up with Sharg and we'll hit atmosphere in twelve hours. Just how deep did you bury their patrol ship?"

"It was forty feet from the top of the Lumbricus ship to the surface," AJ said. "Then another thirty feet to the bottom side. Seventy feet or so."

"I kind of feel bad for 'em," Darnell said. "How do you suppose they'll report this?"

"What do you mean?" Jayne asked.

"Will they admit they got played by a bunch of raccoons?"

AJ helped Greybeard remove his suit and walked to the galley. "I'm more concerned those patrolmen *won't* get a message off. They're going to need help moving that Lumbricus ship off theirs. I took the remaining Fantastium, so that ship isn't going anywhere."

"There's some chance they could dig out the patrol vehicle and punch their way out," Darnell speculated.

"BB, don't suppose there's any food back here? I'm feeling pretty jacked up about now."

"The manufactory appears to be stocked with basic proteins and carbohydrates," Beverly answered, standing atop the counter. "I believe I could provide it with sufficient instructions to produce something along the lines of spaghetti."

"I'd take some of that," Darnell called.

Following Beverly's instructions, AJ punched a few codes into a small manufactory on the counter in the galley. The machine operated in silence, and a moment later a small light illuminated on its front panel.

"You'll find utensils and bowls in the overhead compartment," Beverly instructed.

"Why would they leave all this on here?" he asked.

"Because it's tainted," Jayne said, brushing up next to him and pulling out a very convincing pile of spaghetti.

"Doesn't smell tainted," AJ said, experimenting with and discovering the operation of a water dispenser. Filling a bowl, he set it down for Greybeard, who greedily lapped at it. Jayne slid a good portion of noodles into another bowl and set it next to the water.

"Does it seem weird that Sharg and Gargun are taking parts off tainted ships and selling them?" AJ asked, picking up two bowls Jayne filled with pasta and walking toward the front of the ship.

"They didn't seem overly concerned about helping us," Jayne said. "As I recall, Gargun's initial concern was the payment he would require for their help. Sharg didn't disagree. Matter of fact, she seemed relieved when AJ mentioned he had a trade in mind."

"They could be exotic pet traders, looking to add raccoons to their menagerie" Darnell said.

"I agree, Sharg's a wily one for all her pacifistic talk," AJ said. "I feel like she's been holding back."

9

KRAKEN

"Join me," Jayne said, patting the synthetic leather cushion next to where she sat.

AJ considered the small rectangular table that held Jayne's meal in place and wondered where it had come from. The table hadn't been part of the couch configuration as he'd last seen it. Setting his plate on the table, he felt the tug of a magnetic connection between his own plate and the table.

"I can't believe they scrapped this ship," he said. "At a minimum, they could have sold it to other species who aren't as sensitive."

"At the end of WWII, the United States dumped military surplus vehicles into the ocean so as not to crash the economy," Jayne said. "Vred are well known for manufacturing ships. Perhaps they didn't want to cause a similar ripple."

"I was talking with Gargun when we were getting loaded," Darnell said, joining the conversation from the cockpit, only a few yards forward. "He said the environmental types didn't like the idea of their poisons being offloaded onto someone else. He didn't sound too impressed."

"But they were okay dumping them on the moon?" AJ was astounded.

"I guess hypocrisy isn't limited to humans. Comforting in a way, if you think about it." Jayne rested a hand on AJ's arm as she slumped further into the chair, her head coming to rest on his shoulder. "How soon before we're on the ground?"

AJ caught Darnell's turned head and the two exchanged raised eyebrows but said nothing on the incidental contact.

"Eight hours," Darnell replied. "You two should get some sleep before we hit the atmosphere. We'll have turbulence. I don't care how nice this ship is, it's still physics."

"Don't you need sleep?" Jayne asked, her eyes fluttering open. "We can take shifts."

"No need," Darnell said. "2-F and I are taking turns. Halfnium-8 doesn't have much space traffic, so there's not much to do."

Ever since waking up on Beltigersk Five, AJ had been on edge, either scheming to escape or actively working toward that goal. With the blue-green planet growing slowly on the monitor, a full stomach, and a comfortable seat, he finally felt like he could allow his guard down, if only for a moment. Turning his hand over, he made room for Jayne's to slip into his own. With a soft murmur, she pushed her arm forward and interlaced their fingers. Not wanting to ruin the moment, AJ rested his head against the soft cushion and allowed his eyes to close.

"AJ, IT IS TIME TO AWAKEN," Beverly said. He blinked in confusion, noticing that she stood in front of him, but instead of ten inches tall, she was life-size.

"You're big," he muttered, having a little difficulty talking.

"You're still asleep," she said. "I've entered your dream cycle."

"I knew lucid dreaming was something!" he exclaimed. "I don't suppose this is the part where I find out you have a kinky fantasy about human men, is it?"

Beverly smiled demurely and shook her head. "I'm afraid not, AJ. I would not want to interfere in your ability to form lasting relationships with more suitable partners."

"I thought we were bonded for life."

"Nice try, soldier," she said. "You need to wake up. The ship is about to enter the atmosphere and Sharg has requested communications."

"I don't know how to wake up."

"This might hurt a little. " Beverly's words were followed by a small jolt of electricity.

His eyes flipped open and he groaned. "Holy crap." Halfnium-8 now occupied the entire view from the ship. He also became aware that the ship was shaking. "Are we there yet?"

"Just entered the outer atmosphere. Sharg's on the line," Darnell said. "She wants to talk with you."

"One second." AJ disentangled his hand from Jayne's and shook out his numb fingers. "I didn't realize I was so tired. Did you get any rest?"

"I was down for a few hours. 2-F woke me up about thirty minutes ago."

AJ gently shook Jayne, who woke easily. "We're about thirty minutes from landing," he warned.

"Thank you."

He took a chair next to Darnell. While the chair had an obvious hole for Vred tails to escape, it was every bit as comfortable as the couch. "BB, can you connect me to Sharg?"

Beverly appeared on the ledge beneath the transparent viewscreen in front of the forwardmost cockpit seats. She wore a smart, wool suit and sat in front of an ancient telephone switching station, complete with hanging wires and stainless-steel plugs. Placing a hand over the single earphone, she pulled one of the wires from its position and relocated it on the panel. "You are connected," she said, grinning.

"Sharg, this is AJ. Go ahead."

"It is perhaps indelicate to mention, but we will need to be rather discreet on our approach," she said. "I request that you ask your pilot to stay close as we negotiate the western sea of Bothas. Also, be notified that your vessel is sealed against water and is capable of submersion."

"The engines can take that?" he asked.

"You have an alternative drive that operates quite effectively. Strictly speaking, however, your ship is forbidden to enter the waterways of Halfnium-8."

"Won't they track our arrival?"

"It is true. While the authorities of Tenebas will be aware of the entry of our ships into their sovereign space, it is unlikely they will respond with sufficient haste."

"How unlikely?"

"Tenebas shuns technology but has a small force used to enforce its territorial boundaries," she said. "My family has used the western border as a quiet port of entry for many decades. I believe you suggested your friend, Darnell, was a pilot of considerable skill. Do you wish to modify this statement? I could ask one of my cousins to meet us and take command of your ship. It would, of course, change our negotiation."

"Big D, how do you feel about going submersible?" AJ asked. "Sharg says the ship is designed for it and we might run into some local heat otherwise."

"Doesn't seem like our engines would work," Darnell said. "Oh, 2-F is showing me a propeller set. How hard could it be?"

"Well, she says she could get one of her cousins over to pilot if we wanted. Says it would change the deal, though." AJ nodded as Beverly gestured to add Darnell to the conversation.

"Can't be harder than flying over the jungles of 'Nam with anti-aircraft fire," Darnell said. "I think we're good."

"Did you catch that, Sharg?" AJ asked.

"My translator was unable to identify 'Nam, but the sentiment was duly transmitted," Sharg said. "It is unlikely we will encounter hostile sentient weaponry. The same cannot be said of the Kraken."

"Did she say Kraken?" Darnell asked, which also drew Jayne's attention.

"It was the closest translation," Beverly interjected, standing up from the telephone switchboard and pulling a festooned pirate's hat and harpoon from behind her back. With a flourish, she tapped the hat into position. "In the ship's data stores, I located references to large marine life forms with minimal skeletal structure, much like the kraken from Earth myths."

"There she goes. Hold on to your butts!" Darnell said, jerking on the flight controls. In response, the sleek Vred vessel twisted as he struggled to stay behind Sharg and Gargun's considerably less aero-dynamic vessel, which had made a sharp turn and disappeared into heavy cloud cover.

"Oh geez, I hate this part," AJ said, his stomach flopping with nausea.

Darnell grunted in appreciation as he shifted the controls again. "She sure can sail that washing machine looking thing. You might want to get some straps on."

AJ was grateful when Beverly illuminated the ends of a restraint harness. Pulling them into place, he checked to make sure Jayne was secure and smiled as he realized she was way ahead of him, having even taken the time to lock Greybeard in place as well.

"We have sensor contact with approaching Tenebas ships," Sharg's tone was conversational.

"Are they armed? Will they shoot at us?" AJ asked, searching the various panels at the front of the ship for information. Again, Beverly bailed him out by projecting a large cartoon arrow at a data display. "Like that helps!"

"Albert Jenkins, it would be helpful if you limited your inquiry to a single question when under duress," Sharg said. "Tenebas govern-mental vessels are armed, but they will not use force unless there is an immediate threat. It is their primary concern that the debris from such action would place unnecessary stress into the natural systems."

As AJ looked back at the sensor panel, the data changed and showed, instead, a three-dimensional projection of his, Sharg's and the two Tenebas ships. The patrol was clearly on an intercept course.

Still several miles above the planet's surface, the display also showed an outline of political boundaries.

"This next part will be difficult," Sharg said. "Once we are submerged, our communication systems are not as effective. It will be imperative that Darnell Jackson keep your vessel within five hundred yards or you risk becoming lost."

"They're going to catch us," AJ said.

"Intercepting a vessel traveling at considerable speed is perhaps less interesting than it sounds," Sharg said. "You must ask yourself, what will these Tenebas vessels do once they have come even with our position?"

"I'll bite," AJ said. "What?"

"They will observe. And at the point in which we are submerged to a depth of eleven hundred feet, they will break off their pursuit and we will be left to pursue our own agenda, free of government interaction," Sharg said. "Also, I will reduce velocity to one hundred twenty feet per second before entering the waters of Bothas. Please prepare for this adjustment."

"This is crazy!" Jayne said as the ship seemed to come to a stop above the roiling waters of the sea below.

"I sure hope this baby can handle the pressure," Darnell said. "Holy crap, those ships are right on top of us."

Two gleaming white vessels sailed into view and appeared as if they were trying to block their ship from entering the sea. The bluff might have worked if not for Sharg directing her ship to continue its original course, missing a Tenebas vessel by yards.

"Do not vary from your cour..." Sharg's words were cut off as her blocky ship plunged into the sea, sending great waves splashing out from her entry point.

"This could suck!" Darnell said, holding firm to his course. At the last moment, the Tenebas ship slipped to the side, narrowly averting a collision. Relief at missing the ship was short-lived, as the surface of the water rushed at them.

The three humans and dog strained against their restraint straps, the impact of the water against the ship feeling like they'd just been in a massive accident.

"Holy crap! What in the hell?" Darnell complained.

"Don't lose her," Jayne urged.

"I can't see anything," Darnell said as the ship drifted from its original course.

"Bubbles," AJ grunted. "Follow them."

The ship lurched forward. "Aquatic engines engaged," Darnell said. "For the record, there are bubbles everywhere."

"Yeah, sorry. She did say eleven hundred feet though." AJ looked at the sensor display and discovered that two ships were directly behind them and Sharg's vessel was ahead, accelerating into the sea's murky darkness. "I've got contact on Tenebas and Sharg."

"How am I doing?" Darnell asked.

"Four degrees to starboard," Beverly said. "I recommend utilizing an exterior lamp. The sensors we're currently using are actively giving away our location. 2-F should have the capacity to provide an indication of Sharg and Gargun's position."

"Yeah, he's got a nice bendy arrow laid out in front of me. Nice job, little man," Darnell said. "Six hundred feet."

"Is there something special about eleven hundred feet?" Jayne asked.

"Would you mind terribly if I were to answer this?" Thomas, Jayne's rider, shocked them all as he made a rare appearance.

"Not at all, you've been a perfect gentleman to date."

"Many thanks, lady," Thomas said, still wearing his white lab coat over woolen pants, dress shirt and bowtie. Although, if one were to look closer, they might observe that the bowtie had sparkling green plankton swimming across a black field. "Eleven hundred feet is the depth twenty percent beyond the published operational specifications of Vred hulls. While it is widely understood that these published specifications are conservative, the Tenebas government has been hesitant to endanger its citizens by ignoring the tolerances."

"That seems like a bad thing to advertise," AJ said.

"The information is readily available in a multitude of publicly available articles dating back as far as two centuries ago," Thomas said. "There was a widely publicized breach of a submerged vessel where forty-two were killed. More unfortunately, before the bodies were recovered, the vessel was split open by a kraken – assuming we're to use Beverly's vernacular. The Vred passengers were consumed."

"So, forget about the Tenebas on our butts and start worrying about *that*?" AJ asked, pointing out the window at an extremely thick and long squid-like leg slowly passing through the external beam of light.

"It's after Sharg," Darnell said, accelerating.

"What are you doing?" AJ asked.

"I'm going to bump it. Let it know it's not alone."

"And then it attacks us?"

"*Kraken* is an unfortunate moniker," Thomas said. "These cephalopods are not believed to be aggressive. It is likely our presence has sparked curiosity."

"But you said one of those things ate a ship's crew," Jayne argued.

"As a scientist, I suspect you would be skeptical of such a report, especially if you knew that no other similar incidents have ever been recorded," Thomas said.

"You think it was a bad report?" AJ asked.

"I know no such thing. I am merely suggesting that an aggressive species will demonstrate its tendencies with regularity. A single incident is not a reasonable basis for conclusions," Thomas said.

"Bump it or not?" Darnell asked, glancing nervously over his shoulder as the compressed hull groaned.

"Many species that are not otherwise violent respond unpredictably to external stimulus," Thomas said. "Perhaps a posture of observation would be more appropriate."

"BB, you need to work with him on the whole *too many words* thing," AJ said. "Big D, see if you can close the distance between us and Sharg. Maybe we only intervene if that monster gets unruly."

"Like it." Darnell accelerated until the very tips of the kraken's slender tentacles were only yards from the front of their vessel. "Man, that thing is flat out flying."

"Turn off the lights," Jayne said, suddenly.

"Hard to keep up if we do," Darnell said.

"I don't think so."

"I'll give you twenty seconds," Darnell said, flipping off the lights. "Oh! How'd you see that?"

Phosphorescent lines ran along the length of the kraken's tentacles. With regularity, glowing patches intersected the lines, bunching up and expanding in rhythm with the tentacles' undulating movements.

"Um, we're not alone," AJ whispered, pointing off into the gloom of the sea where hundreds of glowing lines undulated in synchronicity with their progress.

"Nine hundred feet," Darnell said, his voice low and sweat beading on his forehead. He patted the bulkhead. "Good girl. We're almost done with this."

AJ scanned the sensor scope but found no information. "I have no idea if that patrol is still on us or not."

"She's turning," Jayne said, her finger tracing the graceful curve of the kraken as it adjusted course.

"How do you know it's Sharg?" Darnell asked.

"Do you have a better idea? I think it's likely the kraken are along for the ride."

Darnell chuckled. "Going with your gut, Doc? That doesn't sound like you. How about I nudge up a little closer."

"Careful," Jayne warned. A moment later a dark black fog enveloped the ship.

"Lights!" Darnell exclaimed. "Dammit, I can't see anything."

"They're gone," Jayne said. "They ink just like Earth squids. With our speed, we should be through any individual ink cloud. It's like the entire school of them inked. What fantastic behavior."

"You're gonna need to fix her. She's gone all Wild Kingdom on us," Darnell said as the water cleared and a faint white light appeared in front of them. "That's got to be Sharg up there."

After almost an hour of travel with nothing to see other than the bobbing white light in front of them, Darnell recognized a change. "Losing depth," he announced. "We're at nine hundred. Eight fifty. Eight hundred." He kept counting until they were only twenty feet below the surface. "She's going airborne. Switching to atmospheric engines in three, two, one."

Popping above the waves, the ship lurched forward as powerful engines rocketed the ship forward and thick atmosphere caught the airfoils.

"You are to be commended for your piloting skills," Sharg said once communications were reestablished. "I would ask what you thought of our visitors of the depths."

"They were beautiful," Jayne said. "It was a shame they fled."

"I hoped that you would not panic when I elicited their flight response. Their natural defenses are a perfect screen for our activities," Sharg said. "Most do not understand that the kraken are pastoral creatures who feed on plant matter. In fact, their voracious appetites contribute greatly to the sea's health. While I might complain of the extremes our society has taken in our ecological defense of this great planet, the return of the schools of kraken tugs at the spiritual links we all feel with the majestic beasts."

"You know you could have warned us in advance," Darnell said, irritated.

"Perhaps that would have been the most prudent course," Sharg said. "But it would have deprived you of the wonder of the experience. Not only that, but I learned much of your behavior when faced with the unknown."

"This whole damn trip is *the unknown*," Darnell grumped.

"And you have experienced wonders and established new relationships," Sharg said. "I would ask that you keep your elevation below three hundred feet. It would be a shame to alert those who seek to learn of our location."

"From my read of things, we're no longer in Tenebas territory," AJ said.

"That is correct. We have entered my home waters, the Kingdom of Shlasan," she said. "Yet it would be best if our approach was not discovered."

"How much further?" AJ asked.

"Moments. When we arrive, please bring your vessel to rest next to my own and disembark. There will be those who question your presence. Do not worry, all will be resolved peaceably," Sharg said and closed comms.

"What the hell did that mean?" AJ asked.

Darnell shrugged. "We're about to find out. There's a significant population center forty miles northwest of our position."

"I'm picking up on quite a number of small craft – or crap. Looks likes some sort of structures out in the water," AJ said, focusing on the scope.

"That stands to reason. Vred are amphibious." Jayne released herself from her straps and leaned over AJ's shoulder so she could both look at the external sensor data as well as get a better view outside of the ship.

"We're skirting most of it and … there she goes," Darnell said.

The trio watched as Sharg and Gargun's ship jumped suddenly to the south, away from what was resolving itself to be a sprawling city.

"Water depth eighty... sixty... forty," AJ read off data from the ship's sensors. "Hope she doesn't want to go swimming again."

"She's making a beeline for that group of buildings," Darnell said.

AJ mentally projected the path of Sharg's ship and discovered what Darnell was referencing. Cut out from a densely packed grove of spindly trees, their thick roots planted firmly in tidal pools, a small village emerged.

"Looks like that's home," Darnell said as Sharg gently set her boxy ship onto a circular, raised white-painted steel platform. Burning off his excess velocity, Darnell slowed their own ship and set it down on the same platform.

"And boy did we get their attention," AJ said, pointing out the window as dozens of Vred emerged from the various buildings and raced toward the platform. "Sure hope they're friendly."

10

SEA CHANGE

"The atmosphere is compatible and richer in oxygen than you are used to," Beverly said from the arm of AJ's seat. She was wearing her khaki shorts, shirt, and pith helmet. "You'll find the temperature to be a humid eighty-five degrees. I recommend loose clothing."

"We don't have a lot of choices," AJ said, working his way back to the airlock.

"Are you sure we're good here? Some of the natives don't look friendly," Darnell observed.

AJ looked out over the growing crowd of reptilian humanoids and had to agree with his friend. Understanding the expression of an alien's face was a challenge he'd little experience with. The display of so many jagged teeth throughout the crowd went directly to Darnell's point.

"Oh, for heaven's sake," Jayne said. "The two of you sound like a couple of little girls afraid of the boogeyman. Sharg didn't attack even after you tried to bean her, AJ."

"Dammit," he said, turning back to the airlock and causing it to cycle. Screwing up his courage, he pushed the outer door open and stepped out onto the wide metallic stairs.

"Alien!" a nearby Vred exclaimed. This set off a chain reaction of chitters and hisses as the incoming flow of Vred suddenly ebbed away from the masses on the platform.

"AJ." He hadn't realized that Darnell was right behind him until his friend's nervous pronouncement alerted him. "Those guys look like they mean business."

From the crowd, two large muscular Vred emerged. While most of the aliens were randomly clothed to some degree or another, the two who approached wore matching shorts with wide bands of green leather wrapped at the waist. Of significance were the long-handled knives tucked in the folds of the waist belts.

"You will cease your approach." There was no mistaking the authority in the leading Vred's voice, although he made no move toward his weapon.

"If this goes south, I got the guy on the left," Darnell whispered.

"Their left or ours?"

"I hate you."

"Not looking for trouble here," AJ said, holding up his hands. "We followed our new friends, Sharg and Gargun, back from Farst."

"Sssss," the second Vred hissed. "Speak not of that!"

"It is Sharg's vessel. This is rational," the leader said. "State your intent within Tardish Cove."

AJ spread his hands to include the village. "This is Tardish Cove?"

"It is."

"Trade," AJ said. "I'm Albert Jenkins. The slow one behind me is Darnell Jackson." AJ stumbled forward as Darnell's forearm smacked into his back. He ignored Darnell's affront at being jokingly offered up as an easier target should there be an attack. "We kind of ran into Sharg and Gargun on Far ... you know, up there." He pointed into the sky. "We're trying to get home. We had some extra parts and wanted to make a trade for Fantastium."

"Does the slow one speak?"

"I'm not slow," Darnell said. "And, yes, I speak."

"Brother!" Sharg's tall body emerged from the chittering mass of reptiles hanging back at the edge of the platform. With long legs, she covered the final yards to the ship where a smaller group of at least thirty Vred blocked AJ's descent. Wordlessly she embraced the first speaker, who was wider and thicker than she was but a few inches shorter than her seven feet.

"You have a knack for trouble, sister. Is it true you found alien traders and have brought them to Tardish Cove?" he asked.

"Words for discussion around the hearth," Sharg said. "Albert Jenkins, Darnell Jackson, Amanda Jayne, and Greybeard are friends."

"You would befriend a water snake, dear Sharg. Can they be trusted with the hearth of our elders? And what is an Albert Jenkins? They are tall and communicate with clarity but are clear skinned and petite."

"Geshar, you are looking at humans."

"Humans are myth and if they are not, it is said they are barely smarter than moss," he said. "And they are ugly. How could one swim without a tail?"

"Hey, we're standing right here, alligator boy," AJ said. "You got a lot of chatty moss, do you?"

"Albert Jenkins is correct in his offense," Sharg said. "You have not been a conscientious host. Have you even shared names with him?"

"It is ..." Momentary indecision crossed Geshar's face but then cleared. He nodded and clapped his teeth together twice. "It is my mistake. Albert Jenkins, Darnell Jackson, Amanda Jayne, and Greybeard, I am Geshar, brother to Sharg and one of the founders of Tardish Cove. Would you honor my family by attending to the hearth of our elders?"

AJ stuck his hand out and allowed it to hang in mid-air while Geshar looked dumbfounded. Just as AJ was about to take back his hand, Geshar extended his own, which AJ grasped and gave a single pump. "Human tradition. Shows we're not holding weapons and all that."

Geshar nodded. "Why you used four names? Are there more of you?"

"And he called us the cowards," AJ said, opening the airlock. Greybeard burst through the opening and gave an excited couple of yaps before running down the ramp.

"Your companion escapes," Geshar said.

"Greybeard," AJ eyed a handful of short Vred he thought were probably children race after the dog. "I think he needs to tinkle. Nope. That's a spin down. You got a bag or something to pick that up with?"

"Is he expelling waste?" Geshar asked. Greybeard stopped his spin and eliminated the need for the question. "It is of no concern. My daughter is amongst those that follow. She will see that the waste is cared for."

"Amanda Jayne," Jayne said, extended her hand. Geshar was quick on the uptake and wrapped her hand with his own, shaking it gently.

"I am Geshar and am grateful that you have arrived without weapons."

"Did our travel through the Sea of Bothus raise alarms?" Sharg asked.

"It was not reported, but there is yet time," Geshar said. "How did the humans come into possession of a quarantined vessel? It would be best if their vessel did not remain over land."

"I will send Gargun with the slow one, Darnell Jackson, to down under. He has demonstrated excellence in operating the quarantined vessel," Sharg said.

"Why is he considered slow?" Geshar asked. "Piloting a vessel is often a difficult task, requiring fleetness of thought and dexterous hands."

"I hate you, Albert Jenkins," Darnell grumbled.

"Their speech is often difficult to track. I believe humans often have a multitude of meanings with their words or perhaps our translator circuits need more samples," Sharg said. "I do not believe Darnell Jackson is slow in the way we think of it."

"You should ask for an alien breathing apparatus," Beverly said, a swimming mask appearing over her face and flippers on her feet. "I think you're all about to get wet."

"Sharg, are we going swimming?"

Sharg quirked her head to AJ. "How else would we travel?"

"Humans aren't exactly amphibious. I'm under the impression you have breathing apparatuses?" AJ said uncertainly.

"An interesting request, what mixture of gasses do you require?"

Before AJ could answer, Geshar interjected, "It is as I thought; they have no tails. They do not swim."

AJ considered correcting him but then thought better of it. "We can't breathe in water."

"Perhaps a better description is in order," Jayne said, recognizing Geshar's confused look. "We are unable to expel sufficient carbon dioxide while submerged. We are only able to submerge for thirty seconds, give or take."

"It is only a fifteen second swim to the hearth."

"Maybe for you," Jayne said. "I doubt we can swim anywhere near as fast as you can."

"Oh, then I will assist." Geshar stepped forward, wrapped his arms around Jayne, and lifted her easily. "Tap my shoulder if you become uncomfortable."

Jayne barked a short laugh of surprise. "No, I think this is okay."

"Hold on!" AJ said, surprised at his jealousy.

Geshar either didn't hear him or didn't care. He walked to the side of the landing platform and jumped into the water.

"Do not fear, Albert Jenkins. My brother is most conscientious. He will not release her until she is safely within the under." Sharg said. "Gargun, take Darnell Jackson and their vessel to our family cache and then bring him to the hearth. While outside of the ship, make sure Darnell Jackson is not submerged. You must walk. Do you understand?"

"I understands," Gargun said. "Slow Darnells no swims."

Darnell caught AJ's eye and shook his head. Recognizing it was a good time to move on, AJ turned to Sharg who stood semi-crouched with her arms ready to wrap around him. "Yeah, probably should follow Jayne. See you down below. Okay?"

"You're so dead," Darnell said.

Sharg wrapped AJ up and lifted him. He found the warmth of her skin and the strength of her arms entirely surprising. As she hefted him to the edge of the platform, it became obvious to AJ that she could easily have put him down when they'd met on Farst if she'd wanted to. "Will Greybeard be okay up here?"

"The children will look after him," she said, jumping off the edge of the platform. "We will move more quickly if you hold me."

AJ complied as the warm waters enveloped the two of them. With powerful strokes and a strong kick from her tail, they moved through the water more quickly than AJ would have thought possible. Just as he was becoming used to the sensation, Sharg oriented upward and they broke the water's surface.

"You did quite well, Albert Jenkins," she said. "Did you find discomfort in our travels? There is a ledge you can rest on just ahead of you."

AJ's mouth gaped open as he looked around the chamber. The room they were in was a small sphere, about thirty feet in diameter and entirely transparent. A glowing light was affixed to the top of the sphere, but there was no obvious wiring or source of power. Sharg had already clambered onto the watery ledge leading to the dry annular platform encircling the room. No furniture or objects of any kind were visible.

Most significant, and the thing that held AJ's rapt attention, were the hundreds of bubbles of all different sizes visible through the glass. He felt like he was on a giant Christmas tree surrounded by sparkling lights and ornaments. As he focused on individual details, he was able to locate Vred individuals and families going about their business inside the huge structure.

"Am I to understand this is not a usual sight for humans?" Sharg asked.

"Um, no," AJ said, swimming forward and lifting himself onto the semi-submerged platform. "This is how Vred live?"

"Within the water?" Sharg asked.

"Yes, but more than that. The spheres..." he said. "It's all so..."

"Beautiful," Jayne offered with a reverent hush in her voice, entering from an adjoining sphere. "Fantastic. Surprising. Awe inspiring. Sophisticated."

"Yeah, that," he agreed.

"No," Sharg said, her thin lips pulling back on her elongated snout, an expression AJ now recognized as a smile. "There are many of our kind who live in marshlands or in great space structures. This colony, Tardish Cove, was founded by my family. They adapted the plans of a well-known architect and artist to create a protected cove along the seaside. This place is all the things attributed to it by Amanda Jayne."

"Hard to take it all in," AJ said, turning slowly. So absorbed in his surroundings, he missed Jayne's approach and startled when her hand found his.

"I find a new emotional connection to you, Amanda Jayne and Albert Jenkins," Sharg said. "That you appreciate the art of my species draws us closer and gives me hope to experience what you also find as beautiful. I assure you the view will continue as we walk. Would you allow for my hand to bind with yours as you are doing with Albert Jenkins?"

It took Jayne a moment to realize Sharg was addressing her. "Oh, right, of course," she answered, holding her hand out. "For humans, holding hands is a sign of moderate intimacy."

"Vred have a similar gesture," Sharg said, leading them from the room. "Did Geshar go ahead to prepare?"

"He excused himself when you surfaced," Jayne confirmed of the Vred who had brought her into Tardish Cove.

"How do you manufacture these rooms?" AJ asked. "I don't see any obvious seams and I'm not sure how you're powering those lights."

Sharg snapped her jaw as her lips thinned again. "The tools used to join and cut the habitats are of Cheell construction," she said. "The cost of these devices is considerable and there are few within Tardish Cove. It is the use of this device that has Gargun and I seeking to gather our fortune."

"You and Gargun," AJ said. "You're kind of an unlikely pair."

"AJ," Jayne warned. "Careful."

Sharg bowed as she stopped at the edge of a large room. In the center, chairs and sofas were arranged on two levels, the lowest of which was partially submerged. "Welcome to our family hearth." She watched Geshar heating something on a fire. Flickering flames rose from a large slab of stone that looked out of place. "There is no offense at recognizing the difference between Gargun and myself. It is obvious that he is a unique catch for one as old and ungainly as myself."

"You're saying he's pretty?" AJ couldn't contain himself.

"Oh, yes! And he is young and extraordinarily virile," she said. "Once we have constructed our home, we will bring our own children to bear and he will raise them."

"Did not see that coming," AJ said.

"Sharg, do Vred continue to grow throughout their lifecycle?" Jayne asked.

"It is so," Sharg said. "This slows over time."

"And mental development, does it follow a similar pattern?"

"Your questions are perceptive. Can I assume humans reach a point of maturity earlier in their life cycle?"

"We live for eighty years on average," Jayne said. "Physically, we are at our peaks in teenage years. Of course, wisdom continues to collect as we age."

Sharg snapped her jaws twice in a pattern that suggested agreement. "I believe that is true of most sentients. Gargun is almost nineteen years and has been slow to develop his speech centers. This is not uncommon for one so attractive."

"Shargs good to Gargun." Gargun's growly voice announced his arrival. Following close behind was Darnell, who absently nodded at AJ and Jayne, his attention still on the activity of Tardish Cove visible through the bubble structure.

"What of this trade you have talked of?" Geshar asked, looking up from the fire. "Come, join us for tea. I have sent for grands to join us."

AJ accepted a cup of tea that looked much like the one he'd had in Sharg and Gargun's hideout on Farst. "We shared our list of trade items with Gargun," he said, drinking the tea and doing his best to filter out the swimmers. "We're really just looking for enough Fantastium to get back to Earth."

"What of the tainted ship?" A voice came from another entrance. Everyone turned to see two large Vred shuffling into the room. The pair were nearly identical with their thick folds of skin and chubby appendages. "Would you not pay for this?"

"Grand Mams and Das. You honor us with your presence," Sharg said, solicitously. "I am pleased to introduce our new friends, Albert Jenkins, Amanda Jayne, and Darnell Jackson."

"Technically, we don't exactly need a ship once we get to Earth," AJ said. "If it was possible, I'd like to keep it. I imagine we could work out some sort of further trade. Are the parts offered insufficient to purchase enough Fantastium for the trip? Trading for unused items has always been my stock and trade, but I'm at a loss here. I don't know the value."

The older female accepted a cup of tea and slowly scooched her large body onto one of the lower couches, obviously grateful to submerge her lower body. Comfortable, she sighed and leaned back against the tall cushions.

"Fantastium is the most precious commodity in the known universe." The older male Vred spoke for the first time. "It is the very essence that allows movement between the stars. Tell us, why is it that you must return home. Do not spare details. I am aware that Princess 49231125-0-B is in our presence."

"How?" Jayne asked.

AJ shook his head. "He didn't, Doc. But he does now."

"Most perceptive, Albert Jenkins. Will you tell us your story without obscurity?" Grand Das asked.

"How much do you want to know?"

"There is much tea. The chairs are comfortable. If you seek friendship and trade then it is best if we are honest with each other, is it not?"

"You'll offer the same?" Darnell asked.

"We are a transparent people," Grand Das said, gesturing at the clear windows.

Darnell grinned. "I'm not sure a people who avoid detection by two different governments can be considered transparent. If you ask me, this is a good old-fashioned smuggling operation."

Grand Mas snapped her jaws together. "Let us not start this way," she said. "Tell us the story you would entrust with us. You speak with a maturity not evident in your bodies. I believe the presence of a Beltigersk princess would explain this, however. What a blessing to have such a life alteration. Might I ask your real age?"

"Seventy-eight," Darnell said. "How about you?"

"Ninety-two years," Grand Mas answered. "I sense no deception in your words. Your story, please?"

AJ decided not to spare many details and began his tale at his first meeting with Beverly. He made sure to point out BB's reverence for the Vred crew who had been murdered by Korgul. He finished the story by describing the lengths to which they'd gone to steal the Lumbricus ship and why he'd taken a chance on the Junkyard planet.

"I find it incredible that you would risk yourselves to visit Farst," Grand Mas said. "What if the moon had merely contained debris and Sharg had not been trapped there?"

"My experience with junk is that people will throw away anything – even useful things," he said. "What we really needed to do was dump the heavy Lumbricus ship. We had enough Fantastium to make one more stop, especially if we found a more suitable ship. I also figured we'd be better off if we didn't continue our journey in a hot ship."

"Your plan was equal parts logic and luck," Geshar concluded.

"It was more strategic than that," Grand Das said. "Farst has a multitude of operable ships, but if they had not found another ship, they could still have traveled to Celestarn in the Lumbricus vessel. With a Beltigersk rider, they would have been returned to Beltigersk Five. Indeed, their plan would have worked equally well had Sharg and Gargun not been stranded – that is, until they attempted to sell their trade goods. Most Vred would have alerted the local constabulary, who would have, in turn, contacted the Galactic Police."

"You're assuming we wouldn't have been able to suss out

Celestarn traders like we're doing with you," AJ said. "I'd suggest you haven't considered everything. Certainly, an alliance with humans has some future value? We have an old Earth saying, *the sum is often greater than the parts.* Can we come to some sort of agreement that would get us enough Fantastium to get us back to Earth?"

Grand Das blinked but didn't answer.

"A clever saying," Grand Mas said. "I do believe together we could achieve more together than we can separately."

"That's my girl," AJ said.

"I would not have thought to so easily part with such a volume of Fantastium with so little hesitance," Grand Mas said. "We will make a trade for your return trip home, but I have two additional stipulations."

"This'll be good." AJ rubbed his hands together and grinned at Grand Mas. "Okay, hit me with it."

"I assume that is not a literal request," Grand Mas said.

"Good point." He nervously eyed the old reptilian's massive arms. "Just a saying."

"Sharg will join your employ."

"Grand Mas?" Sharg asked, clearly upset. "Gargun and I..."

"Yes, yes," Grand Mas said. "You are permitted to mate. Once this is complete, you will depart with the humans. You will learn what they have to teach and return when your life's fortune is completed."

"Um, I hate to..." AJ started.

"It is the only way," Grand Das grunted before flipping onto his stomach and disappearing into the water.

"But..."

"It was our pleasure, Albert Jenkins, Amanda Jayne, and Darnell Jackson." Grand Mas followed her husband's example and disappeared.

"What in the hell just happened?"

11

THE OCEAN BLUE

"Tell me, do humans prefer carbohydrates in liquid or solid forms?" Geshar asked, sitting on a narrow backless bench with his thick tail resting on the ground behind him to provide support. As he talked, Sharg strode to one of the room's two above-water exits and placed a broad hand on Gargun's back, pushing him through.

"Sharg? Where are you going?" AJ asked, ignoring Geshar's question. "We have to talk. This isn't how things are done."

Sharg looked over her shoulder. "Geshar will explain, Albert Jenkins. I must now make my family so we may depart for Earth. It is a most unexpected turn of fortunes."

"I assure you, Albert Jenkins, I will alleviate your concerns and answer your questions," Geshar said as she disappeared. "But first, it is our duty to see to the comfort of our guests."

Beverly appeared in front of AJ, wearing a bright white-and-red-striped apron over her normal jeans and white blouse, holding a metal BBQ spatula. "Tell him you would enjoy strek steaks with wheat crust."

"They have wheat?" AJ asked.

"No, but I'll translate," Beverly said. "They have a grain that is similar and a fungi that resembles yeast. Trust me, I believe I have come to a reasonable understanding of your tastes."

"Are you speaking with your Beltigersk visitor?" Geshar asked.

"Yeah, BB and I are talking about the menu," AJ said. "You know, since you all have already decided everything else."

"That is logical," Geshar answered. "Halfnium-8 has not seen a bonded Beltigerskian in a number of years. It is considered quite an honor to have been chosen. I would enjoy speaking to you of how this came to pass."

"Seems like that one is immune to sarcasm," Darnell chuckled. "I'd say tell him about BB, strek steaks and wheat crust."

Geshar turned to Darnell. "Strek steak is not a food often prepared for distinguished visitors. Is this truly what you would prefer?"

"Don't suppose you Vred have invented beer?"

Geshar quirked his head to the side and his lips thinned into what the crew had learned was a smile. "In fact, I excel in the brewing of malted grain beverages. I do not wish to be insensitive, but I would fear sharing with beings of such limited physiques."

"Did he just call us out?" AJ asked.

"I think he did," Darnell answered.

"Hold on. Thomas, show me the likely components of this Vred beverage," Jayne said and went quiet as she reviewed the presented data.

AJ shook his head. "Geshar, you're looking at two professional drinkers and I've seen that one," he pointed at Jayne, "drink straight Scotch before the ice even had a chance to soften. You bring us your home brew and we'll see who has the limited physique."

"This is a challenge of pride?" Geshar asked. "Have I insulted our esteemed guests?"

"No, not insulted," AJ said. "You laid out a challenge, one I intend to accept. Tell me Vred are different."

Geshar's lips thinned again and he clacked his jaws together. "No, Albert Jenkins, we are not different. Younger Vred often boast of their capacity for consuming fermented beverage."

"Younger?" Darnell grinned, ready to seize on the Vred's misstep. "So, when you referred to our limited physiques, you were bragging just a little?"

A short burst of air from the Vred was followed by several clacks of his teeth. Almost a full thirty seconds later he was able to respond. "I had not expected to enjoy our interaction," he said. "I have been justly called out for my behavior. Please allow for the passing of twenty-one minutes. I will return with a feast of strek and beer." He stood and strode from the room.

"He's not wrong, you know," Jayne said.

"About?" AJ asked.

"His beer will be roughly fourteen-point-five percent alcohol. More like a strong wine. The good news is, there is nothing overtly poisonous, although I wouldn't want to drink it without a strong liver."

"Their yeast must be good stuff," AJ said. "I can't brew anything over about six percent without killing the batch."

"The Vred fungi which resembles Earth yeast is indeed more robust," Beverly said. "Vred beer is highly valued within the galactic community. It's curious. Even though Vred population dwarfs that of humanity, they have significantly less variety than I've documented on Earth."

"What can I say? We like our beer," AJ said. "Want to explain the twenty-one-minute thing?"

"It's the Vred equivalent of half an hour," Jayne said.

"This is all great, but I feel like we should talk about the elephant in the room," Darnell said.

"More like alligator," AJ said.

"You should stop with that comparison," Jayne said. "It is not complimentary and the Vred have been nothing but polite to us."

AJ started to argue but Darnell cut him off. "Call it what you want, but we can't take Sharg back to Earth."

"Why?" Jayne asked.

"She'd stick out like a..."

"Like a seven-foot-tall walking alligator?" AJ said, grinning defiantly at Jayne. "Korgul aren't going to put up with Vred on Earth. She'll paint a target on our backs."

"It doesn't sound like they're giving us much of a choice," Jayne said.

"Not exactly friendly to make such a huge decision without talking about it with us. Not sure I agree with them being *polite*."

"According to Thomas, the Fantastium required to get us home has an equivalent value of about eight hundred thousand dollars," she said.

AJ whistled. "That's a pretty penny."

"For that kind of investment, they probably feel like they're due at least a one-way ticket," Darnell said. "Besides, it's not like we can show *our* faces. I'd bet every Korgul in Arizona is looking for us."

"I do not believe that to be the case," Beverly said. "Now that the Beltigersk mission to Earth is complete, Korgul should have little interest in you. In fact, a communication from Korgul High Command says essentially that."

"You've been talking to Korgul?" AJ asked.

"Not directly. No," Beverly said. "A missive was delivered to the Beltigersk royal family. I will share the exact wording if you desire, but it is political speak that you would find difficult to understand. The bottom line is that they appreciate my mother keeping us on Beltigersk Five."

"But she's not keeping us," AJ said.

"It was a missive," Beverly said. "There is no expectation of reciprocal communication."

"Taking Sharg is a good trade for getting us home," Jayne said. "She's extremely smart and will easily understand the danger associated with being discovered. Can you imagine what the resistance would trade to have a Vred's knowledge?"

"Can she do that without disrupting things on Earth?" Darnell asked.

"Who gives a crap?" AJ asked. "Korgul are stealing our future. It's time to wake up. Earth needs to be disrupted."

Darnell frowned. "But what about the balance of power? We could single-handedly set off an entirely new arms race."

"You're not actually suggesting we let this whole Korgul invasion go, right?" AJ asked.

"I just thought we'd go back and deal with it ourselves. Not bring an alien into the mix."

"You mean another alien. We've already done that if you haven't forgotten. Darnell, we go back because that's where our family is," Jayne said.

"I get that," Darnell said, growing frustrated. "It just seems like our actions will have a big impact. We should think about it."

"Your caution is reasonable, Darnell," Beverly said. "Your actions have already had inestimable impact on humanity. You will be lauded in the histories of your world and of the Galactic Empire."

"Laying it on kinda thick, don't you think?" AJ laughed.

"Not at all," Beverly chimed in. "There is a Beltigerskian saying that I believe to be relevant. No vessel has been created that will contain truth."

"Poetic," Jayne said.

"Beltigerskians have a lot of time available for such endeavors. Even now, many of my people discuss the plight of humanity openly with other intellectual communities even though it is forbidden by their queen. News will spread of what the Korgul have done to Earth. You must choose if you will add tinder to these flames or if you will stand by and watch."

"How did I become the bad guy here?" Darnell asked. "I'm not saying we stand by. I'm..."

"You're talking sense, Big D," AJ said. "So far, we've got just one decision to make. Do we accept the decision to send us home with Sharg?"

"Only if the ship is ours," Darnell said. "If Sharg wants to go somewhere else, she's got to convince us to go with her or get another ride."

"BB, how long does it take for Sharg and Gargun to, you know." AJ bobbed his head forward a couple of times.

Jayne laughed. "Procreate?"

"Yeah, that."

"I suspect the task has already been completed," Beverly said.

"You can't grow babies that fast," AJ scoffed. "Vred are warm blooded. Don't tell me she lays eggs in a nest or something dumb like that?"

"Vred are technologists," Beverly said. "Sharg's eggs will be fertilized externally and placed in an artificial womb until viable."

"Kind of takes the fun out of it, don't you think?" AJ said.

"She'll just leave them behind?" Darnell asked. "No way could I see Lisa doing that! Me, maybe."

"It only requires a small change in your thinking," Beverly answered. "In Vred society, it is commonly the male who takes responsibility for raising offspring."

"I hope you are ready for an unforgettable treat. I am not only known for my great fermented beverages but my wheat-coated strek is also favored." Geshar's voice interrupted the conversation. Three smaller Vred followed behind him carrying platters covered with bottles and dishes. Plucking off three of the bottles, he handed one to each of the humans.

"It's weird how many similarities we have." AJ took a long drink and resisted the urge to cough at the liquid's unexpected burn. "Damn decent, like a thick porter with a helluva kick."

"Have you come to a decision?" Geshar asked.

"About?" AJ asked, accepting a plate loaded with what amounted to steak wrapped in a shell of leavened bread.

"Grand Mas presented our family's offer to supply your mission with Fantastium," Geshar said. "It is customary for both parties to agree before consummation."

"I didn't think they needed to do that," AJ said, confused.

Geshar stilled, his only movement the soft clacking of his jaw. "I do not understand."

"Consummate what?" AJ said. "Sharg and Gargun? Or our deal?"

"Are they not one and the same?" Geshar asked. "Sharg is prepared. Your acceptance will allow the process of life to continue."

"We require two stipulations," Darnell said.

"Ah, yes," Geshar said. "This is expected. Please state your counteroffer."

"Same deal as Grand Mas offered," Darnell said. "But we own the ship. Not Sharg. Not your family."

"And the second modification?"

"At the expense of your family, you fully supply and maintenance our ship, including food, water and top-of-the-line space suits for the entire crew, including Sharg and Greybeard."

Geshar clacked his jaw together. "A wise and thoughtful counteroffer." Turning to one of the two smaller Vred who had accompanied him with the food, he continued. "Inform Grand Mas that we have reached accord and then let word pass to Sharg that her family is to be completed."

AJ bit into the strek steak and found it to be flavorful, if not chewy. After Geshar spoke to the smaller Vred, the large reptilian man sat on one of the benches and ripped off a chunk of his own bread-wrapped steak with sharp teeth. With minimal chewing, he swallowed it with a large gulp of beer.

"Can you even taste that?" AJ asked. "You didn't even chew it."

"I will enjoy this meal for most of the evening," Geshar said, ripping off another chunk. "I wondered the same thing about you, given your flat, narrow teeth."

"I feel like we left money on the table," AJ said. "What would the family have accepted in that deal?"

"Do you wish to renegotiate?" Geshar's lips thinned as he set his drink down. He pushed forward on his stool in a not-so-subtle, menacing way.

"Don't get your panties in a bunch, big boy," AJ said, tipping back his beer. "A deal's a deal. Just wondering how bad we did."

"You are certain you will not attempt a renegotiation?"

"Not how we work," AJ said. "Look, Grand Mas figured it out before anyone. We're stronger if we work together. I'll honor that. Just got me wondering."

"The maintenance of the ship and resupply was anticipated and confirmed that we are working with thoughtful partners," Geshar said. "I believe you could have requested some form of convertible wealth. There are a number of rare metals that trade well in most societies."

"Platinum, gold, that sort of thing?" Darnell asked. "I thought about that, but felt it was small-minded."

"We have a similar saying – young-minded," Geshar said.

"What I really want to know is, how soon will we be ready to leave?" AJ asked. "It's a long trip home, and I'd like to get going."

"Without movement, a journey is not completed," Geshar agreed. "It will take three days to complete the maintenance of your ship. During this time, you will have the opportunity to gain familiarity with its systems and be fitted for onboard suits. Does this meet with your approval?"

"Probably gonna need to squeeze some sleep in there at some point," AJ said.

"Indeed." Geshar agreed.

"YOU HAVE a remarkable aptitude for mechanical interaction." Kapaugn, a lithe Vred, had been showing AJ the various subsystems of the single-deck, sixty-five-foot-long spacecraft. During the tour, the two had stopped to replace a multitude of filters, aged lubrication, every external door seal, and a number of questionable circuit boards.

"I'll be honest, you've got my head swimming," AJ said. "This ship is a weird combination of simplicity and backward thinking."

"There are many Vred who would not comprehend most of what you've learned in the last days, Albert Jenkins. If all humans are as you, the species has been underestimated."

"I appreciate the vote of confidence, but everything on this ship is a complete mystery. If you weren't here, I'd be lost," AJ said. "Trust me, there are plenty of humans much smarter than me. I'm plenty good with a wrench and a soldering iron, though."

"I have learned much from your questions. The way humanity views technology is very different from that of Vred. We have much to learn from each other," Kapaugn said. "With that said and with regret, I find that we have addressed the final maintenance of this ship. You are always welcome to use the tools of my shop. I will retrieve Grand Mas' Fantastium and transfer it to this vessel's holding. I wish for you an uneventful return home."

AJ held his hand out and was gratified when Kapaugn shook it. "If you ever get back to Earth, mi casa es su casa."

"My translation has failed on this."

"Just saying, you're welcome in my shop anytime."

"You boys finish up?" Jayne asked, a heavy bag hanging over her shoulder as she climbed into the main cabin from the airlock. "I was just bringing in the last of the provisions. AJ, you'll be glad to know Geshar threw in an entire case of beer."

"Need a hand with that?" AJ asked.

"The beer's already loaded," she said with a smirk. "Although there is a vacuum suit in here for you."

"Safe travels, friend." Kapaugn bowed as he slipped past Jayne and worked the exterior airlock door.

"Be well, Kap."

"Seems like you made a friend," Jayne said.

"If you can get past the whole gator thing, they're really not that different from us," AJ said. "Smart like you can't believe, though. That Kap's gotta have a genius-level IQ. There isn't one system on this ship he doesn't have completely memorized. And I don't mean just their names. He knows every circuit, size of each bolt, tolerances, torques, you name it."

"Might need to upgrade that friend status to relationship." The grin in Jayne's voice was evident as she dropped the bag she carried and pulled out a dark purple pile of fabric. "Try this on."

"With clothes underneath?"

"You can keep shorts, but otherwise, strip," she said.

He waggled his eyebrows suggestively. "Finally, we're getting somewhere."

"As a surgeon, I assure you, I've seen more than my share of naked men," Jayne said. "If you want to impress me, it'll require a white tablecloth, a great meal and an expensive Scotch. Nice music wouldn't hurt."

AJ shucked his clothing into a puddle around his feet. "Seriously, Doc?" he asked, looking down at a body he would have been jealous to have at twenty, let alone while in his late seventies. "I haven't seen my abs in forty years. I'm not too proud to say I still look in the mirror. Tell me you haven't looked at what's under the covers and, well, you know."

Jayne chuckled. "I'm not exactly sure what *you know* might mean but, yes, the changes to my body have been gratifying. Stimulating even. I did not realize how much the hormones of my youth drove my thinking."

He grabbed for the suit and turned around, shoving one foot into the opening. "Tablecloths and Scotch, eh?"

"AJ, your face is turning red," she said. "Are you okay?"

"Fine, Doc."

Wordlessly, she stepped around, noticing that he had bunched material up in front of his body as he wobbled on one leg. "Perhaps it would be best to talk of other things when removing our clothes."

He turned away to put his other foot in the suit, grateful the material was thick. "You think?"

"Don't forget fantastic meal and music," she said once AJ turned back around. She held the neck of the suit up so AJ could slip his arms inside. "Sharg suggests that while in flight, these suits should not be necessary."

"Kapaugn said the same," AJ said. "Apparently, Vred hulls can take quite a beating. If something does get through and it's smaller than about the size of my fist, the hull will just seal right back up. Minimal loss of pressure."

"They are a gentle people. Humans could learn a lot from the way they live in harmony with their planet."

"Don't be too impressed," AJ said. "That might be what Halfnium-

8 is all about, but other Vred worlds sound more like Earth. Conflicts over resources, class warfare, the whole works."

"Aw, don't ruin it for me. Tardish Cove is idyllic."

"Seriously, Doc?" AJ asked. "Have you already forgotten how we got here? These guys are great, but they're a bunch of smugglers. Why in the world do you think they're sending Sharg with us? They want her to find a fortune and bring it home before Earth is discovered and plundered by the next big asshat."

"That's a rather pessimistic way of looking at things. If you believe that, why are we throwing in with Grand Mas?"

"Because the whole family is unfailingly honest. Grand Mas instructed Sharg to find her fortune. Don't you get it? Sharg might as well be Columbus and we're the native Americans. She's on an exploratory mission to find treasure for the queen. Columbus wasn't originally looking for a new place to live. He was an explorer. The whole invasion of settlers came later."

"We can't let that whole *invasion* thing happen," Jayne said. "If word gets out, species we haven't even heard about could decide to kick us off our planet. At least Korgul have the courtesy to just take our stuff without making a mess of things. According to Thomas, they also provide a level of protection against invasive species."

"Almost sounds noble." AJ was surprised when the opening on his back closed by itself. "Good fit. How do I get it off?" Jayne pressed at a hidden pouch beneath his armpit and exposed the top of a seam. Her touch was enough to cause the back to open once again.

"Are we wrong to go home?" she asked.

"Negative," AJ said. "The bad guys are already there. Our job is to kick those snot-ball Korgul off our planet. If a certain family of Vred smugglers wants to make some dough while they bring us up to speed on Galactic technology, I'm all in."

"Is it wrong to wish for solutions that aren't so black and white?"

"I've been saying that for years," Darnell yelled from the ship's cockpit.

12

POISON PILL

AJ pulled a retractable stool away from the counter next to where Jayne was seated. They'd been underway for two weeks and had fallen into a comfortable rhythm. During most of the trip, she'd been focused on virtual images not visible to the others as she worked with the Beltigerskian, Thomas.

"Any progress, Doc?" he asked, setting a cup of Vred krill tea next to her.

Amanda Jayne blinked a couple times, a gesture AJ had become familiar with as she disengaged from her virtual environment. Wordlessly, she picked up the tea and turned to AJ, taking a contemplative sip.

"He's done it," she said, lowering her cup.

"Thomas?"

Jayne nodded. "It needs testing. AJ, I know it's crazy to ask, but are we doing the right thing? Our world will be in chaos when people find out what the Korgul have done. It'll be anarchy. What if we cause a war? Or wars? Do we have the right?"

"Slow down there, Doc," AJ said. "What did Thomas figure out?"

"It's simple, really." She drew in a long breath and slowly released it.

"Big D, you might want to get back here," he called. "Doc has something."

"Do you want to wake Sharg?" Jayne asked.

"Not yet. This doesn't exactly concern her," AJ said.

Darnell walked into the ship's comfortable common area and leaned against a partition that separated the area from the cockpit. "We're about thirty minutes from Mars," he said and then smiled. "Can't believe I just said that. Whatcha have, Doc?"

"More Thomas than me," she said. "Originally, we were trying to come up with a way to attack the Korgul directly. We found something, but in simulation it was fatal nearly sixty percent of the time to the Korgul and about twenty percent to the human host."

"Not sure I care about Korgul fatalities," AJ said.

Jayne pursed her lips. "You agree that twenty percent fatality rate for the human host is unacceptable, though, right?"

Darnell shrugged. "I'd have taken those odds. We're talking about people's freedom here."

Jayne gave her head a small shake. "I took an oath to do no harm. I won't be part of something that kills millions of people, which is what we're talking about, given the number of Korgul on Earth. And that's if you can put aside the idea that you'd kill tens of millions of Korgul."

"Ask me, they got it coming," AJ said.

Jayne started to object but Darnell stopped him. "We get your point, Doc. Not good to kill a million of our fellow human beings."

She shook her head, irritation plain on her face. "Instead of attacking the Korgul, we decided to look at things from the other side."

"Attack the person?" Darnell asked.

"Attack is a strong word," Jayne said. "No, Thomas has been involved with a particular line of research into what makes a viable host for Beltigerskians. I won't bore you with the science, but we believe we can interrupt that bonding and make the host immune."

"How is that bad?" AJ asked.

"Well first, it hasn't been tested," Jayne said. "Second, we don't have a good way to disseminate this *cure*."

"We'll paint a target on our backs," Darnell said. "If Korgul figure out what's going on, they'll come after us. Maybe develop an antidote."

"How soon will you have something?" AJ asked.

"Now," Jayne said, holding up a phial. "Before we think about using it, we need a test."

"Whoa, be careful with that stuff, Doc," AJ said. "If it works, you'll knock out 2-F and BB. Do that and I think it's fair to say we're going to have trouble landing this ship with any confidence."

Jayne smiled. "Actually, this *is* the antidote. I want to dose you, Greybeard, and Darnell so there's no chance you'll be affected by the cure we've developed for Earth. It should be impossible for the cure to spread in its current form, but like you said, it could be disastrous."

"And you need a dose," AJ said.

Jayne shook her head. "I'm the first experiment. I'll expose myself and Thomas should be expelled from my body. I argued with Thomas that it's too dangerous, but he's convinced me that this is the only way."

"I thought you never wanted go through that again," AJ said.

"A side benefit of what we came up with is that we'll be separated with virtually no side effects. He'll simply work his way out through my dermis. It was Thomas' research on harmless separation of Beltigerskian from their host that got us here in the first place. He just adapted his methods to include Korgul."

"Aren't you listening to me?" Darnell asked. "This is an existential threat to the Korgul way of life. It'll be a major escalation in the war between humanity and Korgul. We need to consider the ramifications."

"You mean the war only Korgul are aware of?" AJ said.

"What if they have the capacity to destroy Earth? And what if they think it would stop this new bug that causes separation? What's to stop them from just wiping out humanity?"

"That'd be genocide," Jayne said.

"For humans – a non-recognized species? More like eradication of a nuisance species," AJ's voice was thick with anger. "Do you think the Galactic Congress would even lift a finger to help us?

"We're getting ahead of ourselves," Jayne said, loading a hypodermic from the phial she held. "We don't even know if this works."

"Doc, are you sure?" AJ asked.

"If something happens to me, you need to locate Dr. Jerry Jeffries, a researcher at CDC. It'll take some convincing, but you need to explain what's going on to him," she said.

"CDC?" AJ asked. "For what?"

"Jerry is one of the world's foremost experts on disease transmittal."

"Disease? That doesn't make sense," he said. "And what do you mean, something happens? I don't like the way you're talking, Doc." His words trailed off as she plunged the needle into his arm.

Beverly appeared, wearing a blue sun dress, sitting on the back of the couch. "I've spoken with Thomas. There are risks, but they are low. If his antidote does not work, AJ, it has been my greatest honor to have accompanied you on this mission."

"Not making me feel any better, here, BB." AJ's eyes locked on the tiny projection of the alien woman. "I don't want to sound sappy, but I'd hate to lose you."

Beverly nodded.

"I'm sorry, Greybeard," Jayne said. "I don't even think you need this, but I don't want to take any chances."

Greybeard barked once and sat on the floor as she plunged a second needle into the loose skin on the back of his neck.

"This doesn't make sense," Darnell objected as Jayne loaded up a syringe. "What about Lisa? I was hoping she'd get a chance at a rider."

"Is that what she wants, Big D?" AJ asked. "If you don't do this, you might not be able to fly this ship. Are you sure you want that?"

"It's just... She's my wife."

"Who will love you even if your body looks like you're thirty years old," Jayne said. "Besides, this is an antidote for something that I'm not sure will even spread."

"Humanity needs you, buddy," AJ said. "Maybe one of the riders will be a good match for Lisa. We've brought a couple extra along. I think she'd want a say in it, though."

"You're right. I don't know what she'll think," Darnell said. "She can be hardheaded at times."

"We still need a pilot," AJ said.

"I hate this. Do it."

Jayne finished inoculating Darnell and then without hesitation drained a small phial of greenish liquid onto her tongue.

"Was that the cure?" AJ asked.

Jayne nodded. "My life is inconsequential in comparison to the impact of this cure," she said. "Remember. Dr. Jerry Jefferies. Atlanta, Georgia. Lives with his wife. Marie, I think."

"Stop talking like that, Doc," AJ scooted over and wrapped his arms around the rigid woman. Initially, she pulled away, but he held on. "It's okay, I've got you."

Tears fell as she leaned her head against AJ and sagged into him. "I'm scared."

Beverly walked across the back of the cushion so she could look into Jayne's face. "I've lost contact with Thomas. Is he still with you?"

Jayne's eyes drifted as she focused elsewhere. After a minute, she shook her head. "He's gone. I can't talk to him. Oh, Lord, what have we done? We can't lose him."

Beverly's thin smile revealed her own fears. "I have all of Thomas's research. It would be a great personal loss, but the research will be saved. How do you feel? AJ, hold her wrist so I can calculate blood pressure and temperature."

AJ did as he was told but made sure not to release his hold on Jayne. "How long before you should feel side effects?"

"Now?" Jayne said. "Last time, when Jack separated, the pain was instantaneous."

"Do you feel different?" Beverly asked.

"I miss him," Jayne said. "He was kind and gentle."

"It might take time before he surfaces," Beverly said. "It appears the first test was successful."

"Thomas would not confirm the risk to himself," Jayne said, looking at the floor. "I was so stupid. I knew better."

"Give it time. We don't know how long it will take for Thomas to reappear," Beverly said. "According to his notes, the next step is to test a live, treated subject. We would infect them with Korgul and make sure re-infection isn't possible."

"Is that how you see yourself?" Jayne asked. "As an infection?"

"No," Beverly answered. "Korgul are an infection. They do not ask for permission nor do they benefit their hosts. I consider Albert Jenkins to be my partner and friend."

Jayne smiled as she nodded in agreement. "That was Thomas."

———

"Check that out." Darnell pointed at the viewscreen. Against the black of space, Earth gleamed, a deep glassy blue with swirls of pure white. The lifeless gray moon hung off to the side, half darkened by Earth's shadow.

"Never thought I'd see Earth from this side," AJ said.

"Your planet is as beautiful as Halfnium-8," Sharg said. "What a great boon that much water must be. I am surprised you did not develop as an amphibious species."

"Our oceans are deep," AJ said. "They have a high saline content which means we can't directly consume the water. We're not exactly afraid of the water, we're just not as good at swimming in it as you Vred."

"I am curious about these alligators you speak of. If I am to understand Dr. Jayne correctly, the comparison to Vred is unflattering."

"About that," AJ said. "She's right. I only said it when I was irritated. Alligators and crocodiles are dumb animals. The only real resemblance is skin – well, and that whole tail thing."

"Don't forget about the snout," Darnell said. "Just keeping it real, but, you know, it's a thing."

"BB show her a picture, would you?" AJ asked as he kept an eye on

Jayne. Ever since the extraction and the disappearance of Thomas, she'd withdrawn. "You doing okay, Doc?"

Jayne nodded. "I killed him, AJ."

"I know it feels like that," AJ said. "The risk was one he was willing to take. Thomas believed in something bigger than himself and those types of actions are what define a hero, what keeps a soldier moving forward. The good ones, anyway."

"What if we kill every Korgul? How is it right to commit that kind of genocide? They don't even know this *cure* is coming," she said. "Maybe we need to warn them, give them a chance to escape."

"What happens when they decide to wipe out humanity to cover their tracks? They could launch our own nukes against us. What if we let them believe this is just some new disease? Make 'em believe Earth got poisoned somehow. Maybe they'd leave all by themselves."

She shrugged. "We're playing God."

"You don't even know if this cure will kill them," AJ said. "We don't know what happened to Thomas."

"I know you do not want my input as I am an outsider, but I believe Dr. Jayne is right," Sharg said. "Even though Korgul are a miserable species, they should not be exterminated."

"Would you say the same thing if they took over Geshar, Grand Mas and Grand Das?" AJ asked. "What if all of Halfnium-8 was under their control and they were crapping up the place with their litter?"

"I would be very upset," Sharg said. "I do not know how I would respond. That does not change the morality of genocide."

"If I could, I'd carpet-bomb the whole damn lot of them," AJ said. "The only way to stop a bully is to stand up to them. I want to make those robin's-egg sonsabitches squirm in their juices when they think about messing with humans."

"Your people are in an existential fight," Sharg said. "I understand your passion and will not further inflame the conversation. Vred are familiar with war and its ravages. We have a saying: war brings destruction to even the victors."

"Well, we haven't released anything yet, so there's still time to talk about it," AJ said. "I don't think it's a good idea to let the Korgul know about our secret weapon. It kind of ruins the surprise."

The comment drew an ironic smirk from Jayne.

"What's it going to be? We headed back to Tucson or Atlanta?" Darnell asked. "I've got five Korgul ships on the scope and 2-F has responded to a pair of Korgul challenges. So far, they're buying us as a Korgul merc crew."

"Jerry would probably be able to help," Jayne offered weakly. "I feel bad, like I'm going to ruin his life."

AJ felt like someone had punched him in the gut. "You feel like your life's been ruined?"

She looked at him but had no ready answer.

"Tucson, Big D," AJ said. "We should take the same route we used on the way back from Mexico. I'm pretty sure we'll get picked up on someone's radar if we drop in near any major city in the US."

"I was thinking about dropping into the middle of the Pacific Ocean," Darnell said. "Bump along the waves until we hit the coast of Mexico and then slide in behind the Gulf of California."

"And by *drop in*, you mean above, right?" AJ asked.

"Yeah. Top speed in this baby isn't that good under water. We'll be hard to spot no matter what. Even if we're picked up on reentry, they'll just think something hit the water and sank."

"Why Tucson?" Jayne asked.

"Our plan doesn't work if Korgul can just get loaded back up inside any human," AJ said. "I don't know how bad that fire was at my junkyard, but I'm pretty sure those Korgul we hid in the shelter are still there."

"You want to see if they can infest me now," Jayne said, showing no emotion.

AJ raised his eyebrows. "Wasn't that the original plan?"

"I'll do it," Jayne said, shrugging. "After that test, I'll go back to my apartment. I don't think I can do this anymore."

"How in the hell are we supposed to do it without you?"

"Don't you get it, AJ? I'm nothing now," Jayne said. "I'm immune to

Beltigerskians, probably Korgul too. Beverly has the research. I'm just a third wheel and I'm tired."

"No," he said. "I don't get it. Nothing has changed. Korgul are still attacking Earth. It's all-hands-on-deck time."

"No. You *don't* get it," Jayne answered angrily. "I killed someone in my zeal for this fucking cure. I got lazy. Single-minded. Now someone has died. I can't do this, AJ. You have to find someone else."

"Doc," He reached for her.

"Don't!" She pushed his hand away. "Once we get back, we'll try a few Korgul on me. If they get in, you can taze them out of me or let 'em stay for further testing. I don't care. I just don't want to do this anymore."

"Doc..."

"Give her some room, AJ," Darnell said quietly.

Greybeard whined as he pushed his head beneath Jayne's hand and wormed his way into her lap. Tears trickled down her cheeks as she closed her eyes.

"I believe in you, Doc," AJ said, patting her shoulder before walking forward to the cockpit to join Darnell.

"ALL THAT MAINTENANCE we did on Halfnium-8 kind of took the fun out of re-entry," Darnell said as the craft dropped smoothly into the atmosphere and then tipped his head to where Jayne sat alone and withdrawn. "You think she's going to be okay?"

"She's taking it pretty hard," AJ said. "I get it. BB's part of my family now. Wish Jayne wasn't throwing in the towel, though."

"How long were you married?" Darnell asked.

"You know how long," AJ said. "You were there."

"Yeah," Darnell said. "You gotta give her some space."

"How long before we get to Tucson?" AJ asked.

Darnell chuckled. "You're worse than my kids. Why don't you go make me a snack? And none of that tea with the swimmers in it! I've gotta take it easy. If we break the speed of sound, any number of systems will pick us up, no matter our altitude."

When AJ arrived in the central compartment, he found Jayne asleep on the couch, Greybeard still snuggled against her. He pulled a blanket over her before starting his search of the galley for food he knew didn't exist.

"Dr. Jayne is a credit to humanity," Sharg said.

AJ nodded. It was the last thing he wanted to talk with Sharg about. "What kind of fortune do you think you'll find on Earth?" he asked, not really caring about her answer.

"I have already found my fortune," Sharg said.

"Oh?"

"If you are successful at creating a ward against Korgul, the value of such an item within the Galactic community would be considerable," Sharg said.

AJ knit his eyebrows, irritated by her bald-faced admission. "Not sure we're sharing it."

Sharg clacked her jaws. "Yes, you will."

"I don't follow. Are you threatening me?"

Sharg's jaws clacked twice and she expelled a short whoosh of breath. It was a gesture AJ had learned was equivalent to a laugh. "Certainly not," she said. "You will request that I take it. I believe you will also offer this vessel so that I will leave as quickly as possible."

"I'm totally not following. I'm tired and grumpy, so get to the point."

"Yes, of course," she said. "Once you have verified this remedy's behavior with the parasitical Korgul, you will become endangered. Secrets like what you hold are impossible to keep for long periods. The only safety you will find is if the formula is released to the Galactic community. You are not equipped to do such a thing, but no doubt you will pay me a considerable amount to do just that."

"We've got no money," he said. "You seem pretty sure of yourself."

"Your Earth is rich with Fantastium," she said. "Gathering it is of no difficulty, especially for one with a vessel such as we ride in today."

"Korgul have been mining it for decades, centuries even."

"Korgul are lazy. They have perhaps removed sixty percent of what once was," she said. "Entire nations run for centuries on the dregs of what has been left behind by more diligent species than Korgul. Your world will change greatly, Albert Jenkins, but only if you are successful at ridding it of your Korgul masters. You must free this information. It is your only option."

"And you'll do this for a load of Fantastium?"

"I am not just an opportunist," Sharg said. "I am a mother and I am a friend. Others would seek to profit beyond reason with this information. I can be content in completing my family."

AJ felt a hand on his back. "She's right, AJ," Jayne said. "Thomas said as much. Once we verify that the cure works, this information needs to get out to everyone. Even if Korgul destroy us in a nuclear winter, they will have imprisoned their last victim."

13

FOR MEATLOAF

AJ kicked at a charred beam atop the rubble of the home his grandfather built. A second flashlight beam crossed his own as he felt a hand on his back. He'd spent his life in the junkyard, first as a kid visiting with his parents, then as a teenager working a summer job, and finally with his own wife, who'd died in bed only a few feet from where he stood. He bit back tears.

"Didn't think losing this place would hit me so hard," he said absently. "But this was all that is left of my family."

"We could rebuild," Jayne said softly.

AJ quirked his head and looked at her. "We? I thought you were out."

The glow from the flashlight showed tear stains in the small patches of soot on Jayne's face. She looked into his face and shook her head. "And go where?" Her words were a mere whisper.

"Anywhere but here."

"This," she ran her flashlight beam across the destroyed home, "is why we need to fight, AJ. How many people's lives have been ruined by Korgul?"

"AJ!" Darnell called from forty yards away.

"Wonder what's got his panties all wadded up," AJ said and

squeezed Jayne's hand. "Glad to have you back, Doc, but what about Thomas?"

A tiny smile showed on her face. "He's okay."

"You found him? Talked to him?"

She shook her head. "Maybe? No. Let's go see what's got Darnell all worked up."

"You're going to need to do better than that." AJ tried to make a stand until he got an answer, but was nearly pulled off his feet as she dragged him toward Darnell's voice.

Greybeard barked with excitement, racing back and forth from AJ and Jayne to Sharg and Darnell. In the midst of the workshop's rubble, AJ spotted his best friend and knew exactly what he was looking at.

"Is it still covered?" AJ asked.

"I don't think the fire got to it," Darnell said.

AJ pointed his flashlight at the debris leaning against a small structure which hadn't been affected by the fire. "Wait a minute." He jogged to the shed.

"Darnell explained how the Korgul attacked your home. I am sorry." Sharg's voice was unexpected. "Is this another home? It appears small."

"Shed. Hold this." AJ handed her his flashlight. With hands free, he pulled debris away from the door. It took a few tries and the removal of even more debris, but AJ finally got the door open. From within the darkness of the shed, dozens of amber and green lights flickered. "We've got power!" he called back, pressing a plunger switch which started a small motor just outside the shed.

"A control room," Sharg said. "It is rudimentary."

He chuckled. "Thanks." Back outside, he pulled tin siding away from a nearby vent pipe.

"Ah, a subterranean habitat," she said, sniffing the air.

"Not as fancy as your underwater home, but it'll work. The sound of material being tossed aside drew their attention.

"Let's see what we're into here." Darnell opened a wide door made of steel roofing attached to heavy, rusted hinges, revealing an old cellar entrance.

AJ stepped onto cement stairs and shined his light ahead. Ash dusted the steps, but there was no other evidence of the fire that had ravaged his other buildings. About ten steps down, he felt along the cool cement wall and located a recessed switch cleverly hidden between seams in the cement. Dim lights flooded the remaining stairs which disappeared around the corner.

"Are you sure it's safe?" Jayne asked, following close behind him.

He nodded. "No prints in the ash," he said, pointing his flashlight at the stairs ahead.

As they rounded the corner, Beverly appeared in his flashlight beam, hanging from a rope with her feet against the wall, as if she were rappelling. "Ask Amanda Jayne what she meant about Thomas," Beverly said. "Why has she had a change of heart?"

"Because I can both hear and see you, Beverly," Jayne answered.

Beverly kicked off the wall and released the rope, leaping for and landing on AJ's shoulder. "That should not be possible. Can you speak with him?"

"No. Although, now that you say it, I've been having a weird flashing of my vision. I wonder if he's trying to communicate," Jayne said. "Thomas. Can you hear me? One pulse for yes and two for no."

AJ held Jayne's hand to lead her down the final few steps. They stopped in front of an oval door that looked like it belonged on a submarine.

"Do it again. Can you hear me?" Jayne said, squeezing AJ's shoulder with excitement. "He's doing it."

"That's great, Doc," AJ said, spinning open the circular handle before pulling open the door. "Let's get inside. Sorry about the head-room, Sharg. We weren't expecting seven-footers down here."

"It is quite all right," she said, crouching as she ducked around light fixtures hanging from overhead cement beams. "Is this a normal human habitat?"

"Bomb shelter. Humanity hasn't had nuclear bombs for long. Kind of freaked out an entire generation."

"A reasonable precaution, although it would provide little long-term help if such weapons were used within a distance for which this shelter would provide safety."

"Yup," he said, helping Jayne to one of the musty couches, where she continued her one-sided conversation.

"We need communication devices," Beverly said, swinging into view on virtual ropes suspended from the ceiling.

Darnell appeared from one of the back rooms, carrying an old .22 pistol and a box of bullets. "I thought we left this behind. Not sure I'd trust the ammo, though. Who knows how much humidity it's absorbed."

AJ was busy taking a case of water bottles out of a cabinet. "How hard would it be to make some anti-Korgul rounds for that? It's a small bullet and would cause less damage to the human host if we're careful."

"2-F says it's too small for the battery," Darnell said, handing the gun to AJ. "That's why we chose the 9mm."

"If this is to be our base of operations, it would be wise to have Sharg move the manufactory from the ship. Keeping the ship close to your home isn't smart," Beverly said. "Under the cover of night, the ship is reasonably hidden. The same cannot be said for daylight hours."

"Once Korgul figure out we're back, we won't be safe here anyway. We have about three hours. I bet I can find enough old tarps that didn't get burned up to cover the ship," AJ extracted a small stack of twenty-dollar bills from a drawer and counted it. "We'll need IDs and money. I've got two-hundred forty bucks."

"Assuming I wasn't declared dead, I have money," Jayne said.

"How's it coming with Thomas?" he asked, reading sudden interest on Beverly's face.

"We are communicating," Jayne said. "He suggests that indeed he is unable to re-establish his bond with me."

"Then how are you communicating?"

"Slowly. I believe he has asked to be removed from my tragus. I'm working out a time with him now," she said.

"Tragus?"

Jayne pointed to the protrusion of skin above her ear lobe.

"I want to see Lisa," Darnell said. "I need to know she's okay."

"Why not tell her what's going on?" AJ said. "Get her help. She'd have a phone."

"You're serious?" Darnell asked.

"Why not? Korgul can't really use her against us anymore," AJ said. "Help me get the ship covered. I can't wait to see the look on her face."

"She's gonna kill me."

"I DON'T SEE what you like about these old Subarus," Darnell complained as they climbed back in after purchasing a temporary cell phone and a bag filled with junk food.

"We've had this conversation." AJ grinned as the motor turned over with ease. "Cheap, reliable transportation."

"It feels like we're riding around in a lumber wagon."

"Needs struts," AJ said. "You know, as your friend, I happily eat Lisa's meatloaf. You could at least reciprocate. I don't see why you gotta disparage my ride."

"Because it's crap."

"Which?"

The two men laughed. A few minutes later, AJ turned onto Darnell's street.

"We don't even know if she's home," Darnell said. "What if a neighbor sees me? I'm supposed to be dead."

"You look like you're thirty years old," AJ said. "They'll think you're Toby."

"I look nothing like my daughter's dumb-ass husband," Darnell complained. "Shit, what if *he's* here."

"Relax. There's nobody in your driveway." AJ chuckled as he drove past the home. It was late spring, the sun had already been up for an hour, and the sleepy suburb was bustling with activity.

"You missed it," Darnell pointed back at the house.

"I know. I wanted a drive-by. Doesn't look like there's any activity." AJ pulled into a neighbor's drive and turned around, parking on the street half a block from Darnell's house.

"Why not pull in the driveway?"

"Don't want to draw attention to your house."

"What am I going to say to her?" Darnell asked, as the two walked along the sidewalk and turned toward his house.

"Funny that you think you'll get to talk," AJ said, pushing the doorbell.

Darnell drew in a quick breath when the front door was opened and his wife of forty years, still dressed in pajamas, looked through the storm door. "AJ?" she asked after a moment and then her head swiveled to Darnell and she locked eyes with him. "You're... you're dead."

"Lisa, let us in," Darnell said.

Wordlessly, she pushed open the door. Darnell embraced his wife, tears running down his face. "Oh, baby, it's so good to see you."

Instead of reciprocating, Lisa backed away from him and looked over to AJ. "Your mother was warned not to interfere further in our business, Princess." The voice belonged to Lisa, but she was clearly not in charge.

AJ fired the pistol he held in his pocket, the bullet piercing the light jacket fabric and striking Lisa in the abdomen.

Darnell helped his wife drop to the ground. "AJ? What have you done?"

AJ pushed the two of them out of the way until he was able to close the front door. Withdrawing the pistol, he crouched warily and scanned the room. "First aid, Darnell. I'll clear the house."

"You... how..." Darnell stuttered.

"Didn't think you were up for knowing I was packing," AJ said. "Pull back her shirt, I hit her in the side. Dammit, Darnell, treat the wound. There may be more of them here."

Only then did his friend understand. "There's a first aid kit in the bathroom, get it."

"No. I'll clear. You take care of Lisa." With his back to the wall, AJ worked his way through the home's lower level. He moved fast but was thorough. By the time he got back to Lisa, Darnell had the tails of her pajama shirt up and was dabbing at a free flow of blood. "Pressure. Shit, Darnell, did you lose your brain? 2-F, can't you help him?"

Beverly appeared next to Darnell, wearing her black leather Batgirl suit. "Up or down?" she asked.

AJ looked up the staircase and left his friend again. "Any read on how that stuff's working?" AJ asked Beverly. "I thought Darnell knew we'd loaded the cure and were ready to use it."

"The wound perpetrated on Lisa Jackson was not sufficient to cause her unconsciousness," Beverly said.

"Too many words," AJ said. "Keep it tight."

"The anti-Korgul serum is working," Beverly said. "I am grateful that you and Darnell have taken the antidote. The blood spatter might have been sufficient to infect you both."

"Didn't think about that." AJ spun into the final upstairs bedroom, only then realizing that it looked like the homeless had moved into the once immaculate home. "Geez, it stinks up here. Is this how Korgul live?"

"She's coming around," Darnell said when he reached the bottom of the steps.

"What about the Korgul? Did it come out?" AJ followed Darnell's eyes over to a brownish-green splotch on the marble foyer entryway.

"They pop like ticks," Darnell said darkly. "Little bastard tried to crawl back in. I grabbed him and got a shock for it. Guess he didn't know he was fighting above his weight class." He held up his hand so AJ could see the already healing burn on the fingertip.

"Is that really you, Darnell?" Lisa sat up and reached for the wound her husband was finally tending to correctly.

"Baby. It's me. I'm home." When he pulled her into his arms this time, she clung to him with every ounce of strength in her body.

"But you... they said you were..."

"Dead," he said. "I know. Bad people. It was the only way to keep you safe."

"Darnell, there are strange things happening," she said, choking back tears. "I think aliens. I had this dream, a nightmare really, but now I don't think it was a dream at all."

Lisa pulled back to look into his face and blinked in confusion. "You look so young. I don't understand. What's happening?"

"Who cares?" he said. "I just care that you're okay."

"I THOUGHT the whole thing was a nightmare." Lisa placed three coffee cups on the table. She sat for only a moment before jumping up again to load the dishwasher. "I mean, look at this place. Who would live like this?"

"Baby, you need to sit," He moved her away from the trash can and pulled the full bag out. "You were shot."

"Finally get your chance to kill me and you screw it up!" Lisa said jokingly, placing her hands on her hips and looking at AJ. "I knew you always had it in for me and then you go and miss."

AJ chuckled, savoring the taste of real coffee. "You look good, Lisa."

"Don't be hitting on me while I'm in my pajamas," she said and then turned serious. "You know, they said you killed my Darnell. Said you died in the fire out at your house. I never believed it. Then something happened that I still don't understand exactly. It was like I couldn't see very well and all of a sudden I felt like I had a cold. Worse thing was, I couldn't move – except I did move somehow. When you shot me all the weirdness went away."

"Do you remember it all?" AJ asked. "You know, when you lost control?"

"Every damn minute."

Beverly appeared on the table, her legs hanging off the edge. "That kind of memory is a new wrinkle. For the record, you were listed as a person of interest in Darnell's disappearance but not an official suspect. The investigation was closed after the fire. I've been working on new identities for you and Darnell. You'll like knowing that your long-lost cousin Alvin Jenkins has been found and inherited the family business."

"Alvin?" AJ asked.

Lisa blinked in confusion. "Alvin what?"

"Sorry. Just talking to, well, myself."

"We've got to tell someone," she said. "The government needs to know. This isn't right. People can't go around doing this."

"Lisa, sit," Darnell said. "Cleaning can wait a minute."

"No, it can't. I've been a prisoner for weeks. I trashed, no, they trashed everything. I can't even think in this mess."

Darnell gathered his wife into his arms and held her as she sobbed into his chest. "You need to hear this story, Lisa. There's a lot going on and I don't know if it's safe here. You need to come with us."

"Where?"

"We're at AJ's." Lisa pushed away and looked at him suspiciously. Darnell grinned. "I know what you're thinking."

"What?"

"The whole place burned down but they missed AJ's bunker. Right now, that's our safest place to be. We can't stay here."

"I need to talk to Aubri and Toby," Lisa said, referencing her daughter and son-in-law. "I said the most horrible things to them. They'll never speak to me again."

"We'll talk to them, too, but not yet. It's actually safer for them to be separated from us," Darnell said.

"I don't understand. Are there more of these, what'd you call them, Korgul?"

"Tens of millions."

Lisa blinked several times before answering. "I'm taking a shower. Keys to the SUV are on the floor in the half-bath. You might want to wash them off, though." She held the wound on her side as she walked purposefully from the room.

"Go," AJ said. "I'll get the car started for you."

"Because of your actions, Lisa will not be a viable host for a Beltigerskian," Beverly said, once Darnell and Lisa had disappeared.

AJ nodded. "I know, but I don't think Darnell has thought that through yet. Couldn't be helped. If we'd tried to capture her and shock it out, it might have called for help."

AJ swallowed hard when he looked into the half bath off the front entrance. The floor was covered in dried pee and toilet paper. In the middle of the mess was a key ring. Wordlessly, he plucked it from the floor and spritzed a generous amount of soap from an unused bottle on the sink. He hummed a very long tune as he washed his hands and the keys.

"Korgul have little regard for hygiene or material wealth," Beverly explained as he opened a door to the late model luxury SUV. He pulled an empty trash bin over to transfer fast food trash into it.

"Darnell is going to be pissed about all the dents and scratches," AJ said. "He was proud of this car."

"You will need to ask Lisa for six thousand dollars in cash," Beverly said. "I have located a source that can produce a birth certificate and social security card for Alvin Jenkins and Derrell Jackson."

"Do they have that kind of cash?"

"Lisa's bank account shows forty-two thousand three hundred dollars."

"Wow, that's a lot."

"Unfortunately, it is yet another crime against Darnell's family," Beverly said. "That amount represents the last of their life savings. The Korgul drained their accounts after selling all non-liquid investments. Even the mortgage on this house is in arrears and will return to the bank in a short time."

"Thanks, buddy," Darnell said, startling AJ. Darnell, however, seemed unphased as he opened the SUV's hatch and swung two large suitcases into the back. "Lisa will be down in a minute with her makeup bag and some last-minute items."

"We need to stop by the bank," AJ said. "I need Lisa to get us some cash."

"Sure, how much?" Darnell asked.

"Six grand, but there's a problem," AJ said and explained what Beverly had told him.

"What's another six grand?" Darnell shrugged.

"You're taking this pretty well."

Darnell smiled. "I thought I'd never see her again. She's my girl and I have her back. Nothing in the world can take that away from me."

"I screwed up, Big D," AJ said.

"When you shot her with Doc's anti-bug juice? Yeah, I know. Don't see that you had much of a choice. I knew you were packing."

AJ nodded. "She can't ever be a host."

"Beverly, any chance you know how to heal Parkinson's or cancer or Alzheimer's?" Darnell asked.

"I am not familiar with these specific diseases," Beverly said. "But generally, diseases are easily cured with help from the Galactic community. There is a process for requesting help."

"Can a limited species request that help?" Darnell asked.

"Yes. The board that oversees disease management is apolitical," Beverly said.

"Is Lisa sick?" AJ asked. "You never said anything."

Darnell grinned. "No, she's not. But I think Beverly just said she's going to live a good long while and that's good enough for me."

14

STARTING OVER

The bright yellow temporary advertisement painted on the pawn shop's broad glass windows read *Cash for Gold, Best Prices in Town.* The shop was filled with floor-to-ceiling shelves behind glass-enclosed counters with everything from jewelry, guns, knives, to all things sparkly and shiny.

"What can I do for you, hon?" AJ turned away from a shelf filled with power tools to see a short, older woman whose clothing barely contained her bulk. "Got some gold for old Jenny? Maybe a watch?"

"Alvin Jenkins. I must have left my driver's license in here when I came in yesterday. You didn't happen to find it, did you?"

"Might have," Jenny said. "I'll take a look in lost and found. Maybe you might like to buy something?"

His eyebrows rose. Beverly had told him to ask for a lost driver's license, but that was the end of the script as far as he knew. He shook his head. "Nope, really just looking for the license."

Jenny closed her eyes and shook her head. "Not too bright, though."

"What?"

She sighed and gave him an exaggerated smile. "I just so happen to have that watch you were asking about." She pulled a golden watch from the case in front of her. "Came in last night. Try it on."

"Look, I just need that license."

She closed her eyes and pushed the watch across the counter. "It'll cost you seven thousand. I could do a cash discount, though. Even comes with a certificate of authenticity."

A smile formed on his face and he nodded in exaggerated understanding. "Would you take six? I've got the cash."

"Sure, hon," Jenny shook her head in mild disgust, extracted an envelope from below the counter and set it on the glass. AJ reached for the envelope, but Jenny's thick hand kept it trapped. "Need to see that cash, hon. You understand."

"Oh, right," He pulled out the wad of bills Lisa had withdrawn from her bank and set it on the counter. Thinking better of releasing the whole amount, he pulled half off the top and stuffed it back into his pocket. "I'd like to review the certification."

Jenny released the envelope, picked up the cash and started counting. Inside was an Arizona driver's license for Derrell Jackson and social security cards for both Derrell Jackson and Alvin Jenkins. The picture on the license matched Darnell perfectly.

"Everything in order?" Jenny asked.

"About that license I left?" AJ placed the remainder of the cash on the counter but like Jenny had done moments before, he held it in place with his hand.

"I seem to recall something like that." She extracted a driver's license from a small worn cardboard box and set it on the counter.

AJ released the cash. Aside from the wrong name, the new license looked perfect. "Appreciate it," he said, stuffing the license and envelope into his windbreaker.

"Might get that jacket fixed," Jenny held the watch out to him. "Looks like you got a hole in your pocket."

AJ slid the watch onto his wrist, exited the shop and climbed into his old Subaru. Beverly appeared on the dash and leaned languidly back on her elbows. "I set up a meeting with an estate lawyer at four this afternoon. They're taking care of the insurance claim for the fire damage. Also, I have a pickup order at King V grocery."

"So that's it?" AJ asked. "Korgul are just going to leave us alone?"

Beverly shrugged. "No idea. The threat you posed was dealt with. If Korgul were still looking for you, they wouldn't have a lot to go on. Sure, it's suspicious that someone is taking over your property, but would they want to look too closely? There is absolutely no advantage to pissing off Mother."

"That'll change once they figure out what we're up to."

"Which is why we need to plan carefully and go slow."

"And let them just keep pillaging Earth?"

"They've been doing it for centuries. What's a few more weeks or months?" she said. "If you go too quickly and they figure out our game, they'll take us out for sure."

"You sound like a mobster."

A black fedora appeared on her head and a thin trail of smoke wafted from a cigar between her fingers. "You'z can't be too careful." Her Italian accent made it sound like she was gargling with marbles.

"Do you really prefer that old Subaru to my car?" Jayne asked, turning into the downtown parking ramp beneath the professional building.

"Don't get me wrong, Germans make a nice vehicle," AJ replied, "but your car costs ten times as much as mine and doesn't do anything different."

"It does everything differently, including air conditioning." She rolled down her window to pluck a time-stamped card from the machine. "Most of all, we don't have to shout at each other to be heard."

He grinned. "Can't disagree with that. Nice to be home, don't you think?"

"Sal, my doorman, barely seemed to notice I'd changed. I look forty years younger. My face has no wrinkles, my hair color is back, I stand up straight, and I've lost forty pounds."

"Oh, he noticed," AJ said. "I'm not sure he was looking at your face, though."

It was Jayne's turn to grin as she rolled her eyes. "Men. You're all the same. Sal's married, you know. He shouldn't be looking."

"That's why he kept it covert. It's the difference between appreciating and creeping."

She slid the car into a parking spot. "Not sure I see the difference."

"Most women don't. That's why us men are so good at it."

Jayne stepped out of the car. She'd had time to grab clothing from her apartment when they'd picked up her car. "You're really not. We know you're looking."

"Well, from where I stand, it's a nice view," AJ said, rounding the car, heading for the elevator.

Jayne pressed the call button and turned to him, suddenly serious. "Are we just playing, AJ? I mean, we've been through a tough experience and it would be natural for us to lean on each other, but what are we doing?"

The two were joined by a third person as they stepped into the elevator. AJ grasped her hand and gave her a reassuring smile. The stranger stepped off before they reached their destination.

"I'm in for the long haul, Doc," he said.

The elevator dinged and the doors slid open to reveal a comfortable-looking lobby lined in rich wood paneling. They walked toward the receptionist, a reedy-looking young man sitting behind an elegant desk. He stood and made eye contact with AJ. "Mr. Jenkins? Dr. Jayne?"

"Yup," AJ said.

"Very good. I'll just need to see some identification and I've got temporary security badges for you." He held out a clipboard. "Just sign here." They signed the forms and handed them back in exchange for clip-on badges. "If you'll take a seat, Mr. Skagel will be with you in a moment. He's expecting you."

A distinguished, older man in an expensive suit entered from a side door before they sat down. "Mr. Jenkins, Dr. Jayne? Very good. This way."

Skagel ushered them out of the lobby, offering his hand to both as they moved down the hall and into a meeting room with a panoramic view of downtown Tucson.

"Coffee? Soda?" he asked.

"No, thanks," AJ said and deferred to Jayne, who shook her head. They slid into seats around a long table which took up most of the room. Three others in their late twenties to early thirties quietly entered the room and chose seats at the table.

"I've asked a few of our associates to tag along," Skagel said, gesturing to the associates without making introductions. "But first, let me express condolences on the loss of your uncle. Were you close?"

AJ shook his head. "I didn't think he knew I existed."

Beverly appeared, sitting on the black conference phone in the middle of the table. "Good one," she said, chuckling. "You see that he's Korgul, right?"

AJ blinked. He'd forgotten about the lenses that were available to him. With the lens in place, he noticed the slimy goo behind Skagel's eyes. His associates, however, were all clear.

"It's a simple matter to transition his assets," Skagel continued. "We've spoken to the insurance company on your behalf. There's a matter of taxes and probate, but we should be able to clear that all up by the end of next week since there are no other surviving relatives. Do you intend on selling the property?"

"I hadn't given it much thought," AJ said.

"We're in a position to offer a cash buyout on the property. I think you'd find it quite generous," Skagel said. "You could walk out of here today a wealthy man if you so choose."

"I'm not really in any position to make that decision."

Skagel nodded at one of the associates who slid a folder to AJ. "I've taken the liberty of hiring an independent assessor. You'll see the value of your property is four hundred fifty thousand dollars. We're prepared to make a full price offer."

"Why do you want it?"

"We think development will turn that way over the next few years. It's pure speculation on our part, but I think you'll see it's a solid offer."

"What will I end up with after insurance and probate and all that?"

"We'd keep the insurance money if you accept our offer," Skagel said. "You would get the property value minus damages, taxes, probate and fees. You're looking at a little north of one hundred forty thousand. I'm afraid your uncle's buildings had little real value."

AJ bit his tongue so he wouldn't respond and felt Jayne's hand on his knee.

"No reason to decide all this now," she said. "Can he take some time to think about your offer?"

"Let's see," Skagel said, looking at a paper calendar one of his associates slid over to him. "We'll get a settlement check on the fifteenth. How about I leave this offer open until the eleventh. That'll give you a week to consider it. If it's a matter of money. I'd be willing to sweeten the deal by twenty-five thousand, which would bring you well over market value. That deal is good today, only."

AJ shook his head. "No deal today, Mr. Skagel. I'll think about your offer, though."

Skagel tsked. "Hate to see you walk away from twenty-five thousand. Do you want to take a couple of minutes?"

"No."

"All right then. I've just got a couple of things for you to sign and you can be on your way," Skagel's smile was as fake as his handshake was soft.

"Sign here to give us temporary power of attorney so we can settle with the insurance company," an associate said, sliding a paper to AJ as Skagel left the room.

AJ looked at Beverly for assurance. "It's good, AJ. I've looked at their paperwork. Standard legal documents with language that is all to their benefit. I think their interest in your property is for virgin access to Fantastium and Blastorium."

"You know, you asked how I was feeling," AJ said, back in Jayne's car. "You never said how you feel."

"About us?"

"What else?"

"How about the half million dollars they just offered you?" Jayne said. "Or that we just met with a Korgul who had no idea who you were?"

"Sure, that's interesting. But you got me thinking about other things. I'm having trouble letting it go."

"I told you a while back. A date includes steak and good Scotch."

"What about that place by your apartment?"

"Won't Darnell and Lisa miss us?"

"They've been apart for two months. Lisa thought he was dead and then she was captured by Korgul. I'm pretty sure they need some alone time."

"You should at least call and let them know we're okay."

"I've got it, AJ," Beverly said.

"Satisfied?"

"I'll want to change."

"Think you could wear that little black number you wore last time?"

Jayne grinned as she pulled into the parking lot for her building. "I don't know what you see in me."

"Tell me about your relationships, Doc," he said. "I find it hard to believe you've been a spinster your whole life."

"Would that really be so hard to believe? I've mostly been married to my job. There have been a few remarkable men, but for whatever reason, we never really hit it off. They were like me, married to important careers, so that pulled us apart. I'm friends with all of them, if that's your question."

They held hands in the elevator. In her apartment, she poured them both a single finger of Scotch before excusing herself. A few minutes later she returned from the bedroom wearing a dark blue dress that pulled tight across her hips but was tastefully loose otherwise.

He whistled appreciatively. "Holy cow, Doc."

It must have been the reaction she was looking for because she spun in place, holding high heels in one hand. "You like?"

"I mean, wow," he said, taking in the athletic form that perfectly filled out her dress. Although as far as he was concerned, she'd make a burlap bag look elegant.

"Have I sufficiently answered your question?"

He blinked and tried to form a coherent sentence. In the end, he managed a simple, "Yes."

SUNLIGHT STREAMED into Jayne's bedroom through the southern windows. AJ sighed contentedly, running his hand along her side and bringing it to rest at the top of her hip. They'd spent the night together and while he felt pangs of guilt at thoughts of his deceased wife, he knew she would have wanted him to find happiness.

Jayne stirred and turned, carefully adjusting her silky nightgown. "Did you sleep okay?"

"Is it too early for me to feel this way?" AJ asked.

She smiled, her face lighting up. "I hope not. It just feels so good. I've never really felt like this before, have you?"

He looked away but before he could say anything, Jayne stopped him. "I'm so sorry, AJ. Pam. Of course, you were in love with her. I didn't mean to..."

He placed a finger on her lips and shook his head. "I'll never stop loving Pam, but that part of my life is past. I want you to be free to say what you want. Don't worry about how it sounds. I feel the same way, Amanda Jayne. I'm the luckiest guy in the world to find love twice." He kissed her, causing a new sort of urgency.

JAYNE WALKED INTO THE KITCHEN, a towel wrapped around her head. She eyed a plateful of burned toast. "Aww, you made breakfast."

"There's coffee, too," AJ said, oblivious to the charred carnage. "I'm not sure if orange juice can go bad. It tastes okay to me. I heard from Big D. He and Lisa are going over to their house to do some cleaning. He wants to get together tonight so we can make plans. Apparently, Sharg's been having fun rummaging around in the yard. She's already put out a few Fantastium traps."

"Is that safe, her out in the open?"

"Darnell said she was being discreet. Something about a robe that would cover her tail."

"She's seven feet tall. I'm not sure discreet is going to be her thing."

He shrugged. "We should probably head over, especially if Big D and Lisa are leaving."

"I'll put on some work clothing."

"Don't cover more than you think necessary."

"Is this how it's going to be? You ogling me all the time?"

"Nothing new there, Doc."

"You're incorrigible."

Jayne disappeared back into the bedroom and reappeared a few minutes later wearing a baggy pair of jeans and a t-shirt. "These don't fit as well as they used to."

"Isn't Thomas supposed to show up on your ear pretty soon?" AJ asked, nodding toward the door.

Beverly appeared, sitting on Jayne's left shoulder. "Forty-two minutes, according to his original timeframe. You'll need to scrape her ear when it's time." Beverly mimed sticking her finger just beneath the bump at the front of Jayne's ear.

"Maybe an hour," Jayne answered, locking the apartment behind her while AJ called for the elevator.

"You can't hear Beverly anymore, can you?"

"Not sure. Is she talking?"

"She was."

"Couldn't we make some sort of radio for me so I could hear her?"

Beverly pretended to pull on a strand of Jayne's hair, hoisting herself up until she was standing and peering into Jayne's ear canal. "She's right. It'd be simple. She's got nice big canals. It'd also give her a way to talk with Thomas."

Jayne unlocked her vehicle remotely and they loaded up, driving in silence as she worked her way through the garage and out to the street.

"I've been trying to figure something out," AJ said. "Why did you point us to that guy, Jeff Jefferson, in case something happened to you?"

"Dr. Jerry Jefferies." She smiled at a memory. "He's taken plenty of ribbing for his name."

"What's CDC got to do with this? I know you're thinking of Korgul as a disease, but really they're not."

"Their behavior is more so than you might think. CDC works with parasitical infections, viruses, all matter of things, but you're right. Alien infestations are probably a bit out of their purview. The thing is, even with the Korgul cure we've developed, we need a way to create a huge volume of the serum. Once we've done that, we need to disperse it to a massive number of people."

"And we need to do it all covertly," AJ said. "Something tells me the CDC is anything but covert."

Jayne nodded and tapped her brakes, pointing out the window at a kid walking down the sidewalk. "Is that Diego?"

"Slow down," he said, unnecessarily. "Geez, it definitely looks like him, but something got to him. Pull over."

Jayne did as he asked. He hopped out and she trailed behind him.

"Hey, stop," AJ called as he hurried toward the emaciated child.

The small Hispanic boy turned slowly at AJ's voice, a flash of sludge passing over his eyes. "Hold on, Doc."

"Mr. AJ?" the boy asked, his voice confused. Suddenly he straightened, his voice changing. "You should not have come back to Earth. I will report your presence."

"AJ, hold him!" Jayne said.

Diego started to run, but AJ was faster and grabbed him up. "What are you doing, Doc? I used our last batch."

Jayne grabbed Diego's head and forced her fingers into his mouth, pulling his jaw down. "Do you have a knife?"

He flicked his pocketknife open. "Um, yeah."

"Hold his mouth open."

"Doc, what are you doing?" he asked.

She drew the blade across her forearm. "Hold him still." Droplets of blood formed on her arm and she guided them into Diego's mouth. "I don't know how much of this we need. Make sure Beverly's blocking his transmission."

"Tell her I have done as she asked," Beverly answered, unprompted.

A car skidded in the street and a man yelled from the car. "Hey, what are you doing to that kid?"

"He's having a seizure," Jayne called back. "I'm a doctor."

"Should I call 911?"

"No, I'll take him in my car," she said. "It'll be faster."

"Are you sure? That blood doesn't look like his."

"Get him in the car, AJ," Jayne ordered and turned to the man. "Thank you. I've got this. Call Saint Margaret's and ask for Dr. Boland if you need to check up on him." She hustled around to the driver's seat and slammed her door as AJ wrestled Diego into the back seat.

15

BABEL FISH

"Ah, shit," AJ complained as the now familiar, slimy green robin's egg-sized mass pushed Diego's eye aside and slid out onto his face.

"Hang on." Jayne pulled the car to a stop in front of the junkyard's gates and jumped out.

AJ grabbed at the pulsing glob that was the entirety of the Korgul's body and scooped it into his hand. The sensation rivaled what AJ assumed he'd feel if he picked up a red-hot coal from a fire pit. He dropped the mass onto the luxury car's floor mat. "Dammit!"

"What's going on, AJ?" Jayne asked, sliding back into the driver's seat.

"Snot ball is trying to escape and I think it bit me."

Beverly appeared wearing green khaki shorts, a pocketed shirt and a coiled whip on her belt. "Crikee, the little buggers have a good nip to 'em. You'll need to use a tool if you want to be manhandling 'em," she said in a new Australian accent.

AJ used his boot to block the Korgul's path. "Fastest exit yet. I guess that answers the question of whether or not your blood's packing a punch."

"I suspected as much." She turned off the car and jumped out, running back to close the gate. "Get Diego down to the bunker. I'll be right behind you."

"What about this guy?" AJ pulled his boot back, getting ready to stomp the Korgul who'd taken over his young friend.

"Don't," she warned.

"Geneva Convention doesn't apply to these assholes," he said, but lowered his leg and got out of the car.

She leaned in and scooped the Korgul from the carpet. "You're better than that, AJ."

"This guy's hardly a non-comm," AJ argued, pulling Diego out of the back seat. "Geez, what'd they do to you, Diego?" He lost all interest in the Korgul as he picked up the boy who couldn't be more than fourteen. Diego's thin skin was stretched over his sixty-five-pound frame and he suddenly seemed considerably younger.

Beverly floated along as AJ walked toward the bunker. "He's significantly dehydrated and malnourished. I believe I also detect a variety of Earth-borne parasites. I'm creating a few programs for the ship's manufactory to help with diagnostics and treatment."

Sharg met AJ at the top of the stairs. "Who is this?" she asked, stepping out of the way so AJ could pass. Greybeard barked excitedly, but also made way.

"Diego. He's one of my neighbors and a friend. Korgul got to him. He's just a kid," AJ said with disgust. In the main room, he laid Diego's unconscious form on the closest couch. "Bring some water, Sharg."

"Greybeard, would you be a dear and fetch the items from the manufactory?" Beverly said sweetly. Greybeard barked once and raced off.

"How's he doing, AJ?" Jayne asked, stopping in front of a six-foot by eight-foot translucent cabinet composed of tiny cubes large enough to hold an individual Korgul. The *condo*, as they called it, had room for tens of thousands of Korgul inhabitants. Diego's uninvited captor was only the third permanent resident.

"It's not good, Doc. He should be a growing kid, but he's lost weight since we last saw him."

Sharg handed AJ a glass of water but Jayne intercepted it. "Careful," she warned. "We need to go slowly. Let's prop up his back. We need blankets. Can you turn the heat up to about eighty degrees? He's not maintaining body temperature."

AJ prioritized Jayne's demands and ratcheted up the ancient dial for the thermostat before fetching pillows and blankets. When he returned, he was met at Diego's side by Greybeard who was carrying a bag of small items.

"Dr. Jayne, can you hear me?" Beverly asked, taking over a nearby weather radio that was always on. Jayne nodded. "I've manufactured a course of nano-sized medical machines for Diego. They won't be as effective as having an implanted Beltigersk and I won't be able to directly monitor their progress. Please begin with the red gel. It should be applied to the back of his throat so that he does not disgorge the material."

Jayne pursed her lips. "He's very weak. If he aspirates your gel, it could be fatal."

"Uncomfortable, yes. Fatal, no," Beverly said. "The nano machines are capable of delivering oxygen directly to the bloodstream if necessary. It would be better if the material were to make it to his stomach."

"Do no harm, Beverly," Jayne insisted.

"I assure you, the red gel is entirely safe. It is a common first-aid material for an oxygen-consuming bipedal. The machines are designed to stabilize the circulatory system."

"You will send me the details of these medicines," Jayne said and turned her attention to Diego. "Diego, if you can hear me, I'm going to give you some medicine. Try to swallow it."

"I think he's unconscious, Doc," AJ said from where he knelt next to the boy's head.

"Best not to make assumptions," Jayne said, using her long fingers to pry open Diego's slack jaw as she pulled him from the pillows into a seated position. "Help me hold him."

AJ placed one hand on Diego's chest and wrapped a long arm around his back as Jayne tipped the boy's head back and squeezed a long rope of the red gel onto the back of his throat. Instinctively, the boy's swallow reflex kicked in. "Good, Diego. This will help." Jayne's voice was soothing. "Beverly, does he need the entire course now?"

"You delivered seventy-five milliliters. Given his mass, another seventy-five would be ideal. You can't overdo it."

"Just a little more, Diego," Jayne said, squeezing the tube. After delivering the second dose, she nodded to AJ, who allowed the boy back onto the pillows.

"What about the rest of this?" he asked, looking at a single blue tube and four green tubes.

"I'll monitor his progress with the probe that is still within the bag," she said. "I need you to install it."

AJ opened the bag and moved the tubes around in order to find a two-inch-long device rounded gently on both ends and slightly smaller in diameter than a pencil. He shook his head. "This looks like a suppository. I'm *not* putting that in!" he said. "What is it about you aliens and probes, anyway?"

Beverly had a far-off look for a moment, a telltale sign she was looking for information. Refocusing, she chuckled. "While the anus is indeed a viable orifice for this probe, insertion there would not have the long-term effect of providing a communication link for Diego."

"You can't talk to him, BB," AJ said. "He has no idea you exist."

"You speak truth," Beverly said. "We have discovered that Thomas and Dr. Jayne's cure for the common Korgul, leaves the subject in a state where they remember the Korgul's visit. If you are looking to save your friend from the knowledge that aliens exist, it is no longer possible."

"My presence might be difficult to explain," Sharg grunted after clacking her jaws.

"Where, then?" AJ asked.

"Slide it carefully into either ear," Beverly said. "It will conform to his ear canal and disappear."

AJ did what was asked and watched in amazement. Once the end of the small probe contacted the ear, it slid in as if it were being pulled.

"How long will he be out?" Jayne asked.

"In thirty minutes his body will stabilize. We'll introduce the blue gel at that time. The blue gel is a simple rapid-caloric boost and will feed the machines we just introduced. The green gel will be given every two hours after that," Beverly said. "In answer to your question, I propose we keep Diego unconscious through the night. In the morning, I'll manufacture a final course that will remove the machines from his system. He will awaken quite hungry."

"Are you monitoring him now?" Jayne asked. "Are your red nanos working?"

Beverly smiled. "The second probe in the bag is a neural enhancer that will allow you to make Type-A connections with common Tok machinery."

"Like probes?" Jayne asked.

"Yes, and Galactic terminals. It'll also give us a better connection when you're nearby."

"Oh crap! I forgot about Thomas," AJ said. "Isn't he supposed to be ready for pickup?"

"It is indeed time. I had not forgotten," Beverly said. "Dr. Jayne, if you would allow AJ to touch your ear, I believe we will be able to transfer Thomas."

"Which ear?" Jayne turned her head and leaned toward him.

"Ah, that was quite a journey." Thomas's voice filled AJ's ears.

"I've got him, Doc," AJ said.

The apprehension she'd felt evaporated as the burden of Thomas' fate was lifted from her shoulders. Leaning over, she searched through the bag and retracted a probe similar to what had been installed in Diego's ear. Without hesitation she pushed it into her own ear. "Thomas. Thank you for the messages. I'd been so worried."

"I will not bore you with details, dear doctor," Thomas said. "Being rejected by your body was not a pleasant experience. Had I not hastily constructed fortifications, I might have been lost. Alas, all is well. Have you attempted to introduce a Korgul? Is this a second test subject?"

"Direct blood transfer," Jayne looked at her arm where she'd cut herself and dripped blood into Diego's mouth. "There is a third, too. We utilized a low-velocity gunpowder round to free Darnell's wife. That method also worked."

"That's grand," Thomas said. "Three successful deliveries, then?"

"That's right."

"Have you made contact with your epidemiologist friend?"

"No," she said. "We can't risk remote contact if he's been compromised by Korgul."

"Taking precautions is wise but by my count, we have utilized this cure twice on those who were set in place to monitor your return. Won't Korgul find that too much of a coincidence?"

"What are they going to do about it?" AJ asked. "Sure, it's suspicious, but so what if they don't buy our fake IDs? Kicking a couple more snot balls to the curb after they infested our family is fair game."

"We're not equal. With twenty million Korgul on the planet, they could crush us without even thinking about it," Jayne said. "What happens when they send a group of thugs to kill us?"

"AJ has a point. Without sufficient provocation, they'd have trouble with Mother," Beverly said. "There is no advantage for them to push contact. Korgul have a single objective. Drain Earth of its resources. Mother has agreed to turn a blind eye if I am left alone."

"That is a despicable approach," Jayne said. "She's willing to ignore the subjugation of millions of humans."

"You could decide to do nothing," Sharg said. "Send me home to Halfnium-8 with Thomas's remedy. I'll post the formula in a broad public forum where any species is able to find and replicate it."

Jayne slid her a sideways look. "It's not like humans have access to this forum."

"The Galactic Empire consists of thousands of species, many of whom have suffered because of Korgul," Sharg said. "I could release the information and point them to Earth. Do you not think there would be many who would make it their mission to rid Earth of Korgul?"

"And then what? Some other species shows up and takes advantage of our status as raccoons?" AJ spat. "No. This is a human problem and humans will solve it. Sharg, you'll have to make your fortune another way. Earth doesn't need that kind of attention."

Sharg hissed and rolled her shoulders back. "Perhaps I see logic in your argument. Perhaps I do not."

"What'd we miss?" Darnell asked, entering the family room. "Holy crap! Is that Diego? What happened to him?"

"Had a Korgul buddy," AJ said. "He's getting some R&R."

"Man, he looks bad."

"I didn't think we'd see you until later," AJ said. "You were supposed to be cleaning the house."

"We got some cleaning done." He glanced at Lisa, who looked down.

AJ chuckled. "I see. Well, good thing you did. We've been strategizing ever since Thomas got out."

"I brought meatloaf, salad, wine and rolls that need puttin' in the oven. You do have one down here, don't you?" Lisa said, jostling the bags she was carrying.

"Uh, right," AJ said. "Kitchen's over there."

"No comments about the meatloaf, AJ?" She fixed her gaze on him.

He shook his head. "Sweet Lisa, if you had any idea what we've eaten since the last time you saw me, you wouldn't even ask the question."

She smiled. "'Bout time you learned your lesson."

"Korgul are going to be watching us. They'll want to see what we're up to," AJ said. "I feel like we need to give 'em a good show."

"Like what?" Darnell asked.

"Like cleaning your house – for real. We rebuild my house. I've got money coming from insurance. We can clean up the lot and at least rebuild the machine shed. I always wanted to expand it."

"What's goin' on in that thick noggin of yours?" Darnell asked. "Not like you to play it safe."

"We need to get eyes on Jayne's friend, Dr. Jefferies. See if he's one of *them*. Even if he's not, there's no guarantee he'll be able to help us."

"Why would Korgul infect someone like Jerry?" Jayne asked. "It's not like he has anything to do with real estate. He's not political. He's just a scientist who works against the spread of disease."

AJ shrugged. "Be great if he isn't."

"Rolls are up in five minutes," Lisa announced. She walked up to Sharg without batting an eye and stuck out her hand. "I don't think we've met."

"Greetings, Lisa Jackson," Sharg said, gently shaking the woman's hand. Lisa's eyebrows rose well into her hairline, but she showed no sign of understanding.

"Right, Lisa doesn't have a translator. Any chance we could make a doohickey to help her with that?" Darnell asked.

"You understand her?" Lisa asked.

He nodded. "You will too."

Greybeard barked and ran up the stairs.

"Where's he going?"

"Getting a doohickey out of the manufactory in the spaceship. Sharg's a Vred. She's the one who helped us off that moon I was telling you about."

"You said she looked like a crocodile," Lisa said, eliciting a jaw clack from Sharg. "Have I taught you nothing? You cannot judge a woman by her skin color, even if it is, well, in this light, I'm not exactly sure what I'd call the look. She's obviously fit, intelligent and I just don't see it."

"Thank you, Lisa Jackson," Sharg said, bowing.

"Oh, did she..." Lisa turned to face Sharg more directly. "Did you understand all that?"

With a single clack of her jaw, Sharg bowed again.

"Do you like meatloaf?" Lisa asked.

Greybeard's panting heralded his return from the manufactory. In his jaw was a Tok neural enhancer. AJ retrieved it and stepped between Lisa and Sharg.

When Sharg's eyes fell on the device, she clacked her jaw. "A most reasonable accommodation."

"Need to put this in your ear, Lisa," AJ said.

"Nope," Lisa said. "Isn't gonna happen. There've been enough aliens in this woman's body to last a lifetime."

"It doesn't hurt and it's not an alien," Jayne offered.

"Do you have one? Or are you holding one of those bean-shaped aliens in you too?" Lisa asked.

"Unlike Korgul, the Beltigersk are microscopic in size. I no longer have one of them riding with me. I'll say that I miss my time with Thomas, though," Jayne retrieved the device from AJ and held it on her flat palm for Lisa to inspect. "This device is a neural enhancer that interfaces with your brain and translates alien speech into something you can recognize."

"I know all about it. I've read Adams. You're talking about a Babble Fish."

"Since when have you read Science Fiction?" Darnell asked, a frown creasing his brow.

Lisa gave him a challenging look but was interrupted by a buzzer in the kitchen. She turned and raised her hand. "I told you, I ain't puttin' one of those things in me. This girl is one hundred percent human again and I ain't never turnin' back."

"Perhaps it is not the right time," Sharg said.

"What did she say?" Lisa asked, pulling rolls from the oven and setting them on the cement countertop.

"Please communicate my thanks for her defense of my outward appearance," Sharg said.

"You'd know if you put the doohickey in," Darnell said, irritated.

"And I said, *no!*" she shot back. "Is that too big of a word for your translator?"

"Her name is Sharg," Jayne said. "She's grateful for how you see her."

Lisa turned to Sharg, closed her eyes and nodded. "You're welcome. Now everyone, take a seat."

"I don't know what my issue was with this meatloaf, Lisa," AJ said. "It's fantastic."

"Suck-up," Darnell grumbled under his breath.

"What's that taste?" Jayne asked. "Beef, pork and..."

"Family secret. But since you brought Darnell back, I'll share," Lisa said. "It's lamb."

"Unusually moist."

"It tastes different," Darnell said. "You changed it. It tastes like your momma's now."

"Of course, I changed it from momma's," Lisa said. "She used a cup of lard. I couldn't be feeding you all that. Your arteries would have exploded."

"And now you don't care?"

"Way I understand it, that little bean fella you got in you takes all that outta your system. No reason to make it taste like firewood anymore."

"You despicable woman. All these years." he said.

"I thought they were spouses," Sharg finally said. "Have they separated?"

"No," AJ said. "They like to fight. Best to just stay out of it. Or better yet, take Lisa's side."

Darnell looked at AJ with feigned hurt. "You too?"

AJ shrugged. "So, here's what I've got for a plan so far."

"Fine, anything but this conversation," Darnell sat back in his chair with a bottle of beer in hand.

"Jayne and I get tickets to Atlanta and pay this Dr. Jefferies a visit," AJ said. "We'll just do a quick in-and-out trip, hopefully stay under the Korgul radar."

"Won't they be tracking your travel?" Darnell asked.

Beverly appeared on the table seated atop a large suitcase, wearing sweatpants and a hooded sweatshirt. "Maybe. But Atlanta is a large city. In and of itself, there is no reason to hide the trip from Korgul."

"It's just a quick look-and-see," AJ said. "We might not even make contact. Depends on the situation."

"I suppose," Darnell agreed. "What about Lisa, Sharg, and me?"

"We're gonna need help with Diego," AJ said. "Maybe you could actually clean your house when you go back this time."

"Oh, we're gonna clean some house," Lisa said.

"Seriously?" AJ said.

"As a heart attack," she shot back. She drained her wine glass only to top it off again.

"There is a nonstop flight that leaves just before noon," Beverly said. "I have reserved two seats."

"I was hoping to line up a contractor to haul off the burn damage," AJ said, "but I wanted to go through the machine shed first and see if any of the tools are recoverable."

"I could do that," Sharg said. "I have much interest in the tools of your civilization. Perhaps you have an innovation that has not previously been discovered."

"I doubt it," AJ said, "but I don't mind if you look through everything. I've got another shed where you can store stuff worth keeping."

"Please convey my appreciation to Lisa for her preparations. It was most satisfying," Sharg said. "As darkness has fallen, I will once again venture forth so that I might uncover the mysteries of Albert Jenkins' junkyard."

"You know, it's getting late," Darnell said. "We'll get cleaned up and probably take off too. Do you need a ride to the airport?"

"Nah, we'll call a car service," AJ said. "And since Lisa cooked, we'll clean up. Probably good if you can make it back by nine tomorrow morning. We'll be headed to the airport about then. Thank you, Lisa."

"Glad to have you back, AJ. Thanks for taking care of my boy," she said.

16

IN A FLASH

Diego stirred under the dim lights, still on the musty couch. "Is that really you, Mr. AJ?" he asked, smacking his lips tenderly.

"He's thirsty. Take it slow." Jayne handed AJ a glass of water.

"It's Dr. Jayne and me, Diego," AJ said. "How do you feel?"

"I had a bad dream, Mr. AJ. I could not make my body work. I could not speak, even to mi madre. She was very angry."

Diego accepted the water and greedily drank.

"A little at a time," Jayne urged, stepping in to hold the glass firmly.

"Where am I?"

"Bunker in the yard," AJ said.

"Was it a dream, Mr. AJ?" Diego's voice was far off, like he wasn't sure he wanted to wake up.

"No, Diego. It wasn't a dream. There was an alien. It took over your body," AJ said, eliciting a look from Jayne that told him she was certain he'd lost his mind.

Diego nodded. "I talked to people I did not know. I was mean to my sisters. Rosario will never forgive me. I struck her. Momma says I am not allowed to come home."

"I'll talk to her, Diego," AJ said.

A tear leaked out onto Diego's face. "Is the alien gone?"

"Yes."

"I thought it was el diablo but when I prayed, it did not care. I prayed that you would come back. God sent you back."

AJ swallowed hard. While not an outwardly religious man, he believed in his mother's God. "I suppose he probably did. Look, Dr. Jayne and I need to take a trip. It's just for a couple of days. Big D will come over before we leave, but I need you to know something. There's another alien.

Diego visibly retreated into the covers.

"No, she's a good alien, but you might think she's scary looking. I think it'd be better if you could talk to her," AJ said. "Can I put something in your ear so you can talk with her?"

"Will it hurt?"

"No."

"Will it let me talk to your invisible friend?"

"You know about her?" AJ asked.

"You talk to her when you think I am not looking. I trust you, Mr. AJ."

AJ picked up the neural enhancer from the end table where Lisa had left it and slid it into Diego's ear.

"Diego, do you know that it's important we don't tell people about the aliens?" Jayne asked. "The mean aliens will come back if we do."

"I know this, Mrs. Doctor. My family made me leave. I have no one to tell."

"Call me Amanda," Jayne said.

"Or, *Doc*, like everyone else does," AJ added.

Jayne ignored him. "Are you hungry, Diego?"

"I am tired."

Jayne breathed a sigh of relief when she sat next to AJ in the MARTA subway car at Atlanta's bustling airport. "They're everywhere," she said under her breath and into AJ's ear.

AJ set the medium roller bag onto the floor and gave her a reassuring smile. At three in the afternoon, MARTA was crowded and like Jayne, he'd identified at least three Korgul hosts within their car alone.

AJ shook his head. "Hotel first? We'll need to grab the gold line."

"It's getting late," Jayne said. "Maybe go right to the CDC?"

AJ nodded. "We'll change trains in about twenty minutes."

"I'm not really sure what I'll say," Jayne said. "I've been trying to reverse our roles. It's just crazy."

AJ sighed. They'd been having masked conversations for most of the day as they'd always been within earshot of Korgul-infected people. While they didn't believe any Korgul were specifically watching them, they really had no idea.

"One step at a time, Doc," he said, swaying with the train as it moved down the tracks.

An hour later they exited the station and stood in the bright sunshine of an Atlanta suburb. One of Beverly's blue markers appeared, showing a route that would take them to the CDC building where Jefferies worked.

"It's humid," AJ said, removing his light jacket.

"Haven't been this far from a Korgul all day," Jayne stretched her long legs as they walked down the wide sidewalk. "It's so cloying. Almost wish I didn't know."

He paused and took two ballcaps from his suitcase. If Arizona had taught him anything, it was that you couldn't have too much protection from the bright sun. "Says patient zero."

"I wouldn't let anyone hear you talking like that. These folks take that sort of thing pretty seriously," Jayne said.

"I suppose."

The two fell back into step, pulling the wheeled suitcase behind them. It had already turned into a long day and AJ was starting to question Jayne's decision to go straight to their destination.

"That's the building he worked in when I visited a few years ago," she said.

"I thought you met at a conference."

"We did. How much do you want to know?"

AJ sighed. "How are you going to introduce me?"

Jayne smiled as they continued walking. "Of all people, I never pegged you as the feeling-awkward type. I haven't talked with Jerry for a couple of years. I don't think he'll have any expectations about renewing a past relationship."

"Great. You had a past."

Jayne's giggle took AJ off-guard. "Over before it started. Besides, he probably won't even recognize me."

A campus of glass, steel, and stone buildings grew ahead of them as they continued past a small airport. "I was expecting something nicer," AJ said as the aged buildings came into view.

"Your taxes at work," Jayne said. "We can try the lobby. Who knows, he might actually be here this afternoon."

Beverly appeared on Jayne's shoulder, a hand looped around a loose strand of hair. "Dr. Jefferies is in town, but I was unable to extract his personal calendar."

"This doesn't look good," AJ said, stopping as a group of white lab-coated people walked from the campus talking animatedly, unaware of AJ and Jayne's approach. A nudge from one of them caused the entire group to quiet.

AJ nodded as he made eye contact with one of the men in the group. "Did you see that, Doc?" he asked.

"Three out of five were Korgul," she offered. "Interesting that they seemed part of the conversation. That's kind of surprising."

"Korgul can ride along passively. Like a surveillance bug," Beverly offered. "It makes sense. The CDC would likely be the first governmental agency to discover Korgul, but the Korgul don't want to disrupt normal operations."

"Are we talking about a higher level Korgul?" AJ asked.

"Not necessarily," Beverly said. "Surveillance would be a lower level task."

"No guards outside," he observed as they crossed onto the property.

"We are in view of a multitude of security cameras," Beverly said. "It is reasonable to assume we're now being recorded. I'd recommend limiting the conversation."

"Hopefully, I can convince him to go to dinner with us tonight," Jayne said.

"Wait a minute, isn't he married?" AJ said. "What were you two doing down here if he was married?"

"*Recently* married," Jayne said, smiling at his discomfort.

The wash of air-conditioning was a welcome reprieve from the humid spring day. The building's atrium soared several stories high and artwork in the shape of large paper airplanes hung from cables above.

"I'm surprised there isn't more security," AJ said, noticing the bank of elevators.

"Security is controlled by elevator access. According to my research, there are more floors beneath us than above," Beverly said.

"We'll have to ask for Dr. Jefferies at the desk," Jayne said, leading AJ to a freestanding station where two uniformed guards monitored a bank of displays.

"Ma'am?" a middle-aged guard asked pleasantly as they approached.

"I was wondering if Dr. Jefferies was available," she said.

"I'll need you to sign in," he said, holding a clipboard to her. "Is he expecting you?"

Jayne accepted the clipboard. "Would you call his office for me?"

"Third floor, Terry," the second guard said. "He's already gone for the day."

"That's too bad," Jayne said handing the clipboard back. "We were in the neighborhood and thought we'd drop in. I'll give him a call."

Terry nodded, looking at the blank clipboard. Jayne guided AJ away from the check-in desk.

"Now what?" he asked, once they were clear of the front doors.

"Hotel," she said.

"We need to pay Jefferies a visit at home." AJ tossed their shared bag onto one of two queen beds in the room. If he thought it odd that Jayne would share a bag but not his bed, he didn't voice it.

"His address won't be public. I'll call his office in the morning and see about an appointment."

"Twelve Fourteen Minot Circle." Beverly had donned a blue polka-dotted sixties-era swimsuit and was holding a folded towel. "We should take a dip in the pool first."

AJ grinned. "You don't actually swim."

"Hotel pools are notorious for germs. I'd rather swim in the toilet," Jayne said. "How'd you get that address?"

"The MG Jefferies Revocable Trust purchased it twelve years ago, shortly after Marie and Gerald Jefferies were wed. All real estate transactions are public record." Beverly grinned as her outfit switched to a long black evening gown. She held a cigarette lazily in one white-gloved hand. "So, drinks then?"

"Are you bored, BB?" AJ asked.

"It's all Korgul bad, blah, blah, blah," she said. "I need a little entertainment once in a while."

"We just went to dinner two nights ago," AJ said. "Steak, scotch, dancing. Don't you remember?"

"I was trying to give you two some privacy."

"How about this," he said, pulling out a dark pair of jeans and a blue t-shirt. "Rent us a car and we'll go on a stakeout."

"Ooh, do you mean it?" A fedora appeared at a slant on her head, but she'd kept the ballgown. She took a long dramatic drag on the cigarette.

"We need to know if he's Korgul or not."

"I could use something to eat," Jayne said.

"We'll get takeout on the way."

"I'd rather stop at a grocery," Jayne said. "I haven't had much access to fresh fruits and this area is ripe with opportunities, if you don't mind the play on words."

"Absolutely," AJ said. "Cooler and a six pack is just what the doctor ordered."

She rolled her eyes. "I do not believe I have ever ordered that."

"Car will be dropped off in forty minutes," Beverly announced.

"Good," Jayne said. "Just enough time for a quick shower."

"Want company?" He was disappointed when she ignored his question, grabbed a fresh set of clothes, and disappeared into the bathroom.

"NICE NEIGHBORHOOD," AJ observed as they drove deeper into a subdivision where sprawling brick homes sat behind expansive green lawns.

"Maria is a lawyer," Jayne said. "I think they do pretty well between the two of them."

"These houses have to go for better than a million, wouldn't you think?"

"Twelve years ago, they paid nine hundred and forty thousand for their home," Beverly said. "It is just ahead on the left."

"We're going to be conspicuous if we park on the street," AJ said. "Can't imagine how many surveillance cameras are pointing at us right now."

"Only three," Beverly said, her hat still firmly in place. Cigarette hanging limply from her lips, she typed madly on an ancient-looking computer. "I do so love civilian security systems."

A quad-display of video screens appeared on the windshield. The only activity at a kidney-shaped pool where an olive-skinned woman slowly kicked her way to one end. On the side of the pool, a slightly chubby, older man sat drinking a fruity drink.

"That's Jerry," Jayne said. "He's coloring his hair."

AJ chuckled at her observation. "Maria's quite a catch. She has to be at least fifteen years younger than him."

"Try seventeen. But I'm not bitter," Jayne said, laughing at herself.

"Looking pretty good for a gal in her fif ...."

"She was thirty-nine when they married. That'd make her fifty-one," Jayne said.

"Dr. Jefferies is definitely not carrying a Korgul," Beverly said, zooming in on his face.

Jayne pulled a cellphone from her pocket and swiped at it, finally holding it to her ear.

"What are you doing?" AJ asked.

Jayne held a finger to her lips. In the projected video, Jerry Jefferies turned his attention to a table next to his chaise and picked up his phone. Looking at the display, he smiled and then answered.

"This is Jerry," he answered.

"Jerry, Amanda Jayne," Jayne said.

"Amanda, so great to hear from you. I heard you stepped down from surgery," he said. "How have you been?"

"Good. Better than good, actually," she said. "Say, I just happened to be in town on some business and I wondered if you could spare a few minutes. I've got something I need to run by you."

"Oh?" He grabbed reading glasses and a notepad from the table next to him. "Work related?"

"More of a private matter. I can't really say on the phone."

"You've got me intrigued, Amanda," he said. "Would you like to come by the office tomorrow?"

"Actually, a friend of mine and I are at the Ramada near your office. I was hoping we could talk this evening, yet."

"Are you sure you're okay, Amanda?" He sounded worried and his face showed genuine concern, which AJ both hated and appreciated in equal measure.

"Fine, really. Better than you could imagine."

"Well, yes, do you have a piece of paper handy? Maria and I were just getting ready for dinner. I'm sure we could set another plate." Jerry Jeffries rattled off the address for his home.

"Oh, no, I couldn't," she said. "We'll give you time to eat. Is eight too late?"

"Not at all. I look forward to it."

"It's good to talk to you, Jerry," Amanda said.

"Lovely to hear your voice, Jayne."

Through the camera, a woman's voice could be heard. "Who was that?"

"An old friend of mine," he said. "You remember Dr. Jayne?"

"Your old girlfriend?"

"Pish posh, hardly a girlfriend. You know I never had eyes for anyone after I met you."

"For the love of all that's holy, turn that off," Jayne said.

The woman had just started to emerge from the pool in a daring bikini when the image stilled and then blinked out.

"Not fair," AJ complained and then turned to Jayne. "Why eight?"

"We need a change of clothing," Jayne said.

"AMANDA JAYNE?" Dr. Jefferies was in good shape for a man in his late sixties, but it was evident from the surprise etched on his face that he wasn't prepared for her rejuvenated physique.

"Jerry, I'd like to introduce my very close friend, Albert Jenkins," Jayne said, embracing the older doctor and pecking him politely on each cheek.

"Close friend, you say?" Jefferies made no move to hide his bald appraisal of AJ. "You ... you're ... how ...? You look like you're twenty, Dr. Jayne. Dear! Come and meet my old friend, Amanda Jayne."

"I'll be right there, dear," a woman called. "I'll find you in your study."

"Quite so." He looked away and then back again at Jayne, maybe to see if she'd changed. "Um, you look amazing, Amanda. I'm afraid I'm stumbling for words."

"I understand your confusion, Jerry. Perhaps we could talk somewhere less public."

Jefferies nodded and then shook his head as he raised his hands in confusion. "Yes, yes, of course. Follow me, please," he said. "Dear, we'll be in the study."

"Of course," Maria called back. "I'll be in shortly."

"I'm not sure what's possessed her," Jefferies said. "She's usually so interested in visitors.

The doctor led Jayne and AJ down a short hallway and through frosted-glass doors into a wood-paneled office. Jayne recognized most of the multitude of medical texts that adorned the wall behind his desk, although some were unfamiliar.

"I'm afraid I lost your name," Jefferies said, looking pleasantly at AJ.

"AJ."

"Of course. Short term memory is the first casualty of age. Are you a Scotch man? I just picked up a Macallan 18 I'd like to try out. Amanda, I assume you haven't lost your taste?" he continued affably.

"Over ice if you don't mind."

"Wouldn't have it any other way," Jefferies said, his hand shaking as he attempted to open the expensive Scotch. "I must say, my mind is racing. AJ, would you mind pouring?"

AJ accepted the bottle and held it up for inspection, whistling appreciatively. "This is a nice bottle, Doc."

"Yes. And if you ask me, indiscernible from the twenty-five," Jefferies said. "I don't mean to be rude, but Amanda, help me out. What's going on? You show up here, looking like a woman half your age. Why, you look more like your granddaughter."

Jayne nodded. "It's actually why we're here. Tell me Jerry, have you seen anything unusual at the CDC in the last few years."

"Mostly, I can't talk about my work. You know that," he said. "Even if I could, you'd have to qualify the term *unusual*. Unusual is generally just a Wednesday at the CDC."

"Unusual on a global scale," Jayne said.

"Like a pandemic?" Jefferies asked. "At any moment, we're tracking at least a dozen possible outbreaks, from flu to Ebola. I wish it wasn't the case, but I wouldn't consider any of that unusual. Concerning? Sure. But somehow, I don't think that's where you're headed. I just can't get past how you look, and I mean that as a scientist. Is this *unusual happening* related to some new medicine you've discovered?"

"You should sit down, Jerry," Jayne said, taking a seat in front of his desk.

He nodded and sat in the seat next to her. "Okay."

Jayne sighed. "You know me, Jerry. You know I'm not crazy, right?"

Jefferies took a long drink of Scotch and then set the glass on the desk. "You're not crazy, Dr. Jayne. I know you to be a woman of great intellect and character."

"Earth has been invaded."

Jefferies slapped the desk and stood up. "You're barking mad, Amanda Jayne!"

"It's a parasitic species called Korgul," she said, standing with him. "I'm not crazy. We were at the CDC this afternoon. The place is crawling with the infected."

Jefferies turned away and bobbed his head, bringing a finger to his mouth. "Parasites," he said. "You mean *extra-terrestrial* parasites?" He shrugged as he processed the information and looked momentarily indignant as he argued internally. "How could you know that? Parasites can come from just about anywhere."

"They're intelligent, Jerry," Jayne said. "And, there are a lot of them. They've all but taken over and we need your help."

"Seriously bat-shit crazy," he said, looking to AJ for help. "Are you going along with this? Are you hearing what she's saying? It's absolutely nuts."

"I'm a seventy-two-year-old Vietnam veteran," AJ said. "I met Jayne back during the war when she operated on me. Saved my life, far as I know. It's a lot to take in, but she's shooting you straight."

"Prove it."

"It's not really that hard," AJ said. "Doc, take the neural enhancer out for a minute, would you?"

Jayne nodded, touching her ear. In response, the slim probe reformed and popped out into her hand. "This is a Tok neural enhancer," she said. "It'll allow you to communicate with the aliens – the good ones who are helping us. Both varieties are too small to see."

"How small?"

"Nanometers."

"And I put this in my ear?"

"Oh, dear," Maria said. A clatter of dishes drew their attention as Jefferies' wife dropped a silver platter filled with pastries and drinks.

"It's okay, Maria," Jefferies said. "We're just having a hypothetical conversation."

Maria tipped her head to the side, but not fast enough. AJ caught the telltale sign of a Korgul behind her eyes.

"She's a sleeper. AJ, Jayne, get down! She has a gun," Beverly exclaimed.

A flash of skin preceded the glint of steel as Maria Jefferies withdrew a pistol from a thigh holster between her perfectly tanned, fifty-one-year-old legs. AJ's eyes flitted to the Tok neural enhancer in Jayne's hand and knew she hadn't heard Beverly's warning. He threw himself at her, wrapping his arms around her as he slammed her to the floor.

The sound of a single gunshot filled the room.

17

PLAN B

AJ rolled to his feet even as he heard Jefferies' body hit the floor. Old combat instincts had kicked into high gear and he recognized the danger he and Jayne were in if he didn't act. Unfortunately, Maria expected his aggression and backed away, leveling her weapon at his chest.

"Advance no further," she demanded, her voice sluggish. "The death of Dr. Jefferies is your doing. You were warned not to interfere in our Earth-based operations. I am within my right to defend this conquest."

"Speak for me, AJ," Beverly said, appearing suddenly, wearing the long black gown he'd come to associate with her formal duties as Princess of Beltigersk Five.

"I speak for 49231125-0-B or Beverly, as she is known to me," AJ said, holding his hands up to show he was unarmed.

Scuffling sounds from behind caused AJ to glance back. Jayne had crawled to where Jefferies lay unmoving on the floor of his den.

"It is permitted," Maria said.

"Why did you kill Dr. Jefferies?" Beverly asked through AJ's translation.

"For his part in interfering with our operations. The governmental agency known as CDC provides a valuable service, but the one known as Jefferies is not sufficiently important that his duties cannot be replaced. It is an object lesson," Maria said.

"Object lesson?" AJ asked, without Beverly's prompting.

"CDC in this nation is the only viable threat to Korgul," Maria said. "You should know that we will kill anyone you contact. Currently, they do not possess sufficient skills to eject us from human hosts, but there are many clever humans. We will take no chances with this."

"What are your plans for the humans, Amanda Jayne and Albert Jenkins?" AJ asked, translating for Beverly.

"They are to return to their home," Maria said. "Do not attempt further contact with this organization or there will be many who perish. Do not continue your liberal bleating for the human cause. We are not harming this semi-sentient species and are merely mining material they know nothing of. If you continue to interfere in what is rightfully ours, you will be removed, regardless of the impact it has on Korgul-Beltigersk relations. Is this communication clear?"

AJ started to respond, his face full of rage, when Beverly grew to the size of a human, standing between him and Maria. "AJ, do not engage this one. There is no advantage and you could well disclose information we can't afford to share. You must walk away. We cannot win this fight. She's already communicated with others."

AJ glanced over at Jayne, who was sitting on her knees stunned, her hands covered in Jefferies' blood. "He's dead, AJ," Jayne said.

"And you'll let us go, just like that?" AJ asked, turning back to Maria.

Maria shrugged. "Humans only seem to learn lessons when it involves pain. We hope you will not continue to require new lessons. I am surprised a Beltigersk princess requires such dramatic demonstrations. Korgul is a powerful nation and should not be challenged."

"I'll take that as a *yes*," AJ said, leaning over to help Jayne to her feet.

"We can't leave him here like this," Jayne said, looking forlornly at her dead friend.

"We can't help him, Jayne," AJ said and turned to Maria. "You will see his remains are treated respectfully. There should be a service. You will see to his burial?"

"You are in no position to negotiate, worm," Maria said.

"We're not leaving him without your agreement," he said. "It's a small price to pay to get us out of your hair."

"Fine," Maria said. "His death will be attributed to a break-in. He will be buried in a human cemetery and I will allow my host to mourn him."

"AJ, we can't." Jayne resisted AJ's attempt to pull her from the room.

He wrapped an arm around her shoulders and firmly guided her from the den. "We're leaving."

Dazed, she allowed him to place her in the rental car and remained silent until they were back in their hotel room. "What will we do without CDC?" she asked. "Without them, there is no machinery for broad distribution."

"What was your plan? I didn't think CDC actually distributed anything."

"They don't, but they have direct communication with drug companies. I hoped to add our cure to next year's flu vaccine or attach it to some sort of weak viral strain which we could release. I don't know. It's just that these CDC scientists are really good at this kind of thing. I don't know what to do next."

"Can't Thomas just make a virus that we could spread?"

She shook her head. "Maybe, but it'll take more time and research. I just don't know what to do in the interim."

"We go home and regroup. We learned a couple of things. First, they know about us now, if they didn't before. Second, we have some level of protection from the Korgul as long as we don't cross whatever imaginary line they've drawn in the sand."

"I don't understand why you're so calm."

"We've fought this kind of war before," he said. "Most of the time, we're on the other side. We might be outnumbered and outgunned, but we have freedom of movement and we didn't expose Thomas's research. The two of you need to turn your attention to the problem of dispersing the agent."

"I have no expertise in that," she said.

"Then develop it." He shoved his clothing into their combined bag. "Don't be drawn into the lie of urgency."

"But every moment we hold this secret, there's a chance we'll be discovered."

"Agreed. And if we let it loose and it's defeated, we're in even worse shape."

"Why are you packing?"

"Did I ever tell you about that time I was captured?" he asked.

She nodded. "You didn't say much. Only that some Rangers found you."

"Lefty Johnson, Bob Adams, and Maury Thompson," AJ said. "Bob and Maury died about twenty years ago."

"Sorry to hear that. What about Lefty Johnson? I refuse to believe any mother would name their child Lefty."

AJ shrugged. "He was left-handed. We weren't always that creative with nicknames. I have no idea what his real name is."

"Why are you bringing this up?"

"Lefty lives two hundred miles southeast of here down in a Georgia swamp," AJ said. "I was thinking we'd pay him a visit."

"Kind of an odd time for a social visit, don't you think?"

He shook his head. "Is there anyone in your line of work you feel stands a head taller than everyone else?"

Jayne nodded. "Sure, depending on the specialty."

"Lefty Johnson was one of *those* soldiers," AJ said. "Nobody quieter, more lethal or better equipped to fight a war than Lefty."

"I'm not sure why we're having this conversation. He's an old man."

"This thing is likely to get ugly before it gets better. We need to bring in some real pros. BB, how many little nuggets do I have riding around in my skin, aside from Thomas?"

"Eighteen," Beverly said. "It is not known if your friends would be good matches, though."

"Eighteen? That's right. I'd forgotten it was so many," AJ said.

"Many more volunteered. I brought only those I felt were completely trustworthy."

AJ sat on the side of the bed and shook his head. "This changes things."

"You don't want to visit Lefty, then?"

"No, I do. Would you mind driving? I need to think."

She shrugged. "Of course. I'm so keyed up, I could drive all night. It'll be nice to have something to occupy my mind."

"I'm sorry about your friend."

Jayne merely nodded as she packed the remainder of her clothing into the bag.

"ARE YOU SURE THIS IS RIGHT?" Jayne asked, pulling to the side of a gravel road where a faint outline of a trail headed into the dense Georgia undergrowth.

"Lefty is one hundred percent hillbilly," AJ said. "This has his name written all over it."

"You really don't want me to come with you?"

He shook his head. "Stay here and get some sleep. If I'm not back by sundown, you need to leave. Whatever you do, don't come looking for me."

"That sounds pretty dramatic."

AJ pointed to a tree on the other side of the ditch. The posted sign read, *No Trespassing, Violators will be Shot on Sight.*

"That's not legal," she complained.

"If a body disappears in the swamp, was it really ever there?"

She gave him an exasperated look. "Yes. This *Lefty* has to be in his seventies. Surely he's slowed down by now."

"That'd make him almost mortal," AJ said, opening the car door. "Remember, under no circumstances should you follow me."

"I got it. Just for the record, I don't like it."

AJ closed the car door behind him as quietly as possible. As he turned around, he might as well have been back in the jungles of Vietnam for all the humidity and smell of rotting vegetation. He grimaced at the old work boots he was wearing. They'd be soaked within minutes, a sensation he'd always hated. Tying a cut up t-shirt around his head, he settled two water bottles into a makeshift back-pack and started along the narrow game trail.

"Scanning publicly available geo-imagery, I've located a building two thousand yards east-northeast," Beverly said, appearing in front of AJ wearing safari gear, complete with pith helmet and rocket pack.

"We need to replace my rocket pack." He pushed on the top strand of a barbed-wire fence and swung his leg over the top. He gave Jayne a friendly wave before striding toward the tree line.

"The governmental agents at the airport would have likely seized your device," Beverly said. "I'm overlaying your view with an elevation overlay. It's from a recent survey, so it should be reasonable."

He nodded in agreement and scanned the area. "Hear that?"

"I am not sure," Beverly said. "I hear many things."

"It's too quiet," he said, choosing his steps carefully as he searched for the game trail that had already disappeared. "Can you pick up that trail I was on?"

"It follows a natural ridge," she said. A white line appeared over the top of the grass. With the hint, he was just able to locate the tell-tales of the path.

He became frustrated that the path led further away from the only building on the property, according to Beverly. As he walked, the swamp grasses to his right gave way to patches of water filled with spindly growth and deadfalls. After forty minutes of traversal, he stopped.

"We're getting too far away. We have to double back."

"There was no high-ground that allowed for the north-easterly travel you sought."

"Sounds like Lefty. He's using the swamp against me." AJ slapped at a particularly pesky mosquito as he leaned against a thin tree. "Show me that topo again. I bet I missed something."

He studied the map she presented. Indeed, there was a small

bridge of land that joined what looked like long fingers of higher ground. He'd have to get his boots wet, but that was part of the price of walking through the swamp.

Twenty minutes later, he inspected the unassuming ridge of land and smiled to himself. Without Beverly's topographical display, he'd never have located the way across. Smiling, he noticed that an old tree had fallen just perfectly across the water to create a bridge across the lowest point. Where Lefty was concerned, AJ didn't believe in coincidence.

Stepping onto the log, he carefully walked across the rotting bark. His boots were wet but so far, he'd successfully avoided allowing water over the top and completely soaking his feet. He felt the vibration through his boot at the same time he heard the click of a metallic plunger. His heart dropped into his stomach and he froze.

"Shit," he whispered, looking down. He couldn't see the device, but he knew better. If he continued, he'd be blown to bits.

"What was that sound, AJ?" Beverly asked.

"Pressure plate," he said. "The tree was a trap and I walked right into it."

A wavering red dot flashed over his face and settled on his chest. Scanning the trees in front of him, he was unable to find the gun attached to the laser until Beverly outlined a hunched figure covered by brush.

"Are you blind?" The old man's voice seemed to come from a different direction. "No trespassing signs. You ain't welcome. I don't allow hunting, now skedaddle."

"And get blown up?" AJ answered. "What am I standing on, a Betty?"

"First one's a dud. Just turn around and go. I don't want what you're selling," the man answered, his voice now coming from yet another location.

"I'm a friendly," AJ said. "Not selling anything. I need to talk to you about Albert Jenkins."

"Don't know any Albert Jenkins."

"Bullshit. You pulled him out of the jungle in '67," AJ said. "I know for a fact you sent him a letter when Big Bob Adams died."

"Who are you?"

"I told you, I'm a friend," AJ said. "I'm not even packing."

"Who'd you learn your bush craft from? You a soldier? I didn't think they were training jungle warfare anymore."

"I hope you aren't lying about this M16," AJ said and stepped off the log onto dry ground on the other side of the low spot.

"Who in the hell would wear those boots into the swamp?" the old man asked, sliding away from his cover. "Keep those hands up. My mine might be a dud, but this thirty-aught-six is hot loaded. You copy?"

"I copy," AJ agreed, keeping his hands in the air as the older man shambled across the uneven ground.

"Do I know you?" He kept his weapon leveled at AJ.

"Put the gun down, Lefty," AJ said, recognizing the man's aged face behind hastily applied camouflage paint. A cloudy eye, reddened nose and an uncontrolled tremor were signs of a hard-lived life, but there was no doubt of the man's identity.

Lefty narrowed his good eye as he pushed the hood back from his head. He looked into AJ's eyes as he lowered the weapon. "Didn't think Jenkins had a kid. You're the spitting image of him, though. He dead?"

AJ reached under his shirt, pulled off his dog tags and held them out. "Sergeant Albert Jenkins, reporting for duty."

"Don't mess with me kid, I'm in no mood," Lefty said. "Jenkins was a good man. I'm not gonna take any disrespect, you hear me?"

AJ grinned. "Lefty, you old coot. At least invite me in for a beer. If you don't like what you hear, you can send me packing."

"It's eight o'clock in the morning."

"So, we've missed at least two good hours of drinking."

Lefty peered into AJ's eyes. "You really do look just like him. Can't be, though."

"Lefty, I need you to trust me for an hour. After that, I'll leave. I promise I won't make a move. You can keep that gun on me the whole time."

"Like I need a gun."

"Won't get any argument from me. I saw you take out a Viet Cong with that K-Bar knife you got strapped to your back."

"Stop shittin' me, kid," Lefty said. "Jenkins mighta been younger than me, but he's still in his seventies and you ain't seventy."

"I'll be seventy-three in April."

"Bullshit. What's this about?"

"Really? Not gonna offer me a beer?"

Lefty rolled his eyes. "Fine. One beer. You've got exactly fifty-two minutes to make me a believer."

"You said an hour."

"Been talking for eight minutes."

"Lead on. I'll get right to the point."

"This oughta be good." Lefty walked back into the dense foliage.

"Earth's been invaded by aliens and they're stealing our crap."

Lefty chuckled. "Good. Get it all out, kid. No sense leaving all that crazy inside."

"They're called Korgul. They're parasites, about the size of a robin's egg. They take over the host and make 'em do whatever they want."

"And?"

"And they're stealing a couple of elements that we humans haven't discovered yet."

"Elements?"

"Called Fantastium and Blastorium."

"Holy crap on a toadstool, did you run into a tree while you were walking through the woods?"

"Negative, Lefty," AJ said. "Thing is, I can prove what I'm saying."

"Sure you can, kid." Lefty stepped through a seam in the foliage exposing a small wooden cabin on the edge of a clearing that backed to open water. "Couple of cans in the fridge. Grab me one. I'll be out in a second." He nodded at a small refrigerator on the edge of the porch. AJ looked at the cabin and found the electrical wire that ran off into the woods in a different direction from which they'd arrived.

He pulled two cold beers from the refrigerator and assessed the seating. There were two chairs, one considerably more worn than the other. He chose the other chair and sat down, popping the beer as he did.

"All kinds of crazy in this world, kid," Lefty said, exiting the cabin, sans camouflage and weapon. To AJ's surprise, the man had a considerable gut on him. "No sense in being ashamed of it."

AJ handed his old friend a beer and watched as he flopped heavily into the chair. "I get it, Lefty," AJ said. "I'd think I was crazy, too. Thing is, I'm not. I'm shooting you square and I need your help. Hell, the good old US of A needs your help. We're in big trouble."

"So you said. Aliens," Lefty said. "Not sure what that's got to do with me and you've got something of a credibility problem."

AJ took a long drink of the beer and settled into his chair. "I remember when you pulled me out of that hole in 'Nam. Thought we were good and screwed."

"You were good and screwed," Lefty agreed, drinking his beer.

AJ pushed his hand into his pocket. Quick as lightning, Lefty drew his K-Bar. AJ slowed his movement and displayed Jayne's neural enhancer, holding it between his forefinger and thumb. "I can prove I'm telling you the truth. I just need you to do something first."

"Not likely," Lefty said. AJ sighed and placed the device next to his own ear, allowing it to slide home. "What in the hell?"

"Just showing you it doesn't hurt," AJ said, tapping at the rim of the device so that it slid back out and reformed.

"You want me to put that in my ear? Feel like maybe your time's up." Lefty adjusted forward in his seat and held the K-Bar menacingly.

AJ set the device on the wooden arm of the chair he was sitting in and reclined, tipping his beer back. "No need to get like that. Just look at it and tell me you've seen its like before."

Lefty cut his eyes to the device. "Kind of like what those kids do with their phones."

"Ever see one of them change shapes like that?"

"Don't suppose I have." Lefty set his knife on the table in front of him and drank heavily from his can. "Why me? I've made it tough to find me. Gotta be plenty others to talk to."

"You really have to ask?" AJ said. "Think about it. What if I really am Albert Jenkins? Pretty elaborate hoax just to get close to an old guy like yourself. Could have just dropped napalm on your cabin while you were sleeping."

"Don't sleep in the cabin," Lefty said.

"Bullshit."

Lefty shrugged. "Well, sometimes."

"That's more like it," AJ said. "Put that thing in your ear."

"Why?"

"Because then my friend can talk to you."

"Friend?"

"Alien friend. Name's Beverly. She's from Beltigersk Five"

"God save me, I'm an idiot," Lefty said as he picked up the Tok neural enhancer and slid it into his ear.

A ten-inch-tall Beverly appeared on the edge of the table, wearing a red polka-dot dress, her hair styled in a '50s bob. "Greetings, Sergeant Thomas Johnson. I'm Beverly, from the planet Beltigersk Five."

"Sonnavabitch."

18

IN THE FAMILY

"That's one helluva story, Jenkins." Lefty had just finished watching the updated video Beverly created. She explained the basics about the major players, Korgul, Vred, Beltigersk and the Galactic Congress, ending with general back-story about how the team arrived on his doorstep. "Not sure what this has to do with me."

AJ opened a second beer and chugged off the first third before setting it on his knee. "Lefty, you're the best damn soldier I ever knew."

"Got that right."

AJ grinned and took another pull on the beer. "I'm gonna tell you something only three other people know. I need you to promise you won't tell anyone."

"Who would I tell? Aside from the fancy light show, I'm pretty sure you're a couple bricks short of a load."

"I need you to say it."

Lefty held up his hand. "Won't ever leave my lips."

"We've developed a vaccine that makes a human incompatible for Korgul. In truth, it makes 'em incompatible for both Korgul and Beltigersk." Lefty nodded, leaning back in his chair. "Thing is, we don't have a good way of getting it distributed. It's like a million people have a headache and we've only got one bottle of aspirin."

"That hard to make?" Lefty asked.

"Not so much that, exactly. It's more like Korgul would stop at nothing to make that bottle of aspirin disappear, so we need to be careful, if you know what I mean. Plus, once they figure out the cure is out there, they'll attempt to develop a counter to it."

"I seem to recall your video suggested there were twenty-some million infected. I see where you're comin' from, but I still don't know how I can help. I shoot pretty good, but I'm not as quick as I used to be. Good enough for the likes of you, though, so don't be gettin' any ideas."

"I'm offering you a chance to turn back the clock, Lefty," AJ said. "I'd be able to offer the same for a couple more, if you know 'em. I need a group of men I can trust, who've been in the shit and who didn't break. This thing's gonna get messy. Thing is, you and me, we've done messy."

Lefty's grin was lopsided. "I put that behind me, Jenkins. Don't want to be killin' anymore."

"You've been holding a gun on me for the last hour."

"Trespassers are different."

"That ban on killin' go for aliens too? We'd like to keep our fellow mouth-breathers upright."

Lefty looked at the watch on his wrist and shook his head. "Time's up."

AJ nodded and stood. "Appreciate you giving me a chance to present my case. I'd like to get that neural enhancer back before I go. Belongs to a friend of mine."

"Who else you got with you?"

"Darnell Jackson. Met him after you pulled me outta that camp," AJ said. "He flew a gunship. I was his door gunner and did mechanicals for him. Oh, and Doc Jayne."

"And you're gonna leave? Just like that?"

"No sense in wasting my time or yours. Guy like you knows what he thinks. No sense in beating a dead horse. Got too much respect for you."

"You're kind of a jackass."

"It's come up."

"If I say *yes*, what's that mean I gotta do?"

AJ walked to the refrigerator, took out a third beer and popped the top. "BB needs to run a couple tests to see if you're compatible with any of the Beltigersk we brought along. If she finds a match, you'll be paired, but not until you agree. We aren't forcing you to do anything."

"How do I do that?"

"It'll make sense when it happens."

"Then what? Do I get a cute little thing dancing around in my head, too?"

Beverly reappeared, still wearing her red dress. "It is unlikely. Beltigersk don't usually communicate visually as I am doing just now. It requires significant effort and, to be completely honest, most consider it to be beneath the dignity of their bond."

"That so? But you'd run the crap outta my system?"

"We would. The pairing would allow us to restore optimal biological functioning. You'd also gain communication with your rider, most likely aural and in some cases visual via textual representation. It depends on the situation. Also, as long as you are within reach of one of Earth's many communication networks, you'd have direct communication capabilities with any other Beltigersk-paired person. Like AJ, for example."

"Who?"

"Albert Jenkins."

"Oh, right. You call him AJ?"

"It's my nickname."

Lefty scratched his neck. "Guess I didn't know that. What's involved in the test?"

"I've actually been performing those tests as we've been speaking. It's not invasive," Beverly said. "Several riders from Beltigersk would make good candidates."

"Feel like I'm acting like an idiot," Lefty grumbled to himself. "Talking to little fairies on my table."

"I guess the real question is, whatcha got to lose?" AJ asked.

"My sanity." Lefty took a deep breath. "You haven't told me what my mission would be."

"Your mission would be to put together a team that can take down positions crawling with Korgul. I'm thinking half a dozen or so. Didn't you have a captain you liked back in the day?"

"You want me to recruit Barnhardt?"

"Whoever you like. Probably best if they're loners. Family will get suspicious when their bodies suddenly regenerate by forty or fifty years. Hard on marriages, too, if you know what I mean."

"That eliminates a bunch."

"Just need a solid squad."

"I know some guys." Lefty blew out a breath. "This is just plain nuts."

"You can still tell me to leave."

"Like you said. I don't have much to lose and what if you're not actually blowin' wind up my skirt? Be nice to have one last mission."

"Lefty, AJ is going to touch the corner of your eye," Beverly said, pulling on a rocket pack and puttering up so she was hovering in front of Lefty's face. "He's first going to transfer 39835687-7-R from the dermal layer of his finger to your tear duct. The process is painless. Over the next few minutes, 39835687-7-R will figure out the best mechanism for establishing communication with you. Like we discussed earlier, it will likely be aural at first and then possibly some sort of projected screen, like a phone display or tablet. Is that acceptable?"

Lefty shrugged. "Go for it."

The process took only a moment and AJ stared at his old friend expectantly.

"She wants me to give her a name," Lefty said a minute later, his voice louder as if he were talking to someone who had hearing problems. "It's a girl, right?"

Beverly smiled. "Yes. We've found that using familiar names helps the transition period."

"Rebel," Lefty said.

"You want to call her Rebel?" AJ asked.

"She says she likes it," Lefty said, still overly loud. "Can you hear her?"

"You're yelling, Lefty," AJ said. "And no, she's only talking to you."

"Wasn't sure how well she could hear... oh... not sure what that means... oh... subvocal..." Lefty went quiet, aside from little grunts, as he learned how to speak without using his vocal cords.

"Hey, while you're getting settled, I need to go grab my partner," AJ said. "I left her back on the road."

"Be faster if you had her come back to the bridge. We can take my fan boat over. Crap, why am I so hungry all of a sudden?"

"Ask your girl," AJ said and chuckled as Lefty grabbed his stomach and gave AJ a pained look. "You sure you're in any shape to drive a fan boat?"

"I'll be right back." Without further explanation, Lefty scooted around the side of the cabin and made for the outhouse.

Sweat poured down Lefty's face as he gulped water from a large plastic cup and alternatively shoveled rice, beans and cured pork into his mouth.

"It'll take a couple weeks for your body to fully settle," Jayne explained, rocking back on a wooden chair as AJ cooked over an old propane camp stove in Lefty's kitchen. "Believe it or not, you're using substantially more calories right now than you're consuming."

"You were in the war?" Lefty asked, but continued before she could answer. "Is it really possible I'm seeing better already?"

"Surgeon," she said. "And, yes, Rebel is manufacturing a variety of nano-sized biological machines to repair all sorts of things throughout your body. The cataract in your left eye looks like it's thinning. You know, you could have had that fixed at the VA."

"Didn't seem that important." He shrugged. "You know, Captain Barnhardt is gonna take some convincing. Be best if you guys came along. Queenie'll be a pushover, he's already batshit crazy. Good operator, but he's got some impulse control issues."

"That's just it, Lefty," AJ said. "I picked you because I knew you lived out here in the crack of nowhere."

"That so?"

"Korgul are on to us," AJ said. "We need a team that's not connected to me, Darnell or Doc."

"What should I be doing?" Lefty asked.

"For now? Build the team. With Rebel in your head, we can communicate," AJ said. "Beverly and I will leave you with six Beltigersk riders."

"I still don't know how we're going to take on millions of aliens with what amounts to a single squad."

"For now, that's the way it needs to be."

"But you have a plan?"

"Wouldn't be here if I didn't."

"Am I gonna have the runs for the entire two weeks?" Lefty asked.

"You might, if you don't improve the quality of your food," AJ said. "I can't believe you've lived so long on this crap."

"Okay," Lefty sighed. "Give me a few weeks. If this works like you say, I'll see what I can do to round up some of the boys."

"We'll be in touch," AJ said, setting the steaming cast iron skillet onto the kitchen table.

"Tell me I didn't just lose my mind," Lefty said.

"Won't help if I do," AJ said. "And it won't be the last time the thought crosses your mind."

HAVING BEEN cautious to avoid making plans on their long ride back from Atlanta to Tucson, Jayne was visibly agitated as she pulled into the toll booth that would release her car from airport parking.

"You lied to Lefty," Jayne said. "You don't have a plan at all." While her words were hard, she wasn't angry.

"Caught that, did you?"

"I'm pretty sure Lefty did, too. I can't figure why he agreed to go along. You talked about an assault force. You're not thinking about going back to the CDC with force, are you?"

"CDC was a good idea. It could have worked," AJ said. "But they'll have their defenses up. Even with two squads, we'd probably get our butts kicked."

"Then why'd you recruit Lefty?"

"It's a matter of knowing the man. Lefty bleeds red, white, and blue. If we get taken out, he'll take matters into his own hands. Korgul will be watching us, but they won't know to watch him. Element of surprise is everything when you're as outnumbered as we are."

"What now?"

"We do just what Korgul said; we get out of their business. Beverly, would you call A Plus Rental? I need a fifteen-ton dump," AJ said.

"Dump truck?" Jayne asked.

"Ever drive one?"

"No. Why do we need a truck?"

Beverly appeared on the dash, wearing jeans and a flannel shirt with rolled-up sleeves. She held a clipboard in one hand and a cell-phone to her ear. "They have one available. Do you want it now?"

"Yes," he confirmed. "Turn on fourteenth. Gotta clear the site."

"I don't see how you just turn this whole Korgul thing off," Jayne said. "We need to be doing something."

"What do you know about home design?" he asked. "I need to put some plans together."

"You're driving me nuts, AJ."

"You're right. BB is probably better suited to that," he said, chuckling.

Jayne backhanded him on the shoulder as she pulled to a stop outside a large, fenced construction equipment yard.

"We need a delivery device for the vaccine," AJ said. "Ideally, we need a variety. We can't shoot everyone we suspect and I'm positive we can't drip blood into their mouths."

"Like what? I thought we could attach it to a virus or get it into an upcoming flu vaccine, but that was with Jerry's help."

"Take those ideas off the shelf. People have been trying to poison the masses for centuries. Let's see if they've got anything we can make work."

"You're talking military-type applications?" Jayne was skeptical. "It's hard to affect millions like that."

He nodded. "Good. Now you're thinking. We don't have to solve the problem with one application. We need a bunch of different ways to apply our cure."

"We need access to a weapons research team," she said.

"What we need to do is find out if the US resistance survived the attack on Area-51," AJ said. "But we've got too much heat on us. For now, I need you to figure out more ways to deliver the vaccine while we start looking for evidence of the resistance."

"Was that so hard?"

"What?"

"Communicating your plan. It's not much, but at least it's something we can build on. And this way, I don't end up going nuts sitting around while you're off building your house."

"Good. See you back home?"

"I'll probably go by my condo and take a shower first."

AJ nodded and walked into the main office of the large machine rental shop, only to notice that the man behind the counter had the telltale signs of Korgul sludge behind his eyes.

"What are you doing here?" he asked.

"I've got a rental contract for a fifteen-ton Kenworth."

"All out," the man answered.

"Already have the contract."

"Yeah. No. Computer problem. We're all out of trucks."

"Is that how we're gonna play this?" AJ asked.

"Probably."

AJ scanned the interior of the shop. It was midday and it was empty.

"What are you doing, AJ? We should leave," Beverly said, appearing on the counter between him and the man.

"I was just thinking that there isn't much this guy can do if I decide to shock that smug little shit right out of him. I'm guessing this guy's a contractor and he can't lay a hand on me," AJ said.

"Try it," the burly man responded menacingly.

AJ launched himself over the counter and caught the man mid-chest. Having seen the sluggish behavior of more than a few Korgul, AJ wasn't surprised the bear of a man chose to grapple. However, with his body back in peak physical condition, AJ easily slipped around behind the man, locking him up in a sleeper chokehold.

"You'll never get away..." The Korgul-infested man struggled to talk as he thrashed against AJ.

"Save your breath, big fella," AJ said, ripping an electrical cord from the wall. When the man slumped to the floor unconscious, AJ used the guy's pocketknife to cut the casing open. "Nothing wrong with an old-fashioned extraction."

AJ plugged the cord back into the wall and touched the exposed leads to the man's skin. The lights dimmed, the man stiffened and a moment later, the slimy tendrils of a Korgul seeped from behind his eyes and fell to the floor.

"Hey! What are you doing back there?" a woman's voice called.

"Call for help," AJ said, pulling the electrical cord out and stuffing it out of sight. "He was lying back here when I came in."

"Is he breathing?" she asked.

AJ saw no signs of Korgul behind her eyes. He pulled on the man's arms so he could lay out flat. "I think he's coming around."

"I've got 911 on the line. What should I do?"

"I'd get someone to look at him," AJ said.

"What's goin' on?" the man asked. The Korgul crept back along the floor toward him.

"I think he needs water," AJ said, grabbing a cup from the counter and holding it up to the woman. The gesture gained him a confused look, but she took it and ran off, all the same. He scoured the shelves beneath the counter for something to pick the Korgul up with and located a plastic bag full of pencils. Unceremoniously, he dumped the pencils and scooped up the Korgul, stuffing the bag into his pocket.

"Are you trying to steal our pencils?" the woman asked, returning with a bottle of water. The man moved and drew the woman's attention. "Hank, are you okay? I called an ambulance. You fell over."

Hank looked from the woman to AJ. "Who are you?"

"Just came in for a rental," AJ said.

Hank pushed AJ away and batted at the proffered water bottle, irritated. "I just need a minute and I ain't goin' in no damn ambulance. You got a contract?"

"Al Jenkins," AJ said, not sure if the contract was in his made-up name, Alvin, or Albert.

"They just called in," the woman said. "He's taking the Kenworth for a few days."

"Have him sign the papers and get a copy of his CDL." Hank struggled to get to his feet. "I'm gonna go home for a bit. I'm feeling kinda off."

"That was risky, AJ," Beverly said, sitting on the counter as AJ signed the paperwork and accepted the truck keys.

"We have to push back," said he replied, walking out into the half-empty yard. "If every Korgul thinks they can just take what they want from us, we'll never have any peace."

"It is difficult to get used to the level of aggression you are comfortable with," she said. "I understand that revolution can be bloody. It is a different matter to be a part of it."

"No blood this time," AJ said, hefting himself into the cab of the waiting truck. "And now Hank's free to watch NASCAR and drink beer like everybody else on planet Earth."

After checking out the controls, he pushed the truck into gear and rolled for the gate, tooting his horn as he pulled onto the street and headed for home.

"What do you plan to do with the Korgul in your pants?" Beverly asked, dangling her crossed legs over the dash.

"You're a naughty little sprite sometimes," he said, grinning.

Beverly returned his grin. "You know, this truck probably has Fantastium detectors or even collectors underneath. You shouldn't pull it onto the property until we check."

"What do you suppose they look like?" AJ asked.

"Sharg would know how to find them," Beverly answered. "I've sent a query to her. I believe she sleeps during the daylight hours, though."

"I'll pull through the gates, just far enough to get them closed." He slowed the truck to a stop in front of the gates to his junkyard.

"Mr. AJ! Mr. AJ!" Diego's voice and Greybeard's excited barks greeted him as he approached the tall chain link. He sucked in a contented breath as the sense of well-being at returning home settled on him.

"Help me open the gates wide, Diego," AJ said, unwrapping the chain that held the panels together.

Greybeard pushed on the gate and the thick bulldog wriggled happily around his legs, nearly tripping him. AJ was shocked at how much Diego had changed in the two days since he'd left. Still thin as a board, the boy's cheeks had lost their hollow look. His eyes were bright and he smiled broadly, exposing ridiculously jagged teeth. Like Greybeard, Diego wasn't ready to get right to work, but instead wrapped AJ into a tight hug, his thin arms feeling like bands of steel as they gripped him.

"Glad to see you too, Diego," AJ said, uncomfortably patting the boy on the back. "You sure look like you're feeling better."

"I am," he said. "Mrs. Sharg and Mrs. Lisa have been showing me what to eat to become strong. I do not like all of their food, but I do what they say."

"Grab that other gate and pull it open," AJ said, peeling Diego off. He ran with the abandon only a kid could and opened the second gate wide. "Want to take a ride?"

"Yes!" Diego said and raced out to the truck, followed by an excited, barking Greybeard.

A few moments later, AJ climbed into the truck, pushing Greybeard over so he could access the gear shifter. "What have you been up to while we were gone?" AJ asked, pulling past the gate and shifting into reverse.

"Mrs. Sharg is very wise," Diego said. "She has been showing me how to locate Fantastium and Blastorium. She says you are a very wealthy man but that you do not know it."

"I suppose," AJ said. Oddly, it wasn't as if there was much of a local market for either of the exotic elements. "Have you talked with your mother yet?"

"Oh, no, Mr. AJ," Diego said. "She said I could not come back."

"Would you talk with her if I helped? I could explain what is going on," AJ said. Diego looked at AJ with wide eyes brimming with tears. "I'll introduce her to Sharg and get her a neural enhancer. Diego, family is everything. She needs to know what happened. A mother will want her son back."

The truck bounced as AJ backed into the drive, stopping when he cleared the gate.

"Can I ask you a favor, Mr. AJ?" Diego said.

"We're family, Diego. If I can give it to you, I will."

"Can you offer Momma a job? She does not have her card. She does not make good money and my sisters are hungry."

"We'll talk to her tonight, but first, we need to close those gates and start loading this truck," AJ said. "We've got a house to build."

Greybeard saw his advantage at Diego's distraction and slopped a large tongue over the boy's face.

"He is a very messy dog," Diego said. "But we are family."

GOLDILOCKS AND THE BAIRDS

"I have disabled the truck's Fantastium collection system," Sharg said. "It was difficult to locate. I do not believe Korgul invented this technology on their own. It looks like Tok engineering."

"Tok? Like the guys who made the neural enhancer Lisa's finally agreed to wear?" Darnell asked.

"Yes," she said. "I did not want to remove the collection device. I will, of course, check the reservoirs before you leave to make sure no Fantastium was removed while on these premises. I was able to identify several common Tok components. Fortunately, it is not difficult to add shielding around the device."

"I'm gonna need another one of those neural enhancers," AJ said. "Diego asked me to talk to his mother. Apparently, the Korgul had him acting like a jackass to his family and she kicked him out."

"He looks better, now that he's putting on some weight," Lisa added from the other side of the concrete countertop separating the dining table from the kitchen.

Sharg stood up from the table, walked toward Lisa and extracted a small bag from a drawer in the island, offering it to AJ.

"What's this?"

"I anticipated your need for neural enhancers and have constructed twenty. They are not expensive, so I paid with my own credits. We will need to talk of how to reimburse my family, however," Sharg answered.

"How do they cost anything?" AJ asked. "You manufactured them on the ship."

"Data is passed between the ship and other Galactic conduits," Sharg said. "The nature of the transfer is very technical. Do you wish an explanation?"

"Give me a shot at this," Beverly said, appearing on the edge of the counter. "Are you familiar with Bitcoin?"

AJ shook his head. "Nope."

Beverly pursed her lips.

"Don't even try, BB," Darnell chuckled. "Sharg's making online purchases for refills for the manufactory. The patterns are single use."

AJ held out his upturned hands and shrugged. "Got it. Why do all you Galactic types make this crap so hard to understand? Sure. We'll pay you back on your expenses, Sharg."

"I saw you loading the burned debris into the dump truck. Darnell says you're planning to rebuild. Are you sure you have time for that?" Lisa set a large pan of lasagna onto the table. "Dear, would you grab the bread from the oven?"

"Of course, dear," Darnell said. As he passed her on the way to the kitchen, he trailed his hand along her waist and gave her a smoldering look.

"You two need to get a room," AJ said.

"What'd I miss?" Jayne called out from the stairs as she entered the room.

"AJ was just about to tell us his plans for the property," Lisa said.

"Well, actually, I was hoping I could get your help with some designs, Lisa," AJ said. "BB's drafted a bunch of different possible layouts. I've got it narrowed down to a few, but was hoping for your thoughts."

Lisa gave him a suspicious look. "Why, Albert Jenkins, you've never much cared about my thoughts on things before. Why the change?"

He held up his hands defensively. "Thing is, I need someone I can trust to look after the build. It'll be quiet around here for a couple of weeks, but if I haven't missed the mark, it'll heat up after that."

"Doing what?"

"Saving the world, sweetness," Darnell said, returning to the table with loaves of garlic bread.

"If I hadn't had that alien crawling around in my head, I'd be furious at the idea," Lisa said. "But I can't stand the thought of so many people having to put up with the same thing I did. It just infuriates me. I want to play whatever part I can."

"I'm not sure if that's a *yay* or a *nay* on helping me get a building going," AJ said.

"I don't mind helping," she said, slicing a long knife into the pasta. "Look, I know that since I don't have a rider, I'm not going to be as much help, but I know a thing or two about keeping projects on schedule.

AJ passed the bread along after taking a couple of pieces and held his plate out for a slab of lasagna. "I'm going to talk to Diego's mom. If things go well, I'm going to offer her a job."

"A job? But she doesn't know about Korgul," Darnell said.

"I'm going to tell her," AJ said. "That's why I need a neural enhancer. Diego shouldn't lose his family because of all this."

"This is stupid," Lisa said, raising her eyebrows as she took a long drink of wine.

"Something you want to add?" AJ asked.

"Sure is," she shot back, but then closed her mouth tightly.

"Lisa, honey, maybe this isn't the right time," Darnell said, trying to placate.

"No, I want to hear it," AJ said as everyone at the table quieted.

"You have no idea what you're doing, Albert Jenkins," Lisa said. "You're sitting on your hands while Korgul are infesting tens of millions and ruining our future. Where's your fire, man? Where's your plan of action? Are you seriously taking the time to rebuild your house and placate Diego's mom? People are dying. Wake up!"

"Hon, that was..."

AJ held his hand up. "Hold on, Big D." He locked eyes with Lisa, who might as well have been shooting laser beams at him.

"Something to say?" she challenged.

"You're actually right. Our big plan was to get the CDC involved and that got completely blown up. I'm trying to buy time to come up with a better plan."

"Honesty's a good start. Darnell said you found some US military back at Area-51, but he wasn't sure what happened to them."

"We've got a lot of attention on us right now. I'm pretty sure we're the ones who led Korgul to them last time."

"Only if Korgul are dumb as rocks," Lisa said. "Aliens at Area-51 are the worst-kept secret in the world. There was even a movie about it."

"They bugged out," AJ said. "How are we supposed to find them?"

"Seriously, this can't be that hard," Lisa said. "What was the name of that woman general who died?"

"Major," Darnell corrected. "Major Dittany."

"Good. What's her chain of command?" Lisa asked.

"It's a covert operation," AJ said. "You'll never find it."

"US Army is one of the largest bureaucracies in the world," Lisa said. "Tell me your little gal inside can't find her."

Beverly stood and her clothing shifted to green fatigues. A desk appeared on the table and she pulled out a utilitarian metal chair. She started typing on what looked like an old Kaypro computer, complete with green type on the tiny CRT display. "Challenge accepted, mon capitaine," she said, grinning. "Major Sandra M. Dittany, deceased. Apparently, she died in a training accident. No mention of Nevada or Area-51."

"What about that chubby scientist?" Darnell asked. "What was his name? Macanaw?"

"McAlister," AJ said.

"Dr. Alan McAlister," Beverly added. "Member of the SETI Institute. Early research related to linguistics and ancient languages. Shows up in a few articles put out by NASA on first contact."

"Feels like the right guy," AJ said. "Where's he at?"

"According to the University of Nevada, he died of a heart attack two months ago," Beverly said.

"That's not suspicious," AJ said, sarcastically. "Anyone remember that General's name? I don't recall anyone saying it."

"How many can there be?" Lisa asked.

"There are only 231 active generals in the US Army, of which I've eliminated 162 for various factors: gender, overseas' assignment, that sort of thing," Beverly flashed up a grouping of four pictures at a time and they watched as the photos cycled.

"Number three," AJ said about halfway into her montage.

"I never saw him," Darnell said.

"I only saw the side of his face," Jayne added.

"General Norman Heckard," Beverly said. " It appears that he and Major Dittany crossed paths eight years ago at a conference where Dr. McAlister was speaking."

"Looks like we have a bingo," AJ said.

Lisa raised her eyebrows. "Do I need to keep pushing?"

"No, boss," AJ said, chuckling. "But what about Diego's mother?"

"Loyalty is perhaps your most endearing trait, Albert," Lisa said. "I'll talk to her, mother to mother. I guarantee she'll take him back and I won't need to spill the beans."

"How?" Jayne asked.

"You leave that to me, dear," Lisa said.

"I also promised to help her financial position," AJ said.

"Understood. Diego and I have become friends in the last week," Lisa said. "This is something I can easily handle in addition to helping organize the rebuilding of your home. And on that subject, have you selected a contractor or set a budget?"

"I won't have any money until insurance pays out."

"I could loan you what you need," Jayne said. "You know, until you get paid back."

"He accepts," Lisa said, cutting off AJ's objection. "I'll put together the details and find a respectable contractor. Darnell, I believe I'd like to go home now. We'll take Diego. I don't like a boy spending time in a dungeon. He needs a warm bed. I assume you all can clean this up?"

AJ tried to speak, but no sound came out. His face resembled that of a fish pulled from the stream and left on the shore, its lips opening and closing slowly and no sound escaping.

"She's really got your number," Jayne said, watching the pair disappear up the stairs.

"Lisa Jackson is a powerful woman," Sharg said. "I believe she would fit into Vred society."

"What did I just unleash?" AJ finally asked.

"She wasn't wrong," Jayne said. "We've been dancing around this thing ever since the setback in Atlanta. We need to move forward."

AJ nodded. "BB, keep going on the General Heckard thing. Can you get a read on his location?"

"I have exhausted my attempts to glean information from your Pentagon," she said. "I believe we would need to be onsite with Seamus and Greybeard to break into those systems. However, I believe I have located the nom de plume General Heckard utilizes while traveling."

"He's using a fake name?" AJ asked.

"I'm a little proud that you knew what *nom de plume* meant," Jayne said.

"Not just a pretty face," AJ said, shaking his head. "Problem is, if he's traveling incognito, he'll have a security team. We'll never get close to him."

"He travels with an entourage of four. Three men, ages twenty-four to thirty-two, and a woman, age thirty-six. The men are all special forces. The woman, Captain and Doctor Jackie Baird, is an academic, specializing in emergency planning. "

"Any tie between Captain Baird and Dr. McAlister?" Jayne asked.

BB grew still, which usually meant she was accessing larger and larger sets of data. "I'll continue to search, but I do not find public ties between the two."

"Seems unlikely," AJ said. "They never once went to the same conference?"

"Oh, that's interesting," Beverly interrupted. "Dr. Baird had no obvious contact with Dr. McAlister, but she *was* recruited to Army Intelligence by one Major Sandra M. Dittany."

"Can you get a location?" AJ asked.

"According to her mother's social posts, Dr. Baird is visiting the family in San Diego," Beverly said.

"She's in Military Intelligence and lets her mother post her location?" AJ asked.

"No. She is untagged in the photo at the restaurant in which they visited last night," Beverly said. "I was able to match her face in the background."

"How much .22 caliber antidote ammo did we make?" AJ stood and walked to the storage room.

"They'll never let you on an airplane with a gun," Jayne called after him.

"San Diego is six hours," AJ said. "In your sportscar, we might make it in five, especially if BB warns us about cops along the way."

"That is not difficult," Beverly said.

"We should be able to make it by midnight," AJ called from the supply room. "I've got maybe forty rounds of this stuff. I'll bring that squirrel rifle and the Ruger my granddad brought back from WWII."

"What about Darnell?" Jayne asked.

"Do humans never rest?" Sharg asked. "You spent the entire day digging charred debris from your family home and now you plan to take a considerable trip?"

"Not just us, sweet cheeks," AJ said. "You're coming along."

"She won't be comfortable in my car," Jayne said.

"We'll take Darnell's SUV. That'll piss off Lisa good. I owe her one."

"For?"

"Getting all high and mighty on me," AJ said. "What else?"

"But you're doing what she said," Jayne said. "Therefore, you agreed with her."

"Doesn't make me love it," he said. "She'll never let me live it down."

"Darnell says they are not concerned with you using their vehicle for a trip to San Diego," Beverly said. "2-F says that Lisa is annoyed."

AJ grinned and Jayne shook her head. "I didn't bring clothing. I can't believe I don't travel with extra clothing. I should know by now."

"We'll pick some up in San Diego," AJ said, handing a short, .22 cal rifle to Sharg. "It's unloaded. You good with a ride?"

"I would very much like a chance to see more of your beautiful planet," Sharg said. "I will endeavor to keep my appearance well disguised."

"It's California," AJ said. "I'm not sure it'd matter that much."

"Does California often have alien visitors?"

"You'll need to come too, Greybeard and Seamus," AJ said.

Ten minutes later, they pulled into the Jackson's garage where Lisa, Darnell and Diego met them. Lisa was holding a paper grocery bag in one hand and folded clothing in another.

"You're welcome to use my vehicle while we're gone," Jayne said, holding the keys apologetically out to Lisa. "Sorry about the late notice."

"No worries, girl. Glad to see something got through that thick head of his," Lisa said, cheerfully. "If you're leaving my Darnell behind, I'm all about it. You and I, we're about the same size. I packed a sundress, an extra pair of jeans and a nice top. There's a package of unopened undies in the bag along with sandwiches for the road."

"Seems we're always running off," Jayne said.

Lisa smiled. "I imagine that's what saving humanity looks like."

"Go easy on her, AJ," Darnell said. "I know she looks sporty, but..."

"I won't ruin your car, Big D. You're welcome to come along."

"Why aren't we flying the big ship?" Jayne asked.

"Do you think you can just fly a spaceship, unnoticed, into a suburb in San Diego?" AJ asked.

"Wake up, Doc." AJ nudged Jayne awake. With Beverly's ability to locate State Patrol, they'd made the entire trip in five hours and thirty minutes, including a rest stop which resulted in an awkward moment with a young girl from Iowa meeting Sharg and being more curious than afraid.

"I must have dozed off," she said, sitting up.

"BB, how many live at the Baird house?"

"Basically, we have a Goldilocks type of situation," Beverly said, doing her best to sound like a grizzled, old sergeant while wearing a pale blue dress, long white apron and white stockings. A thick cigar was tucked into the corner of her mouth.

"You're mixing your metaphors," AJ said. "What's a Goldilocks situation?"

Beverly grinned. "Glad you asked. We've got a Baby Baird, a Momma Baird, and a Papa Baird. I checked security. Jackie left last night at about eight o'clock. Security cameras picked her up mentioning an overnight stay but leaving on a flight early this morning. And for the record, Baby Baird is a twenty-two-year-old boy named Jason who attends a local community college where he's in his fifth year."

"I like him already," AJ chuckled. "Kid needs to join up and see the world."

"What kind of security?"

"Good quality for residential property," Beverly said, keeping both the outfit and her grizzled mannerisms. "I've got control of it, though."

"Dogs?"

"Cat."

"What are you thinking, AJ?" Jayne asked.

"I'm thinking we need some porridge." He reached behind his chair and pulled out the crowbar.

"You can't go breaking into their house."

"*Shouldn't* is probably a better descriptor. We can't miss our chance with Dr. Jackie. What did you think we were gonna do at her folk's house?"

"See if she was still visiting?"

"She's not," AJ said. "Sharg, you're with me. Jayne, we'll give you the all-clear once we've made contact."

"I don't like this plan."

"There's literally no plan."

"Albert Jenkins, you are aware that I am a peaceful being," Sharg said. "I will not harm humans. I will not allow the Vred species to be considered a threat due to my actions."

"Trust me, you're a seven-foot-tall reptilian-skinned Amazonian. The last thing I'll need you to do is get violent. Worst case is, I'll need a really good growl." He chuckled and jumped out of the vehicle.

Sharg stepped out and joined him in the street. "I will not growl, Albert Jenkins. I will take no threatening action, regardless of the situation. I do not understand my role."

Greybeard gave a low woof as they climbed the steps to the Baird's front door, secured with a hefty-looking combination lock. AJ lifted Greybeard even with the keypad. "1492," Beverly interpreted, displaying the digits above the lock.

"That's the reverse of their address," AJ whispered. "Do you suppose that drives Dr. Jackie nuts?"

"What is *nuts*?" Sharg asked.

"Long story." He punched in the combination and turned the lock. Pushing the thumb latch on the handle, he smiled as the door quietly opened.

"John and Candy Baird are asleep on the second floor," Beverly said, flying along next to AJ with her rocket pack strapped on, but still wearing her blue and white Goldilocks outfit. "I do not know of Jason's state."

"What does John do for a living?" AJ asked as quietly as he could.

"Lawyer. Candy sells real estate."

"Seriously?" AJ asked. "Isn't that a cliché?"

"Who the hell are you?"

AJ hadn't quite made it to the top of the stairs when he received the young man's challenge.

"You wouldn't believe me if I told you," AJ said, stepping off the last stair and onto the top landing. He turned toward Jason, who stood down the hall holding a baseball bat in one hand.

"I'm calling the cops," Jason said, using his other hand to dial the phone.

"You got this BB?" AJ asked.

"La Mesa police," Beverly intoned, a headset appearing over her golden locks. "What's the nature of your emergency?"

"There's a man and..." Jason glanced down the stairs and got a glimpse of Sharg, who'd stopped about halfway up. "And... I don't know. You need to send someone."

"Of course. Is this Mr. Baird?" Beverly asked.

"No! I mean, yes!" Jason answered. "They're in my house. Send someone quick."

"Officers have been dispatched," Beverly answered. "Are you in immediate danger?

"Well, I'm looking right at them," Jason said, his chest puffing out slightly. "But I've got a bat. I'm gonna kick their asses if they move another step."

"Mr. Baird, please calm down. Are you being threatened?"

"What? Yes! No! They're in my house!"

"What's going on, Jason?" John Baird's voice came from down the hallway.

Jason dropped his phone and wrapped a second hand around the bat. "Burglars," Jason said. "I've called the cops. They're on the way. Get your gun, Dad."

"Ah, don't do that, John," AJ said, resting his hand on the butt of the .22 Ruger in his waistband. "There's no need for violence. I need to talk to you and Candy about Jackie. She's in trouble."

"Don't trust him, Dad," Jason said. "Take your hand off that gun or I'm gonna mess you up."

"Careful, Jason," John said.

"John? What's going on," Candy asked, slipping in behind her husband.

"Wife is Korgul, AJ!" Beverly announced.

"Dammit!" AJ screamed and pulled the Ruger from his waistband.

With practiced ease, he swung the pistol into place, dialed in his aim and fired, tagging the woman in the side.

"Candy!" John threw his body between AJ and his wife.

Jason lunged. Though he swung his bat wildly he managed to make contact with AJ's arm. AJ grunted and bounced against the railing and fell over the top. Fortunately, he was next to the top of the stairs and only fell a few feet on the carpeted stairs.

"I'll mess you up!" Jason said, throwing his bat over the railing.

Adrenaline surged through AJ's body and he lurched up the stairs, grabbing the back of the boy's pajama shirt. Buttons popped as he pulled the kid down, flipping him onto his back. A blue outline showed the position of the gun and AJ scooped it up, quickly bringing the barrel around on the chaos.

"Everyone, just stop moving," he barked.

His anger was enough to send Jason scrabbling backward until he hit the wall.

"This is not a peaceful encounter, Albert Jenkins," Sharg admonished.

Candy Baird cried as her husband turned in place, facing AJ and holding his hands up to shield his wife.

"Where's the snot glob?" AJ growled, gesturing at Candy with his gun.

"What?" John asked.

"You had to have seen it," AJ said. "Glob of goo, came out of her face."

"AJ, it's attempting to enter John," Beverly warned, outlining the goo crawling up John's face.

"Buddy, wipe that crap off your face," AJ said, still using the weapon as his pointer. Fortunately, John's fear of the weapon over-rode his confusion at the order and he brushed the Korgul glob onto the floor. "Candy, for the love of humanity, stop your bawling. I barely tagged you."

"Are you going to kill us?" she asked.

"I gotta be honest," AJ said. "This went a lot differently in my head."

20

GENERAL DISPLEASURE

"We'll do whatever you want," John said. "Please don't hurt her. Take me."

AJ considered the mix of emotions on Candy Baird's face. "You want to tell him?" he asked her.

"I ... It ... I ..." Candy stuttered, blinking in confusion, tears still running down her face. Her gaze turned down as she searched the oak floor next to where she'd fallen. The Korgul that had fled from her body inched toward the edge of the landing looking to slide between the balusters of the stairway railing. "Is that thing real?"

Despite the confusion, John did his best to stay between AJ and his wife. "Let the boy go," he said, negotiating.

"This isn't a hostage thing," AJ said. "We're not going to hurt you."

"You shot my wife!"

"I got her in the side. Barely a flesh wound."

"What *is* that thing?" Jason pointed at Sharg who stood motionless on the stairs.

"Will you all please shut up for a minute?" AJ asked, pushing the pistol back into his waistband. For whatever reason, the dark hallway quieted. "Jason, that's Sharg and she's an alien from the planet Halfnium-8. Please don't call her an alligator woman or anything dumb like that. Candy, yes, that thing is real and it's a Korgul, another alien. It's trying to escape. I'm sorry about shooting you, but that was the only way to get it out."

"That thing?" John asked. In his bewildered state, he reached for the Korgul.

"Seriously, John, you don't want to do that," AJ warned. "Now, if you will all settle down, I'll call in my friend. She's a doctor, a surgeon actually, and she'll get Candy fixed up. Then we can talk like civilized people."

"What do you want?" John asked, returning to his previously near-hysteric state.

AJ sighed. "Galactic peace. But I'd settle for a good cup of coffee. John, help your wife to the kitchen. Don't do anything stupid. Jason, help your dad."

"This isn't over," Jason growled.

"Jason. Don't," his father ordered.

"Cops will be here soon," Jason argued.

Sharg shuffled down the stairs, watching the Korgul slug as it dropped over the edge of the second-floor landing and onto the tile of the entry hall. "I will find something to restrain the Korgul."

"Look in the kitchen," AJ called after her. "They'll have plastic food containers or bags. They seem to work pretty well."

"BB, could you tell Jayne to park in the driveway and bring a first aid kit in?" AJ instructed. "Tell her we have a gunshot wound, but it doesn't look too bad."

"What do you want from us?" John asked, his voice level, clearly trying to avoid antagonizing AJ.

"We'll get to that," AJ said. "Let me ask you something. Have you noticed strange behavior from your wife lately? Last few months, but could have been longer."

"Strange?"

"Oh, John! I was trapped," Candy blurted out. "I couldn't talk. There was something making me do things, say things. I didn't mean all those horrible things I said. I love you."

John looked at his wife, blinking in confusion.

"It's okay, sweetheart. We'll work it out," he said, bracing her with an arm around her back.

"No, it's not okay. That thing," Candy pointed over the railing toward the bottom of the stairs. Sharg was inelegantly using a cottage cheese container, which she'd unceremoniously emptied, to capture the wily Korgul. "That thing was inside me. It made me do things, talk to people I didn't know and do horrible things."

"Shh," John said. "Don't talk. It'll be okay."

"Are you guys going crazy?" Jason asked. "This guy breaks into our house and shoots Mom and now ... now I don't know what's going on."

"Still got the gun, kid," AJ said, lifting his shirt. "Everybody into the kitchen."

John stopped the little progress they'd made down the stairs. "You said you weren't going to hurt us."

"Keep the kid in line," AJ growled.

"Jason, don't make this worse," John said and continued to help Candy forward.

AJ backed down the stairs, keeping a wary eye on both Jason and his father. He didn't find it overly surprising when about halfway down, Jason lunged again, throwing himself in an attempt to grapple with AJ. Having expected the move, AJ swiveled and grabbed the young man, unwilling to let the boy land full force. He grimaced as the kid's momentum pulled him down hard. With clarity and speed only possible from a fresh hit of adrenaline, AJ surged up, subduing the kid at the bottom of the steps.

"AJ, what are you doing?" Jayne demanded. "What's going on in here?"

He ignored her and pulled Jason's arm behind his back, pushing his wrist up. "Are you done?"

"Jason, stop," John said. "Please don't hurt him."

"AJ, let him go," Jayne said. "We're not here to hurt these people."

AJ sat with his legs straddled over the young man, holding his arm in place. "Things went a little sideways."

"I have it," Sharg announced, holding the cottage cheese container out triumphantly.

"I see that," Jayne said. "Who's hurt?"

AJ gestured with his head to the stairway. "Jackie's mother took a through and through to the side. She was carrying the Korgul Sharg just snagged. John's being reasonable. Kid's a bit of a hothead. I was right. He needs to join up. Army needs his piss and vinegar."

"Screw off," Jason said, pulling his head up defiantly.

"See?" AJ asked.

"Mr. and Mrs. Baird, I'm so sorry," Jayne said, stepping over their fallen son. "This is not how our first contact should have gone at all. We're not here to hurt you."

"Could've fooled me," Jason interrupted, making AJ chuckle.

"You broke into our home," John said, reaching the bottom of the stairs. Something about Jayne's manner made him comfortable enough to turn his wife over to her. "Shot my wife."

"On a scale of one to ten, how badly does it hurt?" Jayne asked, lifting the woman's bloody pajama shirt enough to locate the wound.

"It burns. Six, maybe?" Candy said, searching Jayne's eyes for a glimmer of hope.

"The bullet was a .22 caliber," Jayne said, leading the woman toward the kitchen. "There's an exit wound on your back. You're lucky AJ is such a good shot. Think of it like someone stuck you with a knitting needle but took it out."

"Is that bad?"

"No funny stuff, John," AJ said, as the lawyer gave Sharg a concerned onceover.

"Will it hurt me?"

"She," AJ said. "Her name is Sharg. It's a long story, but she came to Earth because she wants to start a family. Despite her size, she's a pacifist."

"I do not understand why my size is relevant," Sharg said.

"Is she talking to you?" John asked. "Is she intelligent?"

"We'll get to all that," AJ said. "Right now, I need you to help me with your son. It's important he doesn't do anything stupid. The thing is, he's young, dumb, and has a hero complex. Turns out, I respect most of that. I need you to take the electrical cord off that lamp there and bring it to me. Make sure you unplug it first."

"You're not going to hurt him?"

"Nope. Just need to reduce the chaos."

John nodded and after a few attempts, pulled the cord from the lamp.

"Traitor," Jason growled in defeat, as AJ secured his hands behind his back.

With the unruly kid restrained, AJ helped Jason to his feet, nudging him toward the kitchen, nodding at John to lead the way.

"Where is it?" Candy's eyes bored into AJ's as he entered the kitchen.

"Sharg, I need the container." He kicked a stool away from the kitchen island and pushed Jason onto it. "And you. I need you to settle down and listen."

AJ accepted the cottage cheese container and opened it, holding it in front of the rumpled realtor after verifying its contents. "Was that really inside me?" she asked.

"This is crazy," John offered.

"I believe you know it was," Jayne said, taping a piece of gauze over the wound on Candy's back. "You saw it, didn't you?"

"It's not crazy, John," Candy said. "They're telling the truth. That – you called it Korgul? It was in my head. I thought it was just a horrible dream, but then I knew it really wasn't. I thought I'd lost my mind."

Tears streamed down her face and Jayne stopped working long enough to embrace the woman. "I'm sorry, Mrs. Baird. I know how horrible it must have felt."

"I'm having trouble with all this," John said, reaching for the container and tipping it so he could look inside. "That thing? That's what we're talking about?"

"How did you get it out?" Candy asked, her chest shuddering against her sobs.

"The only way I could, under the circumstances," AJ said. "The bullets are doped with a vaccine. Makes you immune to Korgul. It can never get back inside. None of them can."

"Why are you here?" she asked. "There are so many of them. You're not just here to rescue me. It's about Jackie, isn't it?"

"Why do you say that, Mrs. Baird?" Jayne asked.

"They talk about her. They think she's bad. She wears a face mask when she sleeps. They can't get under it. They tried. They made me release free Korgul in her room when she was home."

"You wouldn't," John said, scandalized. "She's our daughter."

She spun toward her husband. "I had no choice, John. I couldn't stop my body."

"But it's Jackie."

"Shit, it's always Jackie," Jason grumbled. "Perfect Jackie. Never does anything wrong, Jackie."

"Dr. Jackie," AJ offered unhelpfully. Jason glanced up at him and nodded in wry agreement.

"Yes," Jayne said. "We need to get a message to her. We believe she's part of the US resistance against Korgul."

"We're not giving Jackie to you," John said, firmly.

"Get my phone, John," Candy said.

"No. How do I know this isn't some elaborate trick?"

"Let Jackie decide," AJ said. "All you need to do is take a picture of me and send it to her with a single message. She's the one in Military Intelligence. She's likely better informed than you and could make a better decision."

"It's next to the bed on my nightstand, right side," Candy said.

"I'll get it," Jayne said, standing from where she'd been kneeling by Candy.

"No," John said, stepping in Jayne's way as she moved to leave the kitchen.

"John," AJ said. "I'll take a selfie with me and Sharg in your kitchen. Message will read, *Didn't get much of a chance to talk with Heckard at Area-51. Breakfast?*"

"Who's Heckard?" John asked.

"Your daughter's boss."

"No," John said, shaking his head. "It's a woman. I've met her."

"That was probably Sandra Dittany."

"How do you know all this?" John asked, allowing Jayne to pass.

"Has anyone told you, you're exhausting?"

"MOM? DAD?" Chaos rose again as the sound of a panicked woman filled the house. The front door slammed, and Greybeard barked wildly.

"In the kitchen," Candy called, sipping her coffee.

Captain Jackie Baird burst into the kitchen, a small pistol gripped in her hand, pointed down. While waiting for her arrival, AJ had allowed the family to change clothing and even freed Jason from his chair, although he'd required the young man to stay seated at the table.

"What are you doing in my home?" Dr. Baird demanded, raising her weapon at AJ, her hands shaking.

AJ flipped the final pancake on the griddle, looked over and smiled. "No need for guns. Do you go by Captain Baird or Dr. Baird? Are you hungry?"

"I asked you a question." Her eyes strayed in the direction of Sharg, who'd found comfort on a backless bench. "What in the hell?"

"Jason, show her the cottage cheese," AJ said.

"'Sup, Sis?" Jason said, tipping his head back coolly. "It's pretty badass. Almost got me convinced." He had spent the last ninety minutes opening and closing the cottage cheese container as he inspected the trapped Korgul. "Are you really MI? I thought you were part of some sort of think tank."

Jackie Baird was a trim woman with short black hair and a tanned complexion common with runners. Her bright blue eyes were like lasers as they locked onto AJ. "My family is off limits," she growled, tightening her grip on the weapon.

"Your mother had a Korgul in her," AJ responded casually. "You get enough cakes, Sharg?"

"I am satisfied," Sharg answered. "I believe the human is in distress. It is possible she will activate her projectile weapon and damage you."

"Did that just talk?" Jackie asked.

"Sharg. She. Be nice." AJ flipped the small stack of pancakes onto a plate and moved to the kitchen table. While he'd served pancakes to everyone, he'd been disappointed no one had eaten much. "Did you hear me about your mother?"

"I can't trust you."

AJ reached for his pocket, but Jackie saw the motion and swung her gun back at him threateningly. "Careful, Captain, I'm going to pull a device about the size of a ballpoint pen cap from my pocket. It's an alien device. It'll let you talk with Sharg and BB."

"Who's BB?" Jackie asked.

"How much of this do you want your family to know?" AJ asked. "I assume you recognized my picture from Area-51?"

"How'd you know about Heckard?"

"If you let me hand you the device, this'll be a lot easier," AJ said. "I'll go slow."

"You don't want to see the Korgul?" Jason asked.

"I'm not familiar with that term," Jackie said.

"I can't recall what you guys called 'em – the snotty, robin's-egg-looking aliens. Gets in behind your eyes," AJ said. "I'm pretty sure you know what I'm talking about."

Jackie carefully walked to the table and tipped her head up as Jason held the cottage cheese container over to her. "Shit," Jackie said and glanced at her mom while keeping the gun trained on AJ.

"It was in me. It was horrible, Jackie," Candy said.

"If that's true, you shouldn't be able to remember anything."

"That's how it works when you shock it out of someone," AJ agreed, talking around the pancake in his mouth. "We took a slightly different approach. Are you sure you want your entire family to hear all this?"

"What do you want?"

"Send that picture to Heckard," AJ said. "Tell him anything you like, but I want a meeting."

"You need to put your hands on the table," Jackie said, calmly. "All of you. Even you, Mom and Dad. A team is about to breach this house. Standard protocol is that they'll take everyone into custody. Jason, don't mess around. These guys mean business."

AJ stood with his hands up. "We surrender. Take the pistol out of my waistband. In my right pocket are those neural enhancers I was telling you about – for communication. Don't let them get damaged. We have more equipment in the car. It needs to come with us."

"Don't try anything," Jackie said. "Dad, take his gun."

John withdrew the pistol and turned it on AJ. "Now you're on the other side. How does it feel, asshole?"

"Get the items from my right pocket," AJ said and was surprised when John did as he was told. "Jayne, Sharg, we need to lie on the ground, face down. Heavily armed people will be coming through that door any minute."

"Dad, put the pistol down," Jackie said.

"I'm helping you."

A bright flash and a loud explosion announced the arrival of the tactical team. John didn't get a chance to lower the weapon as two feathered darts appeared in his chest. He looked at them and then sent his daughter a look of surprise as he crumpled.

"No!" Candy screamed as the cottage cheese container was tipped over. In a last, desperate move, she stabbed ineffectively at the fleeing Korgul with a fork, just as darts appeared on her chest. She crumpled.

"That's my mother! Stand down!" Jackie yelled.

"Act like it knocks you out, Sharg," AJ called as twin pricks struck his back.

AJ AWOKE in a featureless white room that had exactly one mirrored glass panel. Jayne lay on the floor next to him, but there was no sign of Sharg or Greybeard.

"Tell General Heckard I'm awake," AJ called, scraping himself off the floor. He gently dragged Jayne with him as he sat back down against the wall. "BB, you there?"

Beverly appeared in front of him, wearing loose-fitting, black-and-white-striped clothing, a metal ball chained to her ankle. "We're in the slammer, AJ. It's a well-shielded room. I cannot establish communication with Seamus or Sharg. No one has visited since you were deposited here over six hours ago."

"Explains why I gotta pee so bad," he said. "Hope they went easy on Sharg."

"The chemicals they used to restrain you would have had a similar effect on her, perhaps even longer-lasting due to her slower circulatory system," Beverly explained.

"Hope they're treating her right."

"Treating who right?"

AJ looked around. The man's voice had come from a speaker near the two-way mirror. He'd heard the voice before.

"Sharg, the Vred that came with us," AJ said. "I know it's you, General. We met a few months back. I doubt you've forgotten already."

"How am I to believe you're not an enemy agent? I hear you speaking to someone. No doubt there is an alien within you."

"I assume this is a secure conversation."

"That's right."

"Did you retrieve the Korgul from the Baird's house?"

"We did not."

AJ rolled his eyes. "You've got to be shitting me! That Korgul knows everything that went down. Could you be any more ham-handed?"

"I didn't like you much last time. You got Dittany killed."

"Major Dittany sacrificed herself so we could complete our mission," AJ said. "She died a hero."

"We lost Area-51 in that battle. Our team was all but nullified after that attack."

"I'm sorry to hear that McAlistair didn't make it."

"Why's that?"

"We came back with tech. That alien, Sharg? She's Vred, a highly intelligent species. She's looking to make some trades. You could put your program back together with help from her."

"I suppose you want me to let you go. To trust you and this alien Vred." Heckard's skepticism was clear.

"No," AJ said. "I want you to make us part of the team."

"Why would I do that?"

"I can think of exactly two reasons. The first is that I know why the Korgul are here. I bet, even with all the time and effort you've put into this, you have no idea why they're here or what they want."

"It's not hard to imagine," Heckard answered. "They want our planet."

"Not exactly."

"Then why? Exactly."

"There are two elements humanity hasn't discovered yet. First one is Fantastium. The other is Blastorium. Basically, one is go-go juice for spaceships. The other powers weapons. Don't give me crap about the names. An alien provided the translations so I could remember what each was used for."

"That's all you have? They want our resources?" Heckard said. "No shit. The Chinese and the Russians want our resources. It's an old story, Sergeant Jenkins. I hardly need your help for that."

"I said two reasons," AJ said. "Are you sure you don't want to hear the second?"

"Sure. Blow me away."

"We've got a vaccine that makes humans incompatible with Korgul. We've got the cure."

21

INSIDE JOB

"T he hell you say!" General Norman Heckard barged into the room where AJ sat on the floor holding Jayne in his lap.

AJ smiled, but his answer was cut off by a nervous-looking man wearing a white lab coat and carrying a clipboard. "General, you can't go in there. Albert Jenkins is infested by an alien parasite!"

"Shut up, Clark." While General Norman Heckard wasn't a large man, an aura of command presence radiated off his five-foot-ten, graying frame. His steely blue eyes locked onto AJ's as he squared off. "Listen, son, your last stunt cost me twenty-five of the finest soldiers ever to don the uniform and our resistance to these shit-heel aliens was nearly destroyed. I don't trust you farther than I can throw you. Now you say you've got a cure? You've got thirty seconds to prove it or so help me God, I'll put a bullet between your eyes so fast you won't see it coming."

AJ carefully set Jayne back on the floor and pulled himself to his feet. An armed soldier burst into the room, pistol aimed at AJ. "You will kneel and place your hands behind your head. Do you hear me prisoner?" The soldier's emphatic words were punctuated by spittle.

"AJ, sleeper!" Beverly said, projecting the outline of a dormant

Korgul moving into the soldier's brain. As soon as the Korgul took control, AJ would be as dead as Heckard had just threatened.

"Dammit." He cursed and spun into the soldier. The soldier's grip on the weapon slackened and he seemed paralyzed. AJ seized the opportunity and stripped the weapon, working quickly to eject the magazine and cycle the hot-loaded round from the chamber. As he felt the soldier's strength and focus return, AJ flung the weapon aside.

A flurry of activity followed as the room filled with officers and soldiers, all watching the exchange from the other side of the mirror. They were not willing to sit idle as the prisoner endangered their commander. Within seconds, AJ was face down on the floor with arms pinned behind his back.

"You're gonna regret that, alien scum," Jackie Baird growled, yanking AJ onto his butt. The rage in her eyes showed she was on the edge of losing it. AJ shook his head as she screamed questions and accusations at him. All the while, he watched the activated Korgul retrieve his weapon and magazine.

"I can see Korgul," AJ said as firmly as he could when she stopped to take a breath. "He's about to put a bullet in my head."

"Time for talk is done," she growled back, her demeanor reflecting frenetic tension.

"Gun!" Someone else in the room saw the danger as the Korgul-infected soldier assembled his weapon, racked a bullet, and raised his weapon.

Jackie Baird's muscles had coiled into tight springs while giving AJ his dressing down. At the shout, her head snapped up and she sprang into action. Launching over the top of AJ, she slammed into the Korgul soldier. The gun belched fire, the sound filling the small room. A second shot rang out and AJ twisted, only to see Captain Baird roll off the attacker holding her side, a blossom of deep red blood forming under her fingers.

"Subdue that man!" Heckard ordered, rushing to Baird's side, behind two additional soldiers. "Baird, hang in there. Medics are on the way."

A medical technician raced to her side and ripped at her uniform shirt, exposing the wound. Working quickly, he applied pressure and worked to stabilize her.

"AJ, Captain Baird is grievously wounded. The location of the wounds and consistency of the blood denotes mortal injury. Human medical technology will not save her," Beverly said, appearing in a white lab coat, standing next to the prone woman.

"What about Thomas?" AJ asked. "She's a scientist. It'd be a good match."

"Not without her permission," Beverly said. "She's lapsing into unconsciousness."

"Let us help, General," AJ demanded.

"You've helped enough!" Heckard shot back. "Get them out of here."

Rough hands grabbed the back of AJ's arms and pulled him to his feet, dragging him toward the door.

"She's dying!" AJ shouted over the chaos. "We can save her. You've seen my history, so you know I'm a damn vet. I served my country and I swear on the honor of my fallen brothers that I'm shooting you square. Don't let her die like I did Major Dittany, dammit!"

A bloody hand grasped Heckard's shirt, finding purchase on his lapel. "Trust him," Captain Baird gurgled.

AJ was pulled roughly from the room and shoved down a narrow hallway.

"Bring him back!" Heckard's commanding voice blew out of the room.

The soldiers pushing AJ down the hallway reversed course and brought him back into the room. AJ's eyes widened as Heckard turned, holding his confiscated Ruger pistol and aiming it squarely at AJ's chest. "Give me one reason," Heckard growled.

Instead of addressing Heckard, AJ looked down at the quickly fading Baird. "A Beltigersk is willing to bond with you. He needs your permission. He's nothing like the Korgul. He and Dr. Jayne developed the vaccine for Korgul. God, please believe me. He'll save your life."

"Dr. Baird has classified secrets." AJ recognized the voice as

Clark's, the soldier who'd entered with Heckard. "You can't let her give that data to a foreign agent. You could be charged with treason."

"Oh, hell, get the damn lawyer outa here," Heckard demanded, never taking his eyes off AJ. "You've got your twenty seconds."

"Thought it was thirty?" AJ knelt next to Baird, still with hands secured behind his back and two agents holding his arms.

"Don't let him touch her!" Clark exclaimed. AJ peered up at the man, fully expecting to see Korgul and was surprised when he didn't."

"Do not let this woman bleed out," Heckard demanded.

"You want incontrovertible proof?" AJ asked. "Give me that Ruger. Put one round in the chamber."

"You can't be serious?" Clark argued.

Baird panted softly, murmuring almost incoherently.

"What'd she say?" AJ asked.

Heckard shook his head, obviously unable to hear over the din in the room. "What are you going to do with the gun?"

"Give you your man back and prove that we have an antidote," AJ said.

"Sounds like you want to shoot my prisoner," Heckard said. "I can't let that happen."

Baird tried again to speak, but her voice was too quiet to make out the words.

"She says she'll accept Thomas," Beverly interpreted.

"Where's Thomas?" AJ asked.

"Left hand," Beverly answered.

"Thomas who?" Heckard looked confused.

"Free my hands," AJ said. "I'll extract the Korgul."

"General, Captain Baird is ready for transport," one of the EMTs said after lifting the wounded woman onto a gurney.

"Just give me the bullet," AJ interrupted, knowing Jackie had precious few moments. "I don't need the gun."

"Take her to medical," Heckard said. "Get him up, take off those cuffs. I'm telling you, Jenkins, I don't care if you make it out of here. You better not be screwing around."

The pressure eased on AJ's arms as the guards removed the cuffs.

He seized the opportunity and swiped his left hand across the failing woman's face, holding it there for as long as possible. The move was met with exactly the response he expected.

"Thomas has moved," Beverly said. "This is going to hurt."

The Ruger pistol crashed into his face as Heckard violently attacked him, pushing him off Baird. AJ accepted the man's blows and crumpled to the floor, fading into blackness.

"YOU'RE DEAD, YOU KNOW THAT?" The Korgul-infested soldier's words were the first thing AJ heard as he awoke. Expecting hands to be wrapped around his neck, AJ was surprised to discover he'd been placed into a cell next to the soldier.

"That's a neat trick – listening in but not taking over the body," AJ said. "How many do you have at this base?"

"How did you know I was there?" the Korgul asked.

AJ sat up and leaned against the concrete block wall. "Lucky guess."

"You really screwed 'em last time," the man said. "I think Heckard wants you more than they want us at this point."

"Why are you admitting your existence?" AJ said.

The man rolled his eyes. "They'll shock me out soon enough. It's standard protocol for suspicion."

"Doesn't work for sleepers, does it?" AJ finally understood the advantage Korgul found by hiding their presence.

"The shock doesn't work when we're not plugged in," the Korgul infested replied. "You broke the treaty, 49231125-0-B. Once I get word out, every Korgul on this jerkwater planet will be coming for you. Hell, they might even drop a nuke – accidentally, of course."

"Knock it off," AJ said. "You know as well as I do that we're being recorded. Are you really threatening Heckard and his team?"

The soldier shrugged. "Not sure why we'd bother. They're pathetic. No wonder even Beltigersk won't sponsor you humans. That said, a deal's a deal. 49231125-0-B broke the rules. She needs to pay the price."

"How many sleepers are there?" AJ asked. "Not like it matters, right?"

"Wouldn't matter if I told you. The resistance is weak. Do you really have something that will kick us outta humans? That'd be a major escalation," the soldier said. "Is Beltigersk ready for the kind of war that'd cause?"

"You talking to me or Beverly?" AJ asked.

"Right. I forgot the humans get to talk if you play nice."

"You're a piece of shit."

The solider was about to respond, when the door at the end of the cellblock opened. "You boys playing nice?" Captain Jackie Baird walked through the door, wearing a crisp new uniform and a bright smile.

Beverly appeared on a middle rung of the cell wearing her prison stripes. The ball connected via chain to her ankle precariously balanced next to her. "Thomas! You made it!" A thrill of adrenaline spiked through AJ's system as Beverly banged a tin cup against the bar she held onto.

Seated on Baird's shoulder wearing a bright white lab coat, the chubby scientist grinned widely back at Beverly. "Why, yes, Princess," he said. "Dr. Baird has been most hospitable."

Baird grinned as she knit her eyebrows together in confusion. "Are you... you're 49231125-0-B?"

Beverly stood up and her outfit changed to her formal black gown. "My apologies, Dr. Baird," Beverly said, holding her hand out as if to shake. "I enjoy the indulgence of exploring your rich culture. I am ever so grateful to make your acquaintance."

"As I am yours," Jackie said, holding out a finger so she could complete the act of shaking hands. Her eyes flicked to AJ. "If I understand correctly, I have you to thank for saving my life."

"All Thomas," AJ said.

"Are you really seventy-two years old?"

"I think that's right," AJ responded. "How's your mother? I probably could have handled that a bit differently. Things turned sideways pretty quickly."

Jackie shook her head. "You broke into my parent's home. How'd you think it would go?"

"Yeah. I get the question," AJ said. "What about Sharg and Dr. Jayne. Are they okay?"

"Perhaps we could move our conversation," she said, opening the cell door as someone remotely unlocked the magnetic door.

"What about him?" AJ asked, walking out to stand next to Baird while keeping his eye on the soldier in the next cell.

Jackie extracted an unusual-looking pistol from the holster on her hip and fired a dart round into the soldier's abdomen. The magnetic lock pinged and with steely confidence, she strode into the cell and scooped the Korgul off the soldier's face with her bare hand. Replacing the weapon into its holster, she dropped the sludgy alien into a black plastic bag, folded over the top and dropped that bag into a second bag.

"What was that all about?"

"Thomas indicated Korgul have an affinity for communication over cellular networks," Jackie said. "Those bags are like mini Faraday cages and block electromagnetic transmissions. Are you quite sure Corporal Turnbull is uncompromised?"

"I do not have much experience with the human psyche," Thomas said before AJ could respond. "It is possible he will need help reintegrating into society after the shock of the invasive pairing with Korgul. If there is one thing I would like to fix, it is that our vaccine should not erase the memory of the Korgul's time within their body."

"I wouldn't fix that," AJ said. "How else will we figure out what those damn snot-balls have done?"

"I understand the tactical advantage of the memories," Thomas said. "I believe the psychological impact to be quite devastating."

"And you know this how?"

"If you recall, I spent considerable time with Dr. Jayne after my predecessor, Jack, attempted a takeover of her being. This event was not insignificant and will have a lasting impact," Thomas said.

"Can I see her?" AJ asked.

"Of course," Baird said. "General Heckard is speaking with her and the alien, Sharg, in the conference room. Suffice it to say, we have learned more in the last two hours than we have in the last ten years. Dr. Jayne explained the great risks you have taken to get word out about humanity's plight. If the story is to be believed, you are a remarkable man, Albert Jenkins."

"Nothing any of my brothers back in the shit wouldn't have done, given the chance."

The smell of garlic and pizza caught AJ's attention as they worked their way up from the basement of what looked more like an office building than a military installation.

"We're right in here," Baird said, pushing through a door into a corporate-looking conference room.

"Looks like I owe you an apology," General Heckard said, extracting himself from a chair. He crossed the distance and offered a firm handshake accompanied by a look of resolve. "Almost can't tell I coldcocked you. Never seen anything heal like that but then, I've been saying that a lot today."

Involuntarily, AJ rubbed his face where Heckard had smashed it. While it no longer hurt, the memory of the pain hadn't yet disappeared. "You pack a pretty good punch for a cake eater, General. Any of that left?" he asked, tipping his head toward the buffet of pizza boxes spread out on the conference room table.

"Captain Baird suggested you might be hungry. Something about Beltigersk converting food energy into repairs. Make yourself at home. We were just doing some brainstorming. Were you serious about joining up? Far as I can tell, you put in your service, soldier."

"I don't know about joining up," AJ said. "Joining forces makes sense, though. Not sure I'd fare very well with a fresh L.T. barking orders, if you know what I mean."

Heckard chuckled. "Know just what you mean. We're not that kind of unit. After that dustup at Area-51, we're running on fumes. We need a team that can operate outside the normal scope, if you know what *I* mean."

"Might be worth talking about. I'd hate to have any confusion," AJ slid as many pieces of pizza onto a plate as it could handle and took a seat next to Jayne. Wordlessly, she gave his hand a reassuring squeeze, her eyes asking if he was okay.

"Suddenly, I find my schedule has miraculously cleared," Heckard said, picking up a Styrofoam coffee cup and tipping it back. He set the cup next to a black dry-erase marker, snagged it and walked to the whiteboard. "Captain, where's McAlistair? We need to call him in."

"McAlistair's not dead?" AJ dropped the pizza back onto his plate.

"No. After Area-51, we put out the story that he died of a heart attack and closed his lab. He was moved to a new location and has continued his research," Heckard explained.

"At 1030 we lost contact with the team we sent to retrieve him," Baird answered sharply. "We sent a second team but have run into resistance from local law enforcement. We suspect Korgul involvement."

"How's that possible? His location is top secret," Heckard protested.

She nodded. "It was. Only three people knew his lab's location. We believe the security team was compromised."

"How's that possible? They're shocked weekly," Heckard looked to AJ for an explanation.

Baird, noticing AJ's mouth was full of pizza, jumped in, "Korgul have found a way around our defensive measures. The alien can enter a human and remain dormant until activated. Jenkins' team refers to them as sleepers. In their sleep state, these Korgul are unable to control the host but to their benefit, electrical stimulation does not remove them."

Heckard waited for AJ to chime in. "I have a Beltigersk rider. BB can easily identify Korgul. That's how I knew your soldier was about to jump me. BB warned me and I saw the sleeper move to engage. They're vulnerable during the transition, so I disarmed the soldier before he fell under Korgul control. I knew you'd take my attack as a hostile action, but I was a goner otherwise."

"It was quite a risk. If Baird's team wasn't so disciplined, you could have been shot," Heckard said.

"His actions saved my life. The transfer of the Beltigersk called Thomas was accomplished when Jenkins touched my body," Baird said and turned to AJ. "You're a hero, Albert Jenkins, and you have my undying gratitude for risking your own safety in pursuit of saving my life."

"I owed Dittany one after she stepped in front of a bullet for me," he said. "Can't think of a better way to pay back her sacrifice than to look after one of her own."

"We need a plan to find McAlistair," Heckard said. "If those Korgul get inside his head, this entire operation will be exposed."

"I think that's already in play," AJ said. "Korgul won't waste time with him."

"That might not be as easy as you think. McAlistair was working on a defense against Korgul. His brain is wired to melt down if it recognizes a Korgul bio signature in his body. If he's still alive, his secrets are his own," Heckard said. "Who led the security team that got taken?"

"Lieutenant Clark," Baird said.

"He sure gets around," AJ said. "Let me guess, he made it out and is helping coordinate the second team."

"He got shocked just like the rest of 'em," Baird said, picking up on AJ's unsaid accusation. "He's a good man."

"Did you talk to him after Thomas and you joined?" AJ asked.

"Not in person." Baird blinked a couple of times as she considered something unsaid. "He avoided me. I thought it was odd."

"Do you have any pull with the Air Force?" AJ asked. "We need to get you and your senior staff out of here."

"We're not calling the Air Force for an extraction. This is the Army, son," Heckard said sternly.

AJ chuckled. "You do know I'm twenty years your senior?"

"Not from my side of the table, you're not."

"I believe Albert Jenkins is concerned with masking the movement of an extremely fast, unidentified vessel," Sharg said. "A Vred ship, if you will."

An explosion rocked the building and was followed by the sound of small-arms fire. A man burst into the conference room. "General, we need to evacuate, the building's under attack by San Diego County SWAT."

Heckard closed his eyes for just a moment. "You guys really know how to stir up the locals. Proceed with evacuation plan alpha. Jenkins, Jayne and... and... the alien. You're with me. Baird, lead the way."

Greybeard barked from under the table as AJ grabbed two slices of pizza from the table and made sure that Sharg and Jayne were ahead of him. At the last moment, he realized his Ruger was still on a table. "I'll be right there, keep going," he directed, dropping the pizza and sprinting across the room.

"Take the stairs," Baird ordered as they exited the room.

Two at a time, the group rushed down the four flights of stairs. The ground shook and dust cascaded down the long stairwell as explosions rocked the outside.

"What the hell are they using?" AJ asked, as they continued into the sublevels.

"Sounds like an RPG to me," Heckard said. "Of course, my ears got blown out in Desert Storm, so I wouldn't count on me."

"Where are we going?" Jayne asked.

"If we learned anything from Area-51, it was that we needed better escape routes," Baird said. "Humanity is relying on us to stay alive. We can't afford to be taken down."

"How far away is your spaceship?" Heckard asked.

"Can you cover for a supersonic flight?"

"Captain, call Gromwall," Heckard said. "Tell 'em we're gonna rattle some windows over Tucson and San Diego. Give me a timeframe."

"BB, can you grab Darnell for me?" AJ asked.

"I'm on the line, Buddy," Darnell answered. "We're five minutes from your house. We can be on the ground in San Diego in twenty-two minutes give or take."

"Can you buy us twenty-two minutes, General?" AJ asked.

22

SWAMP TALK

A squad of soldiers met the team as they exited the stairwell into the sub-basement. A line of four armored Humvees sat idling with the back doors open in an otherwise wide-open underground parking area.

"Won't SWAT close the entrance?" AJ asked, following closely behind Captain Baird.

"Tunnel beneath the street opens to the far side of the opposite building. It's not on any of the city plans," Baird explained. "We'll put the alien and Doctor Jayne in the middle. Jenkins, you're with the general and me, one car forward."

"I'm not getting separated from Jayne," AJ said.

"No room," Baird explained. "Don't have time to argue."

"Go, AJ," Jayne said, directing Sharg and Greybeard to their assigned vehicle.

"Shit," he spat, but dutifully followed Baird, knowing full well that Jackie and her ride-along, Thomas, had just become the most important souls in their hastily formed team.

"Sleeper," Beverly warned, just as a soldier raised his weapon, aiming at the general.

"Sleeper!" AJ shouted, pulling his Ruger and snapping off three quick shots. While his first shot sailed wild, the second two drove home. The soldier's weapon thundered as automatic fire stitched into the garage floor, throwing chunks of cement into AJ's legs. Just before the gun went silent, a bullet hit him in the calf and sent him tumbling headfirst into the side of the vehicle.

"AJ!" Jayne exclaimed, attempting to jump from her vehicle. She was caught and thrown back inside by one of the soldiers.

Baird grabbed AJ and rolled him onto his back. "Are you hit?"

"Just get me in the car," he said, grimacing through the pain while trying to get his battered leg beneath him.

With strength he wouldn't have expected, Baird all but tossed him inside, piling in behind him as fresh gunfire erupted from over by the stairwell. Bullets pinged off the armor. One lucky bullet ricocheted inside the vehicle, but fortunately imbedded itself into a seat cushion.

Scrabbling over the top of Baird and AJ, General Heckard clawed at the door, attempting to close it. "We're in, go!" he ordered, banging the metal door on AJ's hanging foot. AJ grimaced but managed to pull his leg in, the door slamming closed behind him.

"General, I need that first aid kit. Check the boys up front. We had shots inside the cabin," Baird ordered. "Jenkins, where are you hit?"

"Right leg. Just wrap it," he said through clenched teeth, repeating what Beverly was saying as she attempted to calm him.

"I can't give you sedatives until I'm sure we're out of danger," Beverly explained, hovering in front of his face. "You should feel some relief in a moment, though." AJ sighed as painkillers hit his bloodstream and took the edge off.

"Can you see Jayne's vehicle?" AJ asked, squirming out of Baird's prying hands.

"Dammit! Stay still, Jenkins," Baird ordered. "General, where's that kit?"

"Right here," Heckard said, opening a case next to her. "You do know I'm your superior officer, right?" Even through the tension, the smile in his voice was evident.

"And you're doing a bang-up job, sir!" she snapped. "How are the boys up front?"

"Boys and girls, sir!" a young woman's voice responded snappily. "We're squared away, sir!"

"Suddenly everyone's a critic," Baird grumbled, ripping apart AJ's pant leg and accepting unrolled gauze from General Heckard.

For a moment, vehicle's inhabitants were airborne as they crossed a threshold, moving well beyond what could be considered a reasonable speed.

"Shit," AJ groused as Baird's hands flew up and she dropped the bandage.

"Little warning next time, please," she called over her shoulder, never losing sight of her patient. "Call it out, Simpson."

"Hard left, sir," the young woman, Simpson, called out, just before Baird was thrown to the right. "Clear for three count."

"You're going to have to bleed for a couple of beats," Baird said, steadying herself on the seat next to him.

"Coming up to street level, Captain," Simpson said as the Humvee launched skyward. "We're airborne."

AJ half-grinned, half-grimaced at the soldier's continued late delivery of information as the vehicle's armor bottomed out on heavy-duty shock absorbers.

"Hard right," Simpson informed. "All four vehicles clear, sir! We're on fourteenth street on Exfil Plan Alpha."

"Any big parks fifteen minutes away?" AJ asked, as Baird had a calm enough moment to wrap his leg.

"Parks?" Heckard asked. "We're in the open, Jenkins, and I don't know who I can trust. We didn't have time to develop more than those darts we tested. Dammit, we need time to develop a plan. If I was the Korgul and found out about what Baird's carrying around in her head, I'd drop a nuke on the city just to be safe."

"Let her come with us, General," AJ said, handing the man his Ruger even though it only had four remaining bullets. "I've got a team. We'll go after McAlistair."

"What do you want me to do with this?" Heckard asked.

"I wish we had a better answer, but anyone you shoot is guaranteed to be someone you can trust," AJ said. "It's a permanent cure. At least so far. Just make sure you retrieve the Korgul once it exits. They'll just jump to someone else."

"We left one behind."

"It's worse than that. The one from Candy Baird was left at their home," AJ said. "I think it's safe to say Korgul know we have a weapon and they'll be coming hard."

Heckard glanced nervously into the sky. "They can't let us succeed."

"Copy that," AJ said.

"Jackie, this mission is yours," Heckard said. "I'll gather the troops. We're in for a rough ride. Find McAlistair and tell him it's time to open up the Cookie Duster contingency."

"Cookie Duster?" Baird asked.

"He'll know. Just don't repeat that code to anyone else. Pull the convoy over," Heckard ordered. "Simpson, you and ... what's your name, son?"

"Carlson, sir!" the driver answered.

"Carlson," Heckard answered. "The two of you are to accompany Captain Baird. You're officially under her command."

"Accompany where, sir?" Carlson asked.

Heckard ignored the question. "Captain, there's a high school soccer field approximately one mile due east of our position. If you push it hard, you'll be there just in time to meet Jenkins' ride."

"What about you, General?" Concern etched Baird's face. "If you're right, the aliens are gonna hit back hard. They need to stomp this thing out, now."

"My guess is, they're tracking the trucks," Heckard said. "My job is to keep their interest."

"Come with us, General," Baird said, her voice suddenly soft. "You don't have to do this."

"*This*," he said, with finality, "this is exactly what I have to do. Now get out and make tracks. There are a lot of us depending on you."

AJ stared at the convoy as it roared off, leaving Simpson, Carlson and Baird with AJ, Jayne, Sharg, and Greybeard. "You heard the general, we need to move, double-time," Baird ordered. "Carlson, Simpson, help Mr. Jenkins."

"If you would accept a modification," Sharg said. "I am capable of carrying Albert Jenkins."

Baird looked at the seven-foot-tall alien, who had mostly remained quiet in her presence. "Um, right, good," she said. "Move out!"

Taking stock of where they'd been dumped, the group raced into the ditch and crossed a short chain link fence, where they soon ran into a busy suburban street. Horns honked as they ran through traffic. A *whomp* preceded the sounds of shattering of glass and crumpling steel. A driver had lost control, most likely after catching sight of the seven-foot-tall alien accompanied by armed soldiers wearing fatigues.

"Keep up!" Baird urged, knowing they couldn't afford to get tied up in the chaos. With help from Thomas's projection of the neighborhood, she navigated down alleys and side streets.

"I see it," Jayne said. "The soccer field."

The sound of jets passing overhead at high speed drew their attention. AJ, not needing to navigate, locked onto the planes' flightpath with Beverly's help. Zooming in on the fast-moving jets, his heart sank as he discovered the truth of their predicament. "They're carrying bombs!"

"Two minutes out," Darnell gently announced.

"Did you see those F-16s?" AJ asked.

"Didn't look good," Darnell said. "Thought they were coming up after us, but they have somewhere else to be. They were loaded heavy."

Darnell's voice was all but cut off as the earth shook beneath the team's feet and the sound of heavy explosions ripped through the atmosphere. Involuntarily, AJ followed the jets to where they had intercepted the path of the General's convoy. Twin mushroom clouds expanded over the top of the trees.

"Around the gate," Baird ordered as a heavy shadow passed overhead.

"Keep clear," Darnell's voice announced from an unseen speaker beneath the vessel. With ease, he set the ship down midfield.

"Go, go, go!" Baird urged. Her commands were entirely unnecessary. The team was already racing across the freshly cut sod and onto the lowering ramp.

"Did you get clipped?" Darnell asked as Sharg set AJ onto one of two couches in the main cabin area of the small ship.

"Yeah, BB's working a bullet out. Hurts like a mother."

"I see you made new friends," Darnell said.

"Captain Jackie Baird, meet Chief Warrant Officer, Darnell Jackson. Back in 'Nam, I flew door gunner for him. Of course, he wasn't quite so high and mighty back then."

"Honored to meet you, Chief," Baird said.

"Retired, ma'am," Darnell answered. "Nice to meet you, too."

"Any chance we could make nice once we're in the air? If those F-16s figure out where we're at, you can bet they'll give us a nice warm send off."

"Oh, I like her, AJ," Darnell said, scooting back to the bridge. "Where are we headed?"

"How's Georgia sound?"

"Settle in, folks. Short range says we indeed have a couple of birds inbound. Things could get a bit bumpy," Darnell said. He'd no more than made his announcement and started lifting when twin stripes of bullets stitched a line of destruction across the soccer field and along the centerline of the hull. "Should have led with the big boys," Darnell cackled as he flopped the vessel vertical and rocketed into the sky, pushing his passengers gently back into their seats.

"What's negating the g-forces?" Baird asked, unable to contain her curiosity.

"That is a Vred invention," Sharg said proudly. "While it is proprietary, the individual components are not expensive to reproduce as long as you have access to the Galactic Exchange."

She blinked as questions pooled up behind her tongue, each demanding to be released simultaneously.

"Well folks, we're just now crossing into the thermosphere," Darnell announced. "According to US custom, you're all now considered astronauts. We'll take a somewhat circuitous route to Georgia so as to shake off current attention. 2-F is estimating arrival around 0330 local. If you'll direct your attention starboard, you'll see our fair planet passing by."

"2-F?" Baird asked. She nodded as Thomas explained the relationship between Darnell and his Beltigersk rider.

"Are you doing okay, Simpson?" AJ asked. Relief flooded his body as the bullet finally pushed out from his skin and into the bandage.

"We're really doing this," Simpson said, standing next to a window on the side of the ship.

"Ma'am, can I ask what happened to General Heckard?" Carlson asked.

"We don't know for sure," Baird said, her eyes glassy with emotion.

"You think they got him?"

Baird nodded but didn't answer.

"CAPTAIN, HOW'S YOUR JUNGLE CRAFT?" AJ asked, sitting down next to Baird.

Using a path through the Gulf of Mexico to mask their ultimate destination, Darnell snuck the spaceship into Lefty's backyard under the cover of darkness.

"I had the basic training all officers receive," Baird said. "Are you expecting enemy contact?"

"Those shoes you're wearing aren't gonna cut it. BB, do you think you could fashion a few pairs of boots? I can give you an example if you need," AJ said. "Make some for Jayne, too."

Beverly appeared, sitting in front of a sewing machine, picking up a pin cushion. "I believe the Captain could benefit from more practical legwear as well."

"I'll take a pair," Jayne said.

"Of course, Amanda," Beverly said, smiling. "The first pair of boots should be available in the leftmost drawer. The manufactory will produce the remaining items within a few minutes. I suggest loading water bottles and protein bars. AJ, we'll need additional material for the repairs to your leg." True to her word, boots and pants were available almost as quickly as they could retrieve the items.

"Simpson, Carlson, you'll stay with the craft," Baird ordered, joining the rest of the team at the ramp leading into the swamp. "You're not to touch anything. Do you copy?"

"Yes, ma'am," they agreed in unison, clearly relieved not to be heading into the swamp in the middle of the night.

"This is a delightful habitat," Sharg said as the ship's ramp lowered into the muck. "It smells like home, only wild and untamed."

"If you're lucky, you'll get a chance to see an alligator – or forty," AJ said. "I wouldn't suggest trying to make friends, though."

Sharg gave him a long look. "This is humor," she finally summarized.

"Now you're a-talkin'," he said, pulling on his ghillie hat and stepping into the marsh. "BB, I don't suppose you'd like to give me a map of the area, would you? I know things are dark."

"Boy, does this bring back memories," Darnell said, ruefully shaking his head.

Beverly flitted down the ramp wearing jungle fatigues and a matching ghillie hat. A dim green glowing wireframe outline highlighted both vegetation and terrain. AJ winced. Each step Jayne and Baird made behind him sounded like they were walking on loaded mousetraps. Sharg's movement, on the other hand, was impossible to detect.

For nearly twenty minutes they slogged through the swamp, their hopes buoyed by a growing light that represented Lefty's home in the distance.

"Why didn't you just let Lefty know we were coming?" Jayne whispered and then froze as an ice-cold hand grabbed her neck and cold steel touched her throat.

"Not sure why you'd think that was necessary, love." The man's voice held a slight Australian accent and was but a whisper in her ear. "I'd appreciate you keeping still so there's no misunderstandings."

"Freeze, McQueen," Lefty Johnson hissed, stepping between AJ and Jayne, with his hands raised defensively.

"What's that, mate?"

Lefty tipped one of his raised hands, pointing over McQueen's shoulder. McQueen's shoulders twitched as his eyes slid sideways and he slowly rotated his head. Sharg loomed, her clawed hand ready for action only inches behind his ear.

"Hold on, Sharg," Jayne said, pushing what had been the spine of McQueen's blade away from her throat. "If he'd meant to hurt me, the blade would have been reversed."

"Probably lucky she's a pacifist," AJ said, chuckling as he shook Lefty's hand. Even though he knew it would happen, he was shocked at his old friend's transformation from chubby old guy to the lean warrior in front of him. "Don't recall a McQueen in your old squad."

"Picked him up after you and I had our walk through the crap," Lefty said. "One of the best Australian bushmasters you'll ever meet."

McQueen sheathed his blade and warily stepped away from Sharg, only to have Greybeard jump at his leg. "I keep telling you, a bushmaster is a snake, mate," he said, not taking his eyes off Sharg. "I have to know, darlin', is it possible you're unattached? I've never laid eyes on a more beautiful sight."

"Are you serious?" Baird asked, snapping out of her surprise. "We're trying to save the world here and you're hitting on the first alien you meet?"

"Must be an officer." McQueen grinned lopsidedly, tipping his head toward Baird. "Contrary to what you're thinkin', this vision of beauty and death is not my first rodeo with aliens."

"Joshua McQueen, are you proposing to pair with me?" Sharg asked.

"Sorry, pal, she's got a hubby," AJ said.

"Not strictly speaking," Sharg said. "I have my brood mate. He is quite beautiful, but our arrangement is only for the production of descendants. It is true there is an expectation of continued bonding, but Vred enjoy the company of many through their lifecycles."

McQueen's wicked grin looked odd coming from a face painted with green and black camouflage. "That's my girl."

"Mind telling me what in the heck tripped half a dozen of my proximity alarms?" Lefty asked as four more men filtered in from the swampy overgrowth. Most of the men still bore the vestiges of long hard lives. Only Lefty and McQueen had been regenerated by their Beltigersk riders.

"What happened to your old captain? Barnhardt?" AJ asked, not finding the man within the group.

"No good," Lefty shook his head, looking at the ground. "He got put in a home. Rebel and I visited him earlier today. He wasn't doing well."

"Sorry to hear that," AJ said. "Mind if we head back to your place and talk?"

"Things must've escalated, I didn't expect to see you so soon. Most of the boys aren't done percolating. Wasn't expecting to see any brass out this way, either," Lefty said, tossing his head in the direction of his cabin and walking that way.

"At 1430 yesterday, US Resistance Command came under devastating fire in an unprecedented and open attack in San Diego," Baird said.

"Define *devastating fire*," Lefty said, stopping at the edge of the clearing. He gave a quiet, warbling whistle. Answering whistles came from two separate locations.

"Hold on, Captain," AJ said. "How many more did you recruit, Lefty? I'm counting seven and you only had access to six more riders."

"Just because we're old, doesn't mean we're useless, Jenkins. You should know that," Lefty said. "Unless you've got a real good reason to know, I'm not sharing numbers."

"Operational security is important," Baird agreed, stopping on the porch with her hand held up. "Sharg, I don't intend offense, but this next conversation is something we need to work out on our own."

"I find no offense, Doctor Jackie Baird," Sharg said. "I would enjoy an opportunity to explore this beautiful, wild land if such is acceptable."

"Oy, luv, old McQueen'll give you a right good tour." He leaned against a post supporting the grayed wooden porch.

"That's good, Queenie," Lefty said.

"Are you sure that's a good idea?" Jayne asked, following AJ, Darnell, Lefty and Baird into the small cabin. "He seems distracted."

"Don't worry about your girl. Despite how he talks, Queenie'll do right by her," Lefty said. "Now, Captain, I believe you were going to fill me in on what you meant by *devastating fire* and *command*."

"As of 2115 last night, US Resistance Command was transferred to me," she said. "I have independent confirmation that General Norman Heckard and his team were killed in what's publicly being referred to as a horrific training accident. Most of the mainstream news agencies are going with that story because the explosions occurred in a populated area and too much footage is on the internet."

"What kind of *training accident*?"

"Two F-16s dropped five hundred pounders, best I could tell," AJ said. "Looked incendiary, but we were several miles away, so I'm not completely sure."

"And now you're in charge?" Lefty asked, looking at Baird.

"For now. The problem is, without the general, we no longer have shelter from the rest of the Army. We're exposed. If seeing two F-16s drop bombs on San Diego didn't convince you of the Korgul's penetration into our military, I doubt anything will."

"What about the President?" Lefty asked. "Is he one of them?"

Baird shrugged her shoulders. "We didn't think so, but we also didn't know about Korgul sleepers being unaffected by our detection methods."

"What's our play here, Jackie?" AJ asked, purposefully ignoring her rank.

"Korgul are just learning about Thomas's antidote. They wouldn't be out in the open if they didn't know about that. They're right to respond," she said. "I'm certain we've prepared for this contingency."

"That command would be knocked out?" Darnell asked.

"No. Our chief scientist, Doctor Alan McAlistair, has been working to develop something like what Thomas and Jayne created. He wasn't close, but I have to believe if he had a cure, he'd sure as hell have a way to spread it."

"One problem," Jayne said. "Last I heard, McAlistair had been taken by Korgul. There's no way we're getting him back."

AJ chuckled. "Half a century ago, I was stuck in a bamboo hut, staring at the mud, wondering if I was gonna live through the night. I was deep in enemy territory and outnumbered about as bad as a person could be. Only reason I'm sitting here at this table is because of the man sitting across from me. I say, if we need McAlistair, then damn it, we go get him."

23

LOCKED AND LOADED

"While I appreciate the vote of confidence, we're at a significant disadvantage," Lefty said, leaning forward so his elbows rested on the rough-finished wood-plank table. "We have absolutely no idea where they're keeping this McAlistair character. How long has he been missing?"

"Our last contact with him was twenty hours ago," Baird answered. "I suspect I know where he's at, but it's not good."

"What kind of *not good*?" AJ asked. "Last time we played this game, we ended up breaking into a top-secret government base."

"Which one?" Lefty asked.

"Area-51."

"Yeah, that makes sense," Lefty answered and turned to Baird. "Is that it? Are we headed to Area-51?"

"I wish," Baird answered. "At least I know the layout there. No, we've known for quite some time that Korgul took over one of the units at Lewis Correctional Facility."

"I'm not familiar," Lefty said.

"Arizona State Prison up by Phoenix," AJ said. "Why would they take him there?"

"There's a small percentage of the general population who are effectively immune to Korgul," Baird said. "I say *effectively*, because they can be infected by Korgul, but aren't easily controlled. The problem for Korgul is that this small group is completely aware of what's happening to their bodies and, of course, find it disturbing. It takes each person time to understand they have immunity from the alien's control and to assert their free will, and by then the Korgul have exposed themselves."

"So they lock these people up in Arizona?" AJ asked. "Why wouldn't they just kill 'em?"

"We think they do in the majority of the cases," Baird said. "But our intelligence suggests that the Rast Unit within the prison is for high value targets – people with information they need or those who can be leveraged."

"Why take McAlistair there?" Jayne asked. "Why not just kill him?"

"If they crack McAlistair, they get a complete roadmap to US resistance," Baird said. "Funny thing is, all of us right here in this Georgia swamp represent nearly everything that's left. In truth, Korgul should kill McAlistair, but they don't know that. Not yet."

"How do you know they haven't already tried to get that info?" Lefty asked.

"I don't," Baird said. "Fact is, if he's dead, we're screwed ten ways 'til Sunday."

"You said something about McAlistair being resistant to Korgul," AJ said. "Tell us about that."

"Doctor McAlistair carries an implant in his brain that will turn him into a vegetable if they try to implant a Korgul. Trust me, Alan is not a brave man. If Korgul get near him, he'll make sure they know about the implant," she said. "That same implant responds to pain, so if they torture him, they'll end up with the same result."

"So, Korgul need a place where they can break him," Lefty said. "There're a lot of ways to break a man that don't require pain."

"Agreed," Baird said.

"We need to break into a prison on the off chance they haven't scrambled the brains of the one man who can help us *and* we don't have resources beyond what's in this room," Lefty said. "That about sum it up?"

"We have equipment caches in various locations across the US," Baird said. "I don't have any reason to believe that information's been compromised."

"What kind of equipment?"

"Depends on the location," Baird said. "Weapons, light armor, food, computers."

"What about a crop duster?" Darnell asked.

As a group, everyone around the table turned to looked at Darnell.

"That's my boy," AJ said. "Doesn't usually say much, but when he does, it's worth listening to."

Baird shook her head. "I don't recall any crop dusters."

"Hueys?" Darnell asked.

"As far as I recall, there are no aircraft."

"Rebel says she's got a line on an ag service that flies Sikorsky S-300's out of Stanfield," Lefty said. "Not sure how receptive they might be to visitors, but I imagine we could come to an arrangement."

"How are we fixed for cash?" AJ asked.

"Our caches typically have between fifty and a hundred thousand in small bills," Baird said. "There's a cache not far from here."

Lefty pulled a folded map from a kitchen cabinet drawer. "Show me," he said, unfolding a Georgia map and setting a saltshaker on their current location.

When Baird placed her finger on the map, those who had Beltigersk riders were presented with an overlay, tracing various routes. "Damn, that's close," Lefty said. "Rebel, girl, I need you to think more hillbilly, though."

AJ grinned as a six-inch-tall, twenties-something woman appeared on the map, wearing Daisy Duke's red-checked shirt tied off above her belly button, short shorts, and cowboy boots. "I'm still getting my legs about me. What'd I miss?" The southern twang in the woman's voice completed the stereotypical picture.

"Now, that's better," Lefty said, grinning widely. "Tell me, though, what's my favorite mode of transpo?"

Rebel smiled and waved her hand over the map. In response, a new solid blue line appeared, tracing along the waterway that ran past his cabin. "If you stopped there, you'd have to run about a mile over land, but you wouldn't cross any roads," she said with the voice of a southern belle.

"I'll need to go," Baird said. "The caches have bio locks."

"Or we could take Greybeard," AJ offered.

"Boat's only big enough for two, maybe three," Lefty said. "Once we load up, we'll want all the room we can get. I'd prefer to bring the dog, if you'uns don't mind."

"Did you just become more southern?" AJ asked.

"It's those darn Daisy Dukes," Lefty said, referring to Rebel's tight jean shorts. "Rebel's been catching up on her TV watching. I'll let Queenie know we're headed out."

"Are you sure Seamus can break that lock?" Baird asked. Before anyone else could answer, she shook her head. "Oh, I understand. Thomas informs me that he's provided specifications of the locks to Seamus."

"It's generally best to leave field work to grunts," AJ said and turned to Jayne. "Have Sharg take you and Baird back to the ship. Once we get to Arizona, we're going to want as much Korgul vaccine as you can make. It needs to be deliverable via water. Is that possible?"

"Doctor Baird is really the one you should be asking," Jayne said. "She and Thomas are working together now. We'll also need anti-vaccine shots, so we don't accidentally dope our own boys."

"See, that's why I'm talking to you," he said. "Big D, you mind heading back with Jayne and help with manufacturing?"

"I figured that'd be best, too," Darnell agreed. "I got a message from Lisa. Sounds like a bunch of Korgul came by the junkyard. She and Diego are hiding out at his aunt's house. She talked to Diego's mother. They're patching things up."

"Didn't figure Lisa would let that rest," AJ said.

GREYBEARD BARKED EXCITEDLY, following them out to the dock where Lefty's airboat was tied up.

"Just give me a minute to top her off," Lefty said, pulling a pump handle out of a weather-beaten red barrel that was elevated on an equally aged stand.

"Funny how life changes," AJ said, making small talk as Lefty pumped fuel into the boat's tank.

"Funny how it doesn't," Lefty said. "Was this what you had in mind all along when you brought Rebel by?"

"This particular mission? Nah. Did I think we were headed into the shit? Yeah. Korgul have too much to lose. Things been headed this direction for a while."

"I caught wind of the bombing in San Diego," Lefty said, tapping the end of the fuel nozzle to catch the final drips. "Those Korgul are doing a good job of squashing the story, but word still gets around if you know where to listen."

"Can you imagine how this goes once people actually figure out what's really going on?"

"Korgul will have to implement some sort of martial law," Lefty jumped into the flat-bottomed boat and slid into one of three elevated seats in front of the giant fan at the back. He handed a pair of earmuffs, complete with microphone, to AJ after slipping on a pair of his own. "Test, test, test..."

"You know, Rebel and BB can facilitate comms," AJ said.

"I suppose," Lefty said, firing up the oversized engine that was connected to an even larger propeller behind their chairs. "Push us off and then get strapped in. It'll be a bumpy ride. I'm not quite as familiar with some of our path."

AJ unwrapped lines both forward and aft, stepped nimbly onto the boat's deck, and pushed away from the dock. Greybeard jumped in behind him and settled onto the deck between the two main chairs.

"Never had a chance to ride in one of these," AJ said.

"You're in for a treat, then. Most roads around here pick their way through the swamp. This deal gives us a straight shot. You been thinking about what you want to pick up? I figure we'll need ballistic armor and maybe a riot shield or two. I hate the thought of shooting our way into a prison, but if that's what it comes to, we'll need more ammo."

"Focus on 5.56 mm rounds," AJ said. "Be better if we could pick up brass and powder, otherwise we'll be cracking shells."

"I'm not following." Lefty zipped across the open water and headed toward what looked like an impossible-to-penetrate shroud of trees.

"Darnell and 2-F created a low velocity shock round. We can make 7.62mm, but it's hard to keep the velocity in that non-lethal range," AJ explained.

Beverly appeared, grinning with excitement, still wearing her ghillie hat and jungle fatigues, her hair whipping wildly around her head as if she was truly in the speeding boat as it sliced through the humid, pre-dawn air. "2-F modified the pattern so the weapon can deliver vaccine instead of shock," she said. "Just like your .22 caliber bullets."

"That was good thinking," AJ said.

"Okay. M4s, money, ammo, riot shields, armor, frags, smokes, C4 and a comm jammer if we can find one," Lefty said. "Anything to add?"

"Packs, tactical knives, line and some .22 caliber pistols," AJ said. "Good thinking on the comm jammer. Korgul use cellular networks to communicate."

"Thomas has communicated the layout of the cache," Beverly said. "Rebel's split the load into sixty-pound packs. We've got nine of 'em to move."

"And we have a mile hump overland?" Lefty asked, skeptically.

Rebel popped into view, giving Lefty a challenging look. "Aww, don't be a weenie."

"We'll manage," AJ said.

"Hand me a water, would you?" Lefty tilted the airboat as he swung in a wide arc and ran into a previously hidden opening in the tree line.

"Georgia swamp is prettier than I had in my mind," AJ said, twisting off a bottle top.

Lefty pointed at a glow on the eastern horizon. "Gets in a man's blood. Sunrise is a magical time down here."

For twenty minutes, the two men were quiet as the sun rose over the swamp, displaying its beauty in nature's quiet grandeur.

"Do you suppose this is what they were thinking when they put this cache in?" AJ asked, jumping off the bow of the boat and tying it off on a fallen tree.

"What? That it'd get raided by two seventy-year-old hillbillies and a dog?" Lefty joked.

"I think that's probably why they have the bio locks," AJ said, breaking into a slow jog.

The two men picked up speed as the footing underneath became more stable. "Feels good to have my body back," Lefty said under his breath. If not for Rebel and Beverly's connection, AJ wouldn't have heard a thing, but the whispered sounds came through so that he heard Lefty perfectly.

"Never gets old, does it?"

"I see something up ahead."

A glowing outline appeared over a dilapidated farmhouse that had definitely seen better days. "You think that's their cache? I figured it'd look newer. More secure. Maybe brick or a cellar door in the middle of a field."

"Good camouflage," Lefty said. "Greybeard, get on up there and let us know if you smell anyone."

Greybeard barked over his shoulder as he outran the two men. Scrambling onto the porch, the dog avoided the broken boards and raced first around one side and then the other. Once satisfied, he sat unperturbed, by the weathered front door.

"Good boy," AJ said, patting the top of Greybeard's head as he caught up. Inspecting the door, AJ realized it had no handle and when he tried to push it open, the door refused to budge.

Lefty pulled a wicked-looking crowbar from his back. "Let me try." With a hefty swing, he slammed the blunt end of the bar against the space where a handle should be. The door bowed but refused to move. Switching tactics, Lefty eyed the hinge side and took a swing. This time, the bar hit solidly and he was rewarded with a slight cracking sound. Flipping the bar around, he pushed the narrow end in and wiggled it until he had a decent bite. Prying against the jamb, the door finally relented, the bar tearing through the wood. "Two more to go." Working his way up the door, he repeated the process and when he was done, the door was still in place but had three deep gouges along its edge. Lefty was panting like he'd run a marathon.

AJ kicked near the hinges and the door slid back an inch on that side. Several more kicks finally got the door to twist and fall inward onto a dusty floor. "Lot of work for an abandoned building," AJ said, pistol in hand, scanning the room.

"Wanna bet we set off some sort of alarm?"

"Captain Baird shared the frequency of the internal communications," Rebel said, still wearing her country girl attire. "We're blocking the signal, but it would be ideal if you were to disable it. There should be an entrance to the cache in the basement."

Together, Lefty, Greybeard and AJ worked their way through the old but highly reinforced home and down the cellar stairs at the back of the kitchen. For the first time, they were presented with a sight that gave away the true purpose of the building.

"Probably not going to get by with a wrecking bar on that," Lefty said, looking at the heavy steel door at the end of the basement.

Greybeard barked and ran across the basement floor, standing on his back legs next to a keypad. Moments later, a red LED turned off, replaced by a green LED light. At the same moment, the otherwise plain steel slab sprung inward, allowing an arc of light to escape.

"I like Greybeard's approach better," AJ said and pushed the door open.

The room was only twenty feet on each side, but the small space was filled with shelf upon shelf of military hardware. The two men filled packs with the materials they'd previously identified as necessary. In no less than thirty minutes, they'd filled all nine packs.

"We'll take three trips," Lefty said, loading a single pack on his back and holding a second in front of him. AJ helped him slip the pack over his frontside and then loaded a pack onto his own back.

"Every thousand yards, we'll shift the front pack," AJ said. "That'll let us keep a good pace."

"Copy," Lefty grunted as he trudged for the stairs leading out of the basement.

"QUEENIE, YOU THERE?" Lefty called. It was well into the afternoon as the two men approached Lefty's dock.

"Aye, I'm here, mate," McQueen answered.

"Any trouble?"

"Quiet as a newborn joey."

"Good. Round up the boys. We'll need help offloading gear and humping it over to the spaceship," Lefty said.

"Any trouble?"

"Negative."

"That can't be good," McQueen said. "I don't trust the quiet."

"You and me both, brother."

Instead of tying up to the dock, he juiced the engine and came ashore twenty yards south of where they'd taken off. AJ slung a pack over his shoulder and watched with a certain amount of jealousy as Lefty's squad appeared as if by magic from the tree line, each brandishing a weapon and inspecting the newly arrived vessel.

"We're clear, Queenie," a man announced, holstering his pistol.

"Any reason not to get this show moving?" Lefty asked. "We can sort through the gear once we get underway."

"Lead the way," AJ said, knowing he'd make better time with Lefty setting the pace.

About halfway to the ship, McQueen caught up with AJ. "Hey, mate, you have a minute?"

"Sergeant McQueen, of course," AJ said.

"Call me Queenie."

AJ nodded. "What's on your mind?"

"That Vred Sheila. I was wondering if you'd put in a good word for me."

"Didn't sound like you needed a good word last night," AJ said. "Something happen in the swamp?"

"Oi, it sure did, mate," McQueen said. "Rocked my world, she did."

"Did you tell her that?" AJ asked. "I haven't known her long, but far as I can tell, Sharg calls it pretty straight."

"So, you don't think she's just trying to hookup while on liberty?" McQueen asked.

AJ had to fight to keep the smile from his face. McQueen was a lethal warrior from one of the most successful, clandestine units in one of the deadliest wars in American history. And yet, all AJ could find in the man's weathered face was innocent concern and a deep longing.

"You're overthinking this, Queenie," AJ said. "Maybe I misread her, but best I can tell, Sharg says exactly what's on her mind. If I were you, I'd take advantage of that and say what you've got to say. Otherwise, you're likely to miss your chance. She's looking to get home."

"She is?"

"Even before she came," AJ said, slowing as they approached the ship. "Don't dillydally, man. Get in there. Make your case."

"You're a good man, Albert Jenkins, no matter what Lefty says about you."

"Wait, what?" AJ asked, but he might as well have been talking to a tree. McQueen had already disappeared into the ship.

"Good trip?" Jayne asked, greeting AJ as he boarded and unloaded his pack onto the deck.

"Yeah," he said, taking her hand.

"Something on your mind?" she asked, stepping in closer. AJ closed the distance and kissed her softly, eliciting chuckles and a couple of whistles from Lefty's squad. When they finally separated, she knit her eyebrows together. "Where'd that come from?"

"Queenie," AJ said. "Any luck baking a batch of our favorite new aftershave?"

"If by *aftershave* you mean vaccine and anti-vaccine, yes," she said. "Thomas is still working out the concentration for aerial application, but they'll have it together before we get there."

AJ sat on the deck and leaned against the bulkhead. Lefty's crew had swollen to nine, with some of them having only a few hours of transition with their riders. It had been an easy decision to bring them along, even though their presence had caused a certain amount of crowding on the small spaceship.

"Are we all loaded?" Darnell asked, his voice carrying over a public address of some sort.

"Door's closed, Big D," AJ answered. "You know where we're going?"

"Stanfield, Arizona. Buckle up, boys and girls, and make sure to keep your eyes on a window. This is a ride you won't soon forget."

"Buckle?" Queenie asked, his voice pitching higher than it should.

"Do not worry, McQueen," Sharg said. "You will be quite safe as there is no requirement for restraint within a Vred vessel."

McQueen scooted closer to the much larger Sharg and pulled her long arm over his shoulders, his expression a satisfied smirk.

24

BUG JUICE

"We're coming up on the airfield," Darnell announced.

It was well into the afternoon and the team had indeed experienced the ride of a lifetime. First, Darnell had flown nap-of-the-earth on the way down to the gulf coast before plunging into the gulf's warm waters, emerging miles later to skim across the waves. When they reached the coast of Mexico, they'd traveled overland through northern Mexico, finally crossing the border into Arizona.

"I think we got their attention," Baird said, leaning over the forward bulkhead to look out the window at a trio coming from a small hangar. "I want everyone except AJ to stay aboard. We'll call if there's trouble, but I'd prefer to do this as peacefully as possible. AJ, can you grab those cases of money?"

AJ shifted his pistol so it was hidden in his waistband and palmed open the hatch, causing the loading ramp to extend.

"What in the Sam Hill?" The trio was comprised of a man in his late sixties, a woman in her mid-forties, and a young man in his late teens or early twenties.

"Are you Bartell James?" Baird offered her best winning smile as she extended her hand. While en route, she'd manufactured a dress uniform and chose to wear it for the meeting.

"I'm Bartell," the older man said, looking back and forth between Baird and the Vred spaceship. "Are you government folks?"

"Captain Jackie Baird, US Army Intelligence," she answered, tilting her hand to draw his attention. The old man looked down and accepted her handshake.

"What are you doing on my property?"

"You okay, Pops?" the younger man asked.

"Mary, take the boy inside," Bartell said, distractedly. "If I don't come in after ten minutes, I want you to call the cops."

"We mean you no harm, Mr. James," Baird said. "In fact, we're in a bit of a pickle and need your help."

Bartell lifted his hat and scratched his head. After a moment, he seemed to notice that Mary hadn't moved. "Get a move on, Mary. You don't need to be mixed up in this."

"I'm not going anywhere, Dad. Whatever they've got to say, they can say to all of us," Mary said. "Duncan is due back any time now, too."

Bartell shook his head. "Dammit, girl! Government ain't up to no good. Now get back to the house."

Mary pursed her lips but finally led the boy off.

"Maybe we could talk inside?" Baird nodded at the hangar, where a newer helicopter sat, complete with water tanks and boom arms.

"I meant it," Bartell said, leading them toward the barn. "You show up in something like that, I know you're up to no good."

"You served in 'Nam?" AJ asked, recognizing the unit designation on the man's hat.

"Yup. Put in my time," he said, turning as they entered the shade of the hangar. "Now, what's this about?"

"We need to rent your services," Baird said. "I've got a hundred twenty gallons I need to apply over a twenty-five-acre plot about a hundred miles northwest of here. I need it done today."

"That's a pretty long haul. You don't need that much to cover twenty-five acres," he said. "Besides, we're done flying today and tomorrow's all booked up, so I guess you need to take your business somewhere else."

"I'm not sure that you're aware of the government's power to seize property in times of emergency," Baird said. "I'm more than happy to reimburse you for any inconvenience, but this isn't a negotiation."

"What's the emergency?" Bartell asked. "Don't you need some sort of warrant or something?"

"AJ, Mary James is attempting contact with 911," Beverly said, popping into view. "I've taken the call and reassured her that help is coming, but we're going to need to move more quickly."

"Lefty, take McQueen and Jayne and secure the house," AJ said quietly, but Bartell didn't miss the communication.

"Hey, you can't do that!" James stepped forward menacingly only to be intercepted by Baird, who spun the old man around and held his arm against his back.

"We tried asking nicely, Mr. James," she said, pushing him into the hanger and toward a small office. "I respect your right to protect your property. Right now, though, the United States Government requires the use of your helicopter. It's a matter of national security."

"Big-D, go ahead and bring the Bug Juice," AJ said. "Things went south – go figure. Owner's a vet. Were we always this grumpy?"

"You didn't seriously just ask me that?" Darnell answered. "We're bringing the juice now. Make sure Lefty remembers to get his inoculation. We got everyone else."

"I copy," Lefty added. "We're bringing the woman and the kid out to the barn. Might as well keep 'em together."

"Good. Copy," AJ said.

"You're military, too," Bartell said. "I can see it in the way you carry yourself."

"Army," AJ answered. "I wish it didn't have to go down this way. If it's any consolation, we're the good guys in this."

"Doesn't look that way from where I'm sitting."

"I can appreciate that," AJ said, popping open one of the cases. "There's fifty thousand US in this case and another fifty in the other one. We're not sure your bird's gonna make it through, so hopefully you have insurance. If not, this'll help some."

Bartell sighed and settled back. "Can't say I like what's happening, but don't suppose I've got a lot of choice in the matter. Don't hurt the girl or the kid, okay? She's my daughter and the screw-up's her boy. They're all I got left."

"We're not here to hurt anyone," AJ said.

"What's the emergency? Figure I got a right to know."

"You wouldn't believe me if I told you," AJ said.

"Try me."

"Aliens."

"Don't mess with me. I'm old. It makes me mad," Bartell said.

"Do I look like I'm joking?" AJ asked.

"You have anything to do with that thing up at Area-51 a few months back?"

"Yeah, that was us," AJ said and looked over his shoulder. Darnell was working on the helicopter with one of Baird's men. "You good, Big D?"

"It'll take us a few minutes to load the tanks," Darnell called back. "Bird looks to be in good shape, though."

"And she better stay that way," Bartell yelled angrily.

"Hey, no need for that," AJ chastised. "We're keeping things calm. Nobody gets hurt. We'll make it so you can get free in a couple hours. We'll either be dead or heroes by then. If you keep things quiet, I'll make an effort to bring your bird back."

"Damn son, I've seen that look before."

"Which look is that?"

"Boys in my squad would get that look in the quiet moments before all hell broke loose."

AJ pulled the ropes tight enough to hold Bartlett to his seat. He wasn't fooled by the man's outer appearance. There was plenty of strength left in the old man and the ropes needed to be secure.

"If we had time, I'd have tried to recruit you, Bartlett," AJ said.

"That's a strange thing to say. I'm old enough to be your granddad."

AJ chuckled and didn't set him straight, but instead walked over to see how Darnell was coming with the helicopter.

"Infantry?" Darnell asked.

"Probably flew a slick," AJ said. "I should've asked. He's taking it pretty well, all things considered."

"That might be because he thinks I wouldn't find the missing transfer switch," Darnell said. "Probably wouldn't have without 2-F."

"We're a go, Jenkins," Lefty called. "Let's get this show on the road."

AJ looked over and noticed that Jayne was approaching. "Copy that," AJ said. "Big D, why don't you get her fired up and we'll get moving."

"Remember, my speed isn't anything like yours," Darnell said. "Keep things low, but not too low and remember to check on my position once in a while."

AJ held out his hand and Darnell reached past, pulling him into a quick hug. "Be safe, big man," AJ said.

"Back at'cha."

"Our plan feels weak," Jayne said, accompanying AJ back to the Vred spaceship.

"That's because it is," he admitted. "We don't even know for sure that McAlistair is alive, or even here. Back in my day, depending on Military Intelligence was about as dumb a move as a guy could make. Hope things are different now."

"Jackie seems pretty sure of herself," Jayne said.

"They always do."

"You know I can hear you," Baird said, greeting AJ and Jayne as they loaded onto the ship.

"Am I wrong?"

Baird chuckled.

"Lefty, we're forty-nine minutes from target." AJ climbed into the pilot's chair and while he wasn't the expert Darnell was, he'd had more time in the chair than anyone else. Even though he liked Sharg, he hadn't tested her skills enough and wasn't ready to trust her in combat. "Is your team a go?"

"As much as we'll ever be."

"Big D?"

"Just cleared the hangar. I'm firing up the engine now."

AJ PULLED on the armor vest they'd brought from Lefty's cache of goods. Pulling the Velcro straps of the armor across his chest, he seated them in place. AJ thought he'd learned how to take danger and excitement in stride, but he found his blood pressure rising and had to fight to keep calm.

"You got this, Doc?" AJ asked.

"I'm still unsure about being your pilot," she said. "Sharg's much better at this."

"Albert Jenkins is correct," Sharg said, sitting next to Jayne. "I will assist with flight as much as possible, but I have no desire to engage in any sort of hostile actions. Vred are not at war with Korgul. I would not like my actions to modify this status."

"But you'd take the vaccine back and sell it on the Galactic markets?"

"Yes," Sharg answered simply.

"Then promise me something," AJ said. "If this goes south, take Jayne to Halfnium-8 with you and sell the crap out of this vaccine. We're risking a lot and I'd hate to think our mission to free humans from Vred control could end right here."

"I'm not leaving you, AJ," Jayne said.

AJ leaned over and kissed Jayne's head. "You have to promise me, Sharg."

"I will take Amanda Jayne with me back to Halfnium-8. We will make public the recipe for this so-called Korgul vaccine. We will use the wealth generated to benefit both my new family as well as care for Amanda Jayne. This I promise," Sharg said.

"I don't like this," Jayne argued.

"Humanity is depending on you, Doc," AJ said. "I'm depending on you. I can't do this if I have to worry about you."

Jayne sighed. "I don't like how it feels."

AJ pointed out the front window, identifying the landing area they'd chosen. The prison was broken into nine individual clusters spread over a couple hundred acres. Each cluster was comprised of a semicircle of six cellblocks where the prisoners were housed and one autonomous control area with security station, dining hall and public visitation area. While they had no real idea how many guards staffed the entire complex, AJ thought it was an easy bet they were outnumbered by at least twenty to one. He was counting on each of the nine units to enter lockdown upon assault instead of coalescing their forces and swarming wherever the initial breach took place. Everything depended on speed and execution.

"Big D, we're making final approach. Are you in position?"

"Copy that."

"Commence spraying," AJ ordered. "Doc, set us down, right on those steps."

A flash from a tower from a different unit drew his attention just as the sound of heavy rifle round pinged off the ship's armor.

"Sounds like a fifty cal," Lefty said. "Can this thing take that?"

"Do not worry, Lefty," Rebel said, appearing on his shoulder and leaning against his ear. "There are not many handheld weapons on Earth that would pierce ordinary Vred armor. Space debris is quite dangerous and often travels at much higher velocities than your gas-powered projectile weapons."

"We're going to need to dump that tower," AJ said. "Our ship might be able to take it, but I guarantee it'd tear Big D apart."

"But there's a guard inside," Jayne said.

"I bet he'll move," AJ said.

To her credit, Jayne pushed away her initial hesitation and swung the ship around. Without weapons, she had to get inventive, clipping the top ten feet of the tower with the ship. She quickly directed the ship back into position in front of the unit they'd picked to enter.

"Go, go, go!" Lefty called when the ship was within a few feet of the ground. As a team, the squad flowed onto the cement walk and up to the front doors.

AJ raced after them. Some of the men were still not fully rejuvenated by their Beltigersk riders, but even so, AJ had difficulty catching up as they tactically assaulted the heavy glass doors to the *whoop, whoop* of alarms. Their success was confirmed by the addition of ear-splitting screeches from the perimeter sirens.

"Can you cut that noise, BB?" AJ asked.

"Done," Beverly answered, filtering the incoming noise.

Another sound filled AJ's ears. He could hear Darnell's low-flying helicopter flying overhead. For a moment, he was back in Vietnam, his boots covered in mud and his team under fire. Through clouded eyes, he focused on the man in front of him and leaned on years-old training. *One foot at a time. Keep your head down. Keep your eyes open. Trust your team.*

"Grenade!" one of Lefty's team announced, tossing a flashbang into the prison lobby.

"Bug Juice!" another announced, tossing an improvised gas grenade right behind.

"Go!" Lefty demanded. The human train started up again, moving through the doors and spreading out into the room.

A heavy glass window slammed shut in front of them as the guard initiated her safety protocols, only it was already too late. A whiff of Bug Juice had made it beneath the panel. The guard's eyes glazed over as a robin's egg sized snot ball appeared rolled down her cheek. While AJ couldn't hear what she was mumbling, he saw the confusion on her face as reality slammed home.

"Get down!" AJ yelled, approaching the window and gesturing to her. "Explosives!"

She nodded once and dove to the ground even as a squad member plastered a small portion of C4 on the window. AJ hoped like heck she'd be safe, but they had little choice. They couldn't wait for the guard to figure out what was happening and whose side she was on. The unit had to be breached. More armed guards would be arriving within moments.

Pa-ting

A bullet ricocheted through the horizontal bars of the beefy rotating security door that looked more like a meat mixer than a doorway.

"Get me some Bug Juice down that hallway!" Lefty ordered.

"Take cover!" announced the man who'd placed explosives on the window.

"Everyone down," Lefty ordered. "Hit it, Wormie!"

Apparently, Wormie didn't need to be told twice because the thick glass exploded, sending shards of plasticized glass in every possible direction. AJ dove over the counter and into the small room where the terrified prison guard stared incomprehensibly at the Korgul that was attempting to slither away on the floor.

"Yeah, it's real," AJ said, stomping on the blob, catching it between his boot and a pile of glass shards. Blood ran from her ears even as she shouted angry words at the blob beneath his boot.

He moved to the computer terminal that sat on the desk. Beverly, wearing her jungle fatigues but now sporting a black armored vest to match the team, stood over the terminal, shaking her head as she inspected the broken equipment.

"It's dead, Jim," she said, looking at AJ expectantly. When she didn't get any reaction, she shook her head ruefully. "We need another computer."

"Doctor Alan McAlistair." AJ turned to the prison guard who, upon seeing the team in the lobby, was back to cowering against the wall. The woman pointed to her ears and shook her head. "Open door!" He pointed at the wall, beyond which was the metal rotating security door, now firmly locked in place.

"LOCKDOWN!" the woman yelled, obviously unaware of the volume of her voice. "DOORS ARE ALL ELECTRONIC."

AJ scanned the room and found a metal door at the back, which was the only other entrance to the reception desk. Finding it unlocked, he roughly pulled the guard from her cowering position and dragged her through. Three bullets struck into the wall just ahead, missing him but causing him to jump back into the small room.

"I need Bug Juice," AJ called, banking a flashbang off the wall so it bounced into the room from where the shots had been fired.

"Aww shit," he heard from around the corner, just before the flashbang ignited.

"You called for some juice?" McQueen asked, sliding over the counter. In a single smooth move, he delivered a Bug Juice grenade along the same path as the flashbang.

Knowing that speed was their only weapon, AJ and McQueen flowed through the door and searched the room. Two guards had fallen to their knees, familiar looks of confusion on their faces.

"Tie 'em up," AJ said, tossing two zip ties he'd pulled from his belt to McQueen. He went back to drag the guard out of the small guard booth and set her beside the other two. He pinned her to the ground and lashed her wrists together with the zip ties.

"Is this really what we're fighting?" McQueen called over his shoulder as he finished securing his two guards. His eyes were on one of the two Korgul trying to escape the room.

"That's them," AJ agreed, violently smashing a Korgul under his heel. McQueen grinned as he joined AJ and took out his frustration on the fleeing enemy.

"Doctor Alan McAlistair," AJ shouted, kneeling in front of one of the men. He knew the guard was in shock, but also knew the effects of the flash bang weren't long lasting. Unfortunately, like the woman, the male guard didn't seem to be able to hear him. An explosion preceded a blast of dust from the other side of the booth. Rock chips blasted through the doorway, pelting AJ and McQueen.

"Wormie's drilling some holes," McQueen said. "We need to keep moving."

"I need a working computer."

"I remember," McQueen said.

"AJ, you've got a large contingent coming from the north building," Darnell called. "Looks like at least ten guards and they're heavily armed."

"Give 'em a good soaking?"

"About the best I can do is put it on the wind. I'm taking fire and I probably won't be up much longer."

"Shit, D, get safe," AJ said. "Jayne, Big D needs a pickup."

"We've got him," she said, calmly.

Frantic barking drew AJ's attention as Greybeard scrabbled around the corner. AJ winced as blood trailed behind the chunky dog. One of his pads had been deeply cut.

"Seamus needs us to follow," Beverly said. "A group of guards wearing respirators is headed to one of the cell blocks. We think they're going after McAlistair."

"Dammit," he cursed and raced into the hallway behind Greybeard. The debris in the hallway was significant as Lefty's group had blown up key infrastructure to gain entrance, poking holes through cement walls instead of attempting to breach iron gates. "How much C4 did we freaking bring?"

"Not enough. I'm out. We'll have to rely on frags from this point on," Wormie answered, disappointment obvious in his voice.

An overhead view of the prison appeared in front of AJ. "Greybeard found McAlistair," Beverly said, identifying one of the cell blocks with a blue glow. From AJ's peripheral vision, he noticed that he had line of sight to the building through the bank of barred windows on his right.

"We'll have to cut through the yard," he said, running to an emergency door. "We'll never catch those guards otherwise."

"Too dangerous," Beverly said.

Her warning was too late as turf exploded in front of him a few feet into the yard. He dove to the side and rolled, fully expecting the next bullet to punch through his chest. The shot never came. Instead, a shower of bricks rained down across the yard as Jayne flew the Vred ship through the tower.

AJ leaped to his feet and continued the race. From the corner of his eye, he located two of Lefty's men racing through the cell block. He scanned the arc of windows ahead and saw a small knot of well-armed guards in respirators who were running with real purpose. Somehow sensing Lefty's team behind them, four of the six guards spun to a knee and set up a defensive line, firing at and stopping the squad in its tracks.

"McQueen, go!"

"Right on, mate," McQueen answered, branching off to race toward the action inside, Wormie hot on his tail.

AJ cursed under his breath. Without Lefty's men to blow open an entrance, he would have difficulty getting through the reinforced concrete wall. Down to a single frag, he had to make the best of it. Cocking his arm back, he pulled the pin and launched the grenade just as a bullet plowed into his side, spinning him around.

"Oh, shit!" he exclaimed as he flattened out on the ground, hoping he'd tossed the grenade far enough from his body.

"AJ!" Jayne's voice filled his ears before it was drowned out by the grenade's explosion. Pain tore into his shoulder as fragments embedded themselves violently.

"I'm down " he cried out. Confusion clouded his mind, transporting him back in time. "Take cover. We've got Cong on the walls."

25

COOKIE DUSTER

"Get up, you lazy, prepubescent waste of oxygen!" A ten-inch-tall Beverly wearing the Army fatigues of a boot-camp drill sergeant stood inches from AJ's face. With arms behind her back, she leaned forward, spittle flying from her mouth as she screamed orders. "I don't have time to waste on your worthless, lazy hide."

AJ groaned as he reached for his shoulder, his hand coming away slick with blood. "Are we really doing this?" he asked, trying several times to sit up. In the end, he rolled on his side and put his forehead into the rocky dirt before he could get his knees up under his body.

"AJ, get up!" Jayne's call sounded far off, but he heard the urgency in her voice.

"Not you, too," he groaned, testing his good arm. He pushed up from the ground.

"Do you think life owes you?" Beverly continued, still shouting in the cadence of a drill sergeant. "I own your sorry ass, private, and I'm telling you to get it moving! Move! Move! Move!"

The scream of metal scraping stone drew AJ's attention as he stumbled to his feet, searching for his weapon. Miraculously, his pistol was only a few feet away. He managed to stumble without falling and scoop it from the ground.

"AJ, I've got video. Korgul guards wearing gas masks are about to breach McAlistair's cell," Jayne warned. "They're going to kill him. You need to go now!"

"Where?" he asked. A glowing blue arrow appeared, surging toward the building about twenty degrees off from the direction he'd been heading.

Something tore in his shoulder, causing his vision to further narrow. AJ's mind, however, had cleared enough for him to recognize Jayne's voice and understand the urgency she conveyed. Sensing his mission was critical, he stumbled forward. Catching a brick with his foot, the gun flew from his hand in his attempt to steady himself. It took every bit of his concentration to scoop the weapon up without falling over.

"Don't you dare wimp out on me now, boy!" Beverly flew into his face, her eyes alight with anger and purpose.

Despite the circumstances, he grinned, although the grime and blood crusting his face would have prevented anyone from recognizing his facial expression. With each step, he felt stronger. Directly ahead was a rent in the prison wall where it had been violently opened by the Vred ship. He pushed himself through the pain and scrabbled over the rubble.

"I'm here, BB," he finally said, his feet finding purchase on the painted cement floor inside the cell block. "I left the Army a sergeant."

"Nice to have you back, Sergeant," she said, grinning. "Your right shoulder is damaged and you should not attempt to use it."

"Funny." AJ shook his head and raised his pistol as two figures crossed in front of him.

"Friendly!" Beverly warned, just in time for AJ to pull the virtual targeting reticle off the green cotton shirt. His shot barely missed the man's body.

"Not cool," Lefty said, flowing forward next to McQueen, their M4s raised.

AJ pushed himself forward to take up the position on McQueen's left. "On your left." He tapped McQueen's shoulder as the three men came upon the scene of two Korgul guards raising their weapons to fire into a barred cell. Simultaneously, both groups fired.

"They're down. Check the prisoner, Jenkins," Lefty ordered, rushing forward and ripping the mask off one of the fallen. "I need a medic! Get that other mask off."

"Do you have block control?" AJ called, surprised to find McAlistair's chubby body pinned against the back wall, bleeding but very much still alive. "I need number sixteen open."

Greybeard's bark filled the comm channel and was squelched as Beverly appeared, sitting on the prison cell's bars. A loud clack preceded the buzz of magnetic locks. AJ pulled the cell door open and raced inside.

"Doctor McAlistair, where are you hurt?" he asked.

McAlistair was a chubby old scientist with long graying hair. He laughed maniacally. "Did you know they could do this?" he asked, holding a Korgul in his hand. "It was in me the whole time but never bonded. That's so messed up."

AJ recognized he wasn't getting answers from the rumpled doctor. "Captain Jackie Baird sent me. I need you to come with me. Can you stand?"

"What am I supposed to do with this little bugger?" McAlistair asked. "How'd he get pushed out?"

"Not yet, Doctor," AJ urged. "We've got to move. It's not safe here."

"Says the man with blood running down his arm and gravel in his face," McAlistair chuckled.

"Dammit, man, get up!" AJ grabbed the doctor's shirt with his good hand.

"Move it, Jenkins," Lefty called. "Prison has reinforcements coming. We need to clear out."

"What about this alien?" McAlistair demanded.

AJ let go of the doctor, grabbed the Korgul from his hand and tossed it to the side. "Doesn't matter now. We've got a solution, but we need your help."

"How can I trust you? This could all be just some elaborate ruse."

"AJ, tell him *Cookie Duster*," Baird's voice cut in.

"We need Cookie Duster," AJ said.

"Oh," McAlistair said and pushed against the floor so he could stand. "You ... really?"

"Straight from the general," AJ said.

"I saw him die," McAlistair said.

AJ saw blood seeping from a wound on the back of the man's head as he helped him toward the door. "McAlistair has head trauma," he called. "Jayne, I'm going to need you."

"We're bugging out, everyone. HVT is secure. Buggy's in the yard awaiting pickup," Lefty ordered, looping his arm around the chubby scientist.

It was a tense few minutes as the squad worked to extract themselves from the prison. Lefty and AJ were the last ones to load and grateful for eager hands that lifted McAlistair from their tired arms.

"Put him on his side," Jayne ordered, already gloved up and ready.

"We're loaded, Darnell," Baird stood next to the loading ramp as it closed.

"We're taking small arms fire," Darnell confirmed as the ping of bullets hit the Vred ship's side. A moment later, AJ felt the telltale shift in gravity as the Vred ship accelerated well beyond the capacity of any earth-built vessel.

"Drink this," Lefty ordered, pushing a nutrient solution into AJ's hand.

"How are we doing for casualties?"

"Damnedest thing," he said. "We should have lost Wormie. Two more took fire that should have put them on the permanently disabled list. Thing is, they're all just shrugging it off. We're one hundred percent or at least we will be given a few days and a good steak or two."

AJ grimaced as he pushed his right hand forward. "I couldn't have done this without you."

Lefty nodded and shook his hand. "You are one crazy sonnavabitch."

"HOW'S HE DOING?" AJ asked, crouching next to Jayne as she leaned against the outer wall of the spaceship, her knees crossed. She'd insisted on staying close to watch over the unconscious McAlistair.

"Very low pain threshold. He's been out for almost two hours," she said in low tones, so as not to wake the soldiers sleeping off the post-combat low. "I was stitching up a pretty decent wound on his neck and he passed out. I figured it'd be best to let him have some down-time. He's been through a lot."

"Can you wake him?" Baird asked. "I have absolutely no idea what Cookie Duster is or where we should go."

Jayne considered the unconscious man whose face contorted spasmodically as his eyes darted back and forth behind closed lids. "He's running a low-grade fever. I'll try, though. " She tapped on his cheek. "Doctor McAlistair, can you wake up?"

It took a few minutes of cajoling but eventually the man awoke. "Jackie?" he asked. "Who are all these people? Where am I?"

"Alan, you're aboard a Vred spaceship in Alaskan airspace."

"The prison thing. That was real?" he asked, unsteady in his movements.

"Doctor, we have developed a vaccine that makes human bodies reject Korgul parasites," Jayne said.

His cloudy eyes cleared almost instantly. "Delivery?"

"We've tested several mechanisms. The antibodies are extremely resilient and can be delivered via direct injection, blood exchange or aerosol."

"Cookie Duster indeed!" he said, excitement lighting his flushed face.

"This laptop has all the formulation details," Baird said, pushing a laptop into his hands. "What is Cookie Duster or – more to the point *and* assuming it's a protocol for delivering this type of vaccine – how do we get it going?"

McAlistair typed rapidly. "I'll need a satellite connection."

"Give him a Tok neural enhancer," Beverly said, appearing on the edge of the man's laptop, her legs hanging over the side. "Thomas will want to speak with him and it will make this all go more quickly."

"Right," AJ said, surprised when Lefty handed him one of the small communication devices. Extending the small device to McAlistair, he caught the man's attention. "Put this in your ear."

McAlistair clapped his hands together and grinned. "A toy? What does it do?"

"There are other friendly aliens aboard, Alan. Beltigersk," Baird said. "They're only a few hundred nanometers in length, so ordinarily communication is difficult. This device is called a neural enhancer and it will bridge the gap."

"More aliens?" he said gleefully, his fingers trembling as he attempted to slide the neural enhancer into his ear. Fortunately, the device only needed a small purchase before it self-seated. Thomas appeared in front of him, wearing a white lab coat over the top of conservative slacks and collared shirt.

"Greetings, Doctor McAlistair. Jackie has spoken very highly of you and I am pleased to make your acquaintance."

McAlistair poked his finger into the projection that was the ten-inch tall Beltigersk. The image wavered, but provided no resistance. "Fascinating."

"Alan, General Heckard says we need to implement the Cookie Duster protocol," Baird said. "Thomas is the one who invented the antidote."

"Is it true?" McAlistair asked. "Was the general really killed? The Korgul said they'd taken him out. But they said so many things while trying to break me."

"They bombed his convoy while he was in San Diego," Baird said. "He sacrificed himself so we could find you. Tell us that sacrifice wasn't for nothing."

"Oh, my dear Jackie. General Heckard knew quite well what he was doing," McAlistair said. "Such a brave man. Cookie Duster is a man-made variant of an influenza virus," he said. "It's specifically designed to be bonded to an agent for the purpose of delivery. I have no idea if it will work with your antidote, but that was the opportunity General Heckard was providing."

"What do you need?" Baird asked.

"Really not that much," McAlistair said. "We'll need a few vials of my blood. A hundred milliliters of your antidote and some lab equipment."

"And then?"

"The rest is simple. We set the modified Cookie Duster loose in several large urban areas and wait for the virus to spread naturally. If we're lucky, we can reach a quarter of a percent of the population within the first month."

"A quarter of a percent? A month? We don't have that kind of time," AJ said, recoiling. "We need to save the planet, McAlistair. What if the Korgul come up with a way to stop our virus? They have the entire CDC at their beck and call right now."

"First, consider the logistics. A quarter of a percent of the world's population in a month is no easy feat. Second, if we want, we can seed the CDC headquarters in Atlanta with high concentrations. You mentioned aerosol delivery. Really, that's every virologist's biggest nightmare.

"What equipment do you need?" Thomas asked. "This vessel has a manufactory capable of creating complex machinery."

McAlistair typed away on his computer and after a few minutes turned the screen in Thomas's direction. "Can you read that?"

Thomas nodded. "I watched as you composed it. I have instructed the ship's manufactory to create a machine that combines the steps of the process you've outlined."

McAlistair looked at him with surprise. "When?"

"I assume you are asking when the machine will be complete," Thomas said. "Your request was not particularly difficult. The machine already waits in the delivery tray."

AJ plucked a hand-sized device from the manufactory. As he turned to walk back, he became aware of the eyes tracing his every move. The soldiers, once asleep, were all awake and quietly watching the discussion transpire. He nodded in acknowledgement and handed the device to McAlistair.

"How does it work?" McAlistair asked.

"It is already charged with my Korgul vaccine – *Bug Juice*, as it has been named by my companions," Thomas said. "Place the device onto the crease above your elbow. It will extract the requisite blood and separate the Cookie Duster virus from your blood. You took quite a risk with your injection. Even now, your body is creating antibodies to fight the virus. What if you killed this virus?"

"That's the genius of it. The Cookie Duster virus is easily modified and those modifications are not recognizable by our immune systems," McAlistair said. "Which makes it perhaps one of the most terrifying biological agents ever invented. In the wrong hands, humanity could be reduced back to the stone age."

"Good thing you're on our side," AJ said, receiving a quiet rumble of agreement from Lefty's attentive but otherwise quiet squad.

McAlistair placed the device on his arm where Thomas had indicated and yelped as a sharp needle pierced his skin. To his credit, he didn't withdraw the device, even as the needle searched for a vein. A few moments later, the needle was withdrawn.

"It will take four hours for the virus to replicate sufficiently for our first batch," Thomas said. "It is critical that we find volunteers and disperse them widely throughout the world. Korgul command will be on the lookout for those within this ship."

"But they won't know about me and the boys," Lefty said, joining the group. "Now, we've all had an antidote that makes it so we can't be infected..."

McAlistair held up his hand. "Antidote?"

"Yeah, Bug Juice kicks out Beltigersk as easily as Korgul. I can't imagine going without my girl, Rebel, at this point," Lefty answered. Quiet agreement rolled through his squad once again.

"You're immune to Bug Juice, but not Cookie Duster," McAlistair said. "You'd all be excellent carriers. It's the virus that does the dirty work."

Lefty held out his left arm. "Well then, let's get on with it."

"I'M AFRAID DUTY CALLS, doll face," McQueen said, standing at the ship's open hatch, looking up at Sharg. After allowing time for the virus to grow, McAlistair had injected each member of Lefty's squad and dropped them one-by-one at different points throughout the country. Each had several thousand dollars in cash and instructions to make their way to airports and other busy public hubs. At his request, McQueen was the last of Lefty's squad. "If you're ever back in the area, look me up."

"I will be gone for a very long time, Queenie," Sharg said, surprising everyone with the look of longing on her face. "Albert Jenkins will request that I return to my home and make available the knowledge of this Bug Juice Thomas has invented."

"You think?" AJ asked.

"No stopping it now," Darnell said, joining the group. "If Korgul do figure out how to stop the cure, we'll need a backup plan."

"Darnell is right," Beverly said, appearing on Sharg's shoulder wearing her formal black robe. "Now that the Bug Juice has been released on Earth, you must protect the formula's existence by releasing it to the Galactic community."

AJ felt a familiar hand come to rest on his waist as Jayne stepped in next to him. "It's time, AJ."

"Queenie should accompany Sharg," AJ said.

"Go with her?" Queenie asked. "But what about the mission?"

"AJ is right," Baird said, addressing the man. "Lefty's already made it to LaGuardia in New York. Everyone else is so spread out, there's no stopping this thing. Go with her."

Queenies eyes grew wide. "Really?"

"We just need the ship's manufactory and the rest of the cash," AJ said. "There's a hotel about half a mile from here. It's a nice night for a walk."

"Carrying a machine?" McAlistair complained. "Are you crazy? I've got a bad knee and high blood pressure and a fever!"

"It's not far, doctor and you won't need to carry a thing. We'll get you a room to yourself and order a pizza. How's that sound?" Jayne soothed as AJ followed Beverly's instructions on ejecting the critical components of the manufactory. In all, they would carry two hundred pounds of parts, but they could easily split the weight into three packs.

"You owe me a ship, Sharg," AJ said, handing one pack to Baird and another to Darnell.

"I am in your debt, Albert Jenkins," she answered. "But even more, I am pleased to be your friend."

"Oh, get over here, you big softy," AJ said, pulling a surprised Sharg in for a hug.

AJ OPENED the door to the motel room he and Jayne had shared the night before. He'd located a car service and returned with coffee and every newspaper he could lay his hands on. While he'd been gone, Darnell had joined Jayne and both were watching TV.

"Nothing on the national news," Jayne said as he handed her a coffee. "But it's still early yet. I've been thinking about it. I wonder how this is going to roll out. People will be upset as they learn what the Korgul have done. This could be quite an event."

Beverly appeared on the bed, still wearing her formal black robe. "There will be no news," Beverly said, looking from AJ to Jayne.

"How do you know that?" Jayne asked, sipping the hot coffee and eyeing the raspberry Danish he'd set on the hotel dresser.

"I received a communication from Mother," Beverly said. "Two hours ago, Korgul communicated to the Galactic Congress that due to a new understanding of humanity's fragile state as a developing nation, they will cease operations on Earth and depart within seventy-two hours."

"Fragile state?" Darnell asked.

Beverly lifted her eyebrows. "They're crediting Beltigersk with bringing the plight of a previously unrecognized sentient species to their attention. They recommended the Galactic Congress consider diplomatic review of humans for their potential as productive members."

"So lame," Darnell said. "Will they get away with that?"

"You're missing the headline," AJ said. "They're pulling out. We did it!"

"And they're making it sound like they just discovered that humans had brains," Darnell said. "Let me guess, they'll be heroes and nobody will care a lick about what they've done."

"That is often the way of diplomatic solutions," Beverly said. "It is an imperfect victory, but it is a victory, nonetheless. Through these same diplomatic channels, Korgul have requested we slow the dissemination of the virus so they are able to safely recall their citizens."

"Tell them to screw off," AJ said.

"You should rethink that, AJ," Jayne said. "The Cookie Duster virus will take months to really get going and at this point, it's unstoppable."

"Their admission to the Galactic Community could not easily be reversed," Beverly said. "They've admitted to believing humans are sentient and worthy of Galactic recognition. To leave a Korgul presence after this admission would be cause for sanctions."

"So, reading between the lines, they've taken all the easy-to-reach Fantastium and since it's inconvenient to stay, they want to be seen as the good guys," Darnell said. "Are you sure they're not related to humans?"

AJ chuckled. "You are the most cynical man in the history of time."

"Just calling it how I see it."

"I say we toss it over to Captain Baird," AJ said. "We've done our part. Let the cake eaters figure this crap out."

EPILOGUE

"Push that lever until you hear it move just a little," AJ instructed, placing Jayne's hand on the hydraulic control lever. "That's it. When you release the clutch, give it a little bump to get the rock moving. Once it's going, don't stop. It'll come out faster than you think."

"This is crazy. You should be the one doing this," she said.

"Come on, you know you've always wanted to drive one of these things."

She closed her mouth and focused, pushing on the lever. The truck shook as the heavy bed lifted and the gravel shifted.

"Go!" AJ urged as it started to slide backward. Jayne released the clutch more quickly than was proscribed but adjusted as the big diesel chugged against the load. "You've got it."

"Did I get it?" she asked excitedly, stopping only when the nose of the dump truck was sticking through the Junkyard's front gate.

"Perfect," AJ said, leaning over to give her a peck on the cheek. "Go ahead and take it out of gear and turn it off."

The two opened the tall truck's doors and climbed out, meeting at the back of the truck.

"All the gravel's at the back of the driveway," she complained, shaking her head as she recognized her error.

"No problem. You can't expect to get it perfect the first time out," AJ said. "Now you can use those skid-steer skills you've been working on."

"If my surgical staff could only see me now," Jayne said. "Are we taking the truck back tonight?"

"Nah, they're closed. Besides, Diego and his family will be here any minute." He watched her stare off into space. "What's going on in that big brain of yours?"

"It's just so weird. Five months ago, Earth was crawling with Korgul. If the last report from Baird is right, they've completely pulled out. Since they pulled out voluntarily, people don't even know an invasion happened. It's like we're living in a fantasy world."

"I know what you mean. It reminds me of returning from 'Nam. Well, other than all those parades they threw for us for getting shot at and defending our country," he said sarcastically, surprising even himself with the lack of bitterness he felt. "It's hard to see people living their lives like nothing ever happened, because really, that's how it went for them. You know as well as I do, that's really the whole point. I want my kids to grow up in a world where they play baseball, eat hotdogs and don't think about war."

Jayne turned to him with a look of surprise. "Say that last part again."

"Play baseball and eat hotdogs? Come on, Doc, I can eat a few hotdogs, already. They're not that bad for me," he said, defensively.

"No, the part where you have kids," she said, placing a hand on his arm. "Did you really mean that?"

AJ blinked a few times, rolling back the conversation in his head. He was saved when a familiar voice interrupted their conversation.

"Mr. AJ," Diego called as he, his two sisters and his mother, Estela, walked around the front of the big truck carrying a large tinfoil-covered pan.

"Diego, just in time," AJ said, relief evident in his voice. "You want to help me grab a couple of tables from the machine shed?"

"Are those tamales?" Jayne asked, giving AJ a this-conversation-isn't-over look as Estela joined them on the porch.

"Si. Diego says Mr. AJ love my spicy tamales. The girls and I made extra," Estela said, grinning broadly.

"You know you can just call him AJ, right?" Jayne asked.

"It is what Diego calls him and Mr. AJ is my guardian angel," Estela said, smiling. "I will put them on the kitchen table."

"I'll come with you," Jayne said, "I was just going to clean up and get a drink anyway."

"What is that, Mr. AJ?" Diego asked, pointing to the sky as the two walked toward the machine shed.

"That, my boy, is a Vred long-range shuttle craft," AJ said. "If I'm not wrong, they're trailing smoke from one of those engines."

But, of course, that's another story entirely.

ABOUT THE AUTHOR

Jamie McFarlane is happily married, the father of three and lives in Lincoln, Nebraska. He spends his days engaged in a hi-tech career and his nights and weekends writing works of fiction.

Word-of-mouth is crucial for any author to succeed. If you enjoyed this book, please consider leaving a review, even if it's only a line or two; it would make all the difference and would be very much appreciated.

FREE DOWNLOAD

If you'd like to receive automatic email when Jamie's next book is available, please visit http://fickledragon.com. Your email address will never be shared and you can unsubscribe at any time.

For more information
www.fickledragon.com
jamie@fickledragon.com

ACKNOWLEDGMENTS

To Diane Greenwood Muir for excellence in editing and word-smith-ery. My wife, Janet, for polishing myriad rough passages so they are readable and kindly fixing my poor grammatical habits. I cannot imagine working through these projects without you both.

To my beta readers: Carol Greenwood, Barbara Simmons, Chuck Rivers, and Jeffery Shirley for wonderful and thoughtful suggestions. It is a joy to work with this intelligent and considerate group of people. Also, to my advanced reading team, you're a zany, fun group who I look forward to bouncing ideas off.

Finally, to Elias Stern, cover artist extraordinaire.

.

ALSO BY JAMIE MCFARLANE

Printed in Great Britain
by Amazon